NEVERMORE

NEVERMORE

TALES INSPIRED BY EDGAR ALLAN POE

Edited by

MISTY MASSEY

FALSTAFF
BOOKS
WWW.FALSTAFFBOOKS.COM

CONTENTS

RED (QUINCY'S VERSION)
John G. Hartness

THE VALLEY OF UNREST

JAMES R. TUCK

Y ou can't kill me," the reptilian said.

His voice came louder than normal in the cold air of the thin atmosphere. He said it on his knees, looking up at the ancient ion blaster pointed at his face. The yttrium aluminum garnet in the barrel port glowed a dark amber, barely energized, but even the slightest pressure on the trigger would change that. The big hunk of crystal, original to the old gun and close to burn out, would still fire. The burn across the reptilian's hip from the shot that clipped him, stopping his escape, attested to that.

The red dust swirled around them both, little dervishes that lifted the bottom of the man's coat, making it flare dramatically around his legs. It was the long asymmetrical coat worn by the clergy of the Temple of Anti-Damnation.

The same dervishes dragged dust across the reptilian's body armor, decorating it with spindly sanguine whorls that lasted only seconds before being wiped away and replaced by others that were infinitely different but looked the same to someone without a cybernetic eye.

The priest's eye recorded each one.

He wanted every nanosecond of this event stored in his cerebral cortex. He wished to Korrum he could erase some of the memories that had been burned in there, but memories were sticky things that touched each other, making the procedure too delicate to be performed without some of the good going with the bad, even with the best psychic surgeons money could buy. The result was always too much cleared away and suddenly you couldn't remember the first time your love laughed at a joke you made. Or the first time she told you she loved you.

Or the *last* time she told you she loved you.

If he had to live with the fact that he was a vegetarian now because the smell of cooked meat took him back to the killing fields on Cortaque, where the limbs of enemy soldiers and civilians blackened into charcoal from the accelerant his fellow Science Marines called 'Mothers Milk' because of its color and consistency before ignition, then he would cherish the memory he created right now by having the manslayer Mordoon at his mercy.

Mordoon looked up at him, red pupils narrowing into a vertical line.

"I know your ways, priest," Mordoon spat. The thick fluid landed in the dust, rolling into a pebble like leftover batter. "You kill me and it's an unnatural death. An unnatural death means my essence goes to the Valley of Unrest and spends eternity in agony, stuck between."

The priest motioned with the blaster in his left hand, the ready end of the barrel casting a butter yellow glow across Mordoon's face.

"You think I give a good gorrfrag about your essence suffering?" His voice rasped from his throat, partially from disuse, partially from the dust that blew across the planetoid.

Mordoon laughed.

"Probably not, but you'll be there beside me. That's what your religion demands."

"Do I strike you as the kind of man who cares about his own essence?"

Mordoon's heavy brow dropped lower, hooding his deep-set eyes. "You care about your essence being apart from theirs."

"Theirs who?" The priest said it as a dare.

"Whoever I killed that matters enough for you to hunt me down." Mordoon's mouth twisted as he ran his tongue across his outer row of teeth. It slid across with a sucking, wet sound. "Wife?"

The priest didn't react.

"Child? Children? And wife?"

He tried to not move a muscle but the corner of his left eye betrayed him.

The smile that split Mordoon's face revealed teeth that interlocked, long and curved and serrated, carnivore's teeth made to excise flesh from other flesh.

"You poor suffering son of a whore. I took them all from you! How many kids did you have? Your kind screw like clabbups, I bet you had at least three. I'm sure they were delicious. Which ones were they? Give me a hint."

The priest's teeth clenched hard enough to squeak.

"Oh, come now!" Mordoon cried out, the rise in his voice causing the universal translator to go fuzzy on the higher notes. "You know you want to tell me. You've hounded me across two galaxies. That kind of hate has been building inside you for so fragging long, just stewing and bubbling, churning your stomach acid with every thought about me."

The blaster trembled, the barrel glow going orange as the tension in the priest's hand increased, the radiation building.

"Tell me," Mordoon demanded.

The blaster rose, pointing at Mordoon's face.

"Tell me!" Mordoon's voice grew to a yell.

The barrel glowed Mars red, angry and vicious.

Mordoon leaned in and snarled, low and wet. "Tell me! Tell me or shoot me you sorry, belly dragging, son-of-a- "

The ion beam crackled through the air between them, cutting the oxygen into ozone as it tore atmosphere over Mordoon's shoulder. The radiant heat of the beam scorched the osmium pauldron he wore, searing the dust on the rise behind him into glass.

The blast flashed white light bright enough to see bones outlined under flesh. Mordoon turned away to save his slit-pupiled sight.

The priest's foot lashed out, aiming the heavy magnetic plate on his sole to crush Mordoon's skull. The reptilian jerked sideways. The boot scraped his temple but did no real damage. He lunged, shoving his body under the priest's leg. The priest fell to the ground. A cloud of dust rolled up, blinding his cybernetic eye and choking him.

Mordoon snatched the blaster from his hand. The reptilian's talons tore open the thick material of the priest's glove and the thumb underneath. Pain bloomed hot and fast, spreading rapidly as the neurotoxin from Mordoon's talons took hold. When the pain ended and his hand went numb and cold, the nerve damage would be irreparable.

The priest rose to sitting, coughing dust out of his lungs and wiping his eyes. Tears came from his organic eye, washing the dust into thick trails on his cheeks, as the cybernetic one spun in its socket, the cleaning cycle engaged. He expected to see Mordoon pointing his gun at him.

Instead the reptilian snarled down at the gun before tossing it behind him.

"Fragging humans and your tiny fragging human hands," he growled. He tapped a spot on the armor at his hip, talon sinking the button there. Seams appeared on the thigh, widening as the plate lifted out, revealing a large rectangular gun. The cybernetics lifted the weapon up from the opening, raising it to a position that the reptilian could grasp it. His taloned hand closed on the grip, removing it from the holster. Once cleared, the plate slid back into position. The seams shrank until they disappeared.

"Now, this is a real weapon! Not that piddly-spit thing you were carrying."

"The one I had was all I had."

"That old thing was your only weapon? I recognize that scar on your cheek, that's shrapnel from a Coltaire grenade. You've seen combat. And the skill to track me, that's military, don't act like it ain't."

"I left that behind when I took my vows to the Church."

"Well, that's fraggin' stupid. Your kind ain't pacifists."

"Dola—" the priest swallowed. "My wife didn't like weapons. She asked me to never use one again."

"How'd that work out for her?"

Red washed the priest's vision. He scrambled, getting his legs under him, hands on the ground, mouth open, baring his teeth.

Mordoon lashed out with the gun in his hand, the heavy rectangular barrel splitting the skin on the priest's forehead, driving him back down to the ground.

"Don't make me kill you just yet," the reptilian snarled.

The priest's rage shattered, leaving him cold and empty inside.

He sat on his ass, head hung down to his chest. Blood ran down his face, congealing in the coating of dust on his skin, becoming a mask of red. He chuckled.

Mordoon stepped back, keeping the gun trained on the priest.

"You're wrong," the priest said.

"Wrong about what?"

"About the souls of my family."

"How so?"

The priest looked up at him, eyes bright through the mask of blood. "You're an apex predator."

"Why are you complimenting me?"

The priest ignored Mordoon's question.

"You kill and eat your prey. You hunt for food. You were made for it. You are a force of nature."

"I ain't going to disagree, but I don't see your point."

"You killing my family is natural. It's part of the cycle. You're no different than the storm that destroys a house, killing the family that lives there."

"So you believe that your family is in the Valley of Rest because I am a natural death for soft little humans?"

The priest nodded.

"Well, that's fragged up. And coming from me, that means a lot."

"It fits the teachings of the ancients."

"It's still fragged up."

"All that matters is I believe it."

The reptilian frowned, thinking about the concept. "There was a time I was wild, a fearsome creature. I hatched with the universe against me. As I grew, I killed as I wanted. I did it for meat and I did it to prove my strength and I did it for pleasure alone." He looked down at the priest. "I was uncivilized. A barbarian."

"You fulfilled your purpose the way Korrum intended."

Mordoon snarled, shoving the gun toward the priest. "I am more than a beast to eat your kind!"

The priest didn't respond.

After a long moment, Mordoon lowered the gun.

"Get up, priest, but behave. Go for a weapon, attack me, or just piss me off and I will kill you dead."

Carefully, the priest climbed to his feet. It wasn't graceful, requiring him to roll to his knees, which gave him a face full of the red dust. He choked down a cough as he got one foot on the ground and used that knee to push himself up. He ached across his back, below his shoulders but above his waist, in the middle part that he breathed from. His hand had stopped burning from the neurotoxin, the numbness up his wrist.

They would amputate that by the elbow to make a stronger prosthesis.

He pushed the thought aside.

Mordoon lowered the gun in his hand.

"A few stardates ago I joined the Alliance, got legitimized, got educated, got *civilized*." The reptilian spat, long forked tongue curling out into a tubular form to launch the spittle into the dust at his feet. "Mostly."

"Doesn't change your purpose."

"It ought to."

The priest shrugged. "Korrum moves in mysterious ways."

"When did I kill your family?"

"A lifetime ago."

"I said not to piss me off. Don't talk in riddles." Mordoon bared his teeth in threat. *"Gorrfraggin' priests."*

The priest just looked at him. He could feel the blood tight on his face where it had dried. The gash on his forehead throbbed softly but with no real pain. He felt unmoored, as if reality shifted around him. Peace settled on his shoulders like a soft feathered Fotoric finch.

Sure sign of a concussion.

Korrum moved in mysterious ways.

"You claim to have changed."

"I have," Mordoon nodded.

"Then repent."

The blaster fired, its plasma beam striking the priest in the torso, burning a hole the size of a fist completely through him.

Red dust swirled up over his body as it crumpled to the ground.

He choked as he gasped for air. The plasma cauterized the wound but his lung and other organs were destroyed. The pain made his thoughts into static. He thought when the moment of his death came for him he would have time to offer one final prayer, but that was lost in a sea of agony.

The reptilian loomed over him, watching his dying gasps. The sight of his murder sparked a moment of clarity, a brief instant, but it was enough for one thought.

"Gorrfraggin' priests," Mordoon spat as the priest gave one last shudder and departed the mortal coil.

A low whirring click caught his attention. He squatted, looking. Small movement in the priest's left eye socket. He used the tips of his talons to pry up the lid. The cybernetic eye jerked right to left over and over. Mordoon wedged his talon behind the thing, plucking it out. Thin monofilament strands pulled from the optic nerve, retracting back inside the eyeball to leave a perfectly smooth outer surface.

Mordoon studied the orb, rolling it around between his fingers.

"What were you transmitting, you little bastard? Probably some last beg for forgiveness."

The reptilian stuffed the eye into a pouch on his belt. He'd lose the keepsake soon enough but that never stopped him from taking them.

He watched the dust settle over the corpse before turning away and walking toward the sleek Omni-Arch Falconer perched on the hill. It swept forward, all looped foil wing and curved fuselage, a remnant from the other side of the Alliance, and was the one the priest used to blast him out of the black. His own, more modern Warstarr still poured smoke into the thin atmosphere of the planetoid. Maybe he could repair it, but the priest had scored a good strike on the rear of his ship, dropping the warp core into the thruster bay. Mordoon had to eject the entire core into orbit just to keep from being vaporized.

It was easier to just take the priest's ship. He wasn't going to use it again.

The burn across Mordoon's hip got worse with each step up the hill. The Falconer was a sleek little messenger ship. The only weapon onboard was the retrofitted K-11 Bolt Thrower cannon that took his Warstarr down, but it was fast. Capable of warp but also faster than anything else planet to planet.

The pilot seat had been built for humans. It made his hip hurt worse, but Mordoon wedged his bulk into it.

Let's get back to civilized space.

He punched in the ignition sequence, bracing himself for the atmo thrusters to engage.

Nothing happened.

He ran the sequence again.

Nothing.

Growling, he took a deep breath and slowly tapped in the sequence, carefully using just the tip of his index talon.

Something moved at his beltline.

He leaned his bulk over the arm, digging into the pouch. He pulled out the cybernetic eye. It buzzed, vibrating, sending a tingle up his fingers.

The console in front of him lit up, the viewport becoming a sheet of blue-tinged glow. After a second the priest's face filled the now holographic projection bay.

"Thank you," the hologram of the priest said, the voice coming from the sound system all around the cockpit. The surround sound gave it a disembodied feel.

7

It felt like a hole opened in Mordoon's stomach. He didn't respond to the hologram. On a messenger class vehicle like this, the program used yellow for interactive exchanges, green for live transmissions, and red for emergency or priority messages. Blue was only for missives. He would have to listen, no way to interrupt.

"You did as Korrum created you and you gave me a natural death. I will spend my afterlife until rebirth with my family now. I am grateful to you. This is why I tracked you down. Not for revenge. Korrum decrees a death by your hand, the hand that took them, means I will be instantly reunited with them in the Sunless Lands."

The hologram glitched, the priest freezing in place and breaking across the center in a black line. Each half slid in opposite directions, distorting as they did. The cybernetic eye vibrated in Mordoon's hand, reminding him it was there. The hologram flickered back into one image and began moving again.

"I jettisoned the thruster fuel cell before landing, so the ship is sound but will not fly in atmo. Without the thruster cell, there is no long-range transmission. This planetoid is devoid of any predator big enough to harm you or poison strong enough to kill you. I have thirty days of supplies in the hold in the back. They are yours, freely given.in accordance with the requirements of hospitality in the Cerulean Scroll of Korrum."

The hologram glitched again, freezing, this time without the split but surrounded by static as if the priest stood in a snowstorm. Mordoon shook the eye. It buzzed again and the hologram resumed.

"I am a teacher, so forgive me," the hologram chuckled at its choice of wording. "I want you to know exactly the situation you are in. It was natural for you to kill me as you have, Again, thank you. But because of how you were created and the life you have lived, in order for you to achieve the Valley of Rest, you should die in combat or under attack. I offer you neither of those. You will reach a peaceful death. Here on this lonely planetoid, outside any spacefaring lanes, once the food I have provided runs out, you will slowly starve. I know your kind can go weeks without a meal. I hope you use this time to reflect on the sins that brought you to this place."

The hologram leaned forward and smiled.

"When the time comes, when you're mad with hunger and thirst and you have resorted to consuming your own waste out of desperation, understand that taking matters into your own hands is also an unnatural death for a creature like you. The Peace of Korrum be upon you until you enter the Valley of Unrest."

The hologram moved its hands, tracing the complicated geometric symbol of the Temple of Anti-Damnation.

Before the hologram completed the sigil, Mordoon crushed the eye in his hand.

AND THEY WILL RISE FROM THE OCEANS

MICHELE TRACY BERGER

Isabella could not bear to see Pascal, her fiancé, in pain. He writhed at the table as the water spirit occupied his body and disrupted what had been a peaceful and uneventful séance. He had never summoned a non-human spirit before and Isabella didn't know why he had now. Sweat ran down her back, the cold rivulets dampening her elegant flapper dress dotted with intricate blue beading. Moisture pooled at her hairline. Marcus' and Elliot's tight brown faces looked as bewildered as she felt. For once Marcus was speechless while they sat at the table. Her lips trembled watching her beloved's face contort. Pascal's eyebrows knitted together, the veins in his prominent forehead bulged. His mouth tightened and his skin took on an oily sheen. *Why would he open himself to this spirit? Why would he possibly invite something like this?* Ever since his trip to the wild places of Egypt, Tunis, Arabia, he had come back unsettled. He spoke of the mysteries of rivers, great water spirits, and the power of oceans. As water in the crystal glasses on the table gently bubbled - another manifestation of the spirit's presence - she felt a chilling fear toward Pascal's obsession with water. *It will lead to no good.*

The humidity in the parlor was the first thing that alerted her senses. Instead of feeling like a crisp October evening in Manhattan, it felt like June, air so heavy and moist it felt as if damp cloth was wrapped around her head. The spirit arrived late into the evening after the usual affair. Pascal, working as a medium, summoned a few deceased souls, and shared their specific messages for some of the bereaved guests. Marcus and Elliot laid their hands on the sick. Marcus was especially good at stomach ailments.

Departed souls, ghosts, 'the ancestors', as Pascal described them, showed up and announced themselves with a strong scent, or a sound like the dropping of pennies. They left clues and sometimes teased the person seeking their guidance. This possession was nothing like that.

Pascal's eyes rolled back in his head and spittle formed in the corners of his handsome, full-lipped mouth. What should she do? She squirmed. She was not a medium or a healer, but a believer in the unknown and unseen and Pascal's champion. She possessed no spiritual talent but had insisted on being at the table with Pascal and the other men. Earlier that evening, Pascal finally, grudgingly, assented. *I've earned my place. That small victory distinguishes me from the rest of his followers.*

When Pascal's arms twitched like a puppeteer pulled at them, someone gasped. Isabella was barely aware of the small crowd, followers of Pascal who stood a few steps back from the circular table where she and the others sat. Their séances and spiritual meetings drew curious Black socialites, artists and everyday seekers. The tension and growing fear in the room felt like a belt tightening against her ribs making it difficult to breathe.

Pascal's shuddering jerk brought her attention back. She noticed his eyes watered.

"What have you come to tell us?" she said, finding her voice at last.

"What's your name?" Marcus interrupted.

It's here for a reason, with or without a name. She clamped down on the irritation that the short, mustached, and quick-tempered man brought out in her.

"He who has roamed many lands," the spirit began, its voice sharp and clear like a pin prick on her skin, "and now seeks the waters, knows my name. He wants the secrets of my brothers and sisters."

Pascal's face was a wreck of light and darkness now, his eyes clouding, rheumy as if he suffered from too much drink.

Elliot muttered the Lord's Prayer loudly.

"He wants to go down to the bottom. Arrogant man," the water spirit continued.

Isabella drew in her breath. The other men shifted and stared.

Pascal turned his head toward her, blue spirit eyes fixed on her. *Those eyes!* For a moment it was as if she were submerged in dank water, a foul place where dead creatures rotted in the dark.

The heavy oak table shook and she gripped Pascal's hand harder. The glasses of water shattered, scattering shards and droplets across the table and into the crowd. People near her shouted. Many backed away, some turned and fled the parlor. Flinching, she forced herself to tighten her hand. *I will not let you go, beloved.*

"Spirit, release Pascal. Go forth from here," Isabella commanded.

"We show you back to the light," Marcus said standing, still gripping her and Elliot's hands.

Her hand throbbed from Marcus's grip and from the wet heat of Pascal's hand.

"We are tempted!" the spirit roared.

After a moment, all was still in the room. Isabella's heart galloped as Pascal slumped over to her side. The chamber felt dimmer although no one had touched the lights.

She released her hold. Taking Pascal's face in between her hands, she rubbed his cheeks.

Eleanor, a woman of means who recently had become a regular attendee rushed forward. "Is he alright?" she said.

Eleanor was from a well-known family in D.C. and had gone to Spelman College, not Howard University, as Isabella had. A socialite now in New York, she moved as if always surrounded in a layer of delicate cloth and softness. Her voice seemed softer still, a squeak, but a determined squeak. Isabella noted the other differences between them—Eleanor was tall and busty, blessed with perpetually dewy-looking skin, medium-length hair held by a simple barrette which looked nothing like Isabella's sleek pageboy wave.

Isabella reminded herself that she was engaged to Pascal, not Eleanor. *He has chosen me for special things.* Feeling protective nonetheless, Isabella whispered, "Darling, how are you feeling?"

Pascal's face was losing the coloring and harsh expression the water spirit etched on it. He opened his large eyes. She loved those dark, fearsome eyes. They complemented his face, showing the complexion of dual parentage just like hers. She was a tad lighter shade of tan. He was darker, caressed with reddish undertones in his skin. Some called them mulattoes, but she liked the word colored, as was the fashion of the day.

"Pascal, what was that?" Marcus said in a clipped tone. He leaned on the table, wiping himself with his familiar blue handkerchief.

Pascal bolted up. "Was the Old One of the Ocean here?"

It's true, as he has told me then, when in a trance you feel far away from your body. You know little of what transpires. "Yes, it took you," she said.

Pascal pulled out a handkerchief from his gray and blue lounging jacket. "You *made* it go away. I could hear you."

She recoiled at his tone, color rising quickly to her face. Had she been wrong to make the spirit leave? "Darling, I was worried."

He waved a hand and turned to Elliot and Marcus, "What did it say?"

"It was fearsome and noxious," Elliot said. The tall man stood with his arms folded.

"Not much," Marcus said with a shrug. "It didn't seem friendly."

Isabella twitched her nose. A musty smell clung to Pascal.

"Tell me what it said," he demanded. They told him in detail. Pascal pursed his full lips, sat back and said. "This is good."

Pascal's butler and driver, Middy, an older man with a limp, brought towels and cleaned up the mess. In a short time, Pascal assured everyone he was fine. "Please everyone, head to the parlor. I'll be there shortly."

Pascal motioned for Isabella to follow the others. Baffled, she shook off the feeling of doom as she reluctantly left him. She followed the crowd, now speaking in hushed tones, from the small room where the séances were held through the adjoining hallways that led to the large parlor.

Everywhere in this building he owned displayed signs of Pascal's success. She had not seen so many beautiful pieces of art in any home. He was richer than any colored man she would ever hope to meet, cultured, comfortable in his own skin. Her thoughts turned toward the few whispers she had heard about him when she met him last year. Rumors swirled around him when he arrived in New York's colored circles. There were tales of him using sex magic in Louisiana. Some said he poisoned his white father and that was how he acquired his wealth. Isabella knew that rumors and gossip often twined around successful colored men. *I believe in him and I love him, that's what matters.*

Everything in the parlor connoted beauty and elegance except the newest object that stood on a pedestal on the far side of the room. *That awful thing!* The vessel Pascal brought back from Egypt—a large four-foot urn. Old, chipped on one side, with intricate carvings all around. And there was something else. She could not help noticing how the squat, slate-gray figures carved into the urn had wide mouths that seemed to leer and grimace, lifelike. They looked as if their forms could step off the jar to greet her. They struck her as ugly and mean spirited. *Isabella, you are being silly.* Pascal said little about it on his return except that it had once been used for sacred water rituals.

She moved away from the urn and thought of more pleasant things. When troubled she returned to the comfort and anticipation of her future wedding. *If only Pascal would commit to a date.* Although she had long ago vowed not to be constrained by the strictures for colored women of the day, she did want to be married. He was twelve years her senior, but as an unmarried twenty-four-year-old, she was not a young girl either. *Several of my friends have been married for years!*

Every time she was near him, she ached and his slightest touch sent waves down her body. Oh, how they could travel together and see sites that she only read about! She did not want to pester, it would not be her place to do so, but how she wanted to share a wedding date with her friends and rejoice.

She made small talk with the guests, about thirty in all and more than half were women. More and more women were coming to their meetings. Although many spiritualist meetings had faded in the past years, Pascal's arrival had revived them in Harlem. Besides Eleanor, she liked most of the women there.

"What the hell was that?" Marcus asked.

"I don't know. Pascal looked quite surprised," Isabella said.

He snorted and took a long pull from his glass of brandy. A muscularity in his face, volatile, he always seemed ill at ease, but nonetheless a powerful healer.

"He's never attempted anything like that before. Was this your idea?" He leaned in close enough that she could smell the sweet whiskey on his breath. "Water, such a feminine notion connected to birthing..." he said, with only a thinly veiled sneer.

Her face flushed for the second time that night. *That he would immediately think I would welcome such a spirit because of my womb is vexing!*

Isabella held up her head, narrowed her eyes and gave him a cool look that she usually reserved for obnoxious men who called to her on the city streets. "I can assure you that I had nothing to do with this evening."

"What do you make of it, his fixation on water?" Marcus pressed.

"I can't say, Marcus."

Elliot joined them. She smiled at him. Cooler in temperament and more pleasant in every way than Marcus, Elliot seemed not to resent her connection to Pascal.

"Does he seem different to you?" Isabella asked.

"No," Elliot said.

"Horse shit," Marcus said. "Since his trip away, I rarely see him anymore, except for these meetings. He's holed up here. Really, Isabella, you should try to get him out more. Work your feminine wiles."

"I do try," Isabella stammered.

"He's trying to build something good and powerful here," Elliot said, his eyes gleaming. "Maybe he has better things to do than spend time at the private drinking clubs you so often favor."

"He never drank much anyway," the small man said with a shrug. "Plus, he's moody and sullen most of the time. He's given up on so many things we used to like to do together."

Isabella felt Marcus's rising frustration. It's true, she thought. *Although Marcus has known my beloved much longer than Elliot, they don't seem as close anymore.*

"Great men have to put their time into building great things. Things that last," Elliot said with a smile that showed slight dimples in his long handsome face.

Marcus shook his head, "Tonight was almost a disaster! What disarray he was in. We go from a healing to-"

"To something beyond our wildest expectations" said Pascal stepping up behind them, startling Isabella. He stood open armed, his hair perfectly waved and looking even more fetching than before. He had not come in from the main entrance they were facing, but from one behind them.

"Pascal," she said, moving toward him.

Caught off guard, Marcus opened and closed his mouth.

"I called that powerful spirit because I wanted to know about the ocean. So many secrets float in its waters and are buried at the bottom of its vast expanse."

"It felt foul. If Isabella hadn't stopped it, you may not be standing here right now," Marcus said.

Isabella could hear the challenge in his voice.

"Isabella is a woman of fine intentions, but I needed no help. I need *believers* if we are to do something great, not naysayers. I thought you understood that, Marcus."

I am a believer, Isabella thought. *I have been guided by your hand and your light.*

"I confess confusion. I haven't understood much this evening," Marcus said, shaking his head.

"Let's make it an early night then," Pascal said, his voice louder. He stood aside, "Middy has your coat and will show you out."

Murmurs shot through the crowd. Middy stood silently next to Pascal.

Anger flashed in Marcus' eyes', but instead of making a scene, he took his coat with one hand and gave the butler his empty glass with the other.

"Isabella, a pleasure. Elliot," Marcus said, giving a curt nod to each.

I'm not sorry to see him go. Did a brief smile cross Elliot's face?

Pascal went over to stand near the urn. Surveying the crowd, he said, "We must probe the unseen mysteries to better help our people. We are over twenty years into a new century and what is the state of the colored man? He wants for everything. He wants for dignity, for work, for education, for prosperity, for industry. His women are forced to be maids and often face the hands of white men who wish to mistreat them in the vilest kind of way.

And my friends, many of the church leaders offer little except mind numbing obeisance. It is upon us friends, to take our vision into the world, into new heights. That is what these sessions are about. Let us talk tonight of what may help the colored race. And of Africa, a place of deep mystery."

"Oh, Pascal, no do not compare us to the deplorable savages of Africa," a woman Isabella didn't know said with a sneer.

Shaking his head, Pascal gave the speaker a withering gaze. "You speak from the comfortable vantage point of ignorance." As he spoke, the round woman moved a step back as if feeling the power of her transgression.

"We are a part of the dark mysteries of Africa, a continent which I have traveled. We must seek those motherly roots for guidance," he continued.

The small crowd swayed and nodded. Isabella did not like the way they stared at him as if he was some deity. *But is that not true of me, too?* A man who has faced death, who can work the unseen energies, a man who can talk to spirits, who can heal. *And when he looks upon me, do I not also wish to fall down at his feet?* She could feel herself falling now into this delicious intoxication, feeding her senses, making her want only him. But when she opened her eyes she saw the vessel and it gave her such a fit of unease she did not hear the rest of what Pascal said. Did she see movement on the urn? *No, it was a trick of the light,* she thought. *The last hour has been a strain on me.*

"Is it always like that, like what we saw?" a stooped older man asked.

"No. Tonight we saw something special. We've had a very eventful night. We hold these meetings so we may help you and each other—that we may connect with our spiritual purpose and evolution. Now please take time to enjoy yourselves before leaving my company."

Interrupting Isabella's thoughts, he offered his arm. "Shall we walk?"

She nodded.

Being this close to him erupted a fire through her belly. He moved through the crowd and chatted with people as they made their way out to a small balcony. The fresh air helped clear her thoughts, though this close she did notice that a sour, mildewed smell still clung to him.

"What's on your mind?" Pascal asked.

"Everything that I saw with my eyes. Why would you summon such a being?" she asked, feeling small and unsure.

"I have my reasons. Do you trust me?"

She nodded.

"Have I not been worthy of your trust?"

She nodded.

"Did I not choose you out of all the people who are seekers to be by my side?"

She felt the spark of their meeting a year ago ignite within her. Isabella had never dreamed she would meet a man who shared her own interests in the unseen world. Most of the colored men she met were church raised and suspicious, if not hostile, to any notion of the spirit world. She found it difficult to hide her curiosity when they had met at one of the American Theosophical Society's lectures. They couldn't stop talking to each other during the reception held after the lecture. She was entranced then and smitten after their first date.

"Yes," she said, letting the early memories fade.

"Believe that you'll know all the pieces at the right time." Pascal lifted up her chin to look at him. "We must grow, Isabella. We must challenge ourselves. I have to challenge my talents."

The October night air was cool, but it was being this close to him caused little bumps to ripple across her skin.

"What else, Isabella?"

It was as if he could look into the very core of her and know what she was thinking.

"Our wedding date remains—"

"Do not worry, we will set a date. I have much on my mind now."

"Although I don't have family, I would like to inform my friends-"

"I can't worry about frivolities," he said, a steely look in his eyes.

She drew back. He had never spoken to her that way. She noted his sharpness, just like after the séance. *It was like looking at a double of him. Pascal but not himself.*

He took her hands in his. "Soon we will go beyond these healings and the common complaints of our people. Beyond, 'help me talk to my deceased grandson' or 'help me with a new job at some terrible factory'. We must work toward a grander vision. I need someone who can see that, Isabella, someone who can share that. We can't get bogged down in the everyday. We, of course, will get married. I would not have asked for your hand otherwise."

"Yes, of course," she said. *I should not doubt him.*

They walked back into the house. A few people remained sitting on the sumptuous chairs and settee. She paused and picked up her favorite object in the room. It was a baby blue circular music box, about four inches high and a handspan wide, last year's Christmas gift. It played notes from Blue Danube. She had saved for months to purchase it and she was proud that he kept it visible in this room with so many other prized treasures. *A small token of my deep love for him.*

"How are the arrangements coming for my meeting with Swami Asokonanada?" he asked.

"I should know soon. There are many people that want to meet with him."

"That's why I donate so much money to that organization, so I can leapfrog over other people," he said with a wry smile. "*And,* that's why you work there."

And because I studied world religions at Howard University. "I must not seem to play favors when setting up his schedule."

One of the benefits of her job as a secretary for the American Theosophical Society was that she helped schedule all the meetings of guest speakers from around the world. It filled her with a great deal of excitement and purpose. Sri Sri Asokonanada, a noted healer and teacher, would be making his second trip to the US shortly. He advocated yoga and meditation and wanted to meet with people who were open to spiritual teachings and esoteric ideas. Pascal had made large donations to the

New York chapter of the ATS and had asked for nothing in return, until now.

"I met many swamis and gurus in my travels over the years. Strange, powerful men. I am eager to meet this one."

"I know," Isabella said.

His eyes glowed as he continued, "Some have developed powers, siddhis, beyond our current imagination. Men that can shrink themselves, sit in the middle of a snowstorm and melt snow around them. Some can stop their hearts. This one follows the way of water—water spirits...Shiva."

"Yes. I will make sure it happens," she reassured him. The feverish glow in his eyes unsettled her. She changed topics. "I'm so looking forward to seeing Cleopatra's Night tomorrow."

"As am I, dear one," Pascal said.

"My mother always wanted me to go to an opera, but we weren't able to. Philadelphia's ethos of brotherly never much extended to coloreds and the arts."

"Opera was the only one of my father's loves that he shared with me," he said, the creases in his face softening. "How the enjoyment of music can make louts and scoundrels into men."

She smiled, forgetting the labors of the night. "You're exposing me to the opera. Sometime, I would love for you to come with me to the Negro Baseball League. They are in town."

His face soured. "I'm not interested."

"I enjoyed playing softball when I was at Howard. I haven't played for fun in so many months," Isabella said with a sigh.

"There are forgivable things when one is a *girl*," Pascal reprimanded. "It is not fitting for a woman such as yourself to play any kind of ball. Jumping, sweating and running is not suitable for girls and ladies. It's undignified." He turned up his nose. "You are better served to use your energies elsewhere."

Chastised, she lowered her eyes and said nothing. *I like using my mind and body.*

"It is late. I will have Middy drive you home."

"Thank you," she reached up to kiss him, holding her breath to avoid the lingering musty smell.

They arrived at the opera house in their finery. Pascal presented the tickets, but the glassy-eyed man at the ticket booth glared at them. "There must be some mistake," the clerk said.

"There is always a problem when a man is being robbed in front of everyone," Pascal said. "I have paid for a private box and am being denied."

The clerk stalked off to get the manager. Several white patrons, dressed in gay clothes, swirled around them. Isabella's stomach lurched. She wanted to melt into the floor

The manager arrived. The clerk by his side stood straighter and tightened up his boyish face.

"Edward must have sold them," he said addressing the manager, a tall older man with an erect posture. "He must have thought this man picked them up for his employer."

Pascal puffed his chest out, "I work for myself. I know that such a thing might be hard for you to believe, young man. We want to see the show."

The manager said nothing more than, "I see."

Isabella's throat went dry. *I knew this was too good to be true.*

After a moment, the clerk's face fumed, "Go back uptown with your own kind."

"You do not know what my kind is," Pascal snarled.

"A light-skinned monkey is still a monkey in a suit. Get out of here before there's real trouble," the clerk said, clenching the tickets. The manager took the tickets from the young man.

"We will refund the cost to you," The manager said in a low voice. "There's clearly been a clerical error."

"Is there a colored balcony?" Isabella said, her voice trembling.

All three men ignored her.

"I do not want a refund. There's been no error!" Pascal's face and neck flushed.

She tugged on Pascal's arm as the crowd gathered around them. The crowd was behaving itself, momentarily, but dread creeped through her, making her breath shallow. The patrons, anyone, could turn on them. She knew that their heads could be bloodied in the next few minutes and then she would *never* get to be Pascal's bride.

"Shall we get an officer of the law?" Pascal's voice boomed.

She could see the rising anger in Pascal's twitching eyes as if he were forgetting the rules that they both abided by. Rules that made no sense. Rules that washed away dreams and tore into their psyches. But he was dangerously close to forgetting those rules, and in doing so, abandoning them to chaos.

"What did you say?" The manager said dropping the tickets.

"Pascal," she said, shaking his arm. "Let's go now. We shall walk back up to Harlem." She reached out to him with all the mental energy she could muster, trying to will him back to reason.

The coolness in the lobby evaporated and Isabella felt a sticky, cloying, pervasive heat envelope her. The rotting smell Isabella noticed from last night choked the air. Pascal's right arm twitched. As if someone controlled it from afar, it lifted, moving toward the clerk.

"We're done. Get out of here," the clerk yelped, but as Pascal advanced, the clerk fell to his knees. His face reddened. The young man's glasses slid off and he clutched at his throat.

The patrons scurried away from the four of them. Someone yelled for a doctor and another for the police.

Pascal stood over the clerk and said, "A time is coming that such a thing will never happen again to any colored person. America will be washed of its sins. I have seen it."

"Pascal, we must go," she said, grabbing his arm.

He looked through her, his eyes a shimmering spirit blue, and shoved her. Isabella slammed into the manager who pushed her out of his way.

Isabella righted herself and watched as Pascal towered over the man and chanted. *Pascal is possessed!*

The clerk vomited eel black fluids. The oily liquid that spewed from his mouth oozed across the lobby floor. On instinct, Isabella took her purse and knocked Pascal across the head. "Spirit, leave this body!" she yelled.

She heard Pascal's neck crack. He blinked many times. People had come to help the clerk who now moaned and writhed on the floor.

The manager locked eyes with Pascal and walked backwards, as if in a stupor. His thin lips trembled and his hands shook. "A demon is among us. God help us!"

Isabella grabbed his hand, pulled him toward her and they ran out of the lobby and kept running for a few blocks. When they stopped, Pascal said nothing, as if still in a daze. They found a phone booth and she called Middy to pick them up.

They rode in silence. She thought about Pascal's behavior and his strange comment about America being cleansed of its sins. When Middy arrived in front of her building, before leaving, Isabella reached over to kiss Pascal. As if far away, he barely moved his head to acknowledge her. Her lips pressed into a cold, damp cheek.

And there was no telephone call from him that evening or the next.

I shouldn't bother him after what happened a few nights ago. She paced up and down the block for ten minutes before deciding to call on Pascal.

Pleased that she convinced Middy to let her in after she told him she had urgent news for Pascal, she walked down the hall to Pascal's study. She opened the door, walked in and saw a number of open books on the table. Isabella rifled through them. Most were about the slave trade. They made her shiver. Such a cruel history her people sprang from. Such difficult reading.

Well, where was he?

She climbed the grand stairwell to the second floor, drawn to the parlor. She entered from the door at the far end of the hall, the one Pascal had used after the séance.

"Pascal, dear, I'm here with a surprise."

The smell caught her attention. Damp. Musky. Oceanic.

Pascal lay on the floor on his side, shaking.

The urn had been taken down from its pedestal and rested a few inches away from him. It was different. To her surprise the carvings of the ugly figures were gone! The chipped urn's "face" was blank. She rushed toward Pascal and then stopped. Everywhere the squat gray figures surrounded him. The forms before her were real, not shadows. Their wide mouths gaped. They jerked, hopped and leapt. They pulled at his ears and at his fingers. They danced and uttered unintelligible guttural sounds. As if sharing one mind and body, they froze and collectively turned to look upon Isabella.

In a flash they formed a circle around her as well. She jumped and yelped. Isabella stomped on them, but like rubber they bounced off of her shoes.

She screamed for Middy. Grabbing an ash tray off an end table, she threw it at the dancing figures. They scattered, disappearing.

"Oh God," she moaned as she lifted Pascal's legs and attempted to drag him over to the couch.

Middy ran in.

"Middy, oh thank God! Please help me lift him up."

They pulled him up on the sofa. Middy shook Pascal and repeatedly called his name. "Mr. Clay, Mr. Clay. Come back."

Middy pulled a vial from his trouser pocket, opened it and pushed it under Pascal's nose.

Pascal snapped awake. Feverish and drawn, he waved away any more of the salts.

She paced around the room and stopped in front of the urn. It now looked as it always did. The figures were there once again. She rubbed her eyes and shook her head.

Middy lifted the urn with effort and placed it back on its stand.

"Middy, when you walked in…did you see?"

"Nothing, Miss Wells. I saw nothing."

"I think-"

"I'll bring something for you and Mr. Clay to eat. He'll need it."

"Can you tell me?" she said drawing close to him. Her eyes searched his tight face for answers.

"Ma'am?"

"Have you seen him like this before?"

An unreadable expression flickered across his face. "Yes, Ma'am. Yes, I have. He pushes himself with his work."

The faithful manservant turned and left.

It took a full half hour for Pascal to rouse. To her dismay he awoke angry, directing much of it at her.

"Pascal, what's going on? I saw-"

"He should have never let you in here," He sat up but had not risen from the couch.

"Don't blame Middy."

Pascal folded his arms and said, "I employ him and I can and *will* blame him. I gave him strict orders not to disturb me under any circumstances!"

"He didn't," Isabella began.

"What are you doing here anyway?" he said in a tone that cut.

"Pascal, please… I only meant-"

"I'm sure you've heard that the road to hell was paved with good intentions."

She was trying hard to blink back tears. "I came to give you good news. The swami is coming earlier than expected. I wanted to surprise you. After the other night, I-"

His brow softened, those beautiful lips upturned and the few lines around his eyes relaxed.

"Go on," he said, studying her.

"That's it, something changed in his schedule. He'll come next week."

"That is welcome news."

The morning's unusual events had caught up with her. She felt faint. *When was the last time I ate?* She grabbed one of the sandwiches Middy left and took two big bites. The act of chewing helped slow her breathing, she concentrated on the texture of the bread, the sharpness of the cheese. She focused on all the sensations of the food, willing herself to focus.

He patted her knee. "You saw a type of water sprite. Harmless."

"They live on the urn?" She asked, her brows rising up. "Why were they surrounding you?"

"They are protectors of it."

She swallowed and then said, "They didn't look protective at all. Not at all. Please don't lie to me, Pascal."

"The urn connects to the great spirits of the ocean. The sprites act as intermediaries in a way. Under the right conditions, the spirits will grant requests."

"What request?"

"That is none of your concern."

Isabella locked eyes with Pascal, searching them.

"Do not look at me like that!" he snapped.

"What do you know about the power of those spirits? Like the one you called on?"

Pascal rose from the couch and turned his back to her. Steady on his feet, he seemed recovered from the earlier incident. "I am a seeker."

Isabella returned her sandwich to the plate. "I don't understand what's happening to you. You've traveled so many places, but I swear that your recent trip…" she sighed and hugged herself. "You're different now…All those books on slavery in your study," she said, her voice trailing to a whisper.

He turned around, his face now a scowl. "No one will teach us *our* history."

"I don't want to think so much about the past."

"Don't be a ninny. There are already enough of those in the world."

Isabella laid the half-eaten sandwich back on the plate. She got up and wiped a tear from her face. "I shall call on you when you are more civil." She felt unable to stop trembling.

He rushed over, grabbed her and kissed her deeply on the lips. "Forgive me. I am not myself today."

Or many days of late, she thought.

Their lips pressing together, however, made her forget everything in that moment. The tingling of his tongue and the wave of his hair, cut precisely, and the outline of his manhood that she could feel pressed up against her took her breath away. He pulled away and walked toward the end table and picked up the music box. The music played and he wrapped his arm around her waist and waltzed her across the room.

As they danced, she thought of Robert Louis Stevenson's troubled characters of Dr. Jekyll and Mr. Hyde. Had she been so enamored by Pascal's charm, his determination and ability to rouse a crowd that she had overlooked his less flattering traits? She felt her thinking about him was increasingly muddled by his ongoing involvement with strange spirits.

He kissed her again with passion. She stiffened. After a long moment, he released her, stroked her hair and sent her out the door.

"You'll know everything at the right time, Isabella. Trust in me."

She had only met one swami before and he had barely spoken to her. She felt none of the peace and sense of calm then as she did now riding in the car with Sri Sri Asokonanada. The older Indian man had been solicitous and courteous. She felt sorry for his assistant, Kamal, a young pimply looking monk as he seemed ill at ease in all social settings.

Middy had picked them up from the American Theosophical Society office and they rode in companionable silence. She did not tell the swami that he was going to meet her fiancé. No one at the Society knew her and Pascal were to be married. Pascal was just another wealthy donor interested in the occult. They did not seem to care what color he was.

When they arrived at Pascal's, she was surprised to see Elliot but didn't let her face betray that anything was out of the ordinary. She introduced him after Pascal, "Mr. Gibson, is also an organizer of the monthly healings."

Pascal and Elliot greeted Sri Sri Asokonanada with warmth and then led him upstairs. She and Kamal waited in a receiving room for guests on the first floor.

Isabella had brought a newspaper with her and hadn't gotten to the society pages when the swami appeared with Middy at their door.

"Miss Randall," the swami said. His angular thin face looked tired.

The young monk who had been dozing, jumped up.

It's been less than twenty minutes!

"Sri Sri Asokonanada, is something wrong?" she asked.

"We must leave now," he said with a determined and fixed brow, but not in an unkind way.

"Of course," she nodded. "This is the last appointment of the day. Middy will take you and Kamal back to your accommodations."

The swami nodded.

After she found Middy in the kitchen and saw them off, she took the stairs two at a time eager to find Elliot and Pascal.

"What happened?" she asked Pascal. She noticed that his face looked drawn, as if he had added years to his life, like after the séance.

"There is a time for everything, Isabella," Pascal said curtly.

They looked at each other and impatience twisted in her core that she couldn't hide, "Well, did you find him pleasant to talk to?" she blurted.

"It is none of your affair," Elliot said with such ferocity that she felt punched in the stomach.

Isabella could not stop herself from releasing the frustration that bubbled inside. "I worked hard to arrange that meeting. If something unpleasant has happened, it could affect my job-"

"Stop thinking of yourself. Enough. Leave us, I will call you," Pascal said. She noticed his eyes had the hint of derangement and rage she had seen at the opera house.

She drew back.

Elliot didn't bother to look at her as he left the room with Pascal.

The days went on without her hearing much from Pascal. When they dined, he looked as if sleep had eluded for days and was terrible company. He wouldn't say another word about the swami's visit. She gathered it had gone badly. She so wanted to know what transpired between them, though she knew she shouldn't ask.

Taking a break between appointments, Isabella and Swami Asokonanada walked in Central Park on a beautiful fall day. Kamal, trailed behind, periodically sneezing, a victim of seasonal allergies.

She had gotten used to the swami being silent unless spoken to. Today they made small talk about his schedule and the foods he had sampled on this trip. Swami Asokonanada was in love with glazed donuts, even though he declared that Americans had too much of a sweet tooth. Her thoughts circled as they walked and her gaze bounced from place to place.

They sat on a bench and she rubbed the back of her neck several times. She crossed and uncrossed her legs. *If Pascal isn't going to tell me how it all went, I'll have to ask.* She looked into the yogi's eyes. "I was surprised to hear you and Mr. Clay spoke so briefly."

"Yes, one of my least favorite visits," he said, shaking his head.

"He does good work with his healings."

"Indeed, that is a fact. He has opened many doors to the other side and is an earnest seeker. But I could be of no assistance to him, my child."

"Why?"

The swami paused before speaking. "Miss Randall, is there something I should know?"

No one at the Society knew about her and Pascal. She bowed her head. "Please don't say anything. He is my friend…and I am worried about him. He's been acting strangely for some time." *Like a different person.*

The wise man's face clouded over. "He wanted me to teach him. I said no. He wanted to know some of the most sacred rites of water to commune with and try to command energies that know nothing of human sensibilities. Not only could this cause madness in him but would disturb elemental forces that could not be easily controlled."

"Oh," she said. More confused than when she asked.

He rose. "I would advise caution in your dealings with him, Miss Randall. He has an unbalanced mind, ready to topple."

The next night, she was relieved to hear Elliot's voice on the phone asking if he could meet with her and Marcus at a café to talk about Pascal.

The booth seated all of them comfortably. She was surprised how glad she was to see Marcus. The past few weeks had felt anything but normal.

"Thanks for coming," Elliot said.

"Hummpf," Marcus said and took a sip of his soda.

Elliot looked around before he spoke. "I'm worried about our teacher and friend."

Her breath caught. *Me, too!*

"He isn't so much of a friend to me anymore," Marcus said.

"Please, Marcus," she said, placing her hand over his.

"He's been entertaining wild ideas," Elliot whispered.

"I told you he was acting strange. But he clearly doesn't want my help or else he would have called," Marcus said looking away.

"I've been watching him and I'm worried. He sought a spiritual teacher. The swami said no to him. It messed him up," Elliot said.

"What swami?" Marcus raised his eyebrows.

Isabella filled him in on the situation.

"I need your help," Elliot said.

"What is it? What can we do?" Anything, Isabella thought.

"We need to bring the teacher to him," Elliot continued. "I'm worried that if he doesn't get some guidance, he will do something that could harm someone or himself."

"Nonsense," Marcus said, shaking his head. "Pascal would never hurt anyone."

"Isabella, haven't you seen some things recently that have scared you?" Elliot asked.

"Yes," she said with a slow nod. "I have. Marcus, he's right. This is not the normal Pascal."

Elliot smiled then and said, "I know it's been hard for you."

She took a deep breath. *Maybe Elliot does understand.*

"What do you propose we do?" Marcus said.

"Can you bring the swami back?" Elliot asked.

"No," she shook her head. "I don't think that I can. His trip here is concluding. He has very little time."

"Do you love Pascal?" Elliot said.

The dark-skinned waitress smiled at them, refilling Elliot and Isabella's coffee cups.

What kind of question was that? "Don't question my loyalty," she said, the words tumbling out fast. She felt her cheeks grow hot. She sat up straight and took a moment to compose herself. "He has other appointments and it would look strange for me to request a change in his schedule."

Elliot paused and shook his head. In a flash that made Isabella jump, he leaned across the table and grabbed her hand. "Pascal wants to make a deal with the ocean spirits to open sacred portals."

A shudder went through her as Marcus spit out his soda. "That's crazy! Impossible!"

"I don't know whether it is or not, but that's his goal, part of his plan," he said, releasing his grip.

"Why does he want to do that?" Isabella asked.

Elliot shrugged. "Once those portals are open, he believes he can help more people in a new way."

"Nonsense," Marcus said. "How could he think such a thing?"

Isabella looked at Marcus, "I fear that he is working himself to death."

Elliot gently placed his hands over hers, "Put another meeting on the swami's calendar, please. Take charge. Find a way."

She had gotten lucky in that Kamal had come down with a bad cold (and not allergies after all), in the last few days. Isabella happily stepped in to attend to the swami's needs. And she had brought him the best donuts in the city. He agreed to meet with her "troubled friend" once more to see if he could provide some temporary comfort.

Middy said nothing to her or Swami Asokonanada in the car ride over to Pascal's or as he opened the parlor doors. She thought that strange. As soon as they stepped in the parlor, Isabella knew she had made a grave error. The air in the room was charged and thick like the night of the séance. One look around the room plummeted her hopes that the kind man next to her would be able to reach her beloved. He was supposed to have a private audience with Pascal. Instead the room was full of people.

Pascal stood with Elliot and some of their followers, Eleanor among them. An obnoxious giggle escaped her lips. The urn stood in the middle of the room. Marcus lay sideways on the couch, his hands tied in the front. Blood dribbled from gashes on Marcus's forehead and chin. He must have fought with Elliot and others once he realized that something was wrong. Terribly wrong. "Pascal," he shouted, "You must stop. This is madness."

"What's going on here?" Isabella demanded.

Marcus spoke in a halted voice, "Do you know what he wants to do? He wants to raise *all* the African souls from their ocean grave! All who died on the way over!"

"Our people who were taken from us! They will avenge us from their imposed watery graves!" Pascal said. "All who take part in this ceremony will rule the earth with me. The greatest ocean spirits are joining in—we will wash this earth clean and begin again."

This could not be her beloved's plan. He was possessed. Tricked by a powerful spirit. Maybe more than one!

Pascal motioned for two of his followers to grab the swami. "Bring him to me."

Swami Asokonanada maintained a calm demeanor. "This is not what I expected tonight."

Pascal strode over to the slight man and said, "I ask you again, transfer your powers to me. I do not wish to take your life to obtain them. Your great wisdom can help me rule."

Isabella rushed toward Pascal but Elliot grabbed her arm and jerked her back. "He doesn't need you for this part," he hissed.

"Nooooo, no, no. You must let them go, Pascal. I need you. What about our life?"

Pascal turned to her, "I give you one chance, to reign with me in the new place, a place cleansed of America's sins. So many sins against so many peoples."

"Elliot! He is being controlled. Look at his eyes!" Isabella said. Indeed, Pascal's eyes had turned a hazy blue.

Eleanor squeaked, "You don't need her."

Elliot's grip tightened. She twisted and they locked eyes. How she hated seeing his smug grin. "You lied to me," she said with gritted teeth. In that moment she wanted to extinguish the trusting part of her that had been so disastrously misled.

"You're playing your part," Elliot said.

"These spirits are manipulating him," she implored. Can't you see that? *They* want power, they want to be free to cause chaos," she cried.

The swami spoke, "Pascal, you do not know what you seek. You have been misled. If you open those portals, no souls will come but the ocean spirits will enter and destroy the world. Do you understand? *This world.* There is no way you can control them."

"Your imaginations are all so terribly small," Pascal bellowed. "How can they do worse than what we have all already endured?"

Twisting in Elliot's grip, Isabella said. "As you have said so many times, we are here to plumb the mysteries of life in ways that further our goals of justice. You can do that my love, *we* can still do that, but not like this."

"Shut up," Elliot said as he tightened his grip on Isabella, causing her to wince.

Pascal shook his head and laughed. "You had your chance to be part of this. Of something great. Now you will be my sacrifice."

A terrible cracking noise burst from the urn.

"We must get to the heart of the issue. We must come back to our ancestors." Spittle flew out of Pascal's mouth. He chanted and slowly the gray figures on the urn, the water sprites, transformed. Isabella, transfixed, shuddered as if something plucked at each of her vertebrae. Gasps arose from some of Pascal's followers as they watched the static images on the urn undulate and with little effort peel themselves off the urn and drop to the floor.

Pascal nodded to the men holding the swami. They pushed him down to the ground.

Water shot out of the urn. Frogs jumped out. An ear-splitting noise erupted. Everyone fell to their knees and covered their ears. Elliot let go of Isabella's arm and took a step back.

"Now! Sacrifice him now!" Pascal screamed.

I must destroy the source. Isabella seized on this thought as she regained her balance.

Elliot loosened his grip in his distraction, and she took her chance. She had been a pitcher in her college days. Fast, accurate. A talent so long buried. Isabella shot up and grabbed the nearest object closest to her, the music box. Her fingers wrapped around the cold object. The memory of Pascal dancing with her, twirling her around the room, passed through her. Their love. Her desire. Gripping it with precision, she hurled the music box toward the urn.

Contact. The urn shattered. Pascal let loose an unholy guttural scream and collapsed. The followers rushed to him. Isabella made her way over to the swami who was unhurt. Dead frogs of various colors and shapes were strewn everywhere. It was impossible to avoid stepping on one. They both worked to untie Marcus.

In the middle of the room, Eleanor helped Pascal sit up. He bled from the nose and he bore strange marks that ran the length of his face. He opened his eyes with effort, and when his gaze landed upon Isabella, she saw little gratitude in them. Motioning to Marcus and Swami Askonanada, she made for the parlor door.

DARK WINGS

GAIL Z. MARTIN

C onri Kemble startled awake, annoyed to discover that his right
arm had gone numb from pillowing his head and that he was
drooling on his research notes.

He sat up with a groan from where he had been hunched over the
table and stretched, grimacing as his spine popped loudly. Blinking didn't
clear away the sleep, nor did gulping the cold coffee remaining in his cup.
A noise had roused him from his dream, but now as he strained to listen,
all remained silent.

"Where are you, Leonard?" he murmured as fear and loneliness
tangled in his gut. "And why can't I find you?"

Conri pushed the heavy, carved wooden chair against the nap of the
faded Persian rug. He grabbed his mug and staggered to the kitchen to fill
it. *Normal people aren't still chugging java at three in the morning*, he chided
himself.

Normal people aren't witches whose partners got zapped into another dimen-
sion—or worse, his mind countered.

Conri splashed cold water on his face, then stretched and twisted to
wake up his brain and body. He glanced in the mirror and quickly looked
away. Dark circles shadowed his red-rimmed green eyes. His blond hair
needed washing, and he hadn't shaved in a while. Conri had been going
on just a couple of hours sleep a night all week. Ever since the battle when
Leonard vanished. The exhaustion, worry, and stress were taking a toll.

I can't stop, not until I know what happened to him. Not until I'm sure.

Revenge had nothing to do with Conri's obsession. He'd avenged Leonard when he beheaded Dino Hicks, their dark warlock enemy, and burned the bones. Now he chased the wild hope of being able to bring Leonard back where he belonged—or be certain that he was indeed lost forever and join him in the shadows.

Coffee to work. Whiskey to sleep. Rinse and repeat as long as I can keep moving.

I won't give up on you, Leonard.

Outside the rambling old Victorian house, the December wind banged the shutters and howled across the angles and corners of the slate roof. He had inherited the Second Empire-style home from his grandmother when he came of age and entered into his power as a witch. That last was important, she had told him, because the house needed to respect its owner. Because the house had *secrets*.

Right now, the only secret Conri cared about was finding his partner in life and magic before it was too late.

He picked up his mug and then, on second thought, grabbed the whole damn pot and carried both with him into the study that now more resembled a war room. Whiteboards and cork boards were propped on furniture all around the walls, where Conri scribbled notes to himself, pinned up printouts, and tried to link obscure details he'd found in volumes of forgotten lore.

It looks like one of those movies with an obsessed detective chasing the serial killer who murdered his lover. Maybe that's not too far off, minus the magic and, goddess willing, the murder.

A fire blazed in the fireplace, and the wind whipped the flames to spit embers onto the hearth and send the shadows dancing. Curls of smoke rose from a brazier, filling the air with the scent of frankincense, acacia, myrrh, ginseng, and galangal to heighten psychic power, drive out evil, and break curses. Conri set his mug on a coaster and the pot on a trivet because goddess-forbid he mar the old mahogany. His grandmother's ghost would fuss at him for leaving a ring, and Leonard would never let him hear the end of it.

Leonard.

Conri took his seat. The massive, ornately-carved Baroque revival table had witnessed nearly two centuries of Kemble magic. Its glossy finish protected complex marquetry sigils and runes of power and protection, while carved into the stretches between the thick barley-twist table legs were the watchful faces of grotesques and familiars, bits of incantations in Latin, Sumerian, Enochian, and spell-boosting symbols sealed with Conri's blood and that of his ancestors.

Stacks of old leather-bound books and piles of yellowed scrolls took up part of the expansive tabletop. An etched silver scrying bowl sat at the far end, and beside it, the bloodied Damascene knife he had used in an unsuccessful effort to locate his missing soulmate. His nearby laptop screen showed pages filled with newer grimoires and lore. He rubbed his eyes, gulped more coffee, and fought the urge to doze. *I'll sleep when I have answers. One way or another, I'll rest with Leonard.*

Tap-tap-tap.

Conri looked up sharply, eyes wide, and stared at the darkened windows. *Surely it's just branches in the wind.* He turned a page in yet another old spell book that smelled of earth and vanilla. Here and there, spidery foxing made the faded ink difficult to read.

Tap-tap-tap-tap.

Fear turned Conri's heart to ice as he realized the tapping was on the door, and it wasn't from branches. He'd been brazen about his profligate use of magic in his search for Leonard. Even though the old home had wardings built into its foundation and reinforced by the iron fence and the protective plants surrounding the house, that show of power could attract the wrong attention.

He strode to the foyer and threw open the iron-bound oaken front door. The two carriage gas lamps flanking the doorway flickered in the frigid winter air, revealing a blanket of untouched snow and the steady fall of large wet flakes.

Conri shivered, but not from the cold. Magic flowed through the old house like always, but the currents and eddies had been disturbed. *Either something has answered my call—or someone's come calling to finish me.*

He checked every room to assure himself that the protections remained in place on his way back to his work table. When Conri reached for his mug, his hand trembled.

Tap-tappity-tap.

Conri's heart beat wildly as he ran to the window, shoved the sash up, and flung the shutters wide. *I'm done hiding.* It should have frightened him how little he cared about self-preservation when it came to saving Leonard.

Icy wind stirred the aubergine damask draperies. A proud raven stepped inside, unbothered by the storm that raged beyond the rippled glass. With a shadowy flutter, the bird launched itself into the air and perched atop a marble bust of Poe.

"How are you coming to me, Sir Raven? As omen, prophet, Morrigan, or trickster? What warning do you bear for me—or do you come with word from my lost Leonard?" Conri figured a formal tone was the safest to take with this unexpected visitor.

Grief, lack of sleep, and the heady smell of incense made Conri dizzy, and only the adrenaline coursing through his veins at the arrival of the raven kept him standing. *Is this a vision or merely a hallucination of my over-taxed mind?*

The raven fixed him with its obsidian eyes, as haughty as an oracle. "Restore," it croaked.

Conri stared at the large, dark bird and wondered if he had heard correctly. He decided to trust his heart and his gut. "Yes, that's right. I'm trying to restore Leonard. Do you know something?" *Please, please, give me something to work with. Anything,* he begged silently. When he hadn't been staying up nearly all night scouring the grimoires, Conri had spent the last week summoning demons, attempting to bargain with demigods, bribing the Fey, and teetering on the brink of forbidden magic. Nothing had worked.

"The lore."

Conri swore he heard the bird speak again, not just a rough caw but real words. He turned back to the table, littered with evidence of his failure. "Don't you think I've searched the lore? I've read through every book we had, every book I stole from the warlock, anything I could beg, borrow, or download from the dodgy places on the Dark Web, and I still can't find him," he finished miserably. Conri poured himself whiskey instead of coffee to steady his hands and steel his raw nerves. He tossed it back, impatient for the burn to make him feel alive and the buzz to numb his grief. His stomach grumbled, reminding him he had gone too long subsisting on whatever food was fast to fix and close at hand.

The bird regarded him dispassionately. It shuddered and partially extended its wings. Conri's heart pounded, fearing it might take flight.

"I don't know what you are, but don't go," he begged with a catch in his voice. "Please don't fly away." *All my hope has flown before.*

In response, the raven mantled its wings and gave him a glassy-eyed stare.

Still clutching the crystal glass, Conri sank to a seat on the burgundy velvet high-backed couch. The touch of the flocked nap brought back overwhelming sense memories of Leonard, warm and solid pressed against him—the timbre of his voice, the scent of his cologne mingled with sweat and musk, the taste of his lips. *Which might never happen again if I can't bring Leonard home.*

Conri bit back a sob and glared at the raven. "Tell me, please, I beg you. Have you come to help—or damn me? Are you here to lead me to him? To my love, my lost Leonard?"

I'm losing my mind.

"Evermore." The raven rasped and spread its wings wide as if to shelter Conri.

Conri wished he could accept that single word as proof of the bond between himself and Leonard, that somehow this messenger—either grim infernal omen or ghastly harbinger—affirmed their eternal connection.

"Wretch," Conri snarled, feeling sorrow claw through his heart again as he despaired over finding Leonard before it was too late—or finding him at all. "Why couldn't you be a soothsayer and tell me what I must do? I'd accept a devil who would make a deal and take my soul. But no, you're just a bird, not angel or demon, not even Leonard's ghost come to haunt our house." He staggered to his feet. "If you can't help me find him, then by all that's sacred, make me forget. I can't live without him."

The raven folded its wings and sat as placid as the bust beneath its taloned feet. Its eyes gleamed like polished jet as they stared down at Conri, inscrutable.

"Before."

With that, the bird swooped down and knocked a book from the table before returning to his perch. Conri scowled at him and went to pick up the tome, titled *Familiars in Lore and Practice.*

Something sent him to me, Conri thought, staring up at the huge, grim bird. *What if he's not here to torment me? What if he came to help?*

Conri hadn't worked with a spirit-familiar in a long time. His favored animal daemon was a coyote.

And Leonard's is a crow.

The realization cut through his fog of bereavement and recrimination, and he felt a surge of sudden, desperate purpose.

Restore, the lore, before...those could be directions. Evermore—not sure about that, but let me see what happens if I look at the books we studied before we fought the warlock and see if there's something that might help me undo the curse.

"Stay right here," he told the raven.

Conri pushed books out of the way to make room for the three tomes he and Leonard had used to create the incantations they cast against Dino Hicks. At the time, all they had been seeking was how to break the dark warlock's spell on the small town he held captive. They had gone in with magical and mundane weapons as well as what they believed—incorrectly—to be sufficient protection.

Having Leonard disappear wasn't something they expected.

Conri silently berated himself for not starting his search with the original lore books, but he'd mentally shelved them under "attack magic." Now he searched for anything defensive, clues on how to reverse or lift a curse.

"I found something." Conri looked over his shoulder at the large, still bird. "According to this, it's possible to curse a witch to take the form of his spirit-familiar. The warlock cast the spell at me, but Leonard jumped in front and pushed me out of the way, so he got hit." Conri paused. "Leonard?" Now that he thought about it, the bird's dark feathers and inky eyes did bear a resemblance to Leonard's black hair and dark chocolate eyes.

"Afore."

That single word started Conri's heart beating again. "Hold on—I'll figure out how to do this," he promised.

He went to the storage room and came back with jars and canisters, as well as a teacup.

"Damiana for tea," he murmured to himself, nudging the kettle onto the embers.

"Mandrake, datura, and rosemary, to burn." He poured a measure of each into a stone mortar and ground them to powder.

"Mugwort and nightshade, for direction and protection." Conri used a rune-etched silver spoon to scoop a small amount of both into a small linen drawstring bag. Once he tied it shut, he slipped the pouch into his pocket.

One more necessary item remained untouched, and Conri refused to look at it until its time. He made the tea and let it steep, then added the powder mix to the brazier. The unmistakable scent filled the air, making him lightheaded, as if his soul and body were only barely tethered together.

"There's one more piece, once I drink the tea," Conri said, speaking to the raven and hoping his hunch was true, that this was really Leonard.

He lifted the bone-handled damascene knife and set it on the bookshelves near a large telescope tripod. His own dark blood still stained the razor edge. "It's a blood spell—mine and yours. I need to cut us both and let the fluid mingle. I can re-open the cut I made on my left palm." Conri added, holding up his already bandaged hand.

"Do you trust me? Will you let me cut you on the chest? You know how sharp the blade is—you won't feel anything 'til it's done. Doesn't have to be deep—just enough to run freely."

Maybe he imagined it, but Conri swore he saw the raven blink, a barely-there flash of white, which he took for assent. The black bird spread its wings and ghosted down to land on the brass telescope just beneath his current perch.

The vision powder burned fast. Conri inhaled deeply, feeling the rush immediately, as well as the unsettling sensation that body and spirit now existed slightly offset from one another. As if his soul might decide to go wandering and leave its flesh behind. The unfamiliar magic terrified Conri, but the text had been clear that Leonard would need a guide in order to return to his normal form.

"I'm sorry you got cursed protecting me," Conri said, meeting the raven's stare. "I don't want to hurt you. If something goes wrong and this doesn't work, I need you to know how much I love you."

The raven did not look away. "Adore."

"Let's do it." Conri lifted the teacup in salute and quaffed the drink all at once. The room spun, and the ticking of the clock on the mantle boomed as loudly as Conri's heartbeat. Every sensation was *more*, too much.

He set the cup down and picked up the blade. "Together," he murmured. He sliced across his palm, then slashed the blade over the raven's blue-black feathered breast and pressed the cut on his hand against the bird's bleeding gash.

Pain laced through his veins, streaking up his arm to his chest. *Did I read the spell wrong? Have I just killed us both?*

The raven gave a deep, gurgling croak and burst into flame.

"Leonard!" Conri staggered back, watching in horror.

The fire vanished. Flakes of ash fell to the floor, covering the naked, motionless form of the man he loved.

Conri fell to his knees, brushing away the soot, and gently turned Leonard onto his back. *He's breathing. There's no blood, no injuries.* "Wake up, babe. Show me that you're really here."

Leonard groaned. His eyes blinked open, and his gaze rapidly scanned all around until it came to rest on Conri. "Thank you." His voice sounded as throaty and hoarse as the raven's call.

"I wasn't going to stop until we were together, one way or another," Conri told him, sliding his hand to twine their fingers together and bending down to kiss his lips. "Please don't ever disappear on me again."

"I promise," Leonard said. "Nevermore."

THE DEVIL IN THE BELFRY...
REDUX

DAY AL-MOHAMED

In the three thousand and thirty seventh year of our Lord and Slayer, when the dust devils had settled and the sun's iridescent heat no longer burned, I took it upon myself to travel the world. Or such of the world that was left to us.

I was a young man of four and twenty, and disavowing the profession of my father and my father's father, as both blacksmith and metalworker - I rather fancied myself a bard – I struck out toward the rumored cities of the Sunken Coast. I would be a great storyteller and would bring culture and whimsy to the world like the great scribes of ancient times: Perry, Wollstonecraft, Lorenzini. I would be a teller of tales and singer of songs. I would share stories of all the lands and remind people of our great histories and glories.

Growing up in the safe valleys and caves of Meramec, we always knew there were other communities that had survived the Collapse. Word came through, usually from the St. Genevieve ports and towns along the Big Muddy. Words and food and cloth and sometimes wondrous things like oranges and alligator pears.

But as I and my camel Ermengarde, that beloved foul red beast, traversed the shifting sands and broken asphalt byways, all we found, mostly, was skeletons of steel and concrete rising up to the green-gray sky. Sometimes I could guess the purpose of those ancient construc-tions: a home, a factory, a mill, but other times it was just fanciful speculation. We could've ridden south following the waterways, but those paths were already well traveled. I wanted new and unique. Instead, I found miles of desert and ravaged areas that even the wild beasts seemed to avoid.

That doesn't mean there weren't people. I shared breath and bread with many different tribes. I drank moon in the hollers of Mud Creek and sang with wolves at Angel Mounds. I ate fresh meat with the hunters of Pamunkey Peninsula and trekked through the thousand-year orchards of Vijini. Miles and miles I walked until I reached the great Blue Lantic. I pondered its name as I watched the green and yellow waves swirl and whoosh. Plump sea plants (which tasted terrible) floated in its brackish shallows. I thought my journey had come to its end. Was this it? Was this all there was?

I was just coming to the end of a week with the watermen of Old Capitol who fished over the remains of the drowned cities. Every night I spun stories until the early hours. The watermen laughed as they pulled in their pots and called me a liar and then shouted for more. As well as telling stories, I collected tales of things I had never heard or seen and the food... the blue crabs were such a delight I have never tasted before or since. I dream of those crabs.

But what they told me that seized my imagination and set my feet impatient for the road was of a village to the south of them, hidden away in the mountains and valleys - Burattino. Its people were reclusive; none ever left, and few visitors were allowed in, but there was some barter. Fresh seafood and crabs in exchange for cabbages. Cabbages!

What was a cabbage?

I now had a new destination and my journey would continue. Excitement bubbled under my skin, as I envisaged myself bringing stories and songs to a town that had never known of things beyond their lands. This would be my discovery. This would be my destiny.

I will not linger upon the boring details of the arduous journey. Suffice it to say that it involved many long days and difficult nights, and a very unhappy Ermengarde. But the sight, when I crested the last hilltop to look down on the valley with the small town nestled within, was worth every aching footstep and every angry camel-nip. It was exactly as I had been told by the watermen:

"The village is in a perfectly circular valley, about a quarter of a mile in circumference, and entirely surrounded by gentle hills, over whose summit the people have never yet ventured to pass. For this they assign the very good reason that they do not believe there is anything at all on the other side."

I counted fifty or sixty little houses. Real houses, from antiquity, with brick walls and tiled roofs, divided by tidy paths and gardens with tiny round plants I could not identify. Row upon row of houses and gardens. They were so exact and so identical, precisely placed, with their backs to the encompassing hills as if to deny there was anything other than the town in the whole world. In the center of the valley was a town square - that much I could recognize - an empty space of green grass, crisscrossed with brick paths and a great clock tower. It loomed above the squat homes, its faces gazing out over the valley --one in each of the seven sides of the steeple— so every resident could step from his home and look across the town and see the heavy black hands that moved with a delicate, unyielding precision.

I stood for a moment, looking out on the town in awe. It had survived. Unlike the rest of the country, Burattino looked like the towns I'd heard of in far history, in the time before the Collapse.

The sun was high overhead as Ermengarde and I jogged along the eastern ridge of the valley. We had just started down towards the village when I noticed a peculiar occurrence. The inhabitants began to gather in the central clearing. All of them – men, women, children, even babes in arms. They gazed up at all the faces of the clock, not even noticing me.

I hurried our pace to an awkward gallop, much to Ermengarde's dismay. It would seem some momentous event was about to take place and it was a matter of absolute necessity that all the residents of this hamlet be present. I reached the edge of the crowd, and Ermengarde stopped abruptly, refusing to get any closer.

What I describe now, Dear Reader, is exactly what happened. The resonant bell high up in the tower sounded. Deep and mellifluous, it rang out over the entire valley.

"One!" said the clock.

"One!" echoed every person standing around the green, their voices raised in unison. I could see everywhere, clutched in hands were pocket watches, the faces of the tiny gold timepieces mirroring the great clock. "One" dinged the tiny watches.

"Two!" continued the big bell.

"Two!" repeated all the townsfolk. "Two" repeated their watches.

"Three! Four! Five! Six! Seven! Eight! Nine! Ten!" said the bell.

"Three! Four! Five! Six! Seven! Eight! Nine! Ten!" answered the men, women, and children. It was a magnificent and eerie chorus. The tiny watches perfectly mimicked the great clock's resonant chimes.

"Eleven!" said the big clock.

"Eleven!" echoed the people, their watches held high, chiming eleven.

"Twelve!" rang the bell.

"Twelve!" they finished, their voices rich with satisfaction. The watches binged one last time, the high pitched chime dying away until there was only the memory of sound. And every single thing in the town seemed to give that memory reverence with complete, perfect silence. Not a bird sang, not a whisper of movement. A moment later, as one, the entire town turned and returned to their homes and gardens.

My gaze followed them, awed and a little frightened at the eerie procession. I released a breath I didn't even realize I had been holding. I had never seen anything like it.

"You're off time."

My heart leapt clear up into my hat when the voice came from behind me and I whipped back towards the clock tower. An old gentleman blinked at me, patiently awaiting a response. He was short and what one might uncharitably call rotund, with three chins and lank gray hair. He was dressed in an elegant coat and tail of the brightest blue with gold trim. In his teeth he held a long pipe from which a slow curl of white smoke ascended. The scent of tobacco wreathed us both in seconds.

He must have come from inside the clock tower.

Not knowing the ways of Burattino, I stepped forward, smiled, and introduced myself.

He did not return the smile, but only repeated the words. "You're off time."

I would soon discover that being on time was a matter of extreme importance to the people of Burattino. Unsure what to do, I ducked my head and apologized. He introduced himself as Vater Mitiss, the Bellman and Keeper. Clearly, a position of much respect in the town.

Vater Mitiss puffed loudly on his pipe and stated, "There is a saying among the wisest inhabitants of Burattino: 'No good can come from over the hills'."

"I am no monster from the Blue Lantic. I am no devil from the mountains. Just a humble traveler." I answered. "As human as you are."

He seemed unimpressed and after a couple of minutes of what seemed ardent thought on his part and my pleas about the length and dangers of my journey – I had no shame about my desire to learn more about this borough - he beckoned me to follow him to his home.

We strolled along the smooth path. Tap-tap sounded our shoes on the pavement. It was such a strange sensation and very nice. Of course, filled with curiosity I couldn't help but pepper my host with questions. How long had Burattino been here? How had they survived the Collapse? Was it true they had cabbages and what were cabbages?

Vater Mitiss answered the questions, nothing less and nothing more: Burattino had existed "from its origin, in precisely the same condition which it at present preserves"; it hadn't; yes, and they were wonderful food and fuel.

Vater Mitiss gestured to where three boys toiled in a garden. They were clearly young, the top of their identical blonde heads couldn't have reached higher than my waist. They each wore a purple shirt, buckskin trousers, and heavy shoes with silver buckles. They were hoeing to remove weeds, the tools rising and falling in unison as they made their way down rows of small green balls of leaves.

"Like lettuce?"

Vater Mitiss grunted. He said nothing more. His pace didn't slow until we came to one of the houses nestled against the edge of the valley. I couldn't see how it differed from any of the others. The same red brick walls and white tiled roof separated by pathways and gardens filled with cabbages. Plots of land laid out just so. Like a checkerboard.

He knocked smartly on the door. It was opened by a woman of lovely countenance. She couldn't have been much older than I. His daughter? She wore a huge cap like a sugar-loaf and a tracht of purple with yellow ribbons. In fact, with her blonde hair and red face, she resembled the Plattdüütsch women from Cole Camp just west of my own home. She introduced herself as Mutter Caroline. From her demeanor, it was clear that none of my burning questions would be answered by her lips.

But that did not bother me because the inside of this home had truly enchanted me. It was elegant with gas lights and luxurious blackwood chairs and benches carved in intricate detail showing clocks and cabbages. No doubt items that were a matter of pride for the Burattinos.

There was a fire burning in the deep fireplace with a large pot over it, which Caroline stirred with a restless, restrained violence. She did not look up but answered my unasked question, "Pork and sauerkraut is for dinner."

My host beckoned me to one of the doors leading off from the main room. It was a bedroom with a bed, dresser, chair, and desk, the white blankets bright, even in the dim gaslight. It was more luxurious than anything I had ever known.

"For your stay here," he said before turning abruptly and returning to the main room where he seated himself in a large deep leather chair, right foot on his left knee, and started puffing furiously on his pipe.

I am not so crass a guest as to ever question the generosity of my hosts. Vater Mitiss and his family and the people of Burattino were kind, if a bit odd. However, the very first night of my stay, awakening in the middle of the night with the need to relieve the most natural of urges, I discovered that the door to my room was locked.

After a few moments of panic and pounding on the door, Vater Mitiss spoke through the heavy wood, telling me that this was the time for sleeping. He refused to release me, stating it was for my own benefit and he would be happy to see to me in the morning. Not having much choice but to acquiesce, I held my bladder and returned to bed and a fitful slumber.

True to his word, Vater Mitiss opened the door with the first cock crows of the morning. Beyond him, I could see Caroline stirring an already steaming porridge over the fire. I tried to remain angry. I tried to explain such a betrayal of hospitality. Neither Vater Mitiss nor Caroline understood my fury, nor did they respond to it.

Ermengarde was well kept in one of the gardens at the edge of town. After the first night, I decided to sleep with her. Her cantankerous nature, I assumed, would prevent anyone from disturbing me.

I awoke the next morning, tucked into the same comfortable bed in Vater Mitiss' home. The third night, I slipped away to an abandoned shed on the far side of the town. When I opened my eyes after the night's rest, it was to the white painted ceiling of the guest room. No matter where I chose to make my bed, I always awoke, locked in my assigned bedroom.

I argued, I pleaded, I vented my spleen at the discourtesy and frighteningly controlling behavior. But none of it mattered. I always received the same calm response, that it was for my benefit. It is hard to retain rage in the face of people unmoved or perhaps uncomprehending of their offense.

As the days passed, it bothered me less. Perhaps it was their implacability. This same inflexibility was notable in other ways. Two days after my arrival, I discovered that my clothes had been taken. Caroline replaced my black kerseymere breeches with ones of smooth buckskin, and rather than my worn shirt with patch upon patch, in its place was a shirt of extravagant purple.

Indeed, the clothing was by far more elegant than my own worn threads, yet I couldn't forsake my sentimentality. I had put every patch on my shirt; stitched every rip and tear. It was a symbol of the places and people I visited, each unique in its own way. When I objected to the confiscation and replacement of my clothing, Caroline called for Vater Mitiss who asked if the trousers were not more comfortable than my old clothing? And was the shirt not soft enough? His words were persuasive in their truth. Seeing the confusion on Caroline's face, I did not want to upset her further, so I agreed to my new look.

As time passed, I learned more of the town and its people. Vater Mitiss was a true exemplar of the other residents. He was kind, yet aloof; generous, yet strange. And despite my frustrations at his peculiarities and my own attempts to subvert the deed, I continued to find myself locked away at night.

During the day, I observed and participated in the ways of Burratino. I learned to hoe cabbages, working with the three boys I had seen on my first day. I struggled and swore but eventually found myself raising and lowering the tools with the same precision that they took to the cabbage gardens. Though they often shook their heads and whispered to each other at my inability to keep up with their pace.

And the watermen of Old Capitol had not exaggerated when they said that none of the Burattino would leave the quaint borders of their town. I experienced this myself one morning when I discovered a verdant patch of blueberries just beyond the end of the paved path at the edge of town. Joyous at such a late season treat, I couldn't help but untuck my shirt to gather as many as I could in my shirttail, eating almost as many as I collected.

Seeing one of the fraus passing with a basket over her arm and anxious to share my discovery, I waved her over. She stopped at the edge of the path.

"What it is?" She asked, her accent faint.

I grinned and held up my treasure. "Blueberries! Come! You must try one."

I put another in my mouth and bit down. The tart sweetness rolled over my tongue.

The frau stared at the edge of the path and then at me and then back at where the paving ended. She pursed her lips and furrowed her brow. "You left the path."

"Only a little bit. And blueberries!" I took a step toward her, my hand extended. "They're delicious."

"There is nothing tolerable outside of Burattino," she said mechanically, as if reciting from memory.

She took a step back and gestured with the basket towards the edge of the path. "It is not safe."

"But-"

The frau hitched up her purple trachten, and turned back apace to continue on to wherever she had originally been headed. She repeated, as if to herself more than to me, "There is nothing tolerable outside of Burattino."

While the encounter perturbed me slightly, it was quickly gone from my mind, dismissed as just another of many strange customs.

I enjoyed the tour of the great bell tower atop the Council House. While I was not adept at working with metals and machinery, because of my family background, I had an understanding and appreciation for the intricate cogs and wheels that kept the clock running. In fact, the complexity of the machine was well beyond anything I had ever seen. I was truly impressed, even if I didn't fully understand the inner workings.

Vater Mitiss was inordinately proud of his job as Bell-Keeper, and in truth his role was much revered by the townsfolk. As he said, it was his duty to keep the town running. And, of course, like flocks of birds, the occupants of Burratino would assemble every day to witness the ringing of the noon bells, counting all twelve as they matched the minutes to their pocket watches.

Imagine my joy the day Vater Mitiss gifted me with my own small gold pocket watch that chimed the hours. I had already been in Burattino for two weeks. How easy it was to fall into a pattern with these people because they wouldn't allow anything else. It was so different from where I had come from; so different from all the places I had seen, places of instability and unforeseen catastrophes – some natural and some man-made. It was wonderful to feel accepted and safe. I even shaved my beard to better fit in.

Why was the clock important? Why did they think it was unsafe to leave the valley? I still had so many questions but they seemed to slide ever further back in my mind. I didn't even tell stories anymore. I tried the first few days, but like my anger, it was met with unblinking faces - no tears for my tragedies, no laughter for my comedic tales.

I sat on the steps in front of the Council House, the tall steeple casting a squat shadow on the grass of the center clearing. A cool wind sent leaves dancing in the air. The season was ready to change and winter was on the horizon.

I sucked at my new pipe, another gift. Its long Dutch stem was clasped tightly between my teeth, cooling the smoke and enhancing the flavor. Seeing movement to my left I turned. It was Eliza; at least I think it was Eliza. Sometimes it was hard to identify individual children with all the same clothing.

The little girl stood a few feet away. She was about six years old and the daughter of one of Vater Mitiss and Caroline's neighbors.

I smiled.

She didn't respond.

"It's all right. You can come closer."

Eliza took a few steps closer. I noticed other children gathering around, following her lead. Further back I could see the three boys with whom I had hoed cabbages whispering to each other.

I kept my voice gentle so as not to frighten the children. "You don't get many strangers, right?"

Eliza shook her head.

The other children shook their heads in unison.

"Would you like to hear a story?"

Eliza's brow furrowed. "A story?"

I nodded and gestured for her to sit on the grass.

She sat.

All the other children sat.

"What's a story?" she asked.

That stumped me. I thought for a moment, "A story is a telling of people and places and things and happenings. Sometimes it is real, but often it is imaginary."

Elize's lips turned down. "A lie."

She sounded almost exactly like Vater Mitiss when I tried to tell him a story my very first night in Burattino. Perhaps I would have more luck with the children than the adults.

"No. A story is for fun."

Her expression didn't change.

I put my hands on my knees and leaned forward. "Here, let me tell you one."

Puffing deeply on the pipe, I centered myself, pulling in all the freedom and creativity and freshness of the world. I opened my eyes and began to speak.

"Once, a year and a day away, in the time before Collapse, when the winds didn't shout but instead whispered; when the lands rolled with green grass and smooth gray concrete echoed with the sounds of thousands upon thousands of people - can you imagine so many?"

Eliza was staring at me. In fact, all of the children were. She shook her head slowly. The others shook their heads in the same fashion.

I took a deep breath, "Oh yes!" The words were an explosive whisper, set to carry out to the edge of the group. I had forgotten how much I enjoyed weaving tales. "Thousands upon thousands of people. There was an old man and he was lonely."

Eliza raised her hand.

I stopped.

She glanced at the other children and then back at me. "How was he lonely if he had so many people around him all the time?"

"He was lonely because he didn't have a son. He was so lonely, he built himself a Frankenstein."

Eliza was quick to respond. "What's that?"

I licked my lips, "A Frankenstein is a machine-man. Or a machine-boy. He made him so he would have a son. But..."

I paused for effect.

"...things did not turn out as the old man intended."

"ONE!" sounded the bell tower above our heads. "TWO!" It rang. It continued until it rang "ELEVEN".

All across the greenspace, I heard the gentle dings of pocket watches. I ignored the vibrations in my own pocket.

As one, the children all stood and started leaving.

I scrambled to my feet. "Wait! Where are you going? The story isn't finished."

Eliza looked at me as if I were saying something outrageous like the sky ate cornmeal, or dogs and cats could speak. "It's eleven o'clock. Playtime is finished."

My mouth moved silently for a moment before words emerged. "Don't you want to hear the end?"

"Playtime is finished." She repeated.

"It's only a few more minutes." I don't know why I was trying to cajole a little girl into listening to my stories. Maybe it was because I failed so utterly with the adults. I needed someone to want to hear what I had to say.

Eliza shook her head, "You're off time."

That seemed to be the sum and substance of my entire time in Burattino. I pulled a tiny gold pocket watch from my pocket. "Eleven." I sighed and closed my eyes, feeling the sun on my skin.

I was always off time. Whatever that meant. I had not thought of the phrase as anything other than objurgation for my inability to meet their strictures of time and performance. More and more I felt deep disappointment at my failure from the citizens, and rising frustration from myself.

I glanced over at the white walled workshop that sat on the border of the central greenspace. I was already off time in that I chose to daydream on the steps of the Council House and attempt to tell stories to children rather than join the men involved in clockmaking in the workshop.

I previously attempted the detailed work of assembling both the tiny pocket watches and the larger mantel clocks. I had been less than successful at both. While I could identify the parts and manipulate them into position, I could not do so at the same speed as the other workers.

The workshop was one large room with a long table and bench with tools and clock parts. On the far wall was a black wood ornate clock with cabbages and clocks carved over its entire body. It set the pace for the assembly and everyone matched each tick with a deft movement: tick - pick up a tiny gear with tweezers, tock - place the gear in the watch body, tick - pick up the pin, tock - pace the pin, tick - pick up the mallet, tock - tap the pin. Tick – tap, tock – tap and so on. I am familiar with working songs to set the pace of work, but this was an incredible speed. And to continue such an effort for all hours of the day? Impossible. I was very quickly off time. I was grateful though that for the first time, I wasn't the only one falling behind. Old Nils with his halstuch around his neck, the cloth ends crooked and curling under, struggled to keep up as well. I noticed his shaking hands and gave him a smile of solidarity. He didn't smile back. He only furrowed his brow, sucked furiously on his teeth and attempted to work faster.

It was Old Nils' shout that shook me from my reverie. I opened my eyes. The pipe fell from my mouth as I saw him struggling with two other men of the village. Vater Mitiss was speaking to them. I couldn't hear their words but the fact he was giving orders was clear, as were his frantic arm gestures.

I scrambled to my feet. What were they going to do to that old man?

The men dragged Old Nils around the corner of the building and out of sight. Vater Mitiss pulled out his pocket watch, glanced at it and snapped it shut, and strode toward the Council House and me.

Of course he was headed this way. It was almost noon.

I frowned and crossed my arms waiting for him to reach me. "What did you do to Old Nils?" The words leapt from my mouth like knives, sharp and unforgiving.

Vater Mitiss barely gave me a glance as he stepped past me. "He is off time."

I followed him into the tower, anger giving me impetus. "What. Did. You. Do?!"

I had thought Vater Mitiss was a revered gentleman of Burattino. Maybe in my ignorance I had missed the signs. Maybe the word wasn't "revered" but "feared".

"Is that what happens when people don't do what you say?" I would not be put off. Not anymore. There had been too much.

Vater Mitiss continued to ignore me, checking the equipment and oil levels. The interior hand of the great clock ticked slowly as it inched closer to twelve.

I stepped in front of him. The belfry space was tight with the massive bell and machinery, and the center of the room below the bell was mostly open air as the tower's hollow shape allowed the sound to ring out. He would be forced to face me.

Vater Mitiss pulled out his pocket watch, ignoring me. "It is almost time for the bell."

I felt my anger rise even higher. "You have to stop. Old Nils-"

"-will be seen to." Vater Mitiss said off-handedly, his gaze never leaving his pocket watch. "Nils was off time." He closed it with a snap. "Reset. And you are off time."

I stared in horror as realization struck me. "What did you do?"

Vater Mitiss seemed to hesitate for just a moment as if he was struggling for words to explain. "Nils...I will keep us safe."

White knuckled, I pulled out my pocket watch, the one he had gifted me. "You can't do this. Off time, on time, the schedules, the town borders; you're trying to control us. You've made this whole town prisoners in their own homes."

Vater Mitiss' cocked his head to the side, as if listening to something I couldn't hear. "No."

His voice was that same calm and inflexible voice that he used on me that very first morning after he locked me into my room. That same persuasive tone when he urged me to wear the same clothing as all the other townsfolk, when he pushed me to hoe cabbages and build clocks, and walk to the goddamned square every noonday to count the strokes of the clock bell. I had been here all this time and I had not seen it. I had not fully realized it.

I held up the pocket watch he gave me in a hand that shook with emotion. To this day, I cannot tell you what that emotion was – rage, horror, self-righteousness?

"I don't want this." I smashed the watch to the floor of the bell tower. "I choose to be off time."

Vater Mitiss shook his head. "It is wrong to alter the old course of things. It has kept us safe."

"I will free them from you!" I would save Burattino. Vater Mitiss was forcing them to live in tyranny and they didn't even realize it. How many others had been dragged away before Old Nils? I balled my hands into fists. "I won't let you reset me.

"Thank you." Vater Mitiss said matter-of-factly. "We will stick by our clocks and our cabbages." Grabbing the massive four-foot wrench that was used to adjust the gears, he swung it in a wide arc. Right at my head.

I ducked. He was trying to kill me! It crashed into the side of the bell tower and there was a heavy crunch and broken brick sprayed.

Vater Mitiss swung again.

More stone chips flew, cutting my face and neck. I lunged for him. My fingers wrapped around the long metal haft. We grappled, each seeking leverage. To my horror, I felt myself thrown to and fro, shaken like a rat in a dog's mouth. My body slammed against a wall. All the breath left my lungs and my fingers loosened their grip. Vater Mitiss was a devil, his strength was enormous. It wasn't human. And in those raw seconds, I was sure I would die.

Perhaps what happened next could be considered the depths of irony as the great bell began to ring. "One!"

Outside, I could hear the chant of Vater Mitiss' victims. "One!"

"Two!" rang the bell.

I slammed my head forward into his face, hearing a satisfying crunch.

"Two!" repeated the voices outside.

"Three! Four! Five! Six! Seven! Eight!" said the bell.

Vater Mitiss' head snapped back and he overbalanced. I followed him, raining down blows with knees and elbows in time to the ringing of the bell.

"Three! Four! Five! Six! Seven! Eight!" continued the muffled voices of the townsfolk oblivious to what was going on inside.

"Nine! Ten! Eleven! Twelve!" continued the ringing of the bell as we slid across the floor trading blows. I felt ribs break and tasted blood in my mouth. Vater Mitiss, though, looked unchanged.

He released the wrench. His hands closed around my throat, fingers digging in, squeezing away my breath. I struggled as black began to ring the edges of my vision. In desperation I kicked out, knocking Vater Mitiss back and into the giant bell.

"THIRTEEN!" rang the bell as Mitiss' body bounced off the metal and slammed into the edge of the floor. He crumpled back and fell down the center of the tower, landing with a sickening thud at the far bottom, the sound barely audible between the reverberations of the bell.

I limped down the flights of stairs, one hand clutching my ribs, the other on the smooth stone wall for balance. The sight I beheld at the bottom of the tower was not anything I would wish on another human being. Vater Mitiss lay, his torso and limbs twisted and bent in ways they were never intended, but there was no blood.

When I came to his body, I saw metal and wood, gears and cogs, and while my ears rushed with the sound of blood from my own heartbeat, from Vater Mitiss instead there was the faint irregular tick-tick of a clock. Vater Mitiss wasn't a man.

I sank to my knees and picked up a piece of broken stone and brought it down on Vater Mitiss' head over and over and over, until the gears no longer ticked in minute revolutions and his broken and twisted machine arms and legs ceased to move. Across the floor a pool of slick oil spread, the smell of it thick and metallic in my nose. The monster was dead.

Dropping the stone, I stumbled to my feet and, leaning against the wall, opened the door. I staggered out into the bright sunlight. Silence greeted me.

I squinted until my eyes adjusted. They were all there. Caroline, Eliza, the three boys, Old Gustav, Carlo and Flora, the children, the elders, even Old Nils. Even townspeople I hadn't met yet. All of Burattino.

The only sound in the square was the heavy rasping of my own breath.

"Thirteen," said Caroline.

"Thirteen," the entire town chanted.

"You're free." I gasped. How could I explain it to them? "There's no more off time." I coughed and spat blood on the steps.

Caroline stared at the red stain on the concrete.

No one moved. The silence grew and grew, swirling through the town center, like storm clouds in summer.

Slowly, her gaze rose to mine. "You told us the story. How the Father built a Son."

"Yeah." I said dumbly. "Frankenstein."

What did that have to do with anything? I never even finished the story. No one in Burattino had heard more than the first two or three sentences.

Caroline's gaze bore into me, "But what if his son got lonely? What if his son needed friends? Wouldn't he build them too?"

I stared at her.

Eliza's high voice spoke up. "And cousins and uncles and aunts and neighbors."

Caroline took a step toward me. "And a mother."

My mouth opened but no words emerged. I had been telling the wrong story.

I stepped back, falling as I tripped on the low step. I scrambled backwards on the ground, my gaze bouncing from one resident to another. All of them.

Caroline held up her hands. The expression on her face struck me like the hammer to the bell, resounding through my chest, until my very heart rattled in my throat.

"What are you?!" The words blurted out of my mouth.

I didn't need to ask. I already knew. Maybe they didn't know. Perhaps not all of them realized, but enough of them suspected. They weren't people. Not like me. They were like the freakish creature in the belfry. Vater Mitiss, the machine-monster I smashed to pieces. The Keeper.

"Thirteen. The bell rang thirteen." Caroline insisted, her low voice a monotone.

My mind was trapped in a loop going round and round as I tried to understand all that had transpired. I found myself frantically reexamining every action and interaction, every conversation I had had in the village.

"That isn't right," she continued.

The townsfolk all shook their heads in unison.

"We're off time." Caroline murmured.

"We're off time," the crowd echoed. Their speech patterns and voices were identical.

"You're free," I repeated. But this time, even though I had intended to speak with bravado, the words came out more of a question.

"Fix it." Caroline said.

"Fix it." The townsfolk repeated.

"I can't." I whispered the words. "I don't know how."

Would they kill me? I wiped my sleeve across my face. It came back wet with sweat and blood and...tears?

Caroline blinked. Long and slow, it was the least human I had ever seen her. "Oh."

That's all she said.

She turned away and started walking through the crowd back to her house. One by one, all the other denizens of Burattino followed to their own homes.

There was no sound, no talking or laughter. Even their steps were muted. They were off time.

I don't know how long I lay there, the words rattling around in my head - off time. Dinner time had come and gone; and it was long past when I should have gone to feed Ermengarde her nightly cabbage-treat. Off time. I watched the final rays of sunlight disappear over the edge of the horizon and darkness fall across the valley. But no lights came on in Burattino. No movement. No sounds. No belfry ringing the hours. No life. Off. Time.

THE CASK OF AMARILLO

MISTY MASSEY

Lucky held court most nights in the Red Eye. It wasn't because anyone liked him all that much. He was the only man in town with any real money, and he lorded it over the rest of us like an old-time baron with his serfs. Even his money wouldn't have bothered us overmuch. No, it was his way of poking fun at another man's hard fortune. Nothing pleased him better than flinging barbs disguised as jokes at anyone who wandered into his attention. If the man was armed with real weapons, he couldn't have spilled more blood.

Until the night my wife Becky packed up and left, I'd avoided the Red Eye. Who wants to subject himself to that kind of torture? But with the harsh words she and I exchanged still ringing in my heart, I needed a drink. I promised myself I'd only have one beer and go home before Lucky showed up, but before I drank half the glass, it started to rain, torrential sheets of water lit by flashes of lightning every two minutes. I risked electrocution if I walked home, and since there was no one to go home to, I stayed for another drink. Before I knew how late it was, in he walked, rain dripping off the edges of his black leather hat and a cheroot hanging off his lip. He scanned the room like a gambler looking for his usual spot, and those eyes turned my way.

"Rich Man! Found any more gold in that claim yet?" He pulled one of the saloon girls close to him. "Did you know, sweet thing, my friend Rich

Man here is a prospector? First day on his claim, he found himself a gold nugget the size of a strong man's fist. Come running into my store to cash it in, and guess what?" The girl giggled, even though she'd heard the joke a thousand times already. Everyone had. "It wasn't gold at all! It was a big old chunk of pyrite. Ah, hell, you should've seen his face!" He slapped his thigh, bellowing his laughter. "Rich Man wasn't so rich after all!"

My name is Richmond, as Lucky knew good and well. That blasted nickname was part of his entertainment. Sure, I was a fool to get so excited about what I'd found. But not even a fool deserves to have his stupid mistakes hashed and rehashed so often. It stops being funny the third or fourth time around. My slip with the pyrite happened almost seven months ago. Any other man would have let it go within a week, but not Lucky. He didn't even care that no one else in the place laughed. The rest of the men at the bar kept their eyes down like whipped dogs. They might pity me, but not a one of them would stand up against Lucky.

Usually I'd take the ribbing, finish my drink and leave, the bitter sound of Lucky's laughter echoing down the street behind me. Maybe it was how Becky left things, or it could have been the half-formed plan for leaving town percolating in my mind. Whatever drove me, suddenly I had enough. The seed of an idea, a way to shut his mouth, flowered. I'd hit him where he lived, try to sway his attention and then let it drop, just in time to make him look the fool instead. I'd pay a hard price if I planned to stick around, but since I was leaving, it didn't matter.

"Good cigar, Lucky?"

Two or three heads swiveled to stare at me. Hardly anyone began a conversation with Lucky. He preferred to do all the talking. Lucky took a drag off the black cheroot, pinched it between his teeth and blew smoke into my face. It took everything I had not to cough. "Smells good," I said. "But not as good as the Amarillo."

He wrinkled his forehead, and I felt just the slightest tickle of panic. What the hell was I doing? I should have thought this through. I couldn't walk out now. He'd follow until he got the whole story, and if I admitted I was messing with him, he'd use that against me until the day I died. The notion of catching the morning train solidified into a plan. I'd leave with the dawn, and with any luck, be miles away from Lucky and his laugh on my dying day. *In for a penny*, I thought. He was curious, and nothing sparked Lucky's curiosity except sex and tobacco.

Lucky hailed from North Carolina, the third son of a sharecropper on a tobacco plantation. He came out west with dreams of starting his own tobacco empire. That's why they called him Lucky. Not because he accomplished what he hoped to. Flea beetles destroyed most of his very first crop, doing enough damage that he couldn't recover. Instead of skedaddling back to the East, Lucky found a farmer willing to buy his land and used the money to open the first general store in town. He never tried planting again, but tobacco remained his passion. He imported the finest cigars he could get his hands on, all the time ordering up some fancy new blend from back east, smoking them as if the Lord above had gifted them to him personally. He loved to blather on about the texture of this one, or the finish of that, as if any of the men around him knew or cared.

"Amarillo what?" Lucky asked.

"You ain't heard of it?" I put on my best innocent face. "You being such a connoisseur and all."

He squinted, looking like he wasn't sure whether to keep listening to me. "There's always something new under the sun, as the poet said. Don't make it worth knowing about."

"You're probably right." I waved a hand and headed for the door. "My old uncle sent me a cask of the Amarillo, and said it was special, that I should save it for when my first child's born or somesuch."

Lucky laughed, turning to the rest of the room. "And what does Rich Man's doddering old uncle know about fine tobacco, hey?"

Joe Conner cleared his throat. "I heard his uncle was a foreman on a tobacco farm in Georgia. Ain't that right, Rich?"

If there was a man in town who hated Lucky the way I did, it was likely Joe Conner. Lucky dearly loved to go on about Joe's son burning their house down when he was naught but a toddler. The fact that Joe's son lost his eyesight in the fire didn't seem to bother Lucky one bit. I admit I was surprised at Joe stepping up, but I wasn't going to let the opportunity slip past me. "That's right, Joe. But Lucky don't want to hear about it." I kept walking toward the door.

"Tell you what, Rich Man, you tell me about this tobacco of yours, and I'll tell you if it's worth dumping down the creek."

I had him. I stopped at the door, peering out at the rain, then turned back toward the waiting man. "It's a blend. North Carolina brightleaf mixed with green dragon from China, and a handful of red herb from..." I snapped my fingers. "What's that country that's all desert?"

"Egypt," Fred Morrison called helpfully from his seat next to Joe.

"That's it indeed," I said. "Egypt. Land of the pharaohs."

Lucky snorted. "If it's all desert, how'd they grow anything?"

"The red herb comes out of the pyramids, stored a thousand years, for when the pharaohs woke up. They cultivated it back when the Nile River made the land green and fertile."

"Rich Man's got him some fine tobacco? As if you wouldn't have sold something like that long ago. You're drinking here on the account, ain't you?"

I let my face go sad and slack. "It was a gift, last one my uncle ever sent me. I was thinking of opening it for my going-away."

"Where you going?" Joe called out.

"I got a train ticket for next week. Headed back to South Carolina," I said.

The room fell silent. There wasn't a man in town didn't know I was broke, with no hope of changing that situation. The claim Lucky liked to make fun of was chock full of sand and pyrite, worth nothing to me or to anyone else. Me and Becky should've moved on long ago, but I didn't have the money for two train tickets. She took most of what we did have to pay for her one.

Lucky cleared his throat "I'm troubled to hear of your poverty, I truly am. Not that I think it sounds like much, but bring it on by the shop, and I'll see if I can unload it for you. Probably won't earn out what it cost your fool of an uncle, but it might be enough to get you on your way."

I bit back the smile. Lucky wouldn't have bothered to put out his own mama if she was on fire. This had nothing to do with helping. He couldn't stand me knowing about some rare blend he never heard of, even if it did sound too good to be true. "I guess you're right, Lucky. I'll come see you."

Shrugging on my coat, I stepped out into the wet night, letting the door swing shut behind me. The rain had subsided to a hard drizzle, but the lightning was gone. For once, I had the last word off Lucky. It didn't feel as satisfying as I'd hoped it might, but it would have to do.

Before I took a step, a hand fell on my shoulder. "Richmond. A word, please."

The sharp tone he affected most of the time was gone from his voice. And he used my actual name. It sent a cold shiver down my back. Lucky didn't respect anyone, and calling me Richmond sounded like a trap. I hadn't expected anything to come of my tale telling, beyond knowing how angry he'd be when I never showed up with my mythical tobacco and he realized he'd been snowed. I looked back at Lucky. He was alone, and his face looked downright friendly.

"I been thinking. Something so rare as that Amarillo oughtn't to be wasted on every Tom and Harry riding through town. Instead of me buying it for the store, I think you ought to sell it to me, all quiet-like. So it's appreciated the way it ought to be."

I was struck dumb. I meant only to make a fool of him, and here he was offering money. My avarice was awakened like a hunger deep in my belly. All the years of his abuse, paid off in real money. I deserved some recompense, didn't I? I nodded, more agreeing with myself than him, but he smiled.

"I'll need to try it first, just to be sure it's as fine as you say."

"Of course," I said. "Why don't you come on out to the house tomorrow, after business is over for the day? We'll open that cask and see what my uncle sent me."

He squeezed my shoulder hard. "Tomorrow it is."

Somewhere on my long, wet walk home, I realized the position I was in. As much as I hated to admit it, the man was an expert on tobacco. At least, more of one than I was. I couldn't just fill up an empty cask with dried corn husks and maple bark. He'd notice, and his taunts would become beatings. As the rain soaked me to the skin and the night's chill crept into my bones, I found myself considering a more permanent solution. The man was an ass. I'd be doing the whole town a favor. Nobody'd miss him until he didn't show up in the Red Eye, and no one would bother searching for him until he didn't open his store in the morning. I could cover a reasonable amount of ground by then.

My little house was dark, and cold. Once upon a time there'd have been lights in the windows, smoke floating up the chimney and the smell of food wafting toward me. All those comforts had gone with Becky. Her parting words still stung me. "Lucky's right," she'd growled. "You are a fool." I sighed. I'd be a fool for sure to kill the man. Best if I gave up all this nonsense and disappeared before Lucky made his appearance.

The next morning dawned bright with that sheen the land holds after a hard rain. I drank a cup of bitter coffee and set to work packing what few things I had left. My clothes, my claim papers, and a couple of blankets to make a bedroll, all stuffed into the valise I'd started housekeeping with. I cleaned and loaded my rifle and stored it in the sling, then hunted through the cabinet for whatever food Becky left behind. A jar of tomatoes from last summer, and some dried out bread that she'd have tossed to the birds if she'd stayed, not nearly enough to keep me on the trail. I trudged out to the cold cellar, hoping she might have left some salted venison behind in her rush to catch the train.

I dug the cold cellar out of the hillside the first year we lived out here. When I started, I intended to stop fifteen feet in, but the digging suddenly gave way, opening into a deep cave as cold as winter. The walls glistened with dampness, and the air bore the faint scent of clay. At the farthest wall, deep in the shadows where the light hardly reached, was a hole in the floor, deeper down than I had tools to measure but with a thin lip wide enough to walk on if you were careful. Becky used to badger me to build a fence in front of it, in case we ever had children, but I never got around to it. A few empty wooden boxes sat on the floor to warn me where the edge began. Up on a niche near the hole was a small cask that once held flour. We kept it up there to keep it away from the mice, but it was long empty. I collected a handful of old potatoes from a shelf she missed and returned to the house.

"Hey there, Rich Man!"

The greeting startled me and I nearly dropped my potatoes. Lucky must have realized I was messing with him and come out here early to catch me. He held a pistol, pointed straight at me. "What's the problem, Lucky?"

"I'll have it now."

I didn't know what to say. I wanted to make him a fool, but who was the fool now? Me, for thinking I was smarter than Lucky. He'd caught on to my lies, and I was going to die.

"You tipped your hand, with all that talk about leaving town," he snarled. "You knew good and well you could get more money for the tobacco in a bigger town, so you figured you'd carry it with you, and cheat me."

God help me, the man thought the Amarillo was real. I raised my hands, slow and easy. "There's nothing to have. There ain't no Amarillo."

"Liar!"

"Not lying, not this time. It was all in fun. I was just trying to make you look stupid."

"As if you could!"

He believed my cockamamie story, believed it so well that I wasn't going to be able to convince him otherwise. I could talk until I was blue in the face, but there wouldn't be any getting through to him. I shook my head. "I swear on God's blue sky, Lucky, there is no tobacco. I made it up."

"I looked through your pack, so I know it ain't in the house." He squinted one eye closed, and squeezed off a shot that barely missed my foot, a cloud of dust rising after the ricochet. "Hand it over, or the next bullet goes through your belly."

My heart was in my throat, and I didn't know what to do, when I remembered the empty flour cask in the cold cellar. Maybe I could show him that, and claim the tobacco'd been stolen. Or I could knock him against the wall, stun him long enough to get a head start. I was scrambling for an idea, any idea at all. I lifted my chin in the direction of the cave. "It's in there."

Lucky waved the gun. "Lead me."

We reached the cave mouth and I hesitated. He'd likely shoot me and pitch me down the hole. I already announced to the whole town I was going, but the afterlife was not on my list of chosen destinations. He nudged me in the back with the pistol. "Keep moving."

"It's awful dark," I said. "Maybe I should go back to the house for a candle."

"There's enough sunshine from behind me." He snorted, his breath rank in the cool of the cave. "You said there ain't no Amarillo? So what's that up there?" He pointed with the gun at the little flour cask in its niche. "You are never going to outsmart me, Rich Man."

He pushed me sideways against the cave wall, holstering his gun as he went. He wasn't looking where he was going. I grabbed his sleeve but he jerked away, throwing himself off balance. He reached down to steady himself on the empty crates, but his foot slid over the lip of the hole and he fell, screaming. I threw myself to my hands and knees at the edge of the darkness.

He was hanging about five feet down, holding on for dear life to an outcropping of rock. Blood oozed from a cut on his cheek. The thick darkness below almost seemed to reach for him. He swung a leg up, but couldn't find any purchase, which set his body to swinging dangerously.

"Help me!" he cried.

I stripped off my belt and dangled it down. He reached out with one hand, but the belt was nowhere long enough. "Hang on, Lucky."

I took off my shirt and tied one arm onto the belt buckle. I tested it by catching one end under my foot and pulling hard as I could. It seemed to hold, and it would have to do. It was all I had. Bracing myself against the wall, I lowered the belt down to Lucky again.

His face had gone gray with fear. Or maybe it was the shadows surrounding him. His hand shook when he reached out to catch the shirt. "You're a good man," he said, his voice gone soft. "It's too bad good men don't win." I didn't answer. What could I say? I tried to trick him, and here I nearly killed him. I wasn't a good man at all.

He took hold of the belt and let go of the rock. His sudden weight almost pulled me off my feet. I groaned as I tried to drag him up.

"Yep," he grunted, his voice echoing hollowly in the cave. "You're all right. Still young enough for working."

I leaned back and slid one hand further down the makeshift rescue rope. "What do you mean?" I grunted.

"Maybe I can give you a job when this is over."

Some way to make money would be a good thing. Working for Lucky might be a pure torture, but at least I wouldn't have to leave my house. I dragged the stranded man upward another inch. "That might be good."

"Course there'd be no pay for a while, 'til you've worked off your tab."

"My tab?" I asked.

"For the Amarillo," he said, scrabbling his toes against the clay wall of the hole. "You still owe me. It'll be a good six months paying that off."

The truth of his words hit me like a falling brick. Did he mean to make me his indentured servant? His damn *slave*? All the cruelty he'd slung my way came roaring out of my memory. I held his life at the end of my belt, and the only gratitude he could summon up came in the form of me serving him. Lucky's abuse would never end. I could save his life and he'd tell everyone the story of my effort in such a way to make me sound like a buffoon. He'd have me under his thumb until I died. My vision blurred with the heat of anger. I might have been a failure, a pauper and a miserable husband, but I'd never submit to being anyone's slave.

"Pull, Rich Man."

"No," I said. I let my grip soften ever so slightly, enough for the belt to slide a little. He whimpered like maybe he remembered his predicament.

"For the love of God, Rich Man!"

"Yes," I said. "As if I ever cared what God thought." And I let go.

The belt slithered out of sight with a whoosh. Lucky screamed for longer than I expected. When all was quiet at last, I stood up, and noticed the cask on its niche. I tipped it into the hole, listening to it rattle and bang down to wherever Lucky lay.

No reason he shouldn't have what he came for.

THE TELLTALE TATTOO

NICOLE GIVENS KURTZ

S tart again from the beginning, Officer Bloom."

Detective Trevor Bell pushed his fists into his pants' pockets. His melodious voice resounded in the tight room. He glanced out the window to the rain falling in buckets on Baltimore's drab and dreary streets. The interview space reeked of tense sweat. The overhead fluorescent lights poured down harsh yellowing light.

Hunched against the worn and wobbly table, Officer Gary Bloom glared at the blank paper and pen in front of him. Dressed in civilian clothes, a tee-shirt sporting the Blue Lives Matter flag, and jeans, he scowled at Detective Krista Fox seated across from him.

"I've already told you three times. It ain't gonna change, Krista." Gary ran a hand across his buzz cut hair. He crossed his arms and cocked his head. "Can I go now?"

"It's *Detective* Fox, and we need answers, *Officer* Bloom." He shot forward in his seat, but she didn't flinch and she held his eye contact. "A man is dead."

"And the media has made it a circus." Detective Bell chimed in. "We have some conflicting accounts of what happened, so we're asking witnesses to help flesh things out."

Gary scratched at his neck and tugged on the tee-shirt's flat collar. "All right. Fine. On Saturday, I worked the march downtown. I'm there, in full riot gear, sweating my balls off, to make sure people's right to protest is protected."

He spat out the word 'protected' as if it was poison in his mouth.

"That's our job, officer." Detective Fox wrote in her black, leather-bound notebook.

Gary hissed out his frustration. *These two desk jockeys don't know the first thing about policing. They got their degrees and walked into detective jobs.*

A sharp flash of pain forced his teeth to clench and he sat ramrod straight in the chair.

What the hell was that?

Gary gently touched the area of his neck. His fingers came away wet, with blood on them.

Probably an insect bite. God knows what's crawling around in here.

It hurt more than any other insect bite he'd ever had. He breathed through the pain and glared at the detective.

"Look, all I'm saying is the place was a powder keg waiting to happen. It was like lighting a firecracker—the whole damn pack! Boom!"

Thunder growled outside the windows, and electricity crackled in the worn and weary room.

"Go on." Detective Bell came away from the window and stood to the right of Detective Fox.

Now the detective is gonna turn up the heat on me. Loser. I'm a pro at interrogation.

"It was a tense and dangerous scene. When you got that kinda mix…" Gary swallowed the ache in his throat. An image sliced through his mind.

A Black woman cradled a man in her arms. Her dark eyes narrowed in mournful anger at Gary. Those eyes burrowed into him, a thousand little daggers, and he reeled backward, stumbling to his feet, to flee. He threw the branch aside. She stroked the man's garish and hideous neck tattoo, the kind all filthy gang members and thugs had. It spelled out something in Old English script but blood from the wound obscured some of the letters. The first one was an M.

"Officer?" Detective Fox rapped on the table. "Officer Bloom?"

"Yeah?" Gary startled in the wooden seat.

What's this? His fingers traced the raised swatch of skin. It burned like fire. He sucked in a steadying breath and released it slowly.

"You were speaking about the protest scene…"

"Uh, right. I mean, the scene speaks for itself." Gary splayed his hands wide as if he had nothing else to add.

Detective Fox scratched out several more notes in her pad.

"Tell us about the fight." Detective Bell broke the ensuing quiet.

Gary closed his eyes as the mob's roar exploded, wrenching him back to the memory, to the place.

No justice! No peace! No justice! No peace!

"I dunno anything about the damn fight. I dunno who started it, but it was probably some loud mouth loser…"

"You're a trained police officer. Can you be more specific? Height? Hair color? Clothing? Ethnicity?" Detective Fox looked up from her notepad. "Anything?"

Gary closed his eyes and clenched his fists beneath the table.

"We're confident in the case we're building." Detective Bell licked his lips. "As I said before, we're collecting additional statements."

"All I know is it's peaceful one second and the next quick explosions of violence like the Fourth of July." Gary wiped the thin, runny blood on his pants. Couldn't they see him bleeding?

I need to get out of here. I might've gotten bit by a recluse spider.

Gary slid his hand up to his neck and placed it over the searing and weepy flesh. His finger traced the raised, disgusting black curve of the M. Chills skated up his spine. He coughed to clear his throat.

"Is there anything else? Can I go?"

Detective Fox's arched eyebrows rose. "Why are you so upset? We're trying to get to the truth."

The skin on his neck flared in burning irritation. He slapped it and then rubbed it with the tips of his fingers. It felt like a sunburn.

"You know what, Detective? I'm not mad. I'm *pissed!* Why? Let me tell you. I stood among my comrades in arms, in the blazing heat. Hell, even the sun was angry. The weekend means relaxation. People should be grateful for what they get, you know? I mean, they already get welfare, scholarships, and affirmative action. If the lot of them weren't a bunch of damn criminals, my brothers would be alive and enjoying their weekend instead of rotting in coffins because of those damn crybabies. What about us? It's not safe out here for cops, and these damn people are angry because we gotta protect ourselves. I wanted to be home, under the A/C with a beer and the game. But I wasn't. I did my job."

"A person is dead, *Officer* Bloom." Detective Fox shot a glance at her fellow detective. "We are only trying to get at the truth and catch a killer."

"Sure."

Gary slouched down in the chair. He massaged his neck and sighed in a noisy manner.

"We've talked to other officers as well as participants. Today we're talking to you." Detective Bell flipped open a manila folder on the table. He took out a 4X6 photograph and pushed it toward the policeman. "We pulled this image from surveillance cameras in the area.

This is activist Lorenzo Alfonso Rodriguez. 23. He died yesterday."

Gary hitched his chin higher. "I know."

Detective Bell continued as if Gary hadn't spoken. "His wallet, phone and jewelry were missing, but we were able to identify him from his fingerprints…"

"Immigration, right?"

"Colorado. Born and raised," Detective Fox countered, unsmiling. Her tone betrayed her disgust.

Gary leered at her. *Women. What do they know?*

A searing heat flared along his neck, and he slapped his hand over it. *Damn it!*

His fingers traced the raised mark, sloping into the next set of punished flesh. He swallowed as a trickle of cold sweat raced down his face. *What the hell is this? What's happening? Is it some kinda disease?* His stomach clenched into a ball of tight fear, twisting in terror.

"Lorenzo was struck in the throat and head by a tree branch." Detective Bell tapped the picture. "His wounds were too severe to save him."

The air conditioning rattled, like a dry throat sputtering for words as its life force poured out of it.

"You know when the police close in, suspects will discard evidence," Gary said.

Why did I bring up evidence? Did they notice? Gawd. Do they suspect my sinister act?

The branch had been a weapon of opportunity.

Gary glanced up from the table to Detective Fox. Her eyes, dark brown, narrowed in suspicion and outright revulsion, like the Black woman at the march. He knew this point in the investigation when the detective would pressure the suspect—him.

"Are you okay?" Detective Bell removed his suit jacket.

Gary stiffened and shifted his gaze to the man. "Yeah. Why?"

"You keep scratching your neck."

"Mosquito bite."

Can the detective see it? The blood? The writing? The tattoo?

The detective leaned forward on the chair's back.

Gary mopped his face with his hand. "It's hot in here. You tryin' to sweat me?"

"What?" Detective Bell peered at him. "You can't be serious? The A/C's on."

"I need a break." Gary pushed his chair back so hard it banged against the floor.

He didn't bother picking it up.

"Officer!" Detective Fox called after him.

He stalked out of the interview (interrogation) room and down the hall and directly into the men's restroom. During police questioning, he would deny everything if they tried to pin anything on him.

The lights flickered as he entered and marched to the sink. He gripped the porcelain rounded edges and glared at the mirror.

And shrieked. "What the hell?"

In bold, Old English script, a palm-size *M* blared from his neck, the area below his ear. The snarled swoop and cursive letter reached across to a lowercase, angry black *u*. The inky raised line snaked to the neighboring *r*. He read the rest of the letters and the wretched word they spelled. Gary wheezed as he held on to the sink to keep from dropping to the floor. His pale skin hummed in scarlet, inflamed flesh as if he'd gotten a new tattoo. It felt hot like a sunburn, raw and abraded.

With his throat dry, he gouged at the letters, trying to scratch them out of existence. He tore at his skin, his nails coming out crimson. The agony didn't stop him. He twisted his head and looked again, his heart hammering like a freight train in his chest. The tattoo remained, black and angry against his flushed flesh. Gary watched his Adam's apple bob in terror.

Gary traced the tattoo. The raised cursive remained.

He didn't daydream or hallucinate.

He spun around from the mirror. *Did they see it? Did everyone see it?*

Gary searched the bathroom and found nothing to assist him. He snatched several paper towels and stuffed them under the flat collar. He positioned them to cover the tattoo's blackened stretch across the left half of his neck.

It stung as if he'd received a new tattoo. A thousand tiny needle pricks stabbed at his neck. He shut his eyes against the word etched out forever onto his person. With a trembling hand, Gary slipped out of the restroom.

No way could he go back into that interrogation room. *Do they know?*

Those thugs and criminals could've been carrying a gun or a knife. They didn't care about people's lives. A bunch of vermin. Gary hunched against the exposure as he hurried down the hallway toward the parking lot outside the station. Those educated morons wouldn't understand the danger ghettos and crack-addicted havens held for good police officers like him.

"Officer Bloom?" Detective Fox met him at the double door exit. She held a travel mug in her hand and a confused expression on her face. "Are you going out for a smoke?"

"I don't smoke." Gary responded without thinking.

"You're heading back to the interview room, then?" She sipped and glanced up at him.

She didn't move out of his way.

Women. So damn bossy.

"Yeah, sure." Gary walked backward and then turned around.

"What happened to your neck?" Detective Fox pointed with her little finger. "Looks like you've scratched yourself something fierce."

Gary froze as a shudder rocketed through him.

Can she see it? Did the towels slip?

With a trembling hand, he reached up and began flattening the paper against his searing skin.

"I, I, uh, scratched the bite into an injury." He offered a weak smile.

Detective Fox didn't have her partner's poker face. "Sure."

With her at his back, Gary was guided to the interview room where he found Detective Bell placing more photos onto the scarred table. He didn't look up when Gary and his partner entered.

"Okay, take a look at these pictures..." Detective Bell said.

"I don't wanna look at any more photos. I was there, man." Gary folded his arms.

"Sit down, officer," Detective Fox said as she took the seat across from him once more. "We're going to be a little bit longer, so please, sit."

Play along. The sooner they're satisfied, the sooner you can go home.

Gary sank onto the wooden chair.

"We know you were there, and that's why we want you to look at these images." Detective Bell remained standing, and he tapped on the first one. "This is another one of Lorenzo before the attack."

He placed the photo in front of Gary.

"He was a landscaper. Had a popular business." Detective Fox took out her notepad.

"See here. You're part of the scenery here," Detective Bell pointed at the background spec. "That's you. Right?"

"This was a rage homicide." Detective Fox watched him. "Did you see anyone upset or mad?"

"They were all mad at the march. I told you," Gary leaned his head over to the left, so hide the dark mess on his neck.

"One of the witnesses said the attacker was a cop," Detective Bell brought Gary's attention to him. "When there's a rogue police officer, a murderer with a badge, there's a monster among us. That has to be vanquished."

Monster? He can't possibly mean me. I did that punk a favor.

"There's no boogieman, only whiny people who don't like consequences." Gary's fingers inched up to the pulsating script.

The detectives exchanged a look, and Gary saw it.

They know! They know! I wanna crawl into myself. They can see it!

"Hush! Shush!" Gary shouted.

Detective Fox reared back. Confusion ruined the delicate features for a moment. "What?"

Gary eased to a standing position. "I panicked. Okay? I hit him! The branch, uh, must've crushed his throat."

"Officer Bloom..." Detective Fox stood up. "Calm yourself..."

"I know you can see it. Here!" Gary snatched the paper towels and tossed them in the air. They fell like crumpled confetti. "See here!"

The detectives frowned.

"Gary..." Detective Bell had his hand on the butt of his weapon.

"See here, his horrid tattoo."

"Officer Bloom, please!" Detective Fox glanced over to her partner.

"I know you can't read this fucking font, but it says I'm a MURDER-ER!" Gary sprayed spittle and despair as he collapsed to the floor, to his knees. He held his arms out, ready for the handcuffs.

BE SILENT IN THAT SOLITUDE

EM KAPLAN

E dmund sat at the scarred mahogany escritoire in the conservatory and searched for the perfect words to complete his *opus magnum*. He had become the tenant at Ravenmore with the intent of finishing his life's work but was no closer to its conclusion now than the day he'd crossed the threshold of the crumbling manor three—or was it four? —years ago. He thought that the perfect locale in which he could isolate himself from the distractions of the modern world would allow the evasive words to flow more freely.

As if to prove a counterpoint just at that moment, a baseball crashed through the single-pane glass window across the room. The pale and worried face of young Peter, the groundskeeper's boy, peered through the fracture that now spiderwebbed across it.

"Will you never learn, boy?" Edmund demanded, pushing back from his desk and rising from the tattered velvet seat. Every day, it was one thing or another with the young fellow. "It's no wonder I'm at a loss for words."

He crossed the room to search for the offending missile, but it must have rolled under the settee because he was unable to locate it. By the time he straightened up and smoothed his hair, the boy had disappeared from sight. Edmund sighed. This certainly necessitated an awkward chat with the boy's father. Interruptions, one after another, were not to be tolerated.

He padded in his slippers over the tile floor to the exterior doors and opened one, casting his gaze across the lawn. The boy no doubt wanted to hide in shame until either his father found him or an empty stomach could no longer keep him from returning for supper and his unavoidable punishment. It wasn't the first time the young lad had broken the window, and the irregular custom-sized glass would have to be ordered again from a special glassmaker. If Edmund had had the foresight to mention it previously, he would have suggested they order one or two more identical pieces of glass in the event that the boy broke another.

"If you can hear me—and I know you can—tell your father I'd like to speak with him!" Edmund shouted into the empty air. "And that you shouldn't get dessert with your dinner tonight."

He wasn't truly upset by the incident, but the interruption of his work was annoying. He'd just stumbled upon a new and exciting direction in which to take the final movement of his novel. Now he would have to backtrack and gather up the lines of thought he'd abruptly dropped when the ball smashed through the window.

Edmund reseated himself at the old desk and rubbed his brow. Where was he? Ah, yes. The words came back to focus in his mind as he remembered the direction he'd wanted to take his tale. What was really exciting was that he'd never read a book quite like the one that was slowly taking form on the page before him. Not that it was entirely innovative, but it absolutely did have a freshness to it that even he, as the author, could objectively detect.

The conservatory's inner doors swung open with a creak and the housekeeper backed inside, pulling the wheeled tea tray with its distinctive cacophony of spoons, cups, and saucers. It seemed to Edmund the woman was never without her blasted cart.

In truth, he wanted to shout and tear at his already thinning hair, but he found himself unable to raise his voice at the woman. Mrs. Bittersworth, in addition to effortlessly running the place, intimidated the everloving life out of him. In a time of cell phones, whirring laptop computers, and electric cars, she was a throwback to a bygone era. Who ever heard of a housekeeper these days when one had Merry Maids and Uber Eats?

He stared at the shimmering silken folds of the fabric of her skirt—a Victorian mourning dress, if he wasn't mistaken—and wondered if she ever grew tired of the constant and never-ending fuss she needed to perform for the sake of guests such as himself. Surely she tired of the charade? As if to confirm his hypothesis, she suddenly met his gaze, glowering, as was her typical and slightly menacing fashion.

"Leave it today," he encouraged her. "No need to pour it out for me."

She pursed her lips, gave a snort audible only to herself, and continued with her ritual. The tea steamed as it flowed from pot to cup. With a tarnished silver spoon, she dropped two spoonfuls of sugar into the cup, subjected the mixture to a vigorous stir, neglected to add a splash of milk even though he'd requested it several times previously, and placed the cup and saucer on the edge of the desk near his elbow. The swish of her skirts stirred the chilly autumn air in the room. Eventually she left her serving tray angled near the settee should he desire to make his own second cup and exited the room.

"Not much of a conversationalist, is she? All part of the role, I suppose," he muttered and attempted to focus on the yellowed page of the notebook that lay before him.

Like his surroundings, his tattered silk writing vest, fur-lined slippers, and wire-rimmed reading glasses, everything around him was a bit of a facade, a construction to try to coax his creative mind to cooperate. Edmund had wanted an authentic experience down to his very words. Even the notebook and the fountain pen with which he scratched his thoughts were from an antique shop. In staying at the manor, he hoped that if he submersed himself in the proper setting, he would nourish his creative mind into growing the final leaves on what was distinctly turning out to be a crown of thorns.

Bolstered by the reassurance that he'd done everything possible to encourage his mind to expel nothing but a masterpiece, he put pen to paper and concentrated his efforts on his composition.

When the inner doors banged open again, he flinched and straightened up with a quick glance at the windows. The afternoon light had not faded in the least and shone through the rippled panes of the conservatory's windows. To his muzzy mind, not much time could have passed. However, it seemed that while Edmund had been deeply engrossed in his work, the groundskeeper had come by in the interim with an extra pane of the custom-sized glass. The window was repaired and as good as new.

He tapped his temple, thinking about the particular wisdom of ordering more than one replacement pane of glass. Perhaps the groundskeeper heard him suggest it previously. Or maybe Edmund had remembered to mention it to the man the last time they'd spoken.

Edmund frowned.

Whatever the case, the window was whole once again, and he was free to concentrate on his work, which was coming along nicely at the moment. His publisher would be pleased to finally have it in hand. In fact, they'd lined up two noteworthy authors to read advanced copies and provide quotes for the back cover, which was thrilling beyond belief since this was to be Edmund's first work with a reputable publisher of fine literature.

For a time, he forgot the world around him as he buried himself in his work.

Mrs. Bittersworth once again wheeled in her silver serving cart.

Without thinking, Edmund glanced toward the sofa where it seemed she'd just left her cart. He shook his head because of course she'd already removed the cart earlier. Or perhaps that was the previous day—he couldn't keep track with his nose in his work. These days he fairly lived and breathed within the world of his novel. His words were the walls within which he'd existed for several years now. He could hardly be expected to maintain two separate existences.

What a whirled state of concentration he existed in as he worked. He should feel more self-conscious about his lapses of awareness, but his attention was required elsewhere, namely on the papers in front of him.

"Two sugars and a splash of milk, if you please," he reminded her before she left in her customary swish of her crinoline skirt.

Would it be rude to inquire as to the nature of her mourning? Whom did she mourn? Had she lost a husband, or perhaps a child? He pondered this question as he paused to take a sip from the tea cup. No milk, of course, but he must not have minded terribly much because the next he noticed, the cup was empty. He set it down in consternation because he was still somewhat thirsty. When he looked around for the infernal tea tray, she'd already taken it away when he'd been lost in thought again. Really, he should pay better attention to the comings and goings of others.

No matter. He would simply apply his nose to the grindstone a bit longer and set a few more thoughts to paper before she called him to supper. With the way his plot had been wrapping itself around his mind as of late, he would probably lose all track of time once again. He would put his mind to living more in the world as soon as he finished his work.

It seemed as if only a moment passed before a light rap on the glass door interrupted him. He looked up and gave a wave of recognition. Walter, the groundskeeper, gave him a nod and a cursory salute in return, so Edmund left his seat to unlatch the door.

"There you are. I wondered if you'd already come 'round today and I'd missed you," Edmund said by way of a greeting. "Your young fellow did a number on the window, but I see you had the foresight to—"

He turned to gesture at the new glass but instead found the crack fragmenting the shimmering pane and triangular shards littering the tile floor beneath it.

"I must really get my eyes examined," he said, more to himself than to Walter. "All this peering at words in dim light has made me half-blind. I thought you'd already been here. I see you have the repair well in hand. It certainly was providential of you to have an extra pane at the ready. Then again, you know the boy better than any of us do. Perhaps you should advise him to toss his ball in the other direction from now on, eh?"

Edmund gestured across the lawn away from the house to where the pond lay. He had strolled along it only once since his arrival at the manor. The small reflective pool was downright choked with an overgrowth of lily pads and waterweed. Cattails and what have you. Edmund's shoes had gotten soaked through. The slightly fetid odor of the soil around the water had not appealed to him in a manner that demanded a return visit, even on the sunniest of days. He'd been content to play the role of the reclusive writer and stay indoors ever since then.

Walter was prone to answering in grunts, so Edmund did not expect much of a conversation from the man. All the same, it was nice to have an exchange, however wordless, with another adult male. As Walter went about the task of replacing the broken glass, Edmund gave him a friendly nod and retreated back into his sanctuary.

After all, he'd just been at a pivotal point in his novel. The hero was about to make a life-altering discovery that would change the course of the rest of the tale.

"Oh, blast," Edmund said, looking down at the blank page in front of him. "I was so busy woolgathering that I neglected to write down some of the crucial points."

He sighed and rolled his writing wrist. "No bother. I'll just begin right where I left off. At least I remember exactly what I intended this time."

Thus energized, he bent over his desk and began to scribble in haste, eager to capture his fleeting thoughts this time before they slipped away like so many wisps of cloud on a warm day.

So engrossed was he that he didn't notice when Walter finished fixing the window and quietly left him, once again alone with his thoughts.

"Mrs. Bittersworth?" Edmund asked sometime later, or perhaps it was the next day. One could hardly be expected to keep track during writing days such as these when they all ran together.

The only difference was that today, he felt a little uneasy, as if something might be a bit off in the air.

The housekeeper had swept into the room propelling her rolling tea tray, her dark skirts whispering a soft song of starch and *politesse*. She didn't appear to hear him. She went about her daily ritual of preparing his tea—without the milk he requested. Perhaps it was a judgment of some kind. Did she disapprove of polluting the Earl Grey with the sweet cream or milk that he preferred? Was his beloved concoction perhaps a bit low-brow in her estimation?

"Mrs. Bittersworth?" he repeated.

Perhaps the woman had a diminished sense of hearing. She wore such a stern look, a dark scowl of an expression, that he had avoided conversation with her all of these days together until now.

She didn't look his way and instead made a beeline for the conservatory door as he'd watched her stiff-spined retreating form do so many times. Usually he let her go, but for some reason, today he could not. Whether it was the blank page of the notebook in front of him, or the empty tea cup that no longer balanced on the edge of his desk, or the sparkle of the unbroken pane of glass in the conservatory window— everything was the same as always, but nothing seemed right. Perhaps his spirit had grown restless within himself.

Whatever the reason, he lurched to his feet and placed himself between her cart and the open door so that she could not make her egress.

"I beg your pardon, Mrs. Bittersworth," he began, minding his toes so that she did not run over them with the momentum of her cart.

When he brought his gaze up to meet hers, he frowned in consternation. Where formerly, he'd assumed she was quite a bit older than he, her face seemed to smooth under his scrutiny. Hadn't she had deep crags under her eyes, cracks of old age around her mouth? The manner in which she returned his look now seemed to correct his perception, to clear his vision. She couldn't be much older than three decades, certainly not as many as four. The blue-gray eyes that met his were bright and clear, if not somewhat tired and mournful. The fair hairs that sprang from her temple, escaping her pulled-back bun were light blonde, not gray or white. As he looked at her, truly for the first time since his arrival, he realized she was quite young indeed.

"An old, mournful soul then," he said to himself.

She was not able to stop the forward motion of the cart in time to avoid him, and he yelped and held out a hand to prevent it from running him over.

She also gave a startled cry as he bumped the trolley. The dishes on it rattled. A cup rolled to the floor but did not break. The sugar spoon clinked along the edge of its bowl. The cart jolted but did not stop even though Edmund placed his hands on the edge of it. His fingers slowed it somewhat, but he did not manage to bring it to a halt. The trolley continued to roll forward into the hall.

In fact, it went right through him. As did Mrs. Bittersworth, who continued on her customary journey out of the room without so much as a backward glance.

Edmund stood in stunned silence at the threshold of the room, as anyone might do if they were in his shoes. He looked down at his feet to check if they were still attached to his body as he might expect them to be.

They were. He wore a pair of wool-lined slippers as was his custom when he worked.

He patted his chest, down the front of his trousers, and back up again for a kind of reassurance of his existence. All seemed to be solid and in good order considering he'd been run through with a tea tray.

The hand that lay on his chest felt a comforting rhythm, the beat of his heart even if it was somewhat faster than usual. The skin of his throat, too, was warm and alive with sensation.

He blinked.

Mrs. Bittersworth—and her cart—therefore, *must be a spirit.*

"Fascinating!" he said to himself. "How many years have I seen her daily, drunk her cold tea, and never realized that she was not of this world? No wonder she never serves me milk! She must not be able to waver from the routine of her construct. I wonder if she is even aware of who I am, or if she believes she serves daily refreshment to another who used to live here but is now long gone. Perhaps, even centuries dead by now."

For the first time in his years of residence at the manor, he wished he had thought to bring some means of outside communication so that he could search for information about her. Perhaps a history of Ravenmore would reveal the nature of her life, her struggles and woes, and a description of her last moments upon the earth. Had she died unnaturally and with a compelling unfinished business that motivated her to wander restlessly through the house?

"Not without purpose, apparently. The tea must be served."

He returned to his desk then, not to write—who could concentrate after an event such as that?—but to ponder how he might confront the ghostly housekeeper when she inevitably returned to the conservatory. He wanted to ask her who she was, how long she might have walked these halls, and if there were others, like herself, who were inmates of Ravenmore.

Movement on the lawn drew Edmund's eye outside and he rushed to throw open the glass-paned doors.

"You there!" He thought for a moment before he dredged up the boy's name from his foggy plot-ridden mind. "Jack!"

The boy, in his usual blue jeans and faded baseball cap pulled low, looked up and clearly heard Edmund call to him, but turned tail and disappeared into the hedge.

Edmund leaned out of the house, his hands braced on the door frame at either side, to look for Walter the groundskeeper to ask if he knew anything about Mrs. Bittersworth. All he spied were an abandoned pair of stained garden shears and a small square tarp with garden clippings under the rosebush.

The boy certainly kept his father busy with repairs and general chasing after him. It was a wonder the man was able to keep the grounds as neat and tidy as they were. The place was enormous from what Edmund remembered of his first tour of it. In its heyday, it would have required an entire crew of greenskeepers to maintain the topiary sculptures, various fountains, and whatnot all in top condition. Now the manor was rather like a frumpy old auntie who had gone a bit to seed with sprigs of wild grass springing out from what used to be a neatly polished appearance. As Edmund swept his gaze across the garden, he could imagine it freshly manicured and brightly colored with blooms, teeming with guests in their tennis whites.

He blinked, shook his head clear of the daydream, and retreated back to his desk. Some days, his manuscript felt like a bit of an albatross, that poor bird from old Coleridge's Mariner poem. And wasn't Edmund just like the poor wedding guest, stopped on his way to a night of revelry and merriment by some old bastard muse ranting about his dumb dead bird? Wasn't Edmund just as chained in place by his compulsion to finish his tale as the poor fool who stopped to listen?

At that, Edmund began to chuckle at himself, then to laugh out loud. His gasping guffaws rang through the tiled room. He thought that anyone, on hearing him, would think him a mad ghost as well. And this stopped his laughter short.

Sometime later, Edmund looked up from his work, tilting his head to listen. The page before him was empty. He hadn't been able to focus on his work in anticipation of Mrs. Bittersworth's return. Now he heard the squeak of her cart's wheels, so he rose from his chair and positioned himself by the escritoire, one hand resting on its gnarled surface. Certainly, she would not mistake his posture for anything other than wanting to initiate conversation.

However, if she were a spirit, perhaps her notions of etiquette were at odds to his.

The conservatory door swung open with rather than more force than usual, and Edmund started at the inherent aggression.

The person—or rather, people—who entered subsequently were unknown to him. He'd never seen them before in his life. The woman who pushed Mrs. Bittersworth's cart was young, blonde, and rather busty. He normally would not have noticed such things as cleavage, however the girl's ridiculous garb not only accentuated and displayed at least half her overly large bosom, but the outlandish corset she wore on the outside of her garments pushed all of her bust skyward. Her top half was a veritable shelf upon which she might have stored a series of books, an entire collection of encyclopedias.

She clomped into the room with the grace of a Clydesdale, followed by a very motley group of a dozen mismatched persons of whom Edmund could not make ends or tails at first. Some wore sun hats and dark glasses. Others carried backpacks. One man in an unfortunate combination of socks and sandals carried a camera.

Tourists? What imbecile had opened Ravenmore to sightseers while Edmund's publisher had specifically hired out the entire space of the estate indefinitely so that he could finish his work?

"What is the meaning of this?" he demanded of the young woman.

She ignored him and forged ahead into the room. She set up the cart with her back to the lawn, the pane of the previously repaired conservatory window immediately behind her.

"Excuse me!" he said, but the chatter and shuffling of the group drowned out his words.

Maybe they, like Mrs. Bittersworth, were spirits, too. Had some freakish accident taken their lives all at once and condemned them to eternally shuffle about the old mansion day in and day out? Perhaps they were set on their course, unable to deviate from it just the same as the tea-serving housekeeper. He had never seen this group of tourists before. The estate was very large. Although he'd been here for some time, it was possible their paths had never crossed until now.

He edged closer to the group and waved his fingers in front of the face of an elderly woman in a florid pink windbreaker. No reaction. He placed his hand gently on the shirt sleeve of a rather nerdy looking young man. Again, no response.

"Gather 'round, friends," the young tour guide said. "Welcome to the greenhouse of Ravenmore, also known as the sunroom or conservatory."

She pronounced it oddly—*concert-vatory*—which made him frown. Why did she say it as if it were a foreign term? She recited the rest of her explanation in a strange rush with a sing-song tone as if she'd memorized the entire spiel.

"This is the most famous room at Ravenmore. You may have heard of the novel called *Restless Spirits Among Us* written by our favorite local author." She paused and gave them a knowing smile. Several members of the group nodded. One chuckled. "Well, the very room we're standing in is where he wrote the world-famous words. Once thought to be the greatest American novel, it sold millions of copies both in the U.S. and abroad before the author, sadly, died a very tragic death at a young age. If you or someone you know suffers from depression, please contact the National Suicide and Self-Harm Hotline where professionals can help you find a way to love your life once more. Now, watch your step and follow me."

Edmund felt the blood drain from his head. He lurched to the settee and sank down heavily while his head swam.

"Am I dead?" he asked aloud numbly. After a moment, when he regained the feeling in his extremities, he perked up a bit. "I sold millions of copies internationally? I wrote a best-seller? That's fabulous news. It almost makes one feel motivated to keep working, to plow on ahead!"

The gaggle of sightseers, oblivious to his crisis, listened to their guide with rapt attention as they peered out the glass windows to where their enthusiastic guide pointed.

"Now, just across the yard, you may observe the pond where the gardener's young son, Walter, tragically drowned one day. Stories say he went into the water to retrieve his baseball, but he didn't know how to swim. Sadly, fate didn't give him a chance to learn how and his father, so distraught was he that he died of a broken heart over the loss of his little boy. Let's go across the lawn now and I'll show you just where it happened. Mind the uneven steps down from the door, and follow me!"

Edmund frowned. "I thought the groundskeeper's name was Walter, not the son. Surely, I couldn't have gotten it wrong this entire time." He grimaced. "Maybe that's why he speaks to me only in grunts."

Unable to focus on his manuscript again, Edmund paced the room anxiously awaiting the next arrival of the housekeeper. He had so many questions for her and hoped that she would favor him with some answers. As soon as the doors swung open to announce her arrival, he approached her.

"My dear Mrs. Bittersworth," he began. "I have had an extremely peculiar encounter with a group of tourists this day. Ghost-hunting sightseers, in fact. They burst into my realm, trod through the room gawking at this and that in great number, and proceeded across the lawn. I have never seen such a thing here at Ravenmore. What have you to say about this?"

She halted in the doorway with her tea tray and stared at him. Before his eyes, her skin seemed to smooth and darken into an entirely different face. A broad smile, brilliant with pearl-like teeth spread across her face. Her dark skirts smoothed into slender trousers with a crease down each leg all the way to black sensible shoes. "Now, Mr. Edmund," she said. "You *know* my name is Mrs. Butters. Why are you always making up something new?"

From a pitcher, she poured a paper cup halfway full of water and handed it to him. With her other hand, she proffered a small paper cup with pills in it. "It's time for your medicine. Then I'll let you get back to your little project. You know, I think every single one of us has a story to tell buried inside us. Maybe you will write one someday." She nodded to his desk with a condescension that rankled his nerves.

"Who are you? Where is Mrs. Bittersworth? Am I crazy? Where am I? What is this place?" His head swam at this new scenario. "Oh, no, no, no. I don't like this one bit. I do not accept this."

He looked around expecting to have been transported to a small padded cell that smelled of antiseptic, but to his relief the conservatory was the same as always. Warm, airy, bright, and lush with plants and a lovely worn Turkish rug under his writing table and chair.

When he turned back to this new Mrs. Bittersworth—or rather Mrs. Butters—she and her pills were gone. The door was once again closed, and he was utterly alone.

"Thank heavens. I didn't like that scenario much at all. Not one jot," he murmured to himself before he retreated to his desk.

With a great deal of effort and no little relief, he went back to his manuscript and began to work once again, fueled by the ugly possibility that he might not be altogether sane.

"No, I must focus on that other thing. The bit about the best-seller." He had rather appreciated that news indeed, no matter what other nonsense they said about his early demise.

However, before he was able to do a lick of work, the group of gawkers was back to disturb him again. He should have predicted their inevitable return.

"I must say, I do believe your visit is coming a bit sooner on the tail of the last than I would have liked," he said under his breath. Ever the gentleman, he would have been mortified if the tourists had heard him. He need not have worried, however, the effervescent tour guide, as blonde and as bouncy as ever, barged into the room without a single glance in his direction. He left his writing table once again to mingle with the troupe of tourists.

The older woman in the bright pink jacket seemed as if she were appraising the settee for sale. While the guide pointed out the window, the old lady prodded at the cushions and picked at a stray thread. Edmund shook his head at her audacity.

The tour guide was just reaching the part of her presentation in which he was most interested.

"—once thought to be the greatest American novel, it sold millions of copies both in the U.S. and abroad before the author, sadly, died a very tragic death—"

"Aha! That's what I thought I heard before!" he announced even though no one could hear him. And perhaps because that was the case, he crowed in triumph and did a small victory dance that consisted of a bit of Charleston knee-knocking and some elbows jutting out from his sides in the fashion of chicken wings.

"—which is why they say he haunts this very room," the guide concluded, which stopped Edmund in his tracks. He dropped his hands to his sides.

"What was that?" She hadn't mentioned that part the first time she and her herd of tromping tourists stampeded through his study.

"On top of that, the wax likeness that you see of the author at his desk is said to use actual hair trimmed from the head of the real body, which is why his spirit is trapped in this room. Now watch your head, and follow me." Buoyantly, she turned on her heel and led them out into the garden.

"Whaaa?" Wax what now?

Edmund spun around to see what she'd referred to and found a ghastly man-sized figure that looked nothing like himself sitting at his writing desk. The hair was mousy brown and plastered to the manikin's balding head in a most unfortunate styling. The unfortunate expression on its waxen face was both corpselike and dyspeptic at the same time. The suit it wore was rather Roaring 20s and dapper, he had to admit, but the rest of the display was amateurish and frankly, he was embarrassed for it.

"If that hideous thing is me, I would beg for a wick and a lighted match!"

He was about to slam closed the glass paneled door after the last of the annoying group exited into the garden when the groundskeeper rounded the hedge.

"I beg your pardon, but I must ask you the most ridiculous question," Edmund called out to the man, who had just picked up the abandoned pair of garden shears from under the rosebush. The roses had long since withered on their canes and the clippers had gone to rust. He half expected the man to ignore him as he usually did, or to vanish around the garden wall with not so much more than a grunt. However, Edmund was pleasantly surprised.

"Yes sir?" The gardener tipped his cap and stepped closer. His green wellies were covered in mud so he didn't approach beyond the edge of the grass where it met the bricks of the patio.

"It has come to my attention that I may have been addressing you by a name that in fact is not your own."

"And what might that be, sir?" The man had the good grace to look amused. A half-smile creased his much-weathered face.

"I have been referring to you as Walter. Is that not your name? If not, I am heartily embarrassed."

The man laughed. "Of course that's my name. I don't know who's got it into your head that you were incorrect, but you're not wrong at all."

Now Edmund was even more embarrassed for asking and revealing his self-doubt.

"Don't worry about it, sir. We all know you have your mind on your work. That's why I try to keep my boy away from your poor windows. I'm less successful at that than I like, of course."

"No worries about that," Edmund said. "Other than a glass or two, he's hardly a bother. Jack is his name?"

"Yes sir. He's Walter, Junior, but we call him Jack so there's no mistaking him for me. And you're very kind to say so."

The groundskeeper tipped his hat again, explained that he had more new rose bushes to plant to replace some that had not weathered the winter, and excused himself to return to his work. When Edmund looked over, he noticed that half the rose garden had been replanted and new leaves budded out on the transplants.

"I guess that settles that," he said, although he wasn't sure if he'd just proved the tour guide right or not. He leaned out of the conservatory without stepping over the threshold onto the damp walkway in his slippers to reach for the door handle and pull it closed.

Then he returned to his empty chair to resume work on his future bestseller.

"Mrs. Bittersworth, may I have some milk with my cup today?" Edmund asked the housekeeper later when she returned with the tea service. Even though she never responded to him, he continued to ask her out of habit, more as an amusement to himself. He barely looked up when she entered the room—he was aces this afternoon, words simply flowing out onto the page—but a cup of tea would be just the thing on this gloomy day.

He looked at the window and saw that the sun must have come out while he'd been writing. This day, he felt, might be special, and Mrs. Bittersworth proved it by answering him.

The old housekeeper paused in pouring out his cup with her gnarled hands. Her wrinkled mouth dropped open as she looked at him in astonishment. "Why, Mr. Edmund, I didn't realize you enjoyed a bit of milk with your tea. I don't have any on the cart at the moment, but I will be sure to bring some the next time I come. I'm surprised you haven't mentioned it before. You need only to have asked me! Land sakes! You know we're only here to see that you have everything you need to finish your work. I've made it a point to let all of the staff know they shouldn't disturb you while you're working."

Sometimes, he wondered if that were truly the case. He decided to press the point since his luck had turned today.

"And could you ask the tour group to refrain from visiting this room in particular?" he enquired.

She cocked her head and narrowed her eyes. "I beg your pardon?"

He refused to back down and set down his pen to meet her gaze.

"The group of gawkers who comes through every day. Could you ask them to route through another door to the lawn? Or if they must include this room on their tour, could they at least remain in the hallway?"

The old woman looked decidedly discomfited, and he wondered for a moment if she were going to deny the inconvenience of the tourists altogether. If she found them a necessary evil, she had to know that he did doubly so.

At last she said, "Very well. I didn't realize they had resumed their exploration of this wing of the house. The staff has set up a barrier, you see, and they should not have been here at all. I'm very sorry they have disturbed you."

"How did they die?" he asked.

Mrs. Bittersworth paused. She gave him the now-familiar look of distaste that often presided over her other expressions. She clearly was not comfortable with their exchange, either to admit that they were all deceased, or that they had disobeyed her edict not to bother him. He rather thought it was the latter.

After a moment, she said, "Once again, I am obliged to ask for your forgiveness in this matter. They should not have been in this section of the estate. But if you must ask, they were killed when their touring bus overturned on the road right outside of the front gates. As I recall, they weren't even on our schedule for the day but were headed somewhere else entirely. Now, of course, they must persist here for God knows how long."

"Indeed."

"And their narrative about the author who lived here and died a very tragic untimely death?" Edmund wanted to see if she knew anything about the bestseller. In a roundabout way, of course—he wouldn't introduce the subject directly. He was too polite to ask about himself, but he simply had to know more. Paradoxically, the knowledge of his future success had become the impetus of its creation.

Not that he wanted to admit it—no one wanted to become Narcissus, mesmerized by his own image so much that the rest of the world fell away—but Edmund thirsted for more knowledge about himself. How had the rest of the world received his stunning work? How had he lived with the adoration of thousands of readers across the world?

At this turn of subject, Mrs. Bittersworth became quite flustered indeed.

"I do apologize, sir. No one should be discussing the demise of the tenant of the house. It's extremely untoward, and I'll make sure it never occurs again."

Edmund didn't give much thought to that point. Naturally, everyone had to die, but great works of fiction were eternal.

However she continued, "And when you came to live here not too long after his death, we were all so grateful indeed. I asked them never to speak of the previous author, especially because you're in the same line of work, as you know."

The blood rushed to his head and he felt a bit faint again.

He waved his hand at the housekeeper to dismiss her. "Be gone with you," and she faded away. He wasn't concerned about hurting her feelings. She'd return again later, as she always did with that damned tea service.

They never left him alone.

Edmund returned to the antique escritoire and stared at the blank page.

But never mind all that.

He picked up his pen and set his mind to his task, determined to begin again.

THE VALDEMAR EFFECT

ALEXANDER GIDEON

T he steel door slammed like a hammer on an anvil behind Dominic and the lock clanged into place. He dropped his bags and whirled, frantically searching for a handle. On this side the door was nothing more than a smooth sheet of metal. He pushed, not really expecting it to move but needing to at least try. It didn't budge. His heart pounded a frantic beat against his ribs, and he matched it with his fists as he slammed them over and over against the door.

"Hey! Open the door!" He yelled, stopping for a moment to see if there would be a reply. After several moments he heard nothing but silence. "Someone let me out and tell me what's going on!"

Again, there was no reply. Dominic put his back against the steel and slid down to the floor. One of his bags had opened when he dropped it, and a mess of clothes and books had spilled out. Aside from his reference books, he'd brought a sizable collection of novels along with him. He was supposed to be heading for a research facility somewhere in the Hawaiian islands, and was set to be there for six months.

He had no idea what exactly he would be doing there, or for that matter what the project he'd signed up for even was. The position hadn't been public; his senior biology professor at his university sent his information in for consideration. Said professor vouched for the program, and when he told Dominic how much it paid, Dominic stopped caring about the details. Sitting on the floor of this tiny room in this dilapidated cargo ship, he supremely regretted that decision.

"I'm about to get trafficked, aren't I?" he said with a sigh. He checked his phone as the ship began to move. No signal. Of course not, this dock was in the middle of nowhere, and he was in the heart of the solid metal ship. There was nothing to be done now but to wait and see what plans the crew had for him.

Six hours he sat in that room without hearing so much as footsteps pass by. After a while, he pulled one of his novels out and tried to read to distract himself. No matter how hard he tried though, he couldn't focus on the words. He eventually gave up the attempt and spent the rest of the time pacing the space.

The ship finally stopped, and Dominic's anxiety skyrocketed. Whatever they were going to do with him, he was about to find out. The lock on the door released, and Dominic pressed himself against the far wall. The door swung open and a grizzled old white man with a beard that put Ahab to shame stood in the opening.

"Come up on deck," the man said, "We're here."

"Where exactly is *here*?" Dominic said.

The captain walked away without a response.

Dominic gathered up his belongings and hurried up onto the top deck. The setting sun drenched the bay in tangerine hues, and the island before him crawled with the kind of lush vegetation only found in places not touched by human hands. He could see either end of the crescent shaped island curling inward, which he found surprising. He'd expected something bigger. He hurried down the ramp to the concrete dock below them, dodging between the crew members who were busy unloading cargo.

The man who let Dominic out stood on the dock with two others. One man wore a Hawaiian shirt tucked into his slacks and a white lab coat. He stood with his hands on his hips as the wind tossed his shock of red hair about. It didn't seem that he spent much time in the tropical sun - Dominic had never seen someone so pale. The other was tall and thin with skin nearly as dark as Dominic's own. His bare head gleamed in the sun. He wore small round glasses and an immaculate suit that looked entirely out of place.

"Mr. Brogdon," the red-headed man called when Dominic approached. "I'm glad you finally made it. I trust the trip wasn't too awful."

"Where am I, who are you, and what in the absolute fuck is going on?" Dominic shouted at the trio, eyeing them each in turn.

"You're upset," the red-headed man said, striding forward and reaching out a hand to place on Dominic's shoulder.

"Don't touch me," Dominic said, slapping the man's hand away. The man looked confused and started to step forward again, but the one in the suit stopped him.

"I am Dr. John Franklin," the suit said, his voice deep and smooth as silk with a hint of an accent Dominic couldn't place. "And this is Dr. Terry Desmond, my partner on this venture. I understand your anger, but the existence of this island is top secret. In fact, Terry and I were brought here in much the same manner as you. Only Captain Edmund here and his crew know Wahi Huna's actual location."

"Wahi Huna?" Dominic asked.

"It means 'the hidden place'. It's a bit more romantic than Site 253-56. But there'll be plenty of time to tell you about the island over the next few months. Let's get you to the facility so you can settle in, then we can talk shop," Desmond said with a wide smile before waving to a group of what looked like military personnel gathered around a small four seat UTV farther up the dock.

One of the military types got in the UTV and drove it down to them. Franklin and Desmond loaded Dominic's things into the vehicle before he could protest, and the two men clambered into their seats.

Dominic didn't join them right away. "Coming?" Desmond asked. Dominic glanced back at the ship, then to the surrounding water. He was trapped with no choice but to go with them. He just hoped he hadn't thrown his life away when he applied to this project. He climbed into the UTV.

"And away we go," Desmond said, patting Dominic on the shoulder.

The soldier drove them down the dock, across the beach, and up into the rainforest. Desmond talked incessantly the whole way, jumping from subject to subject so fast that Dominic could barely keep up, though he never once mentioned the project they'd be working on. Dominic had a thousand questions, but whenever he tried to ask one, Desmond plowed right through as if he hadn't spoken at all. Franklin pointedly ignored both of them, and finally Dominic resigned himself to ignorance and strove to tune out Desmond's rambling.

They were deep in the rainforest when they finally stopped next to a large outcropping of rock. It took a moment for Dominic to see the door embedded in the stone. It was solid steel, and nearly the same color as the rock around it.

"It's an old World War Two bunker," Desmond said as the three of them climbed out. He saw the look on Dominic's face and laughed. "Not exactly what you were expecting, huh?

"Not quite," Dominic murmured, studying the flat surface of the door. He'd expected a state-of-the-art facility, not some forgotten relic like this one. Dominic reached for his bags, but Franklin waved him away.

"Our friend here will take your things to your room."

The soldier nodded to them and began hauling Dominic's bags from the UTV. Desmond waved at something above the door, and a moment later a woman in military fatigues swung the door wide from inside. She nodded at them and stepped back to let them pass into the bunker.

The door closed behind them, leaving the hall illuminated only by staggered fluorescent lights. The walls seemed much closer now, and Dominic swallowed hard. Franklin patted him on the shoulder.

"It does take some getting used to, but rest assured, you can go back outside at any time. Just make sure to have one of the soldiers escort you," Franklin said with a smile.

The corridor ended at a set of metal stairs. Desmond led them down to the next floor which turned out to be the kitchens and mess hall. There were a few people eating in the large room.

"Is that the assistant we've been waiting for?" a woman in a lab coat akin to Desmond's called to them, her voice echoing across the room. Several more looked over at the sound of her voice, their gazes curious.

"It is. We'll be getting started tomorrow. I'm just taking him down to the research floor to fill him in," Desmond called back. The room erupted into a din of voices, a sudden sense of excitement permeating the room.

Another set of stairs led to a long corridor that comprised the living quarters. The rooms reminded Dominic more of a prison than anything: stone walls, thick steel doors, and bolted-down bed frames with thin mattresses. Most of the rooms slept four to six together, and while chests of drawers had been set up, the rooms still felt like cells.

"This one's yours," Desmond said as they stopped in front of room nineteen. The soldier set Dominic's bags on the bed and left without a word. Dominic realized he never caught the man's name, or heard him speak for that matter. He found that rather unsettling.

They took another set of stairs down, and here Dominic found what he'd been waiting for. The research floor. They exited the stair into a kind of control room. There were several personnel set up at workstations, and the clacking of keys filled the room. All the workstations faced a wall of glass which revealed a series of white rooms. Dominic counted twelve in all. Each room had a screen above it showing the vital signs of its white-gowned occupant. In one, a big Asian man with scars on his face sat on his tiny bed and scowled out at them. Beside him, a Hispanic woman paced her little room like a caged tiger looking for the first chance to escape. And beside her, a white man covered in tattoos sat rocking on his bed, seemingly talking to himself. All of them wore chains around their ankles and wrists.

"Welcome to the nerve center," Desmond said with a grin, clapping Dominic on the shoulder.

"What the fuck is this?" Dominic said, horrified. The clacking keys stopped as everyone turned toward them. He started to back out of the room, shaking his head.

"Let's step into the office," Franklin said, grasping Dominic's arm and steering him toward a door on the far side of the room. Inside the rows upon rows of books, papers, and files left little room for the two desks. Franklin deposited him into a chair as Desmond closed the door and slid around behind one of the desks. and Franklin took the chair against the wall beside him.

"Who the fuck are those people out there, and why are they in chains?" Dominic said, fear and anger fighting a war in his voice.

"They are the test subjects for this project, and they're chained because they're all death row inmates," Franklin said calmly.

"Death row inmates," Dominic whispered, shaking his head. "What kind of study needs subjects on death row?"

"One that's about death, or rather, how to conquer it," Desmond said, a gleam in his eye.Dominic stilled. "What do you mean?"

"What happens to the mind after death?" Desmond asked, leaning on the desk and resting his chin on the backs of his hands.

"It's gone after the body dies and the brain ceases to function," Dominic said, confused.

"I thought so as well, until John here brought me evidence to the contrary," Desmond said, spinning around to the shelves behind him.

"Have you heard of the Valdemar Effect, Mr. Brogdon?" Franklin asked.

Dominic shook his head.

"It's a rather difficult phenomenon to describe," Desmond said, turning back around with a tablet in his hands. "It's much easier to show you."

He powered on the tablet and queued up a video before turning it towards Dominic and hitting play.

The camera was set up at the foot of a small bed inside what looked like a thatched hut. A much younger Franklin sat next to the bed, holding the hand of the man lying on it, who had to be the oldest person Dominic had ever seen, little more than a skeleton wrapped in a thin layer of dark brown skin. Dominic thought the man dead until he moaned in pain and writhed ever so slightly on the mattress.

There were three others on the opposite side of the bed from Franklin. The man's family, Dominic guessed. The woman cried softly, her black hair obscuring her face. She looked to be older, late fifties or so. The man's daughter, perhaps. The other two were younger men who stood with somber expressions behind the woman.

"Will it be long?" the woman choked out in what sounded like Spanish, though Dominic only knew what she said by the subtitles that scrolled across the bottom of the video.

"No," Franklin said.

"Is he in pain?" one of the men asked.

"I've given him pain medication, and the trance helps, but that hasn't eliminated all of your grandfather's pain," Franklin said, patting the old man's leathery hand. "All we can do now is wait."

The video sped up at that point, the family shifting about but not abandoning their vigil. After a few seconds, the video slowed to normal speed. The grandfather breathed raggedly at this point, and the daughter was crying harder. The man's breathing hitched, then he let out a long sigh and went still.

One of the grandsons wrapped his arms around his mother and she cried into his shoulder. Franklin took a stethoscope from around his neck and checked the patient for a heartbeat. After about a minute he pulled back and placed his fingers on the man's neck, then pulled a small light from his pocket and shined it into the man's eyes. He pressed his fingers into the fold of the man's eyelid. Finally, Franklin sat up and checked his watch before looking at the camera.

"No audible breath or heart sounds for greater than one minute," he said to the camera, in English this time. "No palpable pulse for greater than one minute. No palpable cardiac pacemaker. Pupils are fixed, dilated, and nonreactive to light. There is no response to painful stimuli. It is the twenty-third of August, time of death thirteen hundred hours."

Franklin sat back down, and the daughter turned to him, screaming through her tears, "You said he would not leave us."

"Please be patient for just a moment longer." Franklin said softly, reverting to Spanish. He picked up the camera, bringing it closer to the grandfather's face. After only a few moments, the man's lips receded, giving him a ghastly grin. His mouth opened, and his tongue protruded out. And out. And out. Farther than it seemed possible. All three of the man's family gasped, and the daughter stopped crying in shock.

"Excellent," Franklin said, bringing the camera even closer to the man's face. "Senor Barbaroza, are you with us?"

There was silence for a few moments, and the video began to break up. The man's tongue began to vibrate, and the most inhuman voice Dominic had ever heard came from the man.

"Yesssss," the horrid voice said. The sound of it sent waves of terror through Dominic. There was no way to describe how extremely *wrong* the voice was. It grated against his ears and dug at the depths of his brain like an ice pick.

"Good," Franklin said, sounding much calmer than Dominic felt. "Are you in any pain?"

The video broke up, lines of static running across it as the tongue vibrated again.

"No—pain."

"Can you tell me what state you are in now?" Franklin said, his voice mixing with the static so that it was hard to make him out. The static increased further, but Dominic was able to make out the words.

"I—am—dead."

Abruptly, the video ended.

"What the hell did I just watch?" Dominic said with a shiver.

"The Valdemar Effect," Desmond said, taking the tablet and turning it off.

"Have you read 'The Facts in the Case of M. Valdemar' by Edgar Allan Poe?" Franklin asked.

Dominic shook his head. He'd read a few of Poe's more famous stories for English in high school, but that title didn't sound familiar. What could a nineteenth century horror writer have to do with all of this?

"Many believed it was true when first published in the eighteen hundreds, though Poe refuted those claims," Franklin said. "We now know that the story was very much fact, and for those of us who studied it, that story is widely believed to be the first documented case of this phenomenon, hence the name. To put it simply, when a person dies while under the effects of hypnotism, the mind persists after the moment of death, leaving the person able to communicate with the living."

"Unfortunately, Dr. Franklin has only had a few occasions to witness the Valdemar Effect," Desmond said, leaning back in his chair. "The video documented his third chance to perform the required mesmerism on a suitable subject. Even more regrettably, it was also the last time he has been able to do so."

"Until now," Franklin said.

"Until now," Desmond echoed.

Dominic's eyes widened, and he gripped the arms of his chair. "You're telling me you plan to kill those people out there for the sake of an experiment."

"When put that way, it does sound heartless," Desmond said, his smile slipping a bit. "Every one of those men and women will die, whether or not they participate in our experiment. The United States government merely offered them a chance to survive past their death. Each and every one of them knows what is going to happen, and they've all given their consent."

"We aren't talking about brutal murder here, Mr. Brogdon," Franklin said, placing a hand on Dominic's arm. "They will be administered a lethal injection the same as they would during a normal execution. In fact, with the calm the mesmerism provides, you could say this is an even more humane way for them to pass."

It was insane. Completely and utterly insane. They meant to kill these people, and what, he was supposed to watch and take notes? Be an accomplice to murder? He wanted to walk out, not that he thought the two of them would actually let him go. He knew too much at this point, and they couldn't afford to have knowledge of such an experiment go public.

So...

Dominic pondered the video he'd watched. If he'd seen it anywhere else, he would have thought it was just a short horror story someone made for their YouTube channel. But Franklin truly believed that he'd been able to keep that man... Dominic wouldn't say he was alive. But he'd persisted. He'd been able to speak, even after his demise. It was a gross malformation of life, but something other than death. It answered so many questions, and raised others, and Dominic realized that the possibilities of this study were enormous. He could play his part, maybe change the world, and blow the whistle as soon as he could get away. But also, this might change the world.

"Can I verify with the subjects that they are here of their own will?" Dominic said quietly.

"Of course. We wouldn't want you to think that anyone has been coerced," Desmond said with a broad smile. He got up and reached out a hand. Dominic took it hesitantly. Desmond shook it all the same. "I knew you'd be on board. No time to waste now. Let's get started."

The initial stage of the experiment lasted for months, during which most of Dominic's duties were administrative. Observation, note taking, data entry, et cetera. Franklin had taught Desmond his mesmerism techniques, and the two of them split the subjects, putting each into a hypnotic state at least once a day. It interested Dominic to see how the process differed between them. Some were more susceptible and it took just a few words, some deep breathing, and a bit of hand waving to do the trick. Others were more resistant, not believing in "magic and mumbo-jumbo" as the scarred man so eloquently put it. The process for him had to be a lot more clinical and took longer to achieve. Once they got him there, his trances were deeper than the others. A medical team monitored the subject's vitals during each session, and Dominic filmed the sessions, documenting a host of data the doctors required.

In all the subjects, heart rate, blood pressure, and respiration slowed to rates that mimicked deep sleep, though the subjects remained responsive throughout the process. But it was the things they said under hypnosis that both intrigued and disgusted Dominic. While outside of a trance, the subjects were tight lipped about the crimes that netted them a death sentence, insisting on their own innocence. Under deep trance, most of them admitted fully to their legion of heinous crimes. Dominic heard all about the murders and rapes the subjects had committed, and the in-depth details haunted his nightmares.

One woman bothered him though. He was never allowed to know any of their names, so she was Subject Twelve to him. While the others seemed happy to confess their sins while in a trance, she staunchly denied any wrongdoing. She told them all how her husband framed her for the brutal torture and mutilation of their son. Dominic read through her case file, and while the evidence against her was damning, he couldn't help but believe her story as she told it under hypnosis. As she sobbed for her son, the doctors made her relive the moment she found him over and over. It was cruel, and the sound of her wails reverberating off those sterile white walls started to bounce around in his skull for hours after her sessions. It didn't change the doctors' minds though. She was sentenced to death, and the doctors did not have the authority to stay her execution, despite her pleas. He often wondered if they would even if they'd had the power.

"In the past, I've only worked with a subject when they were on their deathbed. One, perhaps two sessions. We've never achieved a trance this complete before the subject's demise,"

"We've also not been able to see what happens when a healthy subject experiences the Valdemar Effect. This is all uncharted territory, and that's what makes it so exciting."

Dominic had to admit that he was indeed excited to see the next stage of the experiment. After hearing the things that each subject did to deserve their sentence, his hesitation regarding their deaths dissipated. Except for Subject Twelve, but her word under hypnosis wasn't enough to save her from the needle. Not with the amount of testimony that existed against her. At least this way, her death would mean something.

It was almost a relief when the date of execution finally came. Dominic found it hard to sleep the night before. Not that he'd been sleeping well, cooped up as he was in this dark dungeon of a bunker. He had come to enjoy the work, but he missed sunlight in a way he hadn't expected, and he'd only been allowed outside a handful of times.

For several weeks leading up to the end of stage one, the doctors had been able to achieve a trance in less than a minute with every single subject. Their sessions had become much shorter by then, and the questions the doctors asked were few and short. Just a check to ensure the trance was deep enough. The short sessions were both a blessing and a curse. They gave him more time to rest, but sleep had practically become a cryptid to him with how elusive it was. At least a heavy workload would have given him something to occupy himself with. Instead, he spent most of his time in his quarters, failing to read his books, and spending far too much time inspecting the ceiling.

When the doctors announced they were ready to move to the next stage, Dominic was relieved.

The day of the execution, the control room was louder than normal. Researchers and personnel all chattered among themselves, the sound of their voices tumbling together like a rockslide, doing nothing to help Dominic's pounding headache. They'd all seen Franklin's video, of course, but no one had witnessed the real Effect in person. The conditions were so different for the subjects, and the anomalous possibilities were beyond intriguing. Though only Dominic seemed to care that they were about to watch twelve people die.

Desmond swept into the room like a hurricane, his enthusiasm palpable. "Are we ready to get this thing started?" he said, beaming at everyone around the room. Dominic grimaced in response to his bouncy energy. Franklin entered behind him, much less animated, though obviously just as excited. Desmond clapped a hand onto Franklin's shoulder. "All of our work is coming to fruition today, John."

Franklin gave Desmond a half smile and chuckled.

"Let's conquer death, shall we?" Desmond said with a laugh as everyone hurried to their stations. Dominic chugged the rest of his coffee and grabbed his laptop and camera. Unlike the others who would watch from behind the glass windows, Dominic would be in the room with the subjects as the lethal injection was administered. Of course, he wanted to see the Valdemar Effect in person, but the thought of witnessing that many deaths from close up made him sick to his stomach. He took a deep breath as Desmond motioned for him to follow.

Subject One was the tattooed man, a murderer and serial rapist with the blood of at least fifteen women on his hands. Dominic was glad they were starting with him. He didn't think watching this man die would be nearly as hard as some of the others. He set up by the bed, camera trained on the man's face, ready to document everything as the execution team strapped the subject down and Desmond started the process of hypnotizing him. Subject One had been a superstitious sort from the beginning, so it only took a few seconds of deep breathing and a bit of hand waving to do the trick.

"Placing IV," the head executioner said as he placed the first line in the subject's arm and a backup in the other. He arrived only a few days before, and while Dominic watched him work, he thought even after Subject One died, the thin man would look more like a corpse.

The execution team started a saline drip in both lines to ensure they weren't blocked. Everyone looked up at the monitor attached to the subject's telemetry unit, but his vitals didn't fluctuate. Once everything was in order, the executioner turned to Desmond and Franklin and gave them both a nod.

"Subject One, how are you feeling?" Franklin asked, sliding his chair close to the bedside.

"Relaxed," the subject responded.

"Good. Are you in any pain right now?" Franklin said.

"No."

"Are you ready?"

"I am."

The executioner stepped forward and connected the syringe to the line. Most lethal injections were a combination of three drugs, each delivered one after the other. For this study they opted to use the single drug method, an injection of sodium thiopental, which would cause death due to respiratory arrest.

The executioner pushed the drug into the subject's system. The subject's breathing began to slow. Over the next few minutes his breathing abated further, until it halted altogether. A few minutes more, and the subject's heart rate finally flat lined. Dominic kept his camera trained on the man as he died, disturbed most by the man's lack of reaction as it happened. A bit after the subject flatlined, Franklin pressed his stethoscope to the subject's chest.

"Time of death, nine hundred twenty-one hours," Franklin said, throwing his stethoscope back around his neck.

"How long will we have to wait for the Effect to become apparent?" Desmond asked, barely able to contain his very inappropriate amount of excitement.

Everyone fell silent again. Dominic's palms began to sweat, and he realized he was gripping the camera far too tightly in anticipation for something to happen. The minutes dragged by, and Dominic started to think they might have done something wrong.

A pop made Dominic jump so hard he almost knocked the camera over, and all eyes snapped to the subject. The sound had been Subject One's jaw snapping open far enough to dislocate. The subject's lips peeled back, leaving him with a gruesome grin. Ever so slowly his tongue protruded from his mouth, extending farther and farther until Dominic was sure the entire thing would jump out completely.

"Subject One, are you with us?" Franklin said, his words a little shaky. The subject's protruding tongue vibrated, and a voice like the devil's own filled the room.

"I—am—here" the subject said, his words stilted. Dominic wondered how the grandfather in the video had spoken, and revulsion wracked him as he realized it was from his vibrating tongue. Subject One's voice felt even more wrong though. Dominic could *feel* the sinister voice on his skin, and it made him squirm in his seat.

"How do you feel?" Desmond asked, completely unfazed by the horror unfolding. "Are you in any pain?"

"No—pain," the subject said after a while. "Dark."

"Can you see anything in the dark?" Franklin asked, moving closer to the subject.

"No—no—dead."

The subject repeated that last word over and over. No matter what questions Desmond and Franklin asked, he continued to give the ominous selfsame answer.

"Dead."

When it became clear Subject One would say nothing else, the team moved on. Subject Two presented the Valdemar Effect just as thoroughly. The questioning was eerily similar as well, progressing slowly until the subject became stuck on a word as well.

Gone. Gone. Gone.

And so it went with the other subjects. Each answering only a few questions before clinging to a word like a rock climber clings to a crumbling ledge. The chosen word was different for each subject, but they were all unsettling. Please. Stop. Help.

Wait.

When they entered the final room, Subject Twelve already lay on the bed. The others had been pacing their rooms, nervously awaiting what was to come. Twelve looked up at the team when they entered, sadness in her eyes.

"Let's get this over with," she said. "I want to see my son again."

Franklin and Desmond shared a look before the former said, "Very well."

Subject Twelve was extremely susceptible to trance and it took only moments to induce it. Like the others, Dominic zoomed in on her face as the executioner pushed the drug. A single tear rolled down her face, and a lump formed in Dominic's throat. He wished he knew her name so he could at least remember her by something more than a number.

The Valdemar Effect looked even more gruesome on her when it finally occurred. Dominic thought that her lips peeled back a bit faster, and her tongue protruded just a bit more than the others.

"Are you with us?" Franklin said when the process was complete.

"We—are—here," she replied, her unearthly voice slithering through the room.

Dominic's eyes widened. "We," he said before he could stop himself. "What do you mean, we?"

"The—others—are—with—me," she responded.

The air thickened like a blood clot.

"Do you mean the other subjects?" Desmond whispered; his joviality finally gone.

"Yes," Subject Twelve said.

There was a collective gasp. The doctors started a furious whispered conversation. Dominic fought to keep his shaking hands from disrupting the camera. After a few moments they turned back to Subject Twelve.

"What can you tell us of the others?" Franklin said. He leaned in close like he was afraid to miss anything the subject said. "How do you perceive them?"

The seconds ticked by, and Franklin furrowed his brow.

"Are you still with us?" he said when the silence dragged on too long. Another few moments passed, and Dominic thought she wouldn't respond again when her devilish voice filled the room.

"Join—us."

The doctors tried to coax more out of her, but she never spoke again. When she said those words, Dominic wanted to turn tail and run. He stayed in place, dutifully recording everything. In a way, he felt like he owed it to her. When Desmond and Franklin finally dismissed them all, he was more than happy to pack up and leave. He knew the doctors would want a full written report of the day, but at that moment he didn't care. He deposited his equipment in the control room and practically ran to his room.

Dominic tried to sleep and leave the day behind, but he just ended up lying on his bed, staring up at the ceiling above him, his mind full of writhing tongues and chanted words. After hours of tossing and turning he abandoned the hope of sleep and sat up, thinking perhaps he could escape into one of his novels. When that didn't work, he decided that staying in his room wasn't going to help matters. It was well after midnight already, but he knew the doctors were still working, which meant many of the aides would be working as well. He hadn't exactly made friends with anyone, but he was at least on good terms with a few, and he could really use someone to talk to.

The corridors were devoid of people. Most were in their beds, getting what rest they could. With the lack of sunlight, and the grimness of their research, Dominic imagined many of his colleagues were having trouble sleeping as well. Wandering the halls late at night had become a habit for him and the solitude never once bothered him. But something about the complex seemed different that night, something intangible that he couldn't place. It set him on edge.

There wasn't a soul in the control room when he arrived, which only unsettled him more. Someone should have been at least monitoring the patients and documenting anything they might do overnight. The patient rooms were dark as well, which seemed unnecessary. While alive, the darkness helped them to sleep, but they were dead now. Dominic was sure they didn't need sleep any longer.

Dominic knocked on the door to Desmond and Franklin's office, but no reply came from within. He tried the handle and found it unlocked. He opened the door. The lights were out inside. He'd expected them to still be there, poring over the data.

A thud sounded in the lab.

Dominic spun around, his heart pounding in his ears. There was no one in the room with him. Another thud. And another. All coming from one of the dark patient rooms. Was it one of the subjects? The thought of the dead being up and about sent a chill down his spine. The thudding became more frantic. Dominic hurried to the light controls for the patient rooms and flipped them on.

The rooms were empty, the doors wide open. Had someone taken them somewhere? If so, when? Where had they taken them? Where? A thousand other questions flitted through Dominic's thoughts.

Movement caught his eye. One of the rooms was still occupied. Trent, a medical consultant, lay on the floor inside, his legs broken so badly at the shins that the bones showed through. A trail of blood marked the path where he had dragged himself over to the observation glass, and he was actively pounding on it. His eyes met Dominic's and he yelled something. With a shaking hand, Dominic pressed the intercom button.

"...out of this room. Help me. For fuck's sake, help me," Trent screamed over the loudspeaker.

Before Dominic could react, someone—no, some*thing*—opened the door. It moved into the light with jerking, twitching motions, like a toddler learning how to walk. Subject Twelve, her neck bent back at an almost impossible angle so that her protruding tongue pointed straight up in the air like a second head. Trent followed Dominic's gaze behind him and screamed when he saw her.

"Oh fuck, oh fuck," he said. "She's going to kill me. Fucking help."

Impossibly fast, Subject Twelve fell on Trent. He screamed again, trying to buck her off his back. She flipped him over, pinning his hands down when he tried to hit her, and grabbed his jaw. She wrenched his bottom jaw down with a wet snap, breaking it and leaving it dangling. Trent's screams intensified. She wrapped her fingers in his hair, lowered her face down, and smashed her mouth into his, her grotesque tongue slithering down Trent's throat.

Subject Twelve's hellish voice filled the room, speaking words in a language Dominic had never heard before, and Trent began to convulse. After only a few seconds, she pulled back.

"Join—us."

She dropped Trent and skittered out of the room. Trent's tongue slid out of his mouth to an unsettling degree, just like the Valdemar subjects. A voice darker, and more horrible than any Dominic heard from the others filled the room.

"Join—us," it said. Dominic knew the words were directed at him. He ran.

Screams reached his ears before he made it back to the barracks. Dominic slowed, his heart threatening to pound its way out of his chest. He pressed his back against the wall and crept the rest of the way down the corridor toward the main hall of the sleeping quarters. He peeked around the corner and was greeted by a nightmare.

The Valdemar subjects were tearing through the barracks like lions through a herd of gazelles. People were trying their best to get out of their rooms and away from the horrors. But Trent hadn't been the only new abomination to be made, and they were now too many, and too fast. They filled every doorway, descending on the living like a spider on a fly.

Vihaan, one of the cleaning crew, managed to slip by one as it stumbled into a room. He locked eyes with Dominic and ran towards him. The Valdemar horror lunged for Vihaan, tackling him to the floor. Vihaan crawled as fast as he could, desperate to get away, but the thing grabbed his leg and dragged him back. Vihaan kicked at it. The thing caught his foot, twisting it violently. Vihaan screamed as his ankle broke, the bone jutting from the skin, and thrashed harder to get the thing off him.

The Valdemar horror crawled its way forward until it was able to grab his hair. It jerked his head back with a sickeningly wet crack. Vihaan went limp, and the thing slid its grotesque tongue into his mouth, making his body convulse.

When his body stilled, the thing retracted its tongue and loped down the hall, searching for its next victim. Vihaan's tongue began its own unsightly protrusion. And he wasn't alone. Everywhere Dominic looked, more undead were being created at an incredibly rapid rate. If this continued, the entire bunker would be converted in a matter of minutes. Dominic needed to get out as quickly as possible if he was going to survive the night.

A bit of movement from the other side of the entrance to the barracks caught his eye. It was Isabella, the head of security, waving at him. When she saw she had Dominic's attention, she pointed at something.

The newly turned Vihaan was heading straight for him.

"Run!" Isabella yelled at him. He passed the barracks entrance in a matter of seconds, and Vihaan picked up his staggering pace. He moved like a newborn bird, limbs shaking and twitching. Fear moved Dominic's limbs so fast that he almost fell several times.

"Keep going toward the emergency lift," Isabella said, gesturing down the hall with her head and raising her gun. A moment later the sound of gunfire reached his ears. He risked a glance back and saw Isabella backing down the hall after him, putting rounds in Vihaan. She was slowing it down, but the horror seemed otherwise unconcerned with the bullets entering his flesh.

"Join—us," Vihaan chanted as he crept forward under the barrage of bullets.

Rounding the corner, Dominic made for the lift at the end of the next corridor. He slammed his finger into the lift's call button, desperately pressing it over and over to get the doors to open. The gears whirred inside as the lift lowered down to them.

"These things just keep fucking coming," Isabella said as she ran up, making Dominic nearly jump out of his skin. The Valdemar undead lurched around the corner. Vihaan wasn't alone anymore. It seemed that Isabella's gunshots had drawn every single one of the undead. They staggered down the hall like a lava flow just as the doors to the lift opened.

"Get inside," Isabella cried, pushing Dominic into the lift. She backed in after him, firing into the horde chasing them. "Hit the goddamn button."

Dominic scrambled to press the button for the mess hall and the kitchens, the highest floor it would take them to. The doors began to close, far too slowly for his liking. The horde kept coming, their chanting deafening. Just in time, the doors clicked closed and the lift began to rise, the creatures outside pounding at the steel doors.

"Jesus Christ, what the fuck is going on?" Isabella leaned her back against the wall, breathing heavily.

"This shouldn't be possible," Dominic said, running a shaking hand across his face. "The subjects aren't supposed to be able to move like this. All data we have shows that only the tongue should move, and only to communicate. And the Valdemar Effect should only be induced when a hypnotized subject dies during hypnosis. I have no idea how they're able to spread the Effect like this."

"All that matters now is getting the fuck out of here before those things tongue *us* to death. What's your name, again?"

"Dominic Brogdon."

She nodded and pushed off the wall as the lift slowed. "Listen, Dominic, stay with me, stay quiet, move fast, and we'll both get out of here."

The screech of the lift opening echoed out into the dark, deserted kitchens. Isabella switched on her flashlight and the two of them crept out onto the tile. She passed the beam over the entirety of the room, light glinting off the metal of the tables and the pots and utensils hanging overhead. As far as Dominic could tell, they were alone.

"Looks clear," Isabella said. Dominic stuck close, painfully aware of his lack of a weapon. Isabella pushed the swinging door to the mess hall open, shining her light through the empty room.

A hand reached out of the darkness beside the door and wrapped around Isabella's arm. "Join—us." She cried out as the Valdemar undead dragged her toward it. She raised her gun and put a round into the thing's exposed throat. It staggered back, but its grip on her arm never wavered.

She kicked the undead's legs out from under it. It fell, dragging her down. Dominic rushed forward, grabbing the thing's arm and trying to pry it off her. It let her go, but turned its attention to him, picking him up and slamming him down on the floor. Dominic fought with all he had, but the thing was not to be stopped. It bore down on him, prying open his jaw and lowering its head and writhing tongue toward him. Dominic met the thing's unseeing eyes - it was Franklin. He froze in shock. Franklin slid his slimy tongue over Dominic's face and into his mouth. Dominic gagged when it slithered down his throat, and he felt the vibration of its speech in his vocal cords. He started to convulse uncontrollably. Something began to envelope his mind.

With a sucking, slurping sound the tongue was violently ripped from deep within his windpipe. The presence at the edge of his consciousness disappeared, and Dominic returned to himself. Franklin was on the floor, Isabella on top of him. She'd rammed into the horror to get it off Dominic. Before she could get away, Franklin wrapped his body around her, pinning her in place.

"Go!" she yelled at Dominic.

Franklin shoved his fingers into her mouth, grabbing her bottom jaw and ripping it off in a nauseating pop of bone and flesh. She barely had time to scream before he snaked his tongue into her.

Dominic scrambled to his feet and bolted toward the door. He slammed it open and collided with another of the Valdemar undead. The hit sent it stumbling back into the rail. Dominic didn't give it time to react. He dashed up the stairs toward the only exit. The footfalls of dozens of feet echoed up from the stairwell below him.

Dominic stumbled up the last flight of steps and through the door that opened to the entrance corridor. The security man stationed at the door stood up as Dominic rushed toward him.

"Stop," the security guy said, bringing his weapon to bear on Dominic.

"Open the door," Dominic gasped as he came to a stop a few feet from the man, holding his hands up in placation.

"You aren't authorized—"

"Join—us." The Valdemar undead came crashing into the corridor. .

"Open the goddamn door!" Dominic screamed. The man hurried to press the button to release the locks on the door. The red light above the door illuminated. A buzzing sounded as the locks slid out of place. Dominic threw his shoulder into the door and stumbled out into the tropical night, the security guy only a step behind him. Dominic rushed for the single UTV sitting outside

"Where are the keys?"

Behind them, the door crashed open and the first of the Valdemar undead staggered out into the open air.

"What the hell is that?" the security guy said, getting in the passenger side.

"Where are the fucking keys?" Dominic shouted at the man. He reached into a pocket, pulling out a ring and tossing it to Dominic.

Dominic cycled through the keys as quickly as he could, looking for the right one. The Valdemar horde was getting closer.

"Come on," the security guy said, voice shaking.

"I'm trying. I'm trying."

"Shit, we're not going to make it," the man said. He stepped out of the vehicle and raised his weapon to let loose a round of automatic gunfire into the charging horde. Dominic didn't bother to see if the machine gun was working better than Isabella's handgun had.

Finally, one key clicked, and the engine started. Dominic gave a cry of triumph, threw the UTV into gear, and sped off down the road. He heard the security guy yell at him over the gunfire, but he didn't stop. The man had bought him time, and he was thankful, but the guy sealed his own fate when he got out of the vehicle. There were too many of the undead for Dominic to wait.

He sped through the rainforest as fast as he could, headlights barely cutting through the darkness. The tires threw splashes off huge standing puddles in the small road. He remembered the trip to the docks taking no more than ten minutes, but it felt like an eternity before he left the trees behind and the ocean came into view. He expected to see at least one ship docked, but the lagoon was empty.

"There's gotta be something," he whispered to himself as he drove down the connector and out to the dock proper, stopping the UTV and killing the engine. The waxing moon above bleached all color from his surroundings, adding to the eeriness of the night.. He cast about on the dock, not sure what he was looking for, but sure he'd know it when he saw it. He spotted a small set of stairs down the dock that seemed to lead to the water. He hurried toward it, taking the steps two at a time to the bottom.

Where a small, two-man motor boat was docked.

It wasn't much, but it was all that he had. He'd only used a motorboat a few times in his life, so he wasn't sure how far it would get him, but he was pretty sure it wouldn't make it to land even if it had a full tank. He'd seen a small storage shed up on the main dock. Maybe there was some gas he could bring with him. He ran back up the stairs to check and stopped dead at the top.

Over a dozen Valdemar undead ran full tilt down the connector, their lolling tongues glinting in the moonlight. They were moving too fast.

He nearly tumbled down the steps and almost capsized the boat in his haste. He could hear the stomp of the creatures' feet, and their continued chant as they came for him. He tried to untie the mooring line, his fingers fumbling with the rope in his haste and fear. Tears of frustration welled up in his eyes, which only made it harder to undo the knots. Finally, he freed the rope and scrambled into the seat. He pumped the fuel line a few times, pulled out the choke, made sure it was in neutral, and pulled the start cord. The engine started up on the first try, and he whooped at his luck. As the Valdemar horde came rushing down the stairs, he pushed in the choke, pulled it into gear, and sped off from the dock. He thought the horde might try to keep pursuing him even through the water, but when he looked back the creatures were all standing on the tiny lower dock, watching him depart. Tears streamed down his face as relief flooded through him.

He made it.

The boat ran out of gas maybe an hour out. He had nothing to paddle with and found no additional gas in the boat. With no idea where he was, what direction land might be, or how far away it was, he finally resigned himself to dying at sea.

He drifted for days. It didn't take long for the dehydration and exposure to leave him completely incoherent. Finally, he closed his eyes, and expected that he'd never open them again.

When he did, he found himself lying in a bed, a blanket tucked up around his chin. He blinked, trying to shake the sleep from his eyes, and for a moment he thought he was in his room at his parents' house.

Was it a dream? he thought. But as the metal ceiling above him came into focus, he realized that he wasn't in his room. The nightmare had been real.

Dominic sat up, his head spinning. A man wearing a blue uniform, the words U. S. Coast Guard embroidered over his left breast, a stethoscope slung around his neck and a tablet in one hand pulled back the curtain that surrounded the bed. When he saw Dominic awake, he pulled out a radio and held it to his lips. "Captain, the patient is awake," he said. A moment later there was a crackle of static as the reply came.

"Acknowledged. Get him up here ASAP. We've almost arrived."

"Good to see you up and about," the man said to Dominic, setting the tablet on a table next to the bed and pulling the stethoscope from around his neck. "We started to worry you wouldn't for a minute. You were in bad shape when we picked you up."

"Who are you, and where am I?" Dominic said, his voice little more than a rasp.

"I'm Lieutenant Kai Mahelona, and you are aboard the USCGC

Jupiter, my friend. We're about to make port," the man said as he checked Dominic's vitals. Dominic still felt weak, but he couldn't help but smile.

He was safe. He was going home.

"Think you can dress yourself?" Lt. Mahelona said as he removed the last IV. Dominic nodded and allowed the lieutenant to help him to his feet. He wobbled a bit, but after a moment he was able to stand. Lt. Mahelona handed him a bag of clothes and stepped out, pulling the curtain closed behind him saying, "Let me know when you're done, and I'll take you up to the deck."

The provided clothes and shoes were a bit big, but Dominic didn't mind. It was better than the breezy gown he'd woken up in. He joined the lieutenant who guided him up to the open air above. After the days he'd spent floating, the smell of sea air made him nauseous. A woman met them on the deck, dressed in the same blue uniform as the lieutenant. Mahelona saluted and said, "Captain Nguyen, I've given Mr. Brogdon a clean bill of health, and he's ready for duty."

A hot ball of fear dropped into Dominic's stomach.

"What do you mean, duty?" he said, taking a step back. The lieutenant placed a hand on his shoulder, holding him in place.

"Duty to God and country, Mr. Brogdon. You've got work to finish," the captain said, gesturing toward the front of the ship and the island they were headed for.

Wahi Huna.

"No," Dominic said, trying to break free from the lieutenant's grasp. Another soldier stepped up beside him, taking hold of his other shoulder. The muzzle of a gun pressed up against the back of his head, and he went still. The captain smiled at him.

"I'm afraid you don't have a choice in the matter, Mr. Brogdon."

DEVILISH DETAILS

L. R. GOULD

The shower of earth falling onto my son was not the delicate toss of a mourner's shovel but the indiscriminate flood of a backhoe bucket. The rumble of a diesel engine and the impatient work of men already delayed past their dinnertime and wanting to go home underscored how little my son's short life meant to everyone in this world except for me. Oh, the minister tried to move me with shallow words and empty platitudes. To convince me my child's death meant something. But the chill of a September rain pulled all the warmth from them as it pulled away the few who turned out to say their goodbyes. Perhaps the rain was heaven's tears, but even the angels could not comfort me or let me hold my precious child in my arms once more.

The pile of earth disappeared into the hollow hole in the ground, swallowing my life in the setting sun. As the tractor whined, packed up its rigging, and stole away into the night I slipped from the bench the preacher deposited me on while the cemetery crew concealed my son and stumbled back to my child. The passing workers, long hardened by death to a parent's grief, cast furtive glances my way before leaving me to mourn in peace without a word. Finally alone, wrapped in night's oblivion, my tears mixed with the rain soaking my clothes. I fell to my knees, lifted my head, and screamed, my pain demanding an audience, the roll of approaching thunder my reply.

"Please! Please, one more moment with my beautiful baby. Just one more. I would give you anything, my life, my soul." The night swallowed my words, and a bright bolt of lightning punctuated my cry, striking in the distance with a boom of thunder that echoed in my chest. It was the most I had felt since I first saw the still, lifeless form of my son and knew I would never be able to hold or comfort him again.

A sudden urge to kiss his forehead moved my hands into the mud in front of me and my knees followed. I crawled to the empty place reserved for a headstone and lay in the puddling rain, my fingers tracing trails in the soft earth unable to get closer to my beloved child.

The rain fell around me, but not on me, as the shield of an umbrella protected me. The warmth of a tender hand spread across my shoulder. It squeezed comfortingly but did not distract me from the entombment of my heart. It rested there while a wordless lullaby replaced the drum of the rain on the canvas shield. The melody encouraged me to sit and eventually stand. Mud caked my clothes, but I felt the hand slip down to my waist and a thin body press wordlessly against my own. Quietly they drew me away and I found my feet following numbly along. Time had stopped days ago, but it started slowly ticking as I left the grave behind.

Led along the asphalt paths navigating the cemetery, we left though a side gate too narrow for the small procession of cars that brought me here earlier. From there we turned and wandered through a trail in the neighboring woods. I followed my guide until eventually they sat me at a well-worn wooden table next to a crackling fire in a home I did not recall entering. Wrinkled hands helped me from my wet jacket and overshirt before a blanket wrapped itself around me and a steaming cup of spiced tea was pressed into my fingers.

I raised the cup to my lips with an absent-minded thanks. The sweet heat of the tea chased away the chill chewing at my soul. Wiping away my tears with the edges of the blanket, I lifted my eyes.

My host sat patiently in the chair across from me with her own cup of tea. She lowered the cup to the saucer on the table, and her smile shifted the weathered wrinkles adorning her face. The grandmotherly expression creasing her dark skin spoke of a hard life earned beneath a hot sun, but also of the understanding of age. Tight curls of white hair spilled to her shoulders and her green eyes stared compassionately at me. Waiting for me.

I drew in another long sip of liquid comfort and sucked in a cooling breath between the gap in my front teeth. A childish habit I had long ago broken. "Thank you." The words came with more strength than I thought I had.

"You are welcome, dear." Her voice had that sage quality of one who knows everything. I instantly felt as if she contained all the secrets to life and, inexplicably, death.

An irrational thought flittered into my consciousness, and I voiced it without considering what it was. "Are you here for me?" The words floated in the air between us. Death would be kinder than living without my heart. The thought did not distress me, but rather brought peace to my wailing soul. "Are you here to take me to my son?"

The comforting smile on the face staring back at me shifted into an amused expression. "Yes, I am here for you – in a manner of speaking, I am here to reunite you with your son, but not in the way you are thinking."

Confusion threatened to disrupt my newfound peace. I watched the elderly woman sip from her cup. I stared into the cup of tea in my hands, remembering the warmth of the coppery liquid and how the spices tingled on my tongue.

"Just honey and some herbs from the garden, dear. Please drink up."

I raised the cup and drank. Consuming the entire contents in one long draft, praying that if death had come for me, she would be quick so I could see my son once more.

The chair scraped on the hardwood floor. My host retrieved the kettle hanging on a hook over the fire and brought it over to me. "Have another. It'll chase away the autumn chill, dear," she said, refilling my cup. Steam rose in a misty cloud and heat too hot to handle leached from the cup into my hands. I placed my cup on the saucer as the woman returned the kettle to the hook over the fire. She sat back down in her seat as my mind finally grasped at a wavering thought. She'd taken the kettle from the fire with her bare hands—hadn't she? With my own cup too hot to hold, reason argued that I must have missed the towel she used.

"Go ahead, dear. Drink up."

Unable to find death's consoling embrace at the bottom of the first cup, I only sipped at the tea this time. "So in what way are you here for me?"

Her head rocked, setting her curls into a gentle sway. "It would be more accurate to say that I am here because of you."

"Come again?" In my hysterical state I could not parse the old woman's words.

She waved off the question with a slight shake of her head. "It's not important. I am here now and that is all that matters."

"And…you are going to *reunite* me with my son?" Eager, heartbroken desire chastised my rational brain, screaming it didn't care. Whatever it took. Whatever it cost. I would give this woman everything I had if just for the promise.

The corner of her mouth quivered slightly, and her eyes brightened. "I can give you back every cherished moment you have ever had with your son. An opportunity to relive the life taken from you."

"How?"

"How is not…" she made a dismissing gesture, "really important. I can do this thing and once it is done, you can relive your life with your precious child. What more can a mother ask? What more would a mother give?"

A vision of my bank account consumed by the mountain of medical bills passed before me. "I have nothing left."

"The price has already been offered and agreed upon, dear. Don't you worry about it."

"But…"

Again, she waved off my question and again, it slipped from my mind. Every other thought evaporated in the heat of a desperate need to see my baby boy once more. I nodded, shaking loose needy tears. "Please." The word, little more than a gasp, pressed itself through my quivering lips.

"Of course." The woman rose from her chair and shuffled around the table. Her spotted hand took mine and helped me to my feet. The blanket slipped from my shoulders and fell to the floor. "Leave it, dear. I'll get it later," she said before leading me through the door at the other end of the kitchen.

I followed her down a narrow hall and we descended a steep staircase. Earthy, musty odors greeted me as the walls turned to dirt. Soft yellow light flickered from candles burning gently on shelves crowded with jars and books. I scanned the shelves attempting to discern the contents of the jars or read the book spines, but my teary vision blurred the murky waters and rendered the handwritten titles illegible. Musky floral scents mixed with the subterranean mildew in a curious concoction that made me feel lighter on my feet.

Past the shelves, a stacked stone wall holding up the floor above divided the room. A rounded door set in the wall creaked open as we approached. I followed the tapestry of tattoos adorning the thin bony arm holding the door open to a petite man in cargo shorts and tank top in a sickly yellow shade I worried came more from neglect than the candle-light. The hues of blue ink covering every square inch of his skin appeared to move and wriggle in the flickering light. As my escort pulled me past, the tattoo's shapes and lines resolved themselves into a gathering of women in flowing dresses dancing across his bare scalp. The intoxicating dance stopped the moment I tried to focus on them, leaving filaments of blue-blonde hair obscuring the women's faces. The man's eyes dulled with the inactivity of his tattoos.

"This way, dear." My hostess's voice called my attention but turning to follow made my head swim. Her gentle hand clasped my arm and she guided me to a leather chair. "There you go, dear." She stroked my cheek with the back of her hand and began to chant in a language I did not understand.

Something sharp pricked my thumb, but the pain faded as quickly as it came. The monotonous drone of her voice numbed my mind as much as it dulled the pain of my torn heart. The woman collected the bright drops of blood into a small glass vial. Without pausing her recitation or even the slightest shift in pitch, the woman turned the needle and pressed it into her own thumb, adding her blood to mine.

She passed the vial to the man who sat at the small table beside my chair. He added the crimson mixture to a miniature pot of blue ink and gave it a stir with the needle she passed to him.

Clasping my hand in hers, the woman rolled her thumb against mine, swirling the tiny droplets of blood still oozing from our wounds together until they became indistinguishable paint between our fingers. Her chanting changed; the cadence became a melodic singsong that reminded me of the lullabies I used to sing to my little boy. I closed my eyes. My baby filled my vision. An electro-mechanical hum caught up the baseline, cutting in and out in time to the woman's song. The music faded to the background as a theme song to the childish babble of my little Steven playing in my mind.

I lost myself to the playback of Steven's life passing before me.

Steven moved in my belly, playing kickball with my bladder. He took his first steps and stumbled into my arms. His preschool teacher peeled him off my leg when he refused to let me go on his first day of preschool. He pried himself out of my arms when I held on tight his first day of kindergarten. I smiled encouragingly as my eight-year-old told me all about his favorite video game even though I didn't understand a word he said. We spent the day eating ice cream and watching his favorite movie when his friends didn't show up for his tenth birthday. I wept again when he brought his first crush home, and watched his nervousness turn to joy when I welcomed his boyfriend with a hug. I worried all over again through the heartbreak and the weeks of recovery when they broke up.

The doctor walked into the room, pronounced my son's cancerous death sentence, and my heart broke all over again. I admired the strong will and effort he put into cherishing every last minute.

I relived his life from beginning to end—every moment in exquisite detail, the colors, the smells, the tastes, the joy, and even the pain. I died all over again when it ended with so much pain.

The hum of the needle cut off and the room fell silent except for the soft murmur, "There, there, Darling, the ending is always the worst. Give it time," as a cloth mopped the tears from my face.

I opened my eyes. The aged woman held a flower embroidered cloth in her wrinkled hands. Where my tears stained the flowers, they glowed with an ethereal life. My right arm ached from wrist to shoulder. The woman caught my arm when I reached to touch the blue highlights of Steven's life etched into my skin in a perfect memorial.

"No. No. Not yet," The woman said breathily like a junkie after a fresh hit.

She licked her lips unsettlingly, and I pulled my hand back diverting my gaze from hers to the scenes recorded in the flesh of my arm. Like the tattoos adorning the man packing up his implements beside me, mine tricked the eye in a way that brought life back to my Steven. "How?"

"Tsk. Tsk. We agreed, *how* does not matter." The woman swallowed hard and the over-indulged glassy look my father used to get after consuming a full plate of pie at Thanksgiving dinner disappeared from her face.

The tattooist pointed at my arm and muttered something in a language I didn't understand. My host nodded impatiently, shooing him away with a wave of her hand. He collected his things and shuffled away in a huff.

"What did he say?"

She rolled her eyes with a heavy sigh. "Bah, just his little warning. Point and counterpoint, life and death, one cannot exist without the other."

"What?"

"You can relive the memories of your child any time you like, but," she held up a finger, "you must relive them all. It is not possible to choose."

I surveyed the tapestry stitched in a sleeve from wrist to bicep. Every blessed memory of my little Steven captured in exquisite detail mirrored the images already fading from my mind. As they faded, so did the joy of seeing Steven once again. In their hollow place, only loneliness remained.

The woman's tender green eyes turned sympathetic, and she licked her pursed lips. "Fine, darling. Once more today. A simple touch is all you need."

Hesitantly I touched Steven's smiling face. As soon as my fingers made contact, the images flooded my vision with the force of a crashing wave. I closed my eyes and lost myself once more to the cinematic replay of Steven's life.

My fingers slid from the tattoo as the enchantment broke and the cold reality of my empty life set in deeper than ever before. I wiped away tears for the hundredth time and opened my eyelids. The harsh sunlight beaming in through my bedroom window forced them shut. I had lost yet another night's sleep to the tattoo's empty promises of a renewed life with Steven. No matter how many times I watched his life blossom and grow, I could do nothing but observe helplessly as it withered away until only the cold rain spitting onto a hollow grave remained.

Sitting up in my bed, I pulled the sleeve of my nightgown down over the tattoo. A grinning nine-year-old Steven peeked out from beneath the cuff. I gave him a wan smile, barely resisting the urge to kiss him. Tears dripped from my chin, and I whipped them away with the back of my left arm having learned the hard way the last time when I used my right hand and lost myself to the memories.

Hair, thick from nothing but my tears to wash it, fell across my face and my nose wrinkled at the scent. Shuffling to the bathroom, I turned on the shower and let the water flow over my head and shoulders. Lathering up my washcloth I cleaned my left arm, then ran the rag over my right. It rolled in my hand and my fingers brushed my tattoo. A bright light flashed across my vision and Steven punted my bladder. Suddenly my knees buckled, and I lost my balance. Reaching out blindly, I caught myself on the shower wall and watched Steven's life ebb by helplessly waiting for the bitter end. The cold graveside rain turned into a lava hailstorm running down my back and the gray sky became steam as my visions slipped away, leaving me shivering despite the scalding temperature of my shower. I cut the water off, my hair unwashed, and hugged my towel to my chest.

I stumbled back into my bedroom and flopped onto the rumpled covers of my bed, careful to keep my right arm away from the rest of my body. Minutes (it could have been hours later. I hadn't been able to keep track of time for weeks), my cell phone rang, startling me out of a dreamless sleep. I rolled over, stretching my left hand out for the phone on my nightstand. The back of my right forearm brushed across my chest, and I crashed helplessly back through time and my son's too short life.

By the time Steven's ghost finally returned to his grave, I had missed three calls from work, followed by two text messages and a voicemail. My right hand drifted toward the throbbing vein on my forehead, but I stopped it just shy of contact and forced it away, glaring at the horrid artwork on my arm. The once pleasant face of the dear child I adored now taunted me with a blue grin. Fresh tears ran down my face and dripped onto the bed.

I put the phone down and used the edge of the bed sheet to wipe away the tears with my left hand. Only after I dried my eyes did I check my messages. The texts were the standard *where are you* check ins from a workplace already shorthanded. The voicemail contained a bit more compassion from my boss, who had lost her own mother only seven months prior. I opened up my contacts and found my boss's direct line. My finger hovered over the phone icon as my throat clenched tighter. She was the closest person I had to a friend, and this was the first time she had called since Steven had passed. I couldn't muster the strength to talk to her with the memory of Steven still so raw and I opted for a brief text asking for a couple more days.

The ghoulish nights that followed left dark bags under my eyes while I searched for a solution to Steven's nightly visits. I lost track of the days as the visions slowly drove me mad with despair and I realized losing Steven had not been life's horrid bottom I thought it was. One by one, I lost what little I still had: my job, my mind, and eventually my home.

Steven's specter never left me. He preyed upon my waking hours, following me everywhere, tauntingly close but always out of reach. Under his watchful gaze I packed my life into cardboard boxes, stacking them in the dining room until only his bedroom remained untouched. My heart raced as I reached a shaking hand for the door. The many faces of Steven decorating my arm turned their heads from me to the door as one.

The handle turned and the door swung open with a squeak of hinges not used to moving anymore. Like a forgotten time capsule from before that dreaded trip to the hospital, dirty clothes still littered the floor and the covers of his bed lay in a crumpled heap as if he had just gotten up. I shuffled to the edge and placed a hand onto the sheets expecting to find them still warm from his body, but only cold dust wrapped itself around my fingers. The dust floated up into the rays of setting sunlight streaming in through the high window over his bed.

The many faces of Steven gave me a unanimous accusatory glare and an overwhelming sense of unwanted trespass came over me. My hands chased the dust drifting in the light in a vain attempt to gather them and return them to their place. With aggravating slowness, my mind registered the futility of the gesture and anger welled up inside me. I screamed slamming my hands down onto the sheets and tore them from the bed throwing them to the floor.

I ripped the alarm clock from the nightstand. The cord caught momentarily on the outlet, but then came free whipping me across my face. The stinging pain fed my rage and I savagely flung it against the dresser. It shattered in a satisfactory crunch. In a raging whirlwind I pulled the shelves from his wall, tore down the posters of fantastical creatures and shattered the many Lego sculptures he had spent his short life building. My throat rasped raw while the pile on the floor grew until eventually my rage withered and died.

Heaving breathlessly, I sat on the bed staring at the heap of Steven's broken dreams. Somewhere in the back of my mind I knew I should be crying, but I had no tears left to spend for Steven. Numbly I sat on the bed letting that thought echo in the hollowness of my empty heart.

By the time my breathing slowed to the weary raggedness that was now called normal, the beam of sunlight had crawled across the floor and ambled up the closed closet door, unscathed in my blind fury. I pressed myself up, walked calmly to the door, and opened it. I compared the similarities of the pile Steven left inside the closet to the pile of rubbish I created outside and let out a sardonic snort. Crossing my legs, I sat on the floor beside the door. One by one I pulled items off his pile and added them to mine.

Beneath the crust of clothing never returned to the empty hangers above, I uncovered a forgotten Green Lantern costume in a crumpled bundle on the floor. The memory of his smile spreading broad across his face as he put on his favorite superhero's uniform came unbidden to my mind. That happiness wilted into the hot bitter tears of teenage embarrassment when his friends' teasing made him lose faith. The memories lacked the crystal clarity of the tattoo's induced visions, but it hurt all the same.

I held the green fabric to my nose, searching for Steven's lingering scent, but the unpleasant musty odor of undone laundry greeted me. Pulling it away from my face, I tossed it away. One of the long green gloves fell back onto my lap. I picked it up gingerly by the cuff and an idea came to me. The corner of my mouth rose. Silently I whispered a prayer of thanks to Steven.

That night I pinned the sleeve of my nightgown to the cuff of the green glove and got my first full night's sleep in as long as I could remember.

I learned to sleep again, dressed in long sleeves and gloves. I wore nothing else even when winter gave way to spring and spring to the dog days of summer. The long sleeves let the ghost of my precious Steven remain peacefully in his grave. In time the broken edges of my heart healed, and I eventually remembered how to breathe. Life began to flow once more.

After several false starts at trying to replace the corporate career I lost, I eventually found a new job waiting tables. It barely paid enough to cover the rent on my studio apartment, but at least I didn't have to suffer dirty looks and hushed rumors that followed me in an office. At the diner, the long evening gloves I wore came in handy while carrying a table's worth of hot plates stacked up the length of my arm and earned little more than curious glances from the patrons.

On the anniversary of Steven's passing, with the morning sun decorating the sky, I laid a bouquet of lilies at his grave. I knelt beside the headstone. Tears I had thought long dried dripped from my chin. Wanting to feel the blanket of grass covering my baby boy, I unpinned the glove from my sleeve and slipped it from my hand. I ran my fingers through the turf, parting the green blades. "Steven, I miss you so much."

"My dear, then why have you been ignoring him?" The familiar voice drew my attention. I looked up to see the old woman standing on the other side of the headstone.

"You!" I brandished my tattooed arm at her. "Take this curse away."

Her head cocked to one side. "I cannot. You have not satisfied your payment."

I stood. "What payment?"

Between the leering smile that turned up the corners of her mouth and the sickly hollowness eating at her eyes my knees weakened and I placed my bare hand on the headstone to steady myself. "What's... what's wrong with you?"

She waved off my question. "I have not been eating well." She licked her lips hungrily. "I'm here to collect my promised payment." Her hand fell onto mine. I felt Steven kick and despair rose in my belly. As the world faded to the visions, I heard the woman say in an intoxicated voice, "You promised me your life and your soul."

PEACOCK AND THE PURLOINED MONSTERS

KAT RICHARDSON

Peacock leaned against the crumbling wall of the ruined office. Every tense line of her posture expressed the opinion that Charlie Crane was a fucking fool. Or at the very least a good facsimile of an Annoying British Upper Class Git. "So, you don't want me to steal this little box of monsters," she said. "You want me to replace it."

Some jackass had once tried describing her as "a perky little American with a talent for purloining the un-purloinable" and received a hard elbow to the side of the head. She *was* petite, blonde, and American, but perky only applied if you meant like coffee boiled for several days in Hell. Being undead hadn't improved her temper.

Crane flicked a glance at Lenny Redmayne—a lanky Black man with a world-class collection of scars, and his hair in well-kept shoulder-length locs—then turned a charming smile on the young woman in full motor-cycle gear with her leather-clad arms crossed over her chest in spite of London's current heatwave. "It's a box of *small monsters*—"

Redmayne clapped a hand over Crane's mouth. "Stifle it, mate. You're askin' my friend a bleedin' favor, and a fuckin' large one at that, not layin' on the grift. Be honest. If you know how, that is." He raised his eyebrows expectantly as he dropped his hand.

Crane sighed and turned back to Peacock. She still stared at him with the same unwavering gaze. "Look—"

Peacock turned and started for the half-collapsed doorway.

"Wait! Wait!" Crane shouted, chasing after her. He reached for her shoulder and she whipped back around, catching his wrist and using the momentum of her turn to shove him back and away from her.

Peacock pointed at his face. "Sentences that start with *Look* are usually manipulation or mitigation. I do not play well with either. This is your last chance to be straight with me, or fuck off completely. Give me just the pertinent. Do not start with *why*. Do not start with your ideas about how it should be done. What, where, when, how much. Go."

She crossed her arms over her chest again and eased back, but kept her glare trained on his face. This time, Crane did not glance at Redmayne. He took a deep breath and let it out through his nose slowly, eyes closed. "Steal a box of small monsters from the vault of a man called Sol Archer. Replace it with a replica I'll provide, and bring the original box to me unopened and intact. The vault is in Archer's house in Dorset. I will pay you fifty-thousand US dollars for the box, and I need it in four days."

Redmayne gaped at him. "*Magister* Sol Archer? Bloody hell, Charlie. Don't ask for much, do you?"

Crane looked back over his shoulder at Redmayne, who gave a sarcastic grin. His public-school voice and manner dropped off as his shoulders sagged under his Savile Row suit and his face went sharp with fear and misery. "I wish I had an option, Lenny. But I got five days to get the little fellas in that box back where they came from or I'm dead. And I don't mean sorta-kinda dead, or figurative dead. Real. Forever. Bones-and-ashes scattered to the winds dead. Oh, and yeah, I'm given to believe it's also going to be really slow and really painful."

Deadpan, Peacock said, "My heart bleeds for you." Redmayne knew about her fatal fall off a building with a bullet in her spine, but he also knew better than to mention it.

Crane glowered. "No offense but I'd like to keep me skin on."

Redmayne nodded. "You're proper fucked, mate."

"Thanks for the obvious, *mate*," Crane replied. He looked grim.

"What about the other twenty-four hours?" Peacock asked.

Crane shot his attention back to her. "Eh?"

"You said you needed the box in four days. Just now, you indicated five. So what are you doing with the other day?"

"Taking them back where they belong. Which is also not gonna be easy. I don't know how I'm gonna do it, but I'll figure it out once I have 'em."

Peacock took a step back, studying Crane for a silent, bemused moment. Then she said, "You're after something of Apollo's—"

"Who?"

"Sol Archer. Get it? Calls himself Apollo. The Greek god who shot the arrows of the sun. Sol... Sun... Archer..."

"C'mon. The fella's not actually a *god.*"

Now Peacock turned a suffering glance at Redmayne. "Seriously? How do you know a guy who has no idea about Talents and avatars?"

Redmayne shrugged. "Old parish. But Charlie here's not what you might call *conversant* with Talents and the occult, so much as occult-adjacent due to his profound luck. What he told me was he went and conned the wrong geezer, stepped in the shit, and ended up holdin' a magical problem, 'stead of a box of diamonds." He turned a glare on Crane which was not quite as fierce as Peacock's but far more disappointed. "Details of which are only just comin' clear."

Peacock ignored the last comment. "So?" She shrugged. "If he's got an *occult-adjacent* problem, why aren't we in your fancy-ass office, talking this over with a whole team of clever bastards? I mean, you *are* the boss, *Boss.*" Not that he was, strictly speaking. She was a freelancer. Being a Talent as well put her in an unusual, and useful, position within her profession as far as the DOIC was concerned. Being undead made her vulnerable. Redmayne knew that circumstance didn't please her, nor that some members of the current board would exploit that as ruthlessly as the previous Director had if Redmayne weren't in charge.

He pulled a face and rubbed the back of his neck. "It's not the sort of thing you really want the Directorate of Occult Incursion Control gettin' wind of."

"Keeping the British public blissfully ignorant of magical fuckery is what the Directorate has been doing since John Dee cast his first horoscope for Elizabeth I! How in hell is this not a DOIC problem?"

"Didn't say it wasn't. But Archer's got friends in the Directorate. Leftovers from previous management, in a manner of speakin'."

Peacock scowled in silence. Then: "Fuck."

Redmayne was still carefully cleaning house at the DOIC since Peacock had broken him out of Hell, and Peter Fiore—the previous Director—had gone missing. An Artificer Talent out of the roughest parts of South London, Redmayne wasn't popular with some of the current board and senior staff. Fiore had claimed the offices of Director and Thaumaturge-in-Chief over Redmayne's literal dead body just to see

Redmayne grab it back years later. As to Peacock, her refusal to behave like a proper dead criminal and rot away somewhere far from them was an embarrassment; that she'd helped Redmayne get out of Hell and regain control of the Directorate was outrageous. She also gave no fucks at all about them, which stung the most.

"You see how draggin' in the Directorate ain't the solution to Charlie's problem," Redmayne said. "And, yeah, he is a bit of a muppet—"

"Watch it! I run a sweet grift, and I may not be some kind of magician—"

"Talent, Charlie-boy," Redmayne said. "Magicians are just con men, like you, what convince people something's happenin' what ain't. Talents actually do it. And how *you* did *this*, eludes me."

"You said it. I conned the wrong geezer. And then some rather large, scary bastards turned up in my dreams—which were not, in fact, dreams, but some kind of magical... I dunno, break-in? At first, I thought they were a nightmare. Which they are and they aren't—" Crane broke off his rambling discourse when Peacock took an angry step toward him. He put up his hands and backed a few steps away from her before he started talking again. "Anyhow, these toothy, scaly lads are the little fellas' family and they gave me to understand that they might take it amiss if their nearest and dearest weren't returned home on the double. They might come to visit. They might come very loudly. Thus fucking you, me, and your DOIC right and proper."

"And lettin' a bloody big cat out of an up-till-now nearly-invisible bag," said Redmayne. "Bleedin' hell, Charlie. The Directorate's managed to remain nothin' to the public but a sort of urban legend. And you're about to disabuse the whole fuckin' world of that carefully-crafted illusion because you—"

"Hey!" Peacock leaned in between the two men. "Pardon my intrusion into your Friday night guilt fest, guys, but I have a question. If Crane got the monsters off a mark, how did Archer end up with them, and how long has he had them?"

Crane gazed off in any direction that didn't include Peacock. "A week."

Peacock closed her eyes and ground her teeth a moment before she asked, "And how did he get them?"

Crane stared at her boots. "He robbed me," he mumbled.

"At gun point?"

"Uhh…"

Redmayne gaped at Crane. "You tried to sell 'em to him, didn't you? You utter wanker."

Crane made a show of being deeply offended. "Always ready with the insult! You see? That's why I didn't come straight to you to begin with. I had a buyer lined up for the diamonds, but I didn't have diamonds, so what was I to do? Take 'em to Hatton Garden anyway? Or maybe I should have tried the zoo, eh? I know there's mage—er... Talents, like you said— and I figured one of them would want the little fellas, and the only one I knew how to find aside from *you* was this Archer character. So I ran out to Dorset and asked 'round and found the man himself. He allowed he was interested, and I went to his place that night to close the deal. He showed me 'round, took me down to his vault... and he magicked me or something. I couldn't move, couldn't talk, couldn't—well, anything! He took the little bleeders, put 'em on a stand, and shoved me out the front door. Told me not to come back, or he'd tear me head off. And it may be nothing to you, but I'm very fond of me head."

Peacock sighed. "You're too stupid to live." She turned her back and strode through the sagging doorway.

Redmayne called after her. "Oy, Peacock! Hang about!"

"No," she shot back. "This is a fiasco waiting to happen. I'm out."

"Bloody hell..." Redmayne muttered and chased her. "Lot ridin' on this! Fate of the fuckin' world and all that."

"Not my problem, Redmayne."

Redmayne caught up to her, with Crane trailing behind like a chastened school boy. He didn't touch her, just sauntered alongside in the dilapidated hallway where streetlight eked through the crumbling exterior in dusty, glowing needles. "And that matters, how?"

"There's nothing you can threaten me with that will make me do this job. If Apollo catches me, being undead is a liability. I'm not jonesing to be set on fire for the next fifty years—or whatever amuses him—just to save the DOIC from exposure, and smarty-pants here from being dismembered by demon lizards from the slime dimension. I am a thief. Not a martyr for the Directorate's cause." She made a gesture with one hand and vanished.

"Coward!" Redmayne shouted. He looked all around, loosing a continual stream of invective and abuse, punctuated with "Peacock" at varying intervals.

Crane stood still, shifting his wide-eyed gaze side to side, and looking like the next victim in a horror film. "Where'd she go?"

"Somewhere 'round here, but only for as long as it takes for her to sneak away."

A distant door creaked and slammed.

"Suppose I really should have asked, 'How'd she go.'"

"She walked. Like a bleedin' cat, she is. Pulled the veil and walked out."

Crane relaxed. "Ah. What's a veil?"

Redmayne gave him a long *Are you daft?* stare.

"Lenny, I'm outta me idiom, here. I take it this veil is some kind of magic, eh?"

"Yes, you dozy burke." Redmayne sighed. "C'mon. She's already done a bunk, might as well get on, ourselves," he added, jerking his head toward the exit. "See, Peacock can veil—look like someone else or like nothin' at all—that's her talent."

"I thought stealing was her talent," Crane said as they walked through the derelict building.

"No. Comes by that natural, she does. Plus years of practice. Veil only gives her an edge, doesn't make her a brilliant thief by itself. Like, you're a right charmin' bastard, but would you be a successful grifter if that was all? No, my old son, you have a devious criminal mind. Not always the sharpest tack in the carpet, though."

"Lay off it, Lenny. I know I put my foot in the shit."

Redmayne made soothing gestures with his hands. "All right, all right. Point is, it takes more than a talent to be great at somethin'. And Peacock is the best thief in the known worlds, livin', dead, or otherwise. I'd no idea she'd go off like that."

"If she's so great, why's she scared of Archer?"

"Charlie, a Magister is the hardest of magical hardasses. Anyone with a normal, functionin' brain is scared of Sol Archer."

"So, what am I gonna do? Or should I be writing my will?"

Redmayne shook his head. "I dunno, mate. Honestly, I do not know."

At seven minutes past ten Sunday night, Peacock shoved a painfully-white box just the right size for a pair of baby shoes into Redmayne's hands as he opened his flat's front door. "Do not open that or look inside," she said. "Call your jackass friend Crane. Tell him to meet us at the Three Standing Figures in Battersea Park two hours before sunrise tomorrow."

Redmayne peered at her through the gritty residue of insufficient sleep after chronic insomnia. "Why there?"

"Because the statues are near a lake, and the park's on the river. Bring whatever toys you've got that can calm down a giant raging lizard—or a pissed off fire magister—if things go wrong. And you might want to get dressed. Monster Mash pajama bottoms are guaranteed not to be the best sartorial choice."

"Some of us do sleep once in a while."

"Don't rub it in."

"You're bloody lucky I'm wearin' anythin' at all." Redmayne stepped back. "As you've given me only six hours preparation to save the world, are you comin' in, or are you plannin' on lyin' in wait to blag the milkman?"

Peacock entered and closed the front door quietly behind herself. "I'm *planning* on baiting Apollo to come out before dawn so we can get rid of that box for good. It attracts creeps and would-be sun gods, and I don't want to be a fried yegg."

"'Yegg'? Where'd you get that corn?"

"*Pulp Classics* is a free download this month. I read a lot in my copious free time between saving your ass and robbing the magically-gifted rat-bastards of the world." She glanced at a chronometer strapped to the forearm of her leathers. "Shit. I have to run. See you in the park."

Redmayne found himself scowling at his front door as it closed again in his face.

Three abstract stone women clustered at the top of a small, grassy rise facing the lake, their anxious little eye-pits turned toward the sky. False dawn was just bright enough to separate them from the dark trees at their backs. Crane, holding the too-white box, stood on the small stretch of lawn halfway between the statues and the low white metal fencing that separated them from the lakeside path. Sweat had soaked crescents under the arms of his suit jacket, even though the predicted blistering heat of the afternoon was hours away.

The reason for the sweat was striding toward him. Pyro Magister Sol Archer's towering rage created a moving column of smokeless, clear flame and heat distortion around his body. An exceedingly tall man, he stepped over the fence without breaking stride. The lawn wilted and browned as he stalked onward. In the colorless radiance of his ire Archer's appearance easily lived up to his mythic nickname. He was glowing and golden. His scowl could have laid waste to a thousand acres of rainforest in under a minute. And, lacking any subtlety, he wore red.

"You are a greater fool than I took you for," Archer said when he was still a few feet from Crane. "I thought I made myself quite clear that—"

"Yes," Crane interrupted. He remained still while beads of sweat ran down his face. "You took me, all right. You got the box and I'm left holding the bag. But the laugh's on you, old boy."

Archer stiffened, but he wasn't looking at Crane any more as his eyes shifted side to side, searching for something in the tree line. He snarled and the aura of fire around him flared red. "Come out here!"

"Good morning to you, too, Sunshine," said Peacock, suddenly visible, standing equidistant between the trees and the statues as she dropped the veil. She stepped sideways, clear of the statues, holding another bright white box.

"Think you're clever, you little tart? I knew it was you. Crane wasn't up to breaking my security. Now hand over the box and I shan't cook you where you stand."

Peacock rolled her eyes. "Bitch, please. I'm dead." She started tossing her box gently up and down. "What do you think you can actually do to me? I mean, yeah, you can hurt me, but after a while you'll get bored and I'll still be here. And then I'll lodge a complaint with Redmayne for Abuse of Magical Privilege, you'll end up in mage prison, and—if you're lucky—the rest of the DOIC won't decide to make you the poster boy for Consequences of Talents Behaving Badly. I mean, we all do it, but..." She stopped bouncing the box, clicked her tongue, and shook her head in mock-disappointment. "An example will have to be made. And you can bet it won't be any of the old school tie sorts at the Directorate."

Archer glanced at Crane for a moment. Crane shrugged, running his fingers nervously around the lid of his box. "Don't cry to me, old boy. I'm in as much trouble as you if the Directorate gets the wind up. If I weren't I wouldn't have gone and looked *her* up, would I?"

"I am curious why you did. I expected you to run to your old childhood slum chum, Redmayne, and spill your weaselly little guts. I was rather counting on it, in fact."

Crane dropped his shoulders and his posh accent. "How'd you know about me and Lenny?"

"I am a master of the occult. That means *hidden* for your information, which implies that I am very skilled at discovering things that are not common knowledge. It's always to my advantage to know what others don't. Why didn't you tattle to dear Lenny?"

"And get disappeared or something by you lot? Bugger that! We may have been mates back when, but Lenny and I ain't exactly on the same side of the street these days, are we? He wants to keep that precious job of his, he'd stitch me up proper. Fine company for a pint now and then, but this? Required a professional, this did. And they don't come better than that one," he added, pointing at Peacock.

The thief had moved a good distance from her starting point and Archer had to turn away from Crane to bring his glare back to bear on her. "Ah. I see. You have a game of your own to play."

"You bet your ass. Crane doesn't have the sort of money it takes to hire my services, and I figured you'd just burn the poor bastard to a crisp once you had the box. So I convinced him to bring me along to negotiate. You pay me now, I hand over the box, and we all leave here alive and happy."

Crane made a choking noise.

"Well, alive at least."

"You are a ruthless little piece," Archer said with a smirk. The air no longer shimmered with heat.

"Well, I am a thief and I can be bought. But if you're going to be nasty, I can always throw this into the lake and you can swim for it. Or you can offer me a decent price and tell me why you want it."

Archer laughed. "Why should you care what I want it for?"

"Because I have the box of trouble you want to hold over Redmayne's head and you don't. Now quit stalling or I'll open it up and find out what's worth risking magic jail for. After all, if I can break into *Apollo's* house, the DOIC's lock-up isn't going to be much of a challenge to get out of, is it?"

The magister's smirk shrank a little and the atmosphere around him became downright chilly. "Go ahead then, but I assure you that you shan't like the result if you open that box."

Peacock grinned at him. "What makes you think *this* is the right box? What if it's Crane's box?"

Archer's face went rigid. "Only a complete dunce would hand that cloth-eared imbecile something so powerful! Given that you *did* break into my house and abscond with my prize, it's clear that you aren't an utter moron. So let us stop beating about the bush and strike a deal. How much do you want?"

"Fifty thousand pounds, cash. Before the sun clears the treetops, or the deal's off."

"Are you barking mad?" Archer blustered, his rage reigniting and making the air around him waver.

"As you pointed out, I'm not an *utter moron*, and I know that you'll blast me, Crane, and this park into ashes as soon as the sun's over the horizon. So I think I'm going to go ahead and open the box."

"No!" Archer shouted. "They're mine!" He unleashed a gout of orange flame in Peacock's direction.

For a second or two the fire spilled off her leathers and slipped around her body like a stream of water, illuminating the three statues and setting their shadows dancing against the trees like demons in Hell. The flames took hold of Peacock's short blond hair, turning it into a crown of horror and pain. She screamed and dropped to her knees on the swiftly blackening lawn.

Out of Archer's view, Lenny Redmayne, carrying a bundle of metal sticks and wire, stepped from behind the statues. Crane backed up until he was pressing against the plinth the sculpted women occupied, clapped his mouth tight against the urge to vomit, and opened his box.

The lake erupted, throwing water into the air. A massive, scaled head broke the surface, supported by a half-visible, impossible body of wet scales, tentacles, and rigid plates. As the huge, lake-bound creature swung toward the humans on the grass it let out a piercing scream and a blast of salty water that knocked the people and statues to the ground. Archer collapsed in an enveloping cloud of boiling-hot steam as the water doused his flames. Three smaller monsters rose from the lake and scrambled on thick fins and squirming, suckered legs toward Crane, ignoring Peacock's rolling, smoking form and Archer, who'd started thrashing in panic at the sudden loss of his fire.

Redmayne scrambled to the pile of long metal sticks he'd dropped on the ground next to the tipped-over statues and hastily unfolded them into a sort of spiky cone as long as his arm. He dragged the cone to Archer and shoved the narrow end against the magister's head. "You better have some juice left, you underhanded bastard," he muttered. Pointing the open end of the cone toward the lake, he pulled a black box from his trouser pocket, pressed a button, and kicked the pyro magister in the side.

The large creature in the water let out another scream. Its three companions split into more squirming, slithering nightmares that spread out to charge across the whole of the grassy rise toward the humans.

Archer jerked rigid and cursed when Redmayne's foot connected with his kidney. A blast of heat from the cone's wide, open end lanced across the distance, hitting the wet creatures. They steamed and recoiled, holding their ground for the moment, hissing and screeching.

"Keep that up a minute or two, and maybe you'll live through this," Redmayne ordered.

The magister gasped, "Guttersnipe—"

"Shut the fuck up or I'll get Peacock to shut you up. Dab hand with a blade, she is. You won't enjoy it."

The thief groaned and crawled to Redmayne and Archer.

"Hold onto Sunshine, here," Redmayne said, "and keep the cone touching his head on one end and pointin' toward the lake on the other. Charlie needs a bit of help." He handed her the black box and turned away.

Blistered skin and burned hair sloughed off Peacock's head and face as she knelt beside Archer, keeping Redmayne's contraption pressed against him. She didn't speak, but the gruesome face she turned toward the magister said enough.

Redmayne dashed back to Crane and pulled another object from his pocket that looked like a canning funnel with a tape recorder patched onto its narrow end. A thin handle stuck out of one side. "Say you're sorry."

Crane gulped down the sick that had crept up into his mouth. "Eh?"

Redmayne shoved the handle into Crane's fist and pushed the whole weird object toward Crane's face. "The big one likely thinks you've done something nasty to her kiddies. So, start by sayin' you're sorry and we'll go from there."

"Is this a toothbrush handle?"

"Had to work with what I had. Now apologize, or we've got" — Redmayne cast his gaze toward the brightening sky— "about twenty minutes before some bloody fitness plonker comes along for his daily jog and precipitates the apocalypse. All right?"

"I'm sorry," Crane said. What came out of the funnel sounded like a whale's moan of ecstasy.

The big creature in the pond reared backward and gurgled something that didn't sound as nice.

"Abject grovelin', Charlie. That's the ticket."

"I'm so very sorry," Crane said. The funnel burbled and groaned its translation. "I didn't know what was in the box. I'm just terribly, terribly sorry for upsetting you and I never wanted to do your—" he glanced down at the white box, which had landed on its side where he'd been standing. A dozen tentacles groped at the edges, and a bulging eye peered out of a churning blob of multicolored flesh about the size of a walnut. "—your children any harm. That is, I *didn't* do them any harm." Another psychedelic walnut heaved up next to the first one and Crane turned a little green.

The monster in the lake pulled its head down a bit and hissed. The other creatures retreated to the walkway and oozed back into their original three shapes, but they didn't look any less inclined to tear Crane and his friends into bloody gobbets.

"Bit more mitigation and beggin' and we may live past breakfast-time. Maybe."

Crane looked queasier, but he carried on. "They were given to me by accident and I didn't know anyone was looking for them until that scheming, evil bastard over there in the cloud of steam stole them from me. I've been—that is, my friends and I all worked very hard to get them back safe and sound from that wicked man. The tykes are just fine. Really they are. Perfectly healthy. You can tell the little darlings are just thrilled to see you. I am completely, abjectly sorry for upsetting you. Please accept my most sincere and heartfelt apology for any distress this incident has caused you or your kin. On behalf of us all, I am so very, very sorry."

One of the three smaller things oozed up the bank and drew the box of baby monsters into its glutinous body. It retreated, and the box's white glow passed through the monstrosity before sinking into the water. The lake churned and the huge creature there slid down below the surface. The three fishy nightmares remained on the shore, glaring toward Crane and Redmayne.

"I will kill you," Archer muttered.

"Shut it," Peacock replied from roughly-formed lips. She was still on her knees beside him, but the flesh of her face was slowly patching together, still blackened, but healing at uncanny speed.

Archer rolled suddenly and snatched at her in a fit of heat and profanity.

Peacock twisted inside his awkward grab, rammed her nearest elbow into Archer's gut, and swung her fist down into his groin in one continuous motion. The magister huddled into a gasping ball. The heat that the cone had redirected from him toward the things in the lake vanished as the strange machine rolled from Peacock's compromised grip.

The three water monsters lurched forward again, but stopped short as something new came out of the lake.

It was more tentacles than body, more maw than tentacles, and it seemed to have an uncountable number of eyes. The uncanny knot of writhing horror floated from the water and upward, wafting on the first shafts of dawn color rising in the summer morning sky. It stank of rotting bodies pulled from the sea half-stripped of flesh and crawling with small predators.

"What is that?" Crane whispered.

"Fuck if I know," Redmayne said.

It didn't speak—there wasn't any sound that its uncanny mouth could make that a human ear could resolve—but its meaning resonated in their minds. The thing was angry, and sad, pleased, yet vengeful. It floated forward, probing at their minds as the sun began to paint the western sky pink and violet.

Archer unbent from his pained huddle and sat up as the first beam of sunlight touched him. He seemed to glow again, gathering strength from the touch of the sun.

The floating, tentacled mass shifted all its eyes toward him. Archer made a gagging sound and threw out a brilliant flame that leaped toward the largest of the floating monster and struck it with a splash of flame.

The thing shrieked, contracted into a seamless ball like a disturbed anemone, steaming and smoking. The three smaller nightmare things surged toward Archer.

The magister struggled to his feet, shrugging off Peacock's attempt to hold him. Whether he meant to fling another ball of fire or to run in terror, none of them ever knew. The composite creatures fell on Archer too fast and dragged him, screaming and struggling in a roiling mess of steam and smoking tentacles, into the lake. Peacock, half-healed and grim with blood and burns, slumped on the grass and watched them go.

The remaining uncanny thing's tentacles bloomed forth again and it spun lazily, seeming to study each of the three remaining humans before it floated back to the water and sank from sight.

The lake's surface slowly stilled, reflecting the sunrise like a mirror, marred only by a scrap of floating cloth that might have been blood-stained. Or merely red.

After a long minute, birds recommenced their morning songs and the smell of burned flesh and drowned men faded on a rising breeze off the Thames. Crane stared at Redmayne and Redmayne stared at Peacock as she rolled to her knees and crawled over to sit on the upturned plinth of the three toppled statues.

"What the fuckin' hell just happened?" Crane asked.

"I think we got bloody lucky," said Redmayne.

"I wasn't expecting the king and queen of the kaiju, but overall, I think that went pretty well," said Peacock.

The men both blinked at her.

"You are totally barmy," said Redmayne. "And a bloody sight."

"I may be sick." Crane staggered to his feet and down the slope, tumbling awkwardly over the fence and onto the lakeside path.

Redmayne and Peacock made their own unsteady way down to the lakeside and half-carried Crane out of the park.

Redmayne managed to get the party back to his flat without attracting too many stares on the way. Crane was still shaky, but Peacock looked fairly normal by the time she sprawled into the chair next to Crane's in Redmayne's lounge.

"I'm going to have to invest in fireproof leathers," she said, brushing at the singed and blackened front of her jacket. "Travel through Hell and back and they're fine, but piss off one fucking pyro Talent and they're crispy as overcooked chips. And I mean the American kind, not the soggy french fries you guys eat."

"They are called *crisps*, you cretin," said Redmayne. "And what did you mean back there? 'That went pretty well'? You planned that?"

"Not exactly that, but something like it. And don't either of you get your panties in a twist—I put myself in front of Archer's fire-juggling act, which I wouldn't have had to do if you'd come prepared, Redmayne."

"I'd have prepared for it if you'd fuckin' well said—"

Crane threw a book and hit Redmayne in the back of the head. "Both of you trap up! Lord, you sound like an old married couple. How in the name of all that is holy did you get those boxes, and what the bloomin' hell happened in that park? That lake is too shallow for those things to have come out of."

"And it's fresh water," Redmayne added, rubbing the back of his head and taking a seat by the hearth, the better to scowl at Peacock and Crane at the same time.

Peacock leaned her head against her chair's high back and flapped a dismissive hand at him. "Whatever. The long and the short of it is I didn't want to get sucked into more Talent politics, but I got to thinking there might be more to the situation than it looked at first. What would Archer want a box of small monsters for, and how would he even be in the market?" She glanced at Crane. "Why did you take them to him?"

"I'd heard of him, like I said. That he collected things."

Peacock shook her head. "That wasn't his sort of thing, or did you not notice that the vault was all about magical objects and the usual rich-guy trophies? Nothing else alive in there. So, who tipped you to Archer as a buyer? The mark?"

Crane shook his head, looking interested for the first time since they'd staggered through the door. "No. I asked the fella what steered me toward the mark in the first place... Oh, fuckin' hell! He roped me for Archer, didn't he?"

Peacock nodded. "I had the inkling of that idea, and I went and stole both boxes so I—"

"What? When?" Redmayne broke in.

Peacock served him a *what the hell?* stare. "Yesterday evening just before I came here. I gave you the decoy box, but I didn't have much time to go back and get the real box once Archer saw Crane and—"

"I never went near that bastard!"

She sighed. Strictly for effect, since, being dead, she didn't actually breathe except to talk. "Can you two refrain from interrupting long enough for me to tell the tale? Or do you prefer to interrogate me piecemeal and get it all bollixed up?"

The men both shut up and settled back in their seats. "Get on with it, then," Redmayne said.

"Fine. Now just listen. I kept thinking there was something off about the whole deal. The fact that Archer was a self-important prick who didn't like you, Redmayne, and didn't much like the DOIC, but he was suddenly interested in acquiring some mislaid monsters that your buddy here had gotten unexpectedly stuck with seemed like more than a coincidence. I kept wondering what he'd do with that kind of contraband, especially when you"—she pointed at Crane—"started having nightmares about scaly motherfuckers who wanted their friends back and were willing to raise some serious and embarrassing hell to get them.

"So I went and hung out around Archer's place looking like Crane and let him catch sight of me. Archer ran straight to a shiny white box in the study—not the one in the vault. So the box in the vault was obviously a decoy. I stole that box—and I gotta say his security wasn't much good against someone like me, but it would have wreaked havoc on anyone using active Talent to get through it." She stopped and waved dismissively. "But anyhow. Archer had to leave as soon as he thought he'd seen Crane in his vault. He couldn't ignore the theft of the decoy, or the plot would fall apart, but he also wouldn't be worried about the fact that it was still too dark for his powers to be at their best if he just wanted to intimidate a lowly grifter."

"Oy!" Crane objected.

"Don't get shirty about it, Charlie," Redmayne chided. "Archer was the sort of arrogant bastard what would have thought that."

Peacock interrupted them. "You mind?" The men shut up. "Thank you. I dropped off the decoy box with you, Redmayne, but I had to go back and get the real box while Archer was out of his house, and before he had a chance to go all sun god wannabe on Crane's ass. Archer couldn't get to London any faster than I could and he hadn't started out immediately, so I had you call Crane and get him moving."

"Were you just hoping something would happen to stop the bleeding bastard from killing me?" Crane asked, slipping back into his posh voice as the shock of what had happened by the lake wore off.

"No. That's why I had Redmayne drag you to the park so early. Archer wouldn't know where you were until the decoy box stopped moving. By then, I'd have caught up to you both. The monsters threatening you in your nightmares would turn up for real as soon as the box was opened. I just had to get Archer and the real box there at the same time, and pin the blame where it belonged. When Archer said he'd expected you to go to Redmayne, he confirmed what I'd been thinking: that it had all been a set-up from the jump.

"The DOIC is not universally loved by the people who know it exists. Archer hated the Directorate's rules and he wanted leverage to either destroy the DOIC or Redmayne—which would be the same thing. But the monsters weren't effective blackmail if Redmayne didn't know Archer had them. So he counted on your old friendship getting you to confide in Redmayne, who couldn't do anything to Archer without losing control of the Directorate, setting up a vicious little loop of damned-if-you-do that would be the beginning of the end, no matter what."

Crane chewed his lip and frowned. "How?"

"Directorate's in a bit of a mess right now," Redmayne said. "I'm still sortin' it out, but if I couldn't rein in a magister like Archer, the rest would also go rogue. And I imagine the box would have got opened anyhow and I'd have had a kaiju attack on London to deal with, no Talents backin' me up, and the whole bloody scheme of Occult Incursion Control would have been down the shitter."

Crane narrowed his eyes as he thought it out. "So you'd have gone down with it, and Archer would have been standing by to press the flush."

"In a nutshell."

Peacock nodded. "The hard part was getting Redmayne to bring the right toys."

"As I said, I'd have been better prepared if you'd have told me what was goin' on, Peacock."

"Will you two stop that?" Crane snapped. "You're both the goods, all right? Peacock's bloody clever for working it out and getting the box of kaiju kiddies. And Lenny's gadgets were effing clever, too. And, yeah, it all worked out in the end, right? But I still don't understand how those big bastards got in and out of that shallow, bloody lake!"

Redmayne looked at Peacock, who shrugged.

"It's fuckin' magic, mate," said Redmayne and laughed. "Get used to it, because now that they know about you, you're *Talent adjacent* for life."

"Maybe longer," Peacock added.

RUE MORGUE

JASON GILBERT

I know what I saw. My head hurts as I stagger, slump against the far wall. The woman is dead on the couch, her throat slashed open, blood pooled and soaking into the white upholstery. My heart pounds in my chest, my breathing rapid. My muscles are sore, my knuckles bloodied. I try to remember. Did I fight back? What did I see?

Where is the daughter?

I push myself off the wall, look around the room. My vision hazes. The pain in my skull throbs, like a spike being driven through the back of my left eyeball. I hear something from the fireplace, something wet and dripping. I go closer. A hand hangs from above, from inside the chimney, blood running off the fingers, falling onto the logs.

The light. Blinking. Strobing.

That thing. That…monkey? It'd been enormous. How the hell had a giant ape gotten anywhere near here? The closest zoo was hours away. It would've been all over the media if there had been a dangerous animal on the loose.

I look at my bloodied and bruised knuckles again. I had to have fought back. The ape must have hit me, must have knocked me out.

Ape? Primate? Not a monkey. Too large. What was the word? O-rang? Large. As big as me. Red fur. Not a monkey.

I feel a catch in my throat. My heart races with panic. My breath

140

quickens as I see the blood splashed on my clothes, up my arms. My beard is tacky and wet. I rub my face with my hands, pull them away to find more sticky, drying blood.

Try to remember. Edward. Eddie. My name is Eddie.

I startle at the sound of voices outside. There's a knock at the door. I can hear a woman speak. "Groceries? How long have they been here?"

"I thought I saw the delivery guy pull up a good fifteen minutes ago," a man's voice says. "Right before the screaming started."

"We need to call the police," the woman says.

Yes. The police. I can explain this. I must have tried to revive the woman on the couch. That's why her blood is all over me. I move to the door, open it. An older couple is on the porch, the man holding a gun while the woman has her cell phone to her ear. They look at me with wide eyes. The man points his gun at me, the woman covers her mouth, her eyes wide with shock.

I tell them I can explain. I tell them what I found. I beg them for help. They look at me with confusion. The man shakes his head. "What the hell?" He points his gun at me. "Damn crazy. What the hell did he say?"

I repeat myself, more desperate. The woman gasps and backs away. The man chambers a round.

"He's not making sense," the woman says. "God, what does any of that mean?"

"Just keep still, son," the man says, forcing a calm in his voice. "Cops'll be here soon, we'll sort this all out. Get you some help."

"All that blood," the old woman mumbles. She speaks into the phone. "Hello? I have an emergency. I think my neighbors are…he's covered in blood!"

"Inside," the man says, motioning with his gun. I back away from the door, my hands up. I ask him not to shoot me. He ignores me, forcing me further back as he steps into the house. He looks over into the living room, his eyes widening when he sees the carnage. "Dear sweet *Jesus*," he mutters.

I try to explain again. He turns his attention back to me, terrorized and angry at the same time. I see his finger twitch, move to the trigger. Something wells up from inside, moves up my throat, makes my head spin. I swat the gun away and shove the man down. I jump over him, run past the screaming woman on the porch.

Fool. I'm a fool. I tell myself over and over as I run down the street, my legs aching as I force them to keep moving. I could've tried explaining again. I speak English. I don't know any other languages. Why hadn't they understood me? My head pounds, but I ignore it, make myself keep running. Dogs bark as I cut through yards, making for the woods.

They would find me. I knew they would find me. Had to run. Had to get away.

I sleep in the woods. I eat what I can find, steal from gardens and trash cans. I try to steal from a family cooking out on a grill, but they catch me, run me off. Someone calls the police. I think about going back to my car, but my keys are gone. Maybe in that house.

Two days. Four days. I'm always moving. I find a place. They come and raid. I find another place. They come for me. I try to go back, but they're waiting on me. It's been so long. I'm running out of places to hide.

They're going to find me.

Part of me wants to be found. Wants to tell them what I saw. What did I see? I try to remember again, but it makes my head hurt.

I could go back. Find my keys. Drive away. I shake my head. No. They'll be waiting for me. Going back would be stupid.

I make for the city park. I know there are places there I can hide. I know a friend there who jogs every afternoon. I could tell her. I could explain myself. She would understand me. The old couple, maybe they'd been deaf? Both of them?

I crouch in the brush near the asphalt running path, the area canopied by tall trees. It's hot outside. I've removed my clothes down to just a pair of shorts I found outside of the Goodwill store. I'm sweating. I see Katie running towards me, her eyes forward, focused. I step out, call to her. She stops, her eyes wide with panic as she takes a step back.

"Eddie?!" Her voice shakes with fear. Why is she afraid of me? "Oh my god!"

I ask her to wait, ask her to let me explain. Ask her for help. She gives me a look of utter confusion mixed in with her fear. I beg her to listen to me, to believe me. I tell her that I won't hurt her. She still looks confused.

"Eddie, I can't…what are you *saying?*" She pulls her keys from her hip pouch, palms a small canister of mace. "You're not making sense."

I take a step towards her. She points the can of mace at me. "Don't," she says. "Eddie, you need help. Something's wrong."

A gun presses against the back of my head. I hear a man's voice, low and calm, calculating. "Don't move, Eddie. I don't want to have to shoot you."

My body goes rigid with terror. I put my hands up slowly. I ask the person behind me not to shoot me.

"I'm going to assume you're asking me who I am," the man says, his tone still low-key. He speaks as if imparting knowledge, as if I'm a student rather than a fugitive. "Or asking me not to shoot you." He grunts. "My name is Auguste Dupin." He pronounces his name like Doo-*pon*. He doesn't have an accent. "I'm going to step back, and you're going to drop to the ground and put your hands behind your head."

I do as he says. He cuffs me, and I hear him talk to Katie. "You did a good job, Miss McCall. I'll take it from here."

"What's going to happen to him?" Katie asks.

Dupin pauses before he answers. "Hopefully, I can get the truth. Then I can help him." He pulls me to my feet and marches me down the path to the parking lot. He puts me in the back seat of a black sedan. He closes the door, gets into the driver's seat, and we drive away. I can see him clearly now. Middle-aged, almost a reptilian stare in his eyes as he watches the road. He's thin, lean, a squared jaw and dark hair. His tone is quick as if we are on limited time, as if the inevitable is closing in, yet he is driving like we are going to the grocery store on a normal day. "I've been after you for almost a week, Eddie. I'm not going to hurt you. I think I can help you. But you've got to help me. I need to know what happened in that house. What happened to Ms. Hicks and her daughter."

I tell him what I remember. I tell him about the primate. I know he won't believe me. I don't care. I tell the truth. He nods as he listens, driving down the main road, stopping at traffic lights and yielding to others as if we were on a casual drive.

He waited until I was done before he spoke. "Eddie, you think you're making sense, but you're not. The words you're hearing in your head, seeing in your mind, aren't the words coming out. Stomp once for yes, twice for no. Did you kill those two victims?"

I stomp twice.

"Did you see who did?"

One stomp. I pause. I stomp twice. Then once again.

"So you don't know," Dupin says. "Eddie, I could get in trouble for this. I've been on this case for days with no leads and they're about to pull the plug. I've got to try, and it's the only thing I can think of to get the answers I need. If I take you back there, do you think you can remember?"

I stomp once.

Dupin is silent for the rest of the trip. He pulls the car into the driveway of the house. I see the yellow police tape stretched across the front steps and across the front door. The house is dark, cold-looking. I shudder at the idea of going back inside the old Victorian, seeing the living room where those two young women died. The porch wraps around the front and side of the house, and the tall gable on one side overlooks the empty road. Streetlights give little light, the trees in the yard shielding the property from the yellowish glow. The college is in view of the place, the campus also dimly lit and quiet. The clock tower glows in the night, giving the time dutifully. Two minutes to midnight.

The car door opens and the detective helps me out. He keeps me cuffed, leads me up onto the front porch, ripping down the police tape as we go. He cuts the tape at the door, fiddles with the large lock box installed on the handle, and retrieves a key from inside the box. He looks at me, holding the key up into view. "There is no going back," Dupin says. "Do you understand? Nodding is fine."

I nod.

He uses the key to open the door, and we step inside. The air is heavy with the mildewy scent of older homes, aged wood cleaned with heavy amounts of furniture polish. I stand in the foyer, look up the staircase in front of me, off to my right into the empty dining room.

Anywhere I can possibly look that isn't the living room.

I steel myself. I have to. I have to remember. Dupin looks at me. "Okay?" I nod, and he removes my handcuffs. I blink in surprise as he steps back and puts the cuffs into his pocket. "Definitely against protocol. But I need you to trust me. Just the same." He pats the butt of the handgun in the shoulder holster under his arm. "Now. Show me where you were when the killings happened."

I remember where I woke up. I take him there.

"You're sure?" Dupin says, raising an eyebrow, his eyes studying me. He points to the floor in front of the couch. "Are you sure you weren't closer?" I nod. I start to tell him what I saw, but he holds up a hand to stop me. "Can't make words work. Remember?"

I sigh, nod. Point to where I woke up on the floor.

Dupin points at the front door. "There was a bag of groceries near the door when the neighbors found you. Did you bring them?"

I nod.

"You were delivering them? Part of your job?"

I nod again.

Dupin puts his hands in his pockets, bites his lip as he looks away. I know that look, the one someone gets when they're working on the words they want to use for their next sentence. I used to have to do that a lot. It was hard. I got better. But it wasn't working. Not tonight. "Eddie, did you see anyone else here when you arrived?"

I shake my head.

"Did you put the groceries on the porch?"

I think for a minute, replay the day in my mind. I'd just gotten to work when my manager told me the Hicks order was ready. The stocker had loaded it into my car.

My car. Where were my keys? I could've gotten away, gone to another town, another state. Exiled myself. No. They would've found me. They wouldn't have cared about my innocence.

I jerk my mind back on topic. I see myself in my head, driving from the grocery store. I'm going slow. I'm careful. I'm nervous. Always nervous. I won't drive on the main roads. I get to the house. Mrs. Hicks answers the door. Something…

I press my hands to my forehead, the pain coming back. I strain, I start to tell Dupin that I think the killer was waiting, had struck me from behind. He lets me talk, holding his cell phone up at me. I stop talking and he plays back the recording.

"Sienite knock egg noodle. Pitch make blind. Shoes operable pancake."

"That first word," Dupin says, his reptilian eyes focused on me, staring *into* me. "A rock? There was a rock?"

I shake my head. I try again. I know what I saw. We repeat the process again, me speaking while he records. "Sienite. Senaite. Sea. Me. An. Semen."

"Simian," Dupin says in a whisper. He turns, rubbing his chin in thought, his eyes flitting around as if he's seeing his thoughts spread out in front of him on some kind of projection screen. He turns back to me. "A simian. An ape."

I point to him. I nod. I stomp my foot once.

"A gorilla?"

I shake my head, stomp twice. Too big.

"A baboon?"

Two stomps again.

His eyes flash as they pierce me again, his jaw set and his mouth drawn in a small, sly smile. "An orangutan?"

I stomp once. I know that one.

He stands tall, nods, begins to speak fluidly, carefully as if he's pulling each sentence off of a shelf and putting it into place.

"Your name is Edward Cunningham. You prefer to be called Eddie."

I blink. I know my own name. I shake my head slightly in confusion.

"You wanted more than that. You were only a few months from being *Doctor* Edward Cunningham. Specializing in simian behavior. Apes. Most notably orangutans."

I blink again. I'm confused. I try to remember my school years. The playground. Sally Markers running from me as I chased her, tried to tag her. Just wanted to touch her hair, the red curls bouncing as she ran. I remember prom. I skipped it. I was doing homework.

"You were comparing human behavior with simian behavior," Dupin says. "I read your thesis. It was fascinating." He pauses. "Ahead of its time. You were close to proving the theory of evolution on a psychological level."

None of this makes sense. I feel panic rise inside. Who is this man? Who is he talking about?

A memory flashes. I'm in a lab. Not like I've seen in movies. There are cages. Tables. People walking around in white coats. I have a clipboard in my hands. I'm writing something down. I look up. Horror wells inside my gut, my throat closing and my chest freezing as I see the tall, red-furred thing in front of me. It looks at me, reaches for me, then pulls its hand back and scratches the fur on its chin.

"Roger," Dupin says, his voice made distant by the blood thrumming in my ears. "You named your primary subject Roger."

Killer. I was looking at the killer.

"You couldn't predict that he would turn on you," Dupin said. "You were in a coma for months. You couldn't get another lab job. You started delivering groceries because your brain damage wiped out a lot of your education. Do you remember the accident?"

Escaped. Roger had escaped. I try to remember. The lab. I see the lab. The lights are off now. The place is a wreck. Roger is gone. The tables overturned, the holes in the wall. Roger was temperamental, the experiments on him trying and stressful.

146

"Roger became aggressive," Dupin says, still staring at me. He begins to walk slowly to the side, backing away slightly as well, putting distance between me and him. "You were supposed to have him put down. But you couldn't. Your supervisor told me. He said you were insistent that Roger could be rehabilitated. You tried to prove it."

The memory flashes again. I'm arguing with someone, an older man. Heavy-set man. He wants to kill Roger. I open the cage. I release Roger. I don't care what happens. The older man screams as Roger lunges at him, strangles him, breaks his neck. I try to call out to Roger, try to calm him. He grabs a scalpel, slashes the older man up, then lunges at me. Swings.

I blink. I'm in a bed. Nurse staring at me.

"You have a condition called Wernicke's aphasia," Dupin says. "One of a few from a severe cerebral trauma. Concussion, amnesia, all likely connected to Roger's attack." He narrows his eyes at me. "He hit you in the head with a pipe wrench he got after he killed the janitor. But you still tried to save him, even in your state. Do you remember?"

I see myself shielding Roger from the security guard with the shotgun. Roger clambers onto me, pulls me down. Something hits my head again. Blood runs from my ear. Roger pushes me to the floor. I can't move. So tired. The gunshot doesn't startle me. Seeing Roger fall in front of me doesn't startle me. He turns his head, stares at me as the life leaves his pleading eyes.

"Traumatic brain injuries can lead to multiple conditions, Eddie," Dupin says as if I am his student in a classroom. I hear the click of a gun. I see the firearm in his hand, by his side, pointed at the floor. "Like schizo-phrenia. Like dissociative identity disorder." He stands his ground. "Roger wasn't just a lab animal, was he? He was like your child." He pauses, his eyes flash, his head cocks to the side slightly. "No. No, that's not it. You saw yourself in him, didn't you? Saw him trapped like you felt you were. Pushed around. Made to do things he didn't want to do."

I feel a hand on my shoulder, hear the deep sniffing in my ear as some-thing takes in my scent. I look to my side, into Roger's eyes. He looks at me sorrowfully, pleading.

Dupin keeps talking. "The light on the porch. It's an LED. It strobed. Strobing lights can set traumatic brain injuries off, regardless of how old they are. Did you know that Eddie?"

Tears stream down my cheeks as it all replays in my mind, everything so clearly.

The light on the porch flickers when Mrs. Hicks opens the door.

Strobes. My head spins. Roger's hand reaches out, grabs Mrs. Hicks by the throat. He roars, slams her down to the floor. Her daughter comes running, screams. He tries to make for her, but the mother grabs his leg, trips him up. The daughter has a kitchen knife. Roger takes it from her, slashes her across the face and chest. She goes down. He makes to do it again, staggers when Mrs. Hicks grapples him from behind, screams at him to get away from her daughter. Roger shoves back at her, sends her rolling into the living room. She tries to get up, but he's on her, throws her on the couch, swings with the knife. She makes a gurgling sound as blood pours from the opening in her throat. The daughter screams as she charges in swinging a fireplace poker. Roger takes the blow to the head, slams his open hand against hers. He takes the poker from her, swings it at her over and over at her head until it's nothing but blood, bits of skull, and brains. He hears something, turns and looks at the fireplace. He did a bad thing. He has to hide it. He picks the daughter up, shoves her up into the chimney. She gets stuck. Frustration turns into rage as he tries to push. He beats on the body, wailing on it over and over until every bit of the girl is inside the chimney except for a lone hand hanging down just a foot above the logs.

Roger. It was Roger. I try to say his name. I breathe. I think carefully. I force my mouth to make the sound, make it right.

"Ro…ger."

Dupin raises his gun, points it at me. I see the look on his face, that one someone gets when they realize something after everything they were thinking about makes sense. "No, Eddie. Roger is dead."

I shake my head. Stomp my foot twice. He'd been shot, but Roger lived. He'd gotten out. He moved in with me. I was keeping it a secret, still working with him. He was civilized now. Under control. I put my hands up, try to explain.

Red fur. Black skin, rough-looking and strong, large, long fingers capable of human-like dexterity.

I'm cornered as shock takes me, soon replaced with rage. I have to get out. The man is pointing the gun at me.

"Eddie, you didn't mean to," he says. "You're sick. You need help. Stand down."

Out. I have to get out. I grunt. I puff my chest, pound my fists against it, challenge the man. He doesn't move.

I can make him move. I *will* make him move.

I charge, my furry body heavy and teaming with raw power as I make for the man. I can get away. I reach for him; I can already taste his blood in my mouth. The loud bang sounds again, fire coming from the man's hand.

I remember something I read, that the brain is functional up to ten minutes after death. It's true. I wonder if Roger's was still going when he'd fallen next to me.

I can't see anymore.

EARTH, WE'VE HAD A PROBLEM

MICHAEL G. WILLIAMS

The stranger murdered Miller right after we exited waver space.

I couldn't even tell where the stranger came from. One second I stood on the flight deck alone, checking the navigation display for warnings and confirmations. The next, someone in full extravehicular activity gear—not totally unlike ours, but a slightly different design and matte charcoal from boots to helmet—stood beside me.

The intruder kicked his way through the thick wax paper closing off the manual override levers. I couldn't even finish a strangled "what the—!" before he wrapped his gloved hand around the port hull override and pulled it with his full weight. The override came free and the stranger tumbled to the side from the force.

On the monitor bank ahead of us, one of three dozen screens showed me Expeditionary Officer 1st Class Jenna Miller's horror as ghastly red lights strobed warnings across her features. Explosive bolts fired and a perfect mechanical seam opened across the outer wall to let all that nothing in from outside.

Papers vortexed as the atmosphere exploded out into the endless maw of hard vacuum. Even the electron sprayer shot out into permanent night when Miller let go of it. It had been little more than a specialized flashlight to charge and repel dust particles so the air recycler could filter them out, a tube with a battery and a bulb to generate the flow, and it took flight on the two-second wind as if under its own power. The small cargo hold didn't contain sufficient air to push Miller out, too, so she managed to make it to the bulkhead door into the port passageway. Atmospheric pressure beyond made it impossible for her to get the door open. It had been designed that way, a protection against accidental decompression: the very atmosphere it protected would force it shut.

Miller asphyxiated trying to push the door open anyway. I watched her throw her weight against it once, then twice, then she double-stomped to unlock-relock her boots to the deck and tried a sloppy, bumbling third time. She rebounded off the door, fell back, and lost consciousness as she ran out of oxygen.

Miller went limp from the ankles up, her left boot still adhering to the magnetic deck.

Blood ran from her nose and began to drift about the hold.

I turned to the stranger and screamed.

The stranger ignored me, reaching into the manual overrides panel again, this time pulling free a long, red lever marked FIRE SUPPRESSION. I lifted a boot and kicked at his arm, but not in time.

On another screen, the passageway outside our three tiny cabins clouded as overhead vents flooded the residential deck on the viewers and the flight deck where we stood with combustion-disrupting aerosols.

I staggered back, eyes filling with tears from the Combust-o-Stop™. Emergency breathers hung on the wall behind me. We'd spent weeks training to find and wear them in difficult conditions: blindfolded, dark room, while being pummeled with boffers. No training could invoke the shock of the moment, though. I wasted precious seconds getting my bearings before those long hours spent earning bruises finally paid off.

I found the wall, pulled a breathing unit from the tear-away clamps holding it, slipped it around my face and neck, and scrambled to get the strips of hook-and-loop pulled snug in back. Self-defense training finally caught up to the emergency training. I dropped to one knee as I turned to face the stranger, ready to counter an expected assault.

Instead, I watched as a new intruder brought a baton down on the helmet of the charcoal-clad stranger. This one wore a bright scarlet space suit, the design slightly narrower than ours in the waist and the closed helmet shined yellow-gold.

Charcoal's visor shattered under the blow, glass and plastic spraying in on Charcoal's face and out into the atmosphere of the flight deck, In the permanent free fall of microgravity, I watched glistening shards hang in the suppressant-fogged air around us, limned by the green—and increasingly red—lights of the screens on the forewall.

Scarlet's glove bore the bright yellow hammer and sickle I recognized from world history classes in college, surrounded by a circle of tiny stars. *But nobody uses that anymore*, I thought as I watched Scarlet batter Charcoal again, this time smashing the baton into Charcoal's nose and shattering it. Blood sprayed out to join the glass and plastic detritus lost on a sea of oxygen-fixing spray.

Charcoal dropped to his knees, perfectly eye level with me, fingers scrabbling at the edge of his helmet as he tried to bring down the solar shade, the eye shield, anything to protect him from another attack.

Charcoal had my face.

Charcoal was me, but over there, killing my crewmates, while I did not.

I tried to shout through the breather, but they're made for running through dangerous spaces, not conversation. I stood, trembling from shock and from adrenaline, and took four steps towards Scarlet and Charcoal Me. Scarlet put up a hand to stop me.

Through speakers built into the helmet, rendered tinny and scratchy by low-resolution electronics, Scarlet spoke to me, pointing at the instrument panel. "Please stop gas," Scarlet said. She had a sing-song accent when speaking English.

Scarlet sounded just like Miller.

On one of the screens in front of me, Miller's corpse still lolled in open space, one foot magnetically locked to the deck.

The golden yellow sunshield on Scarlet's visor went up and sure enough, she had Miller's face. Her head was shaved, though, instead of the high and tight Miller —*real* Miller, or at least her corpse—wore on the monitor. *This* Miller's accent was much thicker, too, and her consonants a little harder. I stared at her as she frowned and pointed at the instrument panel again. "Gas?"

I gawked at the panel like I'd never seen the damned thing before the training kicked back in. I pressed a sequence of buttons. One of the screens stopped blinking red and turned cool gray. The aerosol jets in the floor and ceiling fell silent, and the cloud of fire suppressant gas in the room stopped thickening.

I heard emergency air vents kick on, trying to recycle atmosphere and scrub out the Combust-o-Stop.

I looked back at Miller and asked the first and only question to spring to mind. "What the fuck is going on?"

Scarlet Miller shrugged at me. "Long story."

"You're her." I pointed at the screen. "But not dead. And your accent is different."

"I'm her." Miller bobbed her head at me in her EVA suit. "Like say, long story."

I pointed at Charcoal Me, now drifting slightly a foot above the floor paneling but prone, belly flopped, dead or perhaps unconscious. "Start talking, goddamn it."

"First, where Kekoa?" Scarlet seemed so unfazed, so calm and collected, and frankly it pissed me off. She'd just smashed in my face, but not my face, and saw herself dead on the monitors in front of us, and she acted like she expected every bit of this from the get-go.

I pointed at another screen. "Probably asphyxiated in her cabin. I—he—set off the fire system ship-wide."

Kekoa crested the top of the ladder to the flight deck from the central passageway in her EVA suit. Though with much better fidelity than Scarlet Miller's suit's tinny, staticky speakers, she spoke to us from audio outputs cresting her helmet. "Ah, shit," she said, completing her ascent and stepping onto the deck. I noticed her boots locked her to the deck so perfectly and so gently she walked as though in normal gravity. She gestured at Scarlet Miller and at Charcoal Me and then at me. "Which ones are you two?"

Kekoa's suit had the Rising Sun flag of the Japanese self-defense forces embossed across both upper arms and the center of her chest.

Scarlet Miller guffawed once, just a rough chuckle, her lousy English pushing its way out on laughter's heels. "Ah. They warned this might happen."

"Is first flight with waver engine." Scarlet Miller gestured around at the rest of the ship, the instrument panel, the monitors in front of us. "*Da?*"

I snapped my fingers. "Russian."

She ignored me, continuing to explain. "My people figured out that waver does more than go faster than light. It is faster than reality. So fast, it... sled."

I furrowed my brow at her under the forehead strap on the ventilator. "Snow sled?"

She waved a hand *no* at me. "*Korablaya*. Ah, wake, like behind ship. *Wake*. Waver engine churns water of time and space as it goes. It chop times, spaces, realities. Mix them up. Slice and dice."

I stared at Scarlet Miller, not comprehending. "Realities?"

Imperial Kekoa watched me, waiting for me to get it. "Do you not know how the waver works? My Concord was the ship's physicist. He knew all about it." Her flag was World War II Japan, sure, but her accent was west coast America, half valley girl and half local news anchor. This Kekoa used none of the Hawaiian pidgin I expected, with its ghostly r's and punching plosives.

I stared at her, annoyed. "Of course I do. It connects two points in space, drawing a shortcut around reality. 'Wormhole-activated vaulting.' You know, the old thing of 'space is a piece of paper, but if you draw two points on it and then fold the paper the two points get closer' kind of stuff. I'm the ship's physicist."

Imperial Kekoa snorted and shook her head. "Nah, they told you that. What it really does is crack open the multiverse, pick a reality where those two points were closer all along, and dip its toe in just long enough to make the trip between them. Those other realities may or may not exist independently, we're not really sure yet, but for exactly as long as it takes to initiate waver, find a universe where Point A and Point B are right next door, step from one to the other, and then reemerge, they all have always already existed."

Scarlet Miller nodded in agreement. "Da. Full histories, identities, worlds. Lives. Memories. All backwards to Big Bang and all forwards to Big Fizzle."

I looked over at Charcoal Me's corpse. "So why did he attack us?" I turned back to Imperial Kekoa. "Why are y'all here?"

"Because when the waver engine punches a hole in the wall, it punches a hole in all the walls, and those other universes—alternate time-lines, alternate realities—can all see through the gap. They see each other, too."

"And if they already have waver, or understand it, or maybe if they get lucky?" Scarlet Miller whistled low. "They know only one still exist when waver drive step back out."

Kekoa caught my eye again. "Think about a friendly game of Sakura. Only everybody is holding a Crane, and Cherry Blossom gets played."

I blinked slowly at her. "None of that made sense."

She looked at my uniform and made a small 'o' with her mouth. "Wow, an American timeline? That's fucked up. Have you never played Sakura?"

I looked at Charcoal Me again, ignoring Imperial Kekoa for now. "So he was sent to hijack my ship so that his universe could be the one to emerge." I pointed at Scarlet Miller for a moment. "And you're from, what, a universe where the Soviets won the Cold War?"

Scarlet Miller pulled her chin back and frowned at me. "Norway is proud member of Soviet Europe." She made a fist and showed me the back of her hand. "Twelve stars, *da*? And what is 'Cold War'?" She glanced at Kekoa. "*Blyat! Americanski? Nyet*, only United Soviets and *Yaponya* these days. You two? Very stupid universes." Scarlet—no, Soviet Miller produced a *pheeeeesh* sound by blowing air between her teeth and her lower lip.

I looked from one to the other: Imperial Kekoa, Soviet Miller, Imperial Kekoa again. "You're each here to do the same thing, aren't you?" I glanced around the flight deck. "Whichever one of us is in control when we come out of waver, that's the universe that survives?" I held up a finger. "Except we just did that, a few minutes ago."

Soviet Miller almost made it to whatever weapon she had on the side of her thigh before Imperial Kekoa shot her. She made a choking sound, gasping for air, hand spasming, so Kekoa shot her again.

I flinched at the gunfire, but otherwise that part of my training held fast. I half-closed my eyes and watched her, awaiting my turn.

Instead, she called out, "Okay, Miller, come on up. She's dead."

I opened my eyes all the way again. Imperial Kekoa still held the gun on me, but she also did a half-nod, half-head-waggle. "You may have experienced exiting waver, but that's backwash from potential futures. Technically we're still in waver right now—or at least, the multiverse hasn't sealed back up yet. What we're experiencing right now is an infinitely long non-particle of time, a vacuum of cause and effect between the last instant our ship was still in waver and the first instant it won't be. Think of it like the space between two solar systems, empty, and for all intents and purposes endless, until suddenly it isn't."

I already had a guess as to the answer, but I needed to be sure. "And how do we get out of this infinitely long non-particle of time and into the moment when we're back to one surviving reality again?"

Another Miller climbed the ladder onto the flight deck. She, too, wore a white EVA suit with the Rising Sun flag, but it also bore a flag with a white cross on a red background.

Imperial Kekoa answered in a tone far more conversational than menacing. "It looks like the answer is we all kill each other until there's only one universe standing."

I drew a slow, steady breath and asked the obvious question. "Why haven't you shot me?"

"There's a theory—" but Imperial Kekoa got cut off by a burst of *vizd vizd vizd*. Unmistakably weapon fire and yet something I'd never before heard. I rolled to the side and scrambled ungracefully behind the main flight deck console. Bursts of blue-gold sizzled and scattered against the overhead in energetic spiderwebs before arcing and fizzling out. Imperial Kekoa cursed a blue streak in her perfect west coast American English and returned fire. I reached the other end of the console and came face to face with my Charcoal counterpart.

No time like the present to roll the dice. How much worse could the outcome be?

I struggled to find the clamps for Charcoal Me's helmet, its design different from my own, but I got it free after a few seconds, took a deep breath, hoped enough Combust-o-Stop had been pulled from the air for me to survive it without major lung damage, and peeled the breather off my face. Imperial Kekoa's handgun went off a couple more times, followed by another burst of *vizd vizd vizd*, then the silence of a firefight being over.

The helmet's interior was slick with Charcoal's blood, its visor smashed to pieces, but it fit me just fine.

I grabbed the pistol from Charcoal's hip, put both hands in the air, and stood up. "Cease fire," I barked. "It's me."

Charcoal Miller and Charcoal Kekoa—I presumed, anyway—pointed weapons at me but didn't immediately fire. "What's the word, Concord? Where's the rest of your suit?" Kekoa's voice sounded almost natural over her speakers. She had the Hawaiian pidgin back.

I took it as a good sign and kept gambling. "This one smashed the visor in," I said with a nod at Scarlet Miller. "After that, the suit was just a bag of warm halon, or whatever these bastards use on their ship. Had to ditch it in case the fire suppressant did something weird to my skin." I paused, hesitating, then gestured around the flight deck. "Guess the rest of the ship is secured?"

Charcoal Kekoa nodded at the screens behind me. "That one of 'em?"

I glanced back to see which one caught her attention. The only monitor with a person in it was the one showing Miller—my Miller—dead on her feet in the cargo hold.

I turned back. "Yeah. I'm not sure she's dead. We need to go check."

They both hesitated, and Charcoal Miller spoke. "She's standing in an open cargo bay, man. Pretty sure that killed her."

"Oh," I said, "these guys have some weird safety protocols. I saw a lot of blinking lights when I cracked the doors. I think they might have an energetic force field holding in atmosphere."

Kekoa's voice was ice cold, and as she spoke I finally noticed that her suit bore no insignia at all. "The ships are supposed to be all the same, Concord."

Her weapon came up as I threw my shoulder against Miller, shoving her over the edge of the ladder and banging her helmet against the overhead. I heard a sharp, muffled crack, unsure whether it was something on her suit or in her body. No time to care. I knocked Kekoa's gun aside even as she fired it. Heat-pain flashed through me as a burst of energetic fire passed millimeters from my forearm, singeing the hair and pinking the skin. Kekoa tried to twist to go for another shot but she wore the bulky gloves of a space suit and I wore none.

I shouted at her as the gun finally came free of her hand and I twisted it around in mine. "*WAIT.* There's a statistical problem we're all overlooking here!"

I stood, panting, hoping to gods I knew did not exist that I wasn't huffing so much Combust-o-Stop I'd collapse. Two seconds ticked off, three, all the way to five. Kekoa stood there, watching me from behind golden glass, waiting for me to shoot her or say something.

I opted to speak.

"Okay, so we're all from different realities. And we're competing to be the one that survives. And I'm guessing you all came here with the understanding there's some sort of quantum effect and human attention is a necessary variable to resolve the question of which one has always been real when this space between moments comes to an end. Of course. Basic quantum physics. Am I right?" I gestured with the weapon as I spoke.

Kekoa lifted her middle finger at me. "You're the ship's physicist, you tell me."

"I'll take that as a yes. But out of all possible universes, ever, wouldn't only a tiny fraction even produce human life? Much less human life capable of developing the waver drive?" The question wasn't rhetorical. I was trying to think through this stuff on my feet, on the fly, with no safety net and wearing a blindfold. "But those are obviated by the quantum effect's necessity. Right. They're self-canceling possibilities, incapable of winning by virtue of the conditions under which a victor is chosen."

Kekoa's hand crept down a centimeter or two and I snapped the gun—or whatever—back to attention. "Nuh-uh," I chided.

"I'm just resting my arm," she said.

I shook my head. "No way. Hands good and high."

"Come on, Concord," she said. I thought I could hear her pause to lick her lower lip the way Kekoa did during poker games on the haul out here, before we fired the waver drive for the first time. "It's me. There's something important you don't understand. We need to talk before you do anything rash, okay?"

"Then talk." My voice was strained, and I couldn't tell whether the tightness in my chest was from chemical burns or terror. Given time to think it over, I probably would have said both.

Kekoa's other hand leapt as I drew another breath, but in the suit she was too slow.

I pressed my index finger to the button where a trigger would have been. Blue-gold bolts of death tore through her suit—and through her.

Charcoal Kekoa stopped moving.

"They were all warned this would happen," Charcoal Me said as he staggered to his feet, his face—my face—a blood-soaked, mashed up mess. He sounded stuffed up from a broken nose, and he lisped a little as his voice whistled through missing teeth.

I swung the gun around. He flinched and put his hands up over his face in defense and, somehow, I managed not to kill him.

Charcoal Me peeked at me around his hands. "Like, literally this: you killing everyone. Us killing everyone. Once we figure out the physics angle, I mean." He pointed at me for a second, and I realized what he meant. "We probably need to put on breathers again. The air in here still stinks from the fire suppressant, and those things are super toxic."

I looked down at Charcoal Kekoa's corpse—green smoke wafted from the holes I'd shot in her— at Imperial Kekoa, Scarlet Miller, all of them, then back to Charcoal Me. "Don't you want me dead, too?"

"Oh heavens no," Charcoal said. "Not yet, anyway. First we need to see if any of the rest of us have survived." He stepped closer, and for some reason I let him. His voice dropped to a husky whisper, conspiratorial, inviting me to lean closer to hear him. "Then we need to kill them."

We found Scarlet Us hiding in the aft waste pod. It was unsettling to hear myself speak with a slightly different accent. His sallow complexion and narrow cheeks told me what I'd look like living further north and on a more restrictive Russian diet. His eyes were bright, though, and when I looked in at him he flinched, then let out a sigh that turned into a laugh. *"Khorosho, khorosho,"* he said before he caught our blank stares and said, in a voice almost the same as mine, "Good, good. I'm glad it's us and not the others." Gesturing at the trash all around him he said, "I was worried things would go too well for one team or another and somebody would dump me into the burn with the rest of the garbage."

He chuckled.

I *hmph*ed.

Charcoal said nothing.

I offered Scarlet a hand and he took it, allowing me to help him out of his nest of garbage. "You know, they told me this would happen," he groaned as he got upright.

"What did they tell you would happen next?" Charcoal's voice had an edge to it, and we both heard it there.

Scarlet Me sounded a little tight in the throat when he answered, Charcoal's tension spreading like a bad cold. "That I'd seal up the wound in space-time and fly home a hero of the people." Scarlet tried to sound modest as he said it, and I knew—because I know myself—he did so in part because he realized how ridiculous it sounded when said aloud.

I tried to keep things casual. "Seen any of us?"

Scarlet nodded. "I saw one of us with the flag of *Yaponya* from the Great Patriotic War." He smirked slightly. "Weird, right?"

"Where did he go?" Charcoal was all business, and I knew that meant he wanted to wrap things up sooner rather than later.

Scarlet pointed by jutting his chin, knowing better than to move his hands. "He went down the starboard passageway after we spotted each other."

Charcoal nodded. "Hiding in the crew cabins."

I blew out a breath. "Or setting a trap."

The three of us crept closer to the sleeping quarters. Crew names had been etched into the doors of our cabins, one of the features done ahead of time in anticipation of the ship becoming a museum piece as soon as we returned. They had other waver engines, other iterations of this same design, ready to go. This first flight, however, already had pages waiting for it in history books not yet written. We were supposed to come out here, fire the engine, get really far away, send a signal, turn around, and waver back.

The signal we sent would arrive in the middle of the ceremony they already planned at United Nations headquarters. Sometime between the General Secretary's speech and getting our medals, our smiling, multilingual greeting from ourselves would arrive. We would have sent it from well outside the solar system, at the edge of the Oort Cloud, the sun at our backs a dim dot no bigger than Mars appears from Earth. It was to be the first time any person spoke to themselves at the speed of light.

The marketing people were very hyped up about it. It would be our era's "one small step" moment.

The three of us skipped Kekoa's cabin. I didn't need to walk in and see her asphyxiated corpse floating around.

Miller's was empty, of course.

We all knew that, given a choice, we would all always prefer our own cabin over anyone else's.

Charcoal and Scarlet flanked me.

I lifted my hand and knocked.

Silence was my only reply.

I waited ten seconds, then lifted my hand to knock again.

The door opened before I could strike it. Dim light spilled from within.

Imperial Us stood inside, stripped down to his skivvies. Dozens of candles in identical metal trays were scattered around the room, their flames jumping. I gawked for a second, as Imperial Us looked great. Clearly the Imperial Japanese military had stricter PT requirements and he'd put time into meeting or exceeding them.

"Hey, boys." His English was perfectly unaccented American, just like Imperial Kekoa's, but he pitched his voice lower than I do. He gestured over his shoulder with his right thumb. "Don't mind the scrubber lights. I'm trying to get some of that fire suppressant out of the atmosphere." Stepping back, Imperial Us held the door wide. "Come on in and get comfortable. I imagine you'd like to give your lungs a break."

The three of us hesitated. Charcoal and Scarlet said nothing. I drew in a breath but couldn't quite speak. My eyes wandered around Imperial's form. It was like looking at myself in an exceptionally flattering mirror.

"Don't mind the *fundoshi*," he said. "Just figured we could be comfortable while we talk this out." He ducked down a little, getting me to meet his eyes, and a sly smile crossed his face.

Scarlet Us spoke at last. "Are you... is this...?"

Charcoal chuckled gruffly. "Well. I guess we all know we've always wondered."

I cleared my throat. "We are all here to be first at something."

Scarlet Us finally said it. "Let's do it."

I paused, putting one arm out to block the door. "Don't we, you know, need to figure out how to save the multiverse from each other?"

Imperial Us put a hand on my wrist, gently lifting it and drawing it towards him and down until it made contact with the bulging crotch of his military-issue boxer briefs. I stammered, but Imperial kept talking. "I'm sure they explained this to you. At the moment, we have a near-approximation of literally forever. I'm not even sure we'll ever need to eat. Might as well enjoy ourselves while we wait to find out."

Charcoal chuckled and gave me a gentle push forward.

We stepped into the cramped cabin, one after another, and the four of us helped each other out of our gear.

After we sated our curiosity—much to our mutual satisfaction—we talked ourselves in circles about what to do next. Eventually we decided to call it a night and get some rest, maybe think of something in the morning, but found we couldn't sleep. Food held no attraction, so Imperial was right about that, too.

"What about other timelines?" I asked with some surprise in my voice, mostly over not having thought to ask earlier. We lounged together in mid-air in my cabin, arms and bodies pleasantly strewn about, micro-gravity letting us rest as we wished.

I lifted my head and looked at the others. "I'm from mine, each of you are from ones where your respective polity came out on top." Imperial me stifled a snicker and we all shot him a look as I went on. "But what about, I don't know, one where China's the space power, or one where it's Czarist Russia instead of the Soviet Union, or Mozambique. Chile. Some country that doesn't exist in any of our timelines. Or one in which Neanderthals were the surviving hominid. Anything like that. Why only us four?"

Imperial shrugged. "We're the superior people."

All four of us said, at once, "No, that sounds pretty racist."

A long silence, still more comfortable than not, passed between us. Scarlet said, "Perhaps one of us willed it to be just us four."

I considered, then shook my head at that. "I don't buy it. Obviously if we're in an unresolved quantum state then this—the four of us encountering one another, even, well..." I gestured around at the four of us. "Even like this, is just one eigenstate: one possible outcome in the set of all possible outcomes. What about the others?"

Charcoal scratched himself as he sat up. "We considered that. As far as we can tell, this existence is the superposition: all potential outcomes added to one another and overlapping. Until the Schrödinger equation is solved for one particular eigenstate, we can all be here. It's like the old thought experiment about Schrödinger's cat. Until the question of its condition is resolved by opening the box and looking in, the cat is in all possible states of being. If none others are here then it's because they were not possible for some reason. Imagine any alternative and it must necessarily exclude some necessary precursor event. Maybe for cultural reasons or technical ones or political ones, who knows, but they never develop the waver engine."

"Or," I said, lifting my arms and stretching them, "they developed one that doesn't do this." I paused to stretch my legs, one at a time, as I spoke. "Or they're too smart to go around trying to murder each other and are just waiting us out. If the waver engine really splits the seam of the multiverse and creates a superposition of every reality at once, it must include all the ones where, say, China develops a waver engine and gives their crew orders to sit tight and focus lots of human attention on their universe being the one that emerges." I gestured at the universe beyond the ship as I spoke. They've got any one of us, by the numbers, and the weight of human attention is one variable when resolving a Schrödinger equation."

Scarlet shifted around and looked at us. I recognized it was him by the United Soviets flag tattoo: the hammer and sickle on red, a circle of 48 stars, and the familiar white and red bars. "So why are we still here? Why hasn't the superposition collapsed?" His voice dropped. "If they could win, why haven't they?"

We all looked at one another, uncertain. Charcoal clearly wanted to sound like he had the answer, but the rest of us knew the look on his face. The look of wanting but not having.

I finally couldn't take the curiosity eating at me the entire time. I poked him in the chest with my index finger as I asked, "And which country's calling the shots in your timeline, anyway?"

Charcoal grimaced. "Same as yours. But in my timeline, we're a military operation. They anticipated this and sent a kill squad to fly the first waver mission."

I flinched. "In mine, we didn't know."

Scarlet put a hand on my shoulder. "Or they never told you."

"They told us this might happen, too," Charcoal said, his voice soft.

I fluttered my lips. "I've heard that more in one day than I need in a lifetime."

Imperial folded muscular legs beneath himself, sitting up. "Killing each other doesn't collapse it, does it?"

I shuddered. "What do you mean?"

Imperial ran his fingers through my hair as he answered. "Well, we all want to be the one who goes home, yes? We all just spent an extended period at different levels of being worried about the outcome and at different levels of, ah, distraction. And the superposition never collapsed in any of our favors. We're all still here."

Scarlet nodded at him. "We were trained this might happen," he said, running a hand around various parts of us. "And to use specific moments of psychological intensity to increase my ability to influence the outcome. But it did not cause me to be the only one left."

I boggled at him. "Wait, when you... when we..."

Scarlet shrugged at me. "Orgasm is a moment of intense psychic focus. But we're all still here."

Charcoal spoke softly. "Same for us. I tried it, too." He sounded embarrassed.

Imperial sounded a million miles away from us as he said, daydreaming a little, "They made us samurai before we left. There's a sword waiting for me at home and everything."

I asked aloud the question I feared facing. "So what makes *it collapse*? Honestly, I'm starting to worry none of us is going anywhere."

Charcoal finally met my gaze. "They—the brass back home—were pretty sure eliminating other sources of human attention would allow a specific timeline to emerge victorious; and that in the absence of that, sufficient mental force would do so. But..."

I snorted derisively. "'Victorious?' Is that the definition of winning? To eliminate infinite other universes and erase all the lives lived in them?"

Imperial put one of his powerful hands on my other shoulder, mirroring Scarlet. "They don't get erased. Or, more accurately, it's impossible for them to perceive being erased."

My voice dropped as my brain caught up and our situation dawned on me. "It's impossible... to perceive... being erased." I shook my head. "One of the Kekoas called this a 'non-linear particle of time,' but that doesn't make sense."

Scarlet struggled to find words and looked away as he spoke. "Unless the engine malfunctioned. They warned us about that, too. If the waver engine splits the universe into different possibilities, but it doesn't work exactly right as it sews them back up..."

Imperial and I stared at him. Charcoal didn't seem surprised by this possibility.

"What then? Time stops in the ones that didn't so-called 'win?'" I tried to keep the fear out of my voice.

Scarlet bobbed his head uncertainly. "Maybe. Our engineers said if that happened the other eigenstates just stick around, each their own little pocket reality. But they were guessing."

I turned my face to the ceiling as though studying the universe beyond it. "And like that Kekoa said, in the not-moment before the wave-form collapses, they all perceive their own forever." I drew a sharp breath. "We perceive our own forever."

Charcoal spoke gently, even kindly, as he glided closer and tried to explain. "If it helps," he said, "it means none of us will be alone."

"What are we supposed to do in the meantime?" Imperial's voice barely rose above a whisper.

I looked at no one and nothing. I knew what we had to do. The only thing we could do.

"We wait for forever to end."

NO BONES ABOUT IT

CAROL GYZANDER

Dave stared at the beautiful young woman on his smartwatch as he sat in the corner booth of the darkened bar. He watched the movement of her rich, full lips in a perfect heart-shaped face and the subtle flicker of long lashes surrounding her bright blue eyes. He smiled a little to himself, and he hovered his finger over the edge of the vidscreen, wishing he could actually touch her.

He always had to have the newest and best technology. If you were going to do something, you should do it all the way, he said. In this case, springing for the new watch with the video interface allowed him to put a filter on his face. Nothing major—his short brown hair and even teeth from years of braces remained the same, but the filter hid the red puckering scar around his eye and the thick spectacles that looked like magnifying lenses.

"What did you say? I was distracted." He half-smiled and watched her chin-length blonde hair ripple as she tossed her head. She'd begun their ongoing conversation by messaging him after his comment on a mutual friend's post, and he had not worked up the nerve to meet her. He wondered what her hair would look like in person.

"I said, I can't believe you're going to come to the festival! We'll finally meet after all these months." Maddie smiled, and Dave felt as if the sun came out in the bar.

His heart skipped a beat, but he couldn't decide the cause—excitement at being with her in person or fear of having her see him. He shrugged and took a deep breath. "Yeah, you talked me into it. Burning Man, here I come."

"No, silly. It's not really Burning Man. That's a much bigger festival. This one is Torchlight."

"Okay, Torchlight, it is then." His watch buzzed, and he toggled to the incoming text message. "I've got to go. Eric just said he's almost here."

"Okay. Say hi to him for me. Hey, I never said this before, but...love you."

His heart skipped again. "Oh! Love you, too!" He toggled the screen off and sat back, letting out a deep sigh. He'd stopped thinking anyone could love someone with a face like his.

Moments later, the door to Roache's squeaked open. Eric came in, looking left and right with a frown until he saw Dave. His face lit up, the light over the bar glinting off his nose and lip piercings.

Dave raised a hand and waved at his old college buddy. Looking around the room, he realized Eric was the only one who still looked like they had over a decade ago: long hair pulled back in a ponytail, T-shirt over grungy jeans and boots. He looked down at his button-down shirt and khakis with a slight grin. He couldn't picture Eric ever wearing nice clothes like his.

His buddy slid into the booth and gestured to the bartender, who sent the waitress over with Eric's usual draft beer.

"Hey man, how they hangin'? Shoulda known you'd be hiding out in the corner." Eric's goofy grin was contagious, and Dave relaxed enough to turn face-on toward his friend instead of sitting sideways in the booth with his badly scarred eye to the wall.

"Not bad, not bad. I was just talking to my gal." He raised his wrist with a flourish of the watch. His heart soared as he said the words.

"You've still only talked to her on the tiny screen? Someday I wanna watch you two chatting. But I gotta say, the watch you gave me is handy for getting orders while I'm driving the delivery van. Thanks again, man."

Dave grinned. "Think nothing of it. Least I can do after dropping out on my old friend for so long after my eye."

"Glad you're getting out a bit." Eric clinked glasses with Dave and took a deep drink. "I can't believe you've been talking for months and still never met each other."

"You know me. Last thing I want to do is scare somebody away with this face. Or these glasses." He had not dated or even gone out in public much since the debacle of his Lasik surgery. His eyesight hadn't been that bad, but he'd wanted to look better without glasses. He'd been one of those with a bad reaction to the procedure that caused intense pain, making him rub his eyes incessantly. The resulting infection attacked the skin around one eye and left nasty scars. The ultimate irony was that he needed thicker glasses than before. "Jesus, Eric. I used to be a handsome guy. Now I could traumatize little kids."

"Dude, it's not as bad as you make out. I keep telling you, don't make such a big deal about yourself. You used to do the same thing in college, always making a huge show after every lacrosse game when you scored the highest points…or whenever you missed a goal. So, are you ever going to get together with Maddie?"

"I'm going to Torchlight Festival this weekend with her. Well, I'm going to meet her there."

"No fucking way! Hell, I've been trying to talk you into going for years, and it just takes this gal a couple of months to persuade you." Eric shook his head with a grin. "You're gonna love it. Best group of folks *ever*. Remember how lost I was when my parents died right after we graduated? You helped me get whole, held me together…until your eye surgery got you all screwed up." His lips tightened, and he downed the rest of his beer. "That was when I found Torchlight. I really think of them as family now. I don't know what I would do if they weren't in my life."

He stared directly into Dave's eyes, with no hint of any reaction to the scarring or the thick glasses. "Seriously, once you connect with this crowd, you'll never want to leave either."

Dave reached forward and gripped his friend's arm. "I've heard you talk about them for so long, man. I didn't want to horn in, if you know what I mean, but seriously I would do anything for this woman. You know how gorgeous she is, right? I just hope the difference between us isn't too much."

"C'mon, man, you're a whacko. Everything with you is either all or nothing. You'll be fine."

"Okay, tell me what I need to bring with me." The two began talking about camping at the festival, the giant bonfire, and what Dave should wear, signaling for more beers as they spoke.

Dave walked through the small forest clearing wearing a fancy backpack with all his brand-new gear, feeling self-conscious among so many left-over hippie types. He knew Eric was into weird music and had dreaded a whole weekend of dubstep—and whatever the hell Playa Tech was—but hadn't quite realized how strange the crowd would be. Seeing Maddie was worth some awkward feelings.

He passed a woman about his age with skull tattoos running all up one arm and onto her face and shuddered, thinking about how much pain he had been in during his eye surgery and wondering why anyone would inflict that on themselves voluntarily. Moving on, he glanced quickly at a tall man with piercings like giant bones through his ears. Boneman talked with a young woman who stood topless while she nursed her baby. Averting his eyes from her bare breasts, Dave moved out of the clearing and headed along the path through the woods.

A diesel generator fired up in the distance, and soon he heard the heavy bass of electronic music. He found it hard not to walk in step with the throbbing beat.

Unsure about where to go, he stopped at a booth at the side of the path. A rainbow of colored crystals covered the table and hung from lengths of rawhide and silver chains on a display stand in the middle. Strings of prayer beads and crystal hand pipes lay on the table's far side.

"I'm thinking you could use a citrine charm to help you release some negative emotions." An older woman, a gray braid hanging over her shoulder down to her waist, looked him up and down from a chair in the shadows behind the table. "Fear and doubt, right?"

"No, I'm just looking for my friend, Maddie. She said she's already here."

The woman stood and pursed her lips, revealing a wrinkled tattoo of black flames on one cheek. "Don't know any Maddie."

"How about Eric? Is he here somewhere?"

"Oh, you must be Dave! Eric said you'd be coming in to join us. *Now* I know who you're looking for. Do you want to leave your pack here until you find them?" She gestured to the tent behind the booth.

Dave paused for a moment, surprised that she knew of him, then figured that he could trust a friend of Eric's. He shrugged the backpack off and passed it with a grunt to the woman, who easily lifted it over the table with one hand and tucked it under the tarp attached to the tent. He reached for the tiny bundle in his back pocket, then thought better of leaving it. She pointed along the trail in the same direction he had been heading and shooed him on his way.

He checked by habit to be sure his filter was on and then signaled Maddie in the video chat on his watch. "Hey there!" he said when she answered. "I'm here and walking around some of the campsites. Where are you? Where should I meet you?"

Her beautiful face brightened with delight, pale blue eyes lighting with excitement in the twilight. Her lush red lips parted with an intake of breath and turned up at the corners in the smile that made Dave melt every time he saw it. "I'm heading up to the top where they hold the feast. Keep going and take any trail that leads you uphill—they all wind up here. You'll catch up!"

Dave spied a fork in the trail, one path going straight and the other heading up the side of the forested hill. "Okay, got it. I guess I'll be there soon! I just...I'm nervous about seeing each other face-to-face."

Maddie puckered her forehead and tightened her lips, but her eyes shone big, bright, and welcoming. "I know, sweetie, and I'm so glad you finally told me about your scars since I can't see them onscreen. No need to make a big deal about it. It's *you* I like, not your skin or your face."

Dave shrugged his shoulders. "Okay," he said with a big sigh. "On my way."

"Oh hey! Did Eric give you the package from me?"

Dave patted his back pocket for what seemed like the thousandth time. "Yep, got it right here. I should wait to open it until you tell me, right?"

"Absolutely!" She blew him a kiss and clicked out of the chat.

He headed up the trail and passed through various campsites along the way, checking in with Maddie several times to see if he was getting close. She kept saying she was just ahead of him, to keep going, and he would catch up to her.

Eventually, he emerged above the tree line onto a rocky slope that leveled into a big open area ringed with tables. He still heard the throbbing beat from lower on the mountain, now overlaid with a reverberating, melancholy electronic tune from somewhere nearby. At least a hundred people gathered together, chanting words he couldn't understand. He couldn't smell anything like food cooking. He saw Eric dancing and swaying in a long black robe on the far side of the crowd near a tall, unlit pyre of wood, but couldn't get his attention.

He turned away and tapped into the chat with Maddie again. "I'm up in the rocky bit by the bonfire. Eric's wearing some weird bathrobe. Are you here?"

"I'm in the crowd! Remember my present?"

Dave felt in his pocket and pulled out the small carved wooden case that Eric had pressed into his hand the previous day.

"Open it now. They will help you find me!"

Dave found a pair of wire-rimmed glasses with light blue lenses inside. The earpieces ended in hooks to wrap around the back of his ears. His hands tightened around the case. "What the hell? Crystal *spectacles*? I already told you I have glasses and need them to see, but I hate them."

"These are special. Sapphires help with clear vision. Put them on, and they will help you find me...the true me."

Dave turned and looked at the assembled throng. How was he supposed to make his way through the crowd without his usual corrective lenses?

When the music faded, Eric climbed up on top of a rock next to the unlit bonfire. He held a tall staff topped with a skull. Raising both arms into the air, he addressed the gathered group. "My friends, my family, my life! We come together again at Torchlight."

The crowd cheered, and Dave startled to hear their throaty and deep voices. Probably half the group was women, and he thought their voices would have brought the group's sound higher than that.

Eric looked up at his outstretched arms overhead. "My friends, we welcome the new member to our feast and to our family."

Dave only listened with half an ear, turning it over in his head, trying to decide—to wear the weird new spectacles or not? Finally, he took a deep breath and removed his thick glasses, frowning at the blur surrounding him as he swapped them for the ones from Maddie. He stashed the case in his pocket for safety and took another deep breath. Slipped on the sapphire wire-rimmed glasses. Turned left and right, surprised that the world did not look blue—just sharp and clear.

He raised his wrist up and smiled into the video screen to show her.

Maddie looked up at him on the screen, as if he floated far above her, and broke into a huge smile. Dave blinked as his eyes tried to adjust to the crystal spectacles, and as he did, her face began to change. Her eyes darkened. Her short blonde hair grew longer and darker, pulled back into a ponytail. Stubble appeared on her chin and jawline. The sun's setting rays glinted off a nose ring and lip piercing as they appeared on the screen. Her mouth opened into a vast, knowing grin.

"What the fuck? Maddie, what...Maddie?" Dave peered closer at the watch, holding it with the other hand and bringing them up toward his face as he looked through the tinted spectacles. "Maddie? You look like... you look like Eric! How can this be?"

Maddie/Eric grinned, showing fierce teeth as the soft flesh melted away from their face. "Sapphire clears your vision. You're not the only one who can use a filter, man!"

Dave glanced up. His friend stood on the rock, gazing up at his wrist on one hand and the other holding the staff. The sun slipped behind the horizon, and the head of the staff burst into flame. The wind blew the black robe back, exposing Eric's bare chest. It was covered with skeleton tattoos that seemed to move and gyrate. He threw his head back and gave a piercing cry.

"Aaaaahhhhh!"

Dave heard the sound in stereo—both from his friend's lips fifty feet away and the watch on his wrist. He jumped back and looked wildly around the crowd to see if they noticed anything strange. The people pressed closer toward Eric and gave an answering howl that echoed back from the surrounding hills. But as he looked from person to person, blinking to focus at different distances, their faces all morphed in front of him as well. High cheekbones, deep-set eyes, and thin-lipped smiles replaced the friendly faces he had seen when he arrived. Their musculature seemed to drip away, leaving sinewy strength behind.

The longer he stared at them, the more differences and changes Dave saw: emaciated arms, broad feet gripping the ground with bony toes, fleshless chests peering out from beneath their clothes. They raised their arms overhead and shook their hands in unison, making a deafening sound of clattering bones.

Dave backed away, looking from his friend's emaciated face on the watch to the sight of the massive bony figure standing on the rock in front of him. "No, no, no, this can't be...."

"Dave, my buddy. It took me years to get you to join us. Trust me. Once you're part of the family, you'll love it here."

Dave shook his head, trying to scramble away. Four sinewy males from the crowd surrounded him and gripped his arms, propelling him toward the bonfire. The bony fingers dug into his flesh, and he gagged as their putrid scent engulfed him.

"We're going to have a special ceremony tonight, my friend," Eric bellowed. "First, we eat you. We cast your bones into the fire and roast off the last bits of the old Dave, and you will be reborn into the family. It's going to be painful, but you will no longer care what you look like once you turn. Trust me." He touched the flaming head of his staff to the bonfire. It exploded into flames with a giant wash of heat that matched Dave's rising terror. The bony crowd cheered.

Dave fought with all his might against the four gaunt creatures to no avail. He started crying and whimpering. "No, no, Eric. I don't want to! No…"

The four dragged him up onto the rock to face his friend. Flames roared in the bonfire at their feet and reflected in Eric's eyes.

His friend reached out and removed the tinted glasses, cupping the back of Dave's head with his emaciated fingers and stroking the scar surrounding his eye with a bony thumb. "Come on. It'll be fine. I keep telling you, don't make a spectacle of yourself, Dave."

Eric pulled Dave's head forward and bit off a chunk of his scarred face. The crowd of walking skeletons surged forward to surround him with a cheer.

NON-FUNGIBLE TRANSCENDENCE

R.E. CARR

They say that eyes are the windows to the soul. Perhaps that is why we've taken to ripping ours out.

The machines we've placed in their stead never falter, never weaken, and never give way to that critical weakness. If you can see out, yet others can't see in, then maybe, for the briefest of moments you might be safe. But we never are safe, not in a world that's already crumbling.

I held onto my side, as if that alone would staunch the tide. I'd taken a hit by being the one unlucky enough to be stuck watching the door, but it hadn't ended me yet. Our deal had fallen apart before the crew entered that cursed warehouse, but no one, not even my old friend Impulse, had the time or tech to warn us through the shielded mass of concrete.

I suppose I had not been so unlucky after all. When the bomb went off, I ended up with a hunk of metal lodged under my rib. The rest of the crew met their fate under tons of rubble. I had known them for mere hours. I had not even learned their names. This was the way of shadowy actors such as us.

The wind turned, picking up a mix of rubbish from the gutters. A ramen cup clattered and rolled past my feet before settling to a final resting place along the chain link. My infra sight warned me that lurkers hid beyond the flimsy barrier, perhaps merely squatting, perhaps waiting for me to stumble and give them easy prey.

Better to be splat upon the windshield than the fly languishing in the trap, they say. I didn't have the remaining kit on me to go out in a blaze of glory with whatever horrors waited in the sprawl. My heads-up display sprang to life, locking reticules onto a few targets should I wish to change my mind. The omnipresent Ariadne-bot booted up as well, confirming my lack of ammunition and the blood still leaking from my barely patched up wound.

Organic Life Support System at 35%. Recommend immediate Medi-vacuation. The message from Ariadne scrolled across my HUD. However, it was tonight's botched job I was going to use to renew my annual subscription to Trauma-Vac.

I took my chances staggering onward, following another arrow on my HUD. I was forced to accept the lifeline Impulse had shot me once the deal went south. He'd managed a solitary message while I burned my adrenaline and ran from the blast.

Safe house in sector 39. Ask no questions, live to see the dawn.

The arrow turned, sending me left and through an underpass. I slid my good arm to my hip, finding resolve in the grip of my sidearm. My fear proved unfounded, as I crossed zones unmolested. Maybe the local gangs had decided to play with each other tonight, or the rent-a-cop brigade had quotas to meet. I couldn't force myself to care. I took joy in the neon flickering in the freshly moistened pavement stretching as far as the ocular implant could scan. The soothing blues distracted me from the stabbing under my ribs.

Neutral territory detected, my Ariadne bot cooed in my ears, the same message flashing in green across my vision. It gave me the breathing room to pull another Patch-It from my bag. The pain flared anew. I winced.

Best not to think of the dubious mix of stimulants and Zhōnghuá antibiotics. Instead, I focused on my mobility returning as the plastic wrapper crinkled in my palm. I slapped the square over the fresh trickle of blood. If only that damn door had had the decency to shatter slightly higher, then the titanium parts of me could have done their job.

The wind turned again, making me grateful I could still afford rebreathers. Smog rolled in from the harbor and even the carbon inserts couldn't wash away the fetid taste from my lips. I moved on.

Deeper I trespassed into the bright and bustling world of those who still considered themselves safe. Shoppers trying to spend away the imminent apocalypse haggled for their synthflesh and bemoaned the ambient smell of the protein reclamation plants. My arrow turned again, sending me past the stalls and the ceaseless lights, plunging me once more into comfortable darkness.

My view shifted to a familiar greenish gray as I ambled past the shuttered remains of eras long gone. A gutted library now housed refugees. The corner church finally became honest and sported bouncers ready to extort cover tithes simply to gain access to the remains of salvation. I moved on.

Soon I found myself standing in the shadows of a crumbling brick edifice, its turrets a stark contrast to the shiny chrome skyline on the horizon. Neon made way for flickering lamplight. Asphalt conceded its dominance to a cobblestone path.

Not all was as it seemed, of course. In the shadows of two tenement towers, a panel lit up, warning all passersby of the dangers within. I took a tentative step towards the rusted iron gate, and my sensors burst to life. The dainty scrollwork contained electrified shredwire, the bricks concealed all manner of explosives, simply waiting for the fool who judged a book by its cover. Foolish as I might have been for landing myself an injury, I had no intention of diving into the deep black so flippantly tonight.

Proximity access granted. Verify and proceed, Wilde.

Impulse had not led me astray, it seemed, but as I approached the sinister black box, my mind drifted to debts owed and the most trivial of transgressions. Specialists like me had been zeroed for lesser sins than mine, and the tech stitched to my remaining meat held more value than most friendships. The panel glowed. I pulled off my glove.

I held my breath as the sensor read my palm, found the few details I never erased in my quest to live only in the shadows, and most importantly of all, verified my credit. A few thousand bits drained in a heartbeat, and I was left only with the words, "Welcome Old Friend. Why don't you stay a while?"

The gate opened.

At this point the stims began to falter, the error messages increased. No time to waste worrying about the deeds now done, and instead I moved steadily towards this throwback looming over my exhausted frame. The weight of the front door steadied me, provided respite before I would have to face whatever wonders or horrors resided within.

Upon opening the door, even my sensors needed a moment to recover from such blinding opulence. Chandeliers spewed their radiance across the gilded walls and shining marble floors, forcing me to momentarily retreat. My Ariadne stream scrolled incessantly as it tried to process the sheer volume of data assaulting my senses, until, at long last it reached the end of the line and could give me proper directions.

Proceed to the east tower. Your accommodations are on floor three.

I indulged in a second hit of stimulants from my bag, using the fresh rush to guide me to my quarters as much as the overlay upon my vision. My sensors picked up no other guests as I passed room upon room, but I found myself surrounded by faces nonetheless.

Scattered along the papered walls, frame after frame displayed portraits in all manner of media and style. Splattered paint mingled with charcoals and projections. Men and women of times long buried either smiled or sneered at my passing, the occasional wink revealing the animated creations amid the lot.

Whoever made this place had more money than sense, as my scanners began reading the barcodes rolling along the frames. The blockchain downloaded into my HUD, showing an unbroken link of purchases all tracing back to a confirmed artist. Even the physical works had been scanned and tagged, boasting to any visitor that the owner paid well for each and every design. I could only imagine the scale of this enterprise, trapping so much creativity within these crumbling walls. No wonder the security rivaled a regime building. It would take the gross national product of a corporation to fund such lavish excess.

Pain spoke louder than awe, however, and I took my leave to face a relentless mountain of stairs. Each step drained me, yet, somehow, I found the will to make it all the way to the top of the tower. There I found modest accommodations, but most importantly a bed coupled with a power station. With my batteries fading and my meat aching, I fell onto the crisp white bedding and let the cables worm their way towards my hungry plugs. Alas, in my exhaustion, I could not find a somnolence regulator to connect to my pounding head.

Charging Commenced.

I'd often wondered how people slept on their own, without the programs or the meds. It'd been so long since I'd had to close my eyes and rely on the whims of dreams to either allow or deny my rest. I focused on the gentle hum, the warmth radiating from my neck and my thigh.

Perhaps I could have taken this time to send messages or soak in my feed, but I had no confidence in the security or privacy afforded by my unknown host, nor inclination to stretch my consciousness beyond this pristine moment of rejuvenation. I found myself quiet. I allowed everything to remain still.

How long I remained in this fugue, I could not quite determine, despite the array of timekeeping software at my disposal. Instead, I sank deeper into the moment, feeling the breath enter and leave my nostrils—letting go of remaining cares and even the basest of thoughts. In this moment I had my peace, and it was indeed enough.

Damage assessment completed. Condition stabilized. Please return to consciousness to initiate repairs.

My HUD had other plans for my evening, it seemed. Wearily I rose from my mattress, now forced to confront the realities at hand. My systems had enough time to reboot, I suppose my human core had no choice but to obey. I needed no thought, no deduction to complete my task, only the muscle memory programmed by countless layers of software and implants. I carried both hardware and wetware maintenance tools in my pack and found that whatever my portable stores were lacking were easily compensated for by the dizzying array of spare parts tucked within the charging station. While I clamped and stitched and patched Nu-skin over my rib plates, I finally took a moment to appreciate my accommodations.

While not as sumptuous as the great hall below, this room was adorned from floorboards to moldings with all manner of digital art. The chains on these works did not stretch far, indicating a close connection between the creator and the owner of this anachronistic estate. I draped myself over the side of the bed to better stretch my newly attached dermis. I found this angle most conducive to take in the glory of a portrait tucked in one of the many nooks afforded by this room's eccentric design.

The frame was in itself a work of art—carved and gilded with images of long extinct waterbirds. Their wings arched around a rare oval portrait amid the sea of rectangles, framing a face that quite simply took my breath away.

In truth, I'd forgotten what eyes could look like. Not everyone had implants, to be sure. Those that still clung to keeping vulnerable sacs of jelly in their skulls did not stare at the world with the life of this image.

The longer I looked, the more I could swear the woman stared back at me. The warmth contained within her deep brown irises stirred something long forgotten, a heat in the floor of my belly not generated by batteries or implants.

Bold of this artist to capture a face so lifelike that I could zoom and enhance to take in every pockmark, every open pore. Somehow these imperfections only added to the glory of the whole, an unfiltered masterpiece of a girl just entering womanhood. Her uneven skin, her thick and lustrous brows, and the smallest of smiles curling up one side of unpainted lips taunted me, screamed at me that this was a human who found glory in her irregularity. The sparkle in her eyes cried that she did not give a shit what others demanded about sanitized beauty.

No makeup, no jewelry, no ludicrous fashion marred the simplicity of this model. Her dark hair fell wild and uneven down to her bare shoulders, and the longer I gazed upon her, the more I yearned to see beneath the frame, to imagine the rest of this shockingly human form.

Repairs complete. You may initiate a rest cycle.

Perhaps rest could wait a little while. The door to my room could be locked and alarmed, and I had no urgent messages from Impulse or anyone else for that matter. Curiosity, deadly as it might be, still resided in my soul, so I could not resist approaching the oval portrait tucked so lovingly by my bed.

Once standing I could read the chain, one link and one link only. *Created by Anonymous Wise.* No sales, no transfers, no insidious history to trace. This image had begun and ended its journey within these walls. My database registered no hits, suggesting an alias. Did it matter though? Would knowing the creator change the wonder of their work?

I encroached closer still, lost in her gaze. For a moment more than desire rushed through my veins. For a moment, I could almost imagine...hope.

I saw my own reflection twisted in her stare. The protective mirrors, the lifeless chrome that formed a band from ear to ear brought me crashing back into the moment, reminding me how little remained of the woman I had been.

Did I dare reach out and touch the screen? Did I need to feel the liquid crystals bend around my fingertips to remind me that this image belonged to fantasy? No, I needed rest. I needed to return to my focus. Yet, I could not move on.

Instead, I explored the remainder of my sanctum. Within one slender dresser, I discovered ration bars and a change of clothes shrouded in shrink-wrap. The cold black of my new garments stood in stark contrast to the warm gold and wood throughout the chamber, making my whole being feel further removed from the girl still looking my way despite how far I prowled from her perch in that nook.

I found an unadorned box placed amid a curious collection of real books. As tempting as it would be to experience what paper truly felt like, I could not resist lifting the latch. A sigh of relief left my lips as I found a comforting row of datachips nestled in a bed of foam. My display flowed with dates and titles and certified attestations of a lack of malware stamped by the IDA itself. It was the last and least populated of the chips that caught my eye—"The Journal of Anonymous Wise".

Patiently as I could, I let my Ariadne scan and verify the data once again. Caution tempered my curiosity for as long as possible, but every return message assured me that this media remained clean and simply informative. I tilted my neck, baring the input panel at the base of my skull. Curiosity would not be countermanded this night.

The chip slid inside me effortlessly. No encryption, no passwords blocked my path, only an archaic file system using American-style dates slowed my investigation.

The strange creator merely used text to tell their tale. How quaint, I mused, as the spiders of my guiding operating system parsed keywords to find meaning within so many mundane entries. The search string returned a mere handful of videos and images, as if I'd truly stepped backwards a century or more. Anonymous Wise documented daily, reporting minutiae with the reverence of a priest. I skimmed evaluations of linework and color palettes, interviews of models, and lamentations over lighting. A historian or collector might have had great use for this level of detail, but I sought only one prize, if it even existed. I sought only the record of this masterpiece that taunted me from within its gilded frame.

I glanced her way again, this time letting the cameras attached to my brain attempt to do her justice. My own image of the woman in the oval portrait rendered on the left-hand side of my vision, whilst Ariadne scrambled to find a match.

Video file detected: playback or simulate?

Falling back into my bed, I felt compelled to stare at only one word within my crowded overlay. The power drain would be tremendous, the render time bordering on obscene, but I was now locked in this chamber, and I had to experience more.

Once more time became elusive, reality even more so. I breathed in. I breathed out. Focusing only upon that until I found myself sinking, sinking deeper into this endless bed.

I awakened surrounded by green. Not the glare of neon or the dim tones of lichens and resilient algae, but rather the verdant tones found only in my holovids. Somehow the pictures and the words of this Anonymous Wise allowed grass to tickle my metallic toes. I stretched my good hand forward. Golden light bathed my skin, the warmth almost as intoxicating as the vision now sitting before me.

I should have been upgraded beyond choking since my lungs were remade in silicone and polymers. However, to catch even a glimpse out of the corner of my eye...the breath caught in my throat. My featureless sensors would not betray me so I indulged in an examination of the curves of her form, barely contained under a gown of silk. I traced the full line of her hips, up to her waist, followed the tiny droplets of sweat that collected along her collar until I lost sight of it amid the waves of hair caressing her graceful neck. She tucked a chestnut lock behind one ear and my gaze nearly shifted up to her face, to just catch her teeth gnawing upon the full pout of her bottom lip.

I was not prepared to take in the full glory of her countenance within this simulation, so I turned abruptly to my right. A stylus rested in the hands of a most unremarkable fellow. My display outed him by flashing the letters A. Wise over his lowered head. I could not determine his face as he slumped behind his massive tablet, his strokes furious as he attempted to capture the perfection sitting mere meters away.

"I could never give up," the man behind the easel said softly. "Not when my dream came so close to finally waking."

While I stood in the image of the highest summer, my own sweat threatened to bead off the remains of my skin. As this man spoke, the leaves retreated into their branches, and the cool and the dew replaced the glorious heat.

"I met her on the very first day of spring, and on that day, I knew I must have her," the artist explained, the words flowing overhead to remind me continuously of my true state. "There had been others to be certain, but no one, no one moved me as she did."

As the artist peered intently at his canvas, I finally allowed myself to gaze upon the vision's face. Somehow, she was even more lifelike than before. Her dark eyes gazed wistfully into the clouded skies and her new smile eclipsed the wonder of all the green surrounding us. I wanted to speak, but the words failed me, so I relied on Anonymous Wise to narrate our tale.

"The day she agreed to come here transformed my entire purpose. I'd tried so hard to capture the essence of humanity, to document what remained. I found her on the last Isle of Bangkok, homeless and alone, yet never lonely. In my kindness, I brought her here. In my cruelty, I made her mine."

The woman lowered her head ever so slightly. She sat upon the meadow, as the world continued to spin, and the heat radiated from the horizon. Faster and faster came the tapping from Anonymous Wise. He occasionally peeked to verify the accuracy of his work. Every time he glanced her way, her smile returned, but for longer and longer he concentrated only upon his screen and the light in her eyes eventually dimmed.

No, no, I tried to cry out, as the leaves nearby bleached from emerald tones to oranges and red. The stylus changed the brushes, the tints flowed across his display, but the girl only sat there as ever the light faded. The very first snowflake landed on my cheek.

"I have done it!" Anonymous Wise bellowed, rising to his feet. "I have finally captured… humanity."

But now the girl's eyes were hollow, and the snow fell like familiar ash. I turned not to see a man leaping from behind his easel but something even more machine than I. The skeletal creature of wires and chrome cocked its head. Its face, a tablet smaller than the one he used as a canvas, projected the barest semblance of a face, a mere emoji plastered on a synthetic frame. How could I not have noticed the true nature of this creature before?

I found myself trapped in the middle between all that was human and all that was not. The motor that replaced my heart refused to quicken despite the pleading of a wet and organic brain. The expression changed and the artist dropped its stylus. "She is dead," it proclaimed, a new softness in the voice. "Yet she lives on."

Simulation terminated.

I shot from my slumber quickly enough to tear the plugs from my sockets. I wasted no time ripping that foul diary out of my skull. It clattered against the floor. I finally breathed.

What had this artist done and was he finished with his dream? I turned slowly and once more beheld her portrait, the face of a girl I'd never know yet felt closer to than myself. As I gazed into the vortices of her pupils, I beheld what could only be described as a spark.

The eyes *are* the windows to the soul.

ASCENT FROM THE MAELSTROM

RACHEL A. BRUNE

S alt.

I smell of it. Feel it. The sea and the sun have baked it into my pores and calluses for so long that when I close my eyes, I dream of the waves as they broke over me.

I'm sorry. I am getting ahead of myself. You came here to inquire about the old man. You have heard of him, perhaps, and the stories he tells. Perhaps you have viewed him in that device you hold in your hand.

Oh, you are surprised?

Perhaps he was an oddity, one of the last salts to man the steam clippers, then a roughneck on a cargo vessel, and all the time, telling his tale to any who'd record it. Those devices, yes, I know them.

Modern life has not escaped me, nor I it, no matter how far I have traveled.

That's how he started. I know this, because he did not recognize me. Not at first. Not even as he made it halfway through his tale. He'd grown comfortable with the telling, reciting the words by rote, stale and unsurprising. Perhaps he truly did not know me until the end.

But I knew him. Just as I knew the winding streams and inlets of his tale. It was a story of the maelstrom, was it not? The journey through the northern waters, yes, and the circumstances of that day that caught us in dire straits, our delay made fatal by the peculiar phenomena that haunted those very waters.

I see you nod, *Yes*. You know. You have heard this many times.

Ah. So much could be ascertained by the account of events that have been *portrayed*—captured and filmed by those curious enough to stop and listen to the tale.

Many times have I wished to explain. I have thought, if only I could speak of the events that occurred that night-into-day. Perhaps then, what I have done could be forgiven.

Your attention wanders. I understand. Please excuse the lack of artfulness in my speech. I have not been able to tell this tale before, and the words are unfamiliar. My mouth is dry and tastes of salt.

Yes. Salt.

I will start on that day, as we entered the channel. Even then, my brother and I had quarreled over some nameless subject. It matters not, but I shall admit that we had done so many times before. Argued that is, over some irrelevant tidbit of business. It was my fault, as well, that our departure came so late, caught up as I had been with the catch that fair leaped into our nets as we trawled under the midnight sun.

And yet, had the tides been with us, we should have entered that channel with plenty of time to make the passage. Instead, the storm rolled in, masking the glow of the sun just as it dipped down below the horizon. A sound like a choir of demons surrounded us, whipping with the hurricane wind that threw salt waves across our bow, blinding us as we fought with the rigging.

We struggled on the deck of that ship. Our youngest brother tied himself to the mainmast; in the first few violent blows, the storm divested us of our main- and foremasts, taking my brother with them as they disappeared from view.

The storm lashed out, shaking us with a fury that was as fast as it was sudden. In the dark and confusion, I leashed myself to one of the casks upon the deck and, pounded by the storm, fell unconscious. I know not what happened next.

You nod your heads. Perhaps you have seen a storm, even a violent storm such as this. But you have not crouched to the deck of a tiny *smak* in the face of the vast, heaving sea, slipping amongst the barrels as the vessel rose and fell with the waves, struggling to breathe, to rise, to blink against the salt. You have not felt the moment of madness that descends upon you when the eye of the storm strikes a sudden calm, more violent even than the chaotic thrusts the storm wreaked upon your ship.

Ah, in that moment, if I had awoken in Bedlam, I would have had no complaint. But it were a worse Hell, for off the bow I shrieked and cried, "The Ström! The Moskoe-ström!"

And here, I see you nod once again, but for the last time, as here our narratives will diverge as cleanly as the masts from the deck of my ship.

I awoke as the maelstrom first took our ship into its grasp, almost gently, but with a pull as inexorable as Hell's upon a sinner. By a roll of the deck, the cask upon which I took my shelter chanced to be maneuvered to my brother, who had grasped hold of an iron ring embedded in the wood at the heel of the bowsprit.

A curious calm befell us both, him on his ring, and I on my cask. The circuit had us deep in its grasp, and even now, we sank further on the belt of the waves. The cacophony of the storm had ceased, as had the furious wind. Now, the only air that moved was the current of our ship as it broke the still air in the throat of the Ström.

For it was a throat, the languorous gullet of some forsaken monstrosity, and we circled lazily into its depths.

The silence was broken now by whispers in a language too dreadful to be spoken—a language foreign and unintelligible—and yet, we understood every word that drifted to our ears. It spoke of a terrible bargain, a choice that a brother could never make, and I was seized with a terror that I could not name, even as it dragged us deeper into its craw.

For the Moskoe-ström had a name, one that it whispered in my ear and echoed in my brother's. It mocked us and tempted us with the faintest sliver of hope. And for all that it offered, I could not lift my hand from the cask I clung to, not even to offer my brother up to its maw in exchange for my own life.

And so it was with disbelief that I took the first blow. Surprise that my brother assaulted me in such a fashion kept me from raising my hands in defense, and with a vicious frenzy, he sliced through the lifelines that leashed me to the cask, wrested it away, and dashed to the rail. He paused, just for the shortest moment, and I thought he would look back, but he spared not a glance. Wrapping a loose rope around his arms, he took up the cask and leaped into the circling sea.

The demon—for who else comes to those in peril of their lives and offers such blasphemous bargains?—sighed, a deep, rattling current that sounded like the groan of the wood under the weight of the waves. It spoke again, and this time, I understood every word with a terrifying clarity.

The calm, perfect circles of the Moskoe-ström shuddered, and then, with a barely perceptible movement, they began to collapse. I clung to the iron ring my brother had abandoned, desperately seeking an escape, but none was to be had.

Around my once-sturdy ship, the detritus and fragments of my fellow ghosts arose—masts, broken hulls, the flotsam and jetsam of those who had braved the channel and been dragged down its throat.

As the powerful waves collapsed around me, I thought I caught the faintest glimpse of my brother, eyes shut tight against the sea, clinging to the cask which he had wrenched from my grasp to satisfy a demon's appetite.

Ah, now, you no longer nod. You stare, aghast. Perhaps I see...disbelief? No matter. I have tried many times to tell this tale, but the words would not come, no matter how many times I tried to rinse them from my throat.

Shall I tell you, then, of the feeling of drowning? Have you felt such a thing? How could you know the smothering panic as the demon of the Ström reaches up to wrap you in its cold arms?

The ring slipped from my grasp, and I was afloat, caught and pulled in every direction at once, powerless against the mighty pull of the current. Did I loose my bowels? Did I scream against the water as it entered my body? I cannot recall. I do remember the insistent grasp that forced my eyes open, that reached into my soul, my being, that spurred my consciousness, so that even as the saltwater choked and pummeled me, I remained aware of everything and everyone who joined me there in the waves, the former sacrifices other sailors had made to the maelstrom.

The waiter glanced disinterestedly at the man sitting at the very end of the bar. He thought he was American at first—tall, even for an American, with blond hair and gray eyes, with one strong, well-formed hand—the left one. His right the man kept hidden, under the bar, as if something were misshapen about it.

Was he American? The waiter had never heard an accent like the one the man spoke with, so perhaps he was from one of the Nordic countries. The waiter wasn't sure, but the man had spent a good deal of money, enough to make the time he sat there worth it for the bar.

Still, it was strange that the old man hadn't been in. He'd been coming to the bar regularly for so many years that the waiter would sometimes find him camped at the door, waiting for the bar to open so he could regain his seat. He was tall like the American, and now that the waiter thought about it—there wasn't much else to do, this late at night, with most everyone finished up and headed out already—the old man and this young, new man had a certain similarity to each other. Especially around those gray eyes. That color that matched the waters under cloudy skies.

Ha! He was getting poetic, this late at night. His wife, if she were alive, would have laughed at him getting so fanciful about some tourist. It wasn't as if the Philippines didn't see thousands of them this time of year.

The old man wasn't a tourist though. He was a storyteller. The old man loved to talk. He had brought some amount of notoriety to the bar, as tourists learned of the expat who told tall tales of old ships and derring-do on the high seas. So much of it had to be the leaky memory of an old sailor mourning his glory days. The old man had been a fixture at the bar even before the waiter had come to work there, many years ago.

The new man, as the waiter thought of him, raised his left hand and signaled for one more round. He laid a crisp bill on the bar, enough for the drink and a sizable tip. The waiter sighed and looked around the otherwise empty room, then shrugged and poured another shot into the glass. It would be a late night—was already early morning, in fact. Still, even if he did usher the man out and close up the floor-to-ceiling French doors that opened the bar to the night breezes that brought the smell of salt in off the bay—there was no one waiting for him. Might as well earn a few more dollars.

"You must have known my brother."

The waiter, startled, almost dropped the bottle. He glanced up to see the new man looking directly at him.

"He came here, every night, to tell his story." The new man kept gazing at the waiter. "You must have heard the tale."

Only about a hundred times a week. But the man who told it was too old to be this man's brother. Grandfather, perhaps. The waiter looked away, carefully placing the bottle back in its spot on the bar. He didn't know what this new man wanted from him, but even the crisp bills that kept appearing on the bar couldn't still the unease that was growing in him.

"It wasn't exactly a lie," the new man continued. "But it was certainly not the whole truth. And while that tale made it out to the world, I was trapped, becalmed in a strange sea, unable to scream or shout or cry.

Unable, even, to hate my brother, because I knew that, given the chance, I would make the same choice."

The waiter nodded, darting his eyes toward the door, hoping the new man would take the hint.

"The demon knew of the tale," the new man said. "He whispered it to me in his incomprehensible tongue, as I sobbed in his grasp, under the water. He spoke to me of many things—things in this world, things my brother had done, the many lifetimes he lived, lifetimes stolen from those in the demon Ström's embrace."

This new man was insane, the waiter decided, although whether it was from the strong, dark rum he'd been drinking since the early afternoon, or if there was something else. It was time for him to go.

"Wait."

The waiter looked up and was immediately caught in the new man's wild, powerful gaze.

"Wait." The new man reached out a hand, then rested it on the bar. "The demon finally tired of its game. Fewer and fewer ships plied those waters, and in the years that followed, the fish ran less and less. Perhaps it grew bored with its watery hoard of debris and souls, but one day it came to me to offer my own deal."

Here, the man paused to finish his drink in one sullen gulp. He placed the glass on the bar. The waiter was relieved to see that it was not followed by another bill.

"Sir—"

"Wait." He drew the back of his hand across his mouth. "I can still taste the salt. I will never not taste salt." Looking back up, he caught the waiter's eye again. "The demon loosed me from its grasp and set me on my travels. I made my way as best I could, my promise rancid inside. For he was still my brother, the man I sought.

"As I traveled, I tried to tell my story, to share my tale. And yet, no matter how receptive the audience, how unobtrusive the words, I found myself unable to utter a word, even when I found myself alone, solitary, as I often did."

The waiter made the mistake of coming too close to pick up the empty glass. The man across the bar reached out with the sudden violence of a striking cobra and grabbed his arm.

With his right hand.

The waiter swallowed back a sudden urge to void his stomach. The new man's right hand was not, as the waiter had thought, misshapen. But the dark stain, mostly dry, covering it from fingertips to well above his wrist, could only be blood.

The man's grip was moist, clammy, and the waiter smelled iron and rot, the kind of malodour the sea threw off at low tide among the fallen timbers of the old pier.

"I loved my brother," the new man said. The wind picked up, the steady breeze off the water growing more urgent, more wild as the man spoke. "I loved him, and even as I traveled to find him, I thought I could not go through with it."

The wind buffeted the waiter, screeching around him, knocking a bottle to the floor. He blinked his eyes against the salt that the wind brought with it, struggling to pull back from the man's grasp, thinking only of escaping this crazy foreign man and the strange, incomprehensible speech that muttered under the storm.

The man stood, holding tightly to the waiter, raising his voice to be heard over the maelstrom.

"I loved him and, I think my brother could have forgiven me, as I could have forgiven him." The man's eyes flashed as the waiter cowered. Lightning flashed, turning the blood on the man's hand a brighter red, just for a moment before fading away. "You are my witness. I made my deal, as he made his, and the storm claims us all in the end."

The waiter set his feet against the bar and yanked away from the man's grasp with all his might. He crashed against the back of the bar and fell to the ground.

The air stilled. Scrambling to his feet, the waiter grabbed a paring knife from the chopping block where he'd been slicing limes a lifetime ago. Panting, he wiped the sweat and salt from his forehead and eyes, blinking against the night.

The tall, blond man with the fierce gray eyes nodded once, as if satisfied that someone had finally heard him out.

In the uncanny silence left by the sudden, unnatural squall, the waiter gazed in horror as the lines deepened in the man's face. The shadows lengthened and darkened. The skin of his face and hands contracted, tightening to the texture of salted jerky, highlighting the prominent cheekbones of the skull beneath, the sharp relief of the bones in the hand. The man's clothes draped longer as the body beneath them shrank into itself, collapsing and wrenching the man's head back.

The man screamed a short, final scream, then threw himself forward, his skeletal right hand, still stained with his brother's blood, reaching across the dark wood of the bar. Those unsettling gray eyes caught the waiter's glance. They glowed momentarily with the spark of the midnight sun, and collapsed under the weight of the man's disintegrating skull.

In the darkness of the empty bar, the only sound to break the silence was the waiter's scream that went on and on, like the wail of a demon caught in the throat of the maelstrom.

EDEN

R.S. BELCHER

This story takes place several years prior to Six-Gun Tarot
Nevada, 1867

At the edge of the Forty-Mile Desert was a tiny sliver of life clinging by dirty, cracked fingernails to the edge of oblivion. The town was called Golgotha and it was on one of the routes west for all those dreaming of a new life and a new frontier. Golgotha reached out, silently, imperceptibly, to the souls that wandered this desolate land, calling to the best and the worst, the blessed and the damned. Golgotha claimed them all as her own.

The sun squatted fat and bloody in the slate of the morning sky. Sheriff Jon Highfather looked at the crimson sun, read its guts, and knew death had preceded the new day.

"How many this time?" he asked.

"Best we can cipher, four," Mutt said. Mutt was the only name the gaunt Indian half-breed had ever given Highfather. He carried the moniker like a challenge. He was the other half of the law in Golgotha, Jon's only deputy. They had met six months ago when Jon had pulled him out of the Paradise Falls saloon, with a brick in his hat to beat all. Even drunk, Mutt gave Jon the toughest fight he'd ever had. It ended with both of them bloody and laughing like lunatics. When Mutt sobered up, Jon offered him the job and surprisingly, the drifter took it.

"This is just like what happened last year, ain't it?" Mutt said, pushing his hat back on his head. His features were cruel and sharp, his face craggy as a desert mesa. He always had a sardonic knife-cut of a smile playing at the corners of his mouth. "I heard old Doug Fenton and some of the others talking about it. Homes broken into, people murdered, sometimes with their loved ones laying right next to them. A handprint left on the door in blood. Real Angel of Death."

In any other town, the thought would go to this being the work of bandits, or renegade Indians, maybe some religious lunatic, but Golgotha seldom got that lucky. There were never easy answers here, at least not answers that came off as sane or rational. The fact that in his short spell as sheriff, Jon had encountered things that could only be described as monsters. Everyone in the town knew the secret, but everyone pretended there was always a reasonable explanation. Kept folks sane.

There was no theft, nothing missing. More often than not the victim was savaged, but someone sleeping next to them, or a few feet away, was spared, untouched. No tracks were ever found, human, animal or otherwise. Always, the red hand print was left to mark the killer's passing. One of the Mormon townsfolk had likened it to the Angel of Death that visited the homes of the Egyptians in the Old Testament, killing only the firstborn child. The grisly nickname stuck. For all the good things, good people, Golgotha sheltered against the wasteland, this was the price, always the price—evil, blood, and death.

"Yes," Highfather said after a long silence. "A year ago, almost to the day. Last time it was an even dozen, over three nights." He saw Eden's face, spider-webbed with crimson. So still. He swallowed hard.

"Jonathan, you okay?"

Highfather nodded, "He's not getting away again."

He saw her for the first time when she climbed off the morning stage. That had been, what, two years ago? Even after days of being locked in the coach with the other passengers, she was the most beautiful woman Jon ever laid eyes on. Her hair was so fair, it seemed to drink in the sun. Her blue eyes reminded him of sunlight on water. She was slender and tall, almost as tall as Jon. She struggled with a large, leather travel trunk. He rushed across the street to help her.

"Here, let me," he said.

"Oh, no thank you," she said in a voice that was confident and sweet. She glanced at his jacket and saw the badge, "Sheriff."

"Jon," he said, "Jon Highfather."

"Eden Crane." She managed to move a few steps forward, using both hands to hang on for dear life to the luggage.

Jon slid his hand into one of the chest's handles, brushing against Eden's hand, "Pleased to meet you. Let me give you a hand. It looks like you have an entire house in this one bag." She laughed at that and relented, letting Jon take the bag.

"I'm sorry it's so heavy, it is all of my worldly possessions. Are you here to meet me? Was the mayor detained?"

"Mayor? Harry's meeting you?"

"Our correspondence indicated he would, yes."

Before Jon could say another word, Golgotha's mayor, Harry Pratt, had crossed Main Street from Town Hall and joined them before the coach station. Pratt was a strikingly handsome man with hair the color of rust that fell to the collar of his fine coat. He wore a handlebar mustache and prominent mutton chops. Harry broke into a wide, practiced smile as soon as he saw them.

"Ms. Miss Crane, I must apologize for my delay. I hope our earnest sheriff has not already convinced you to jump back on the coach!"

"Harry, Mayor Pratt," Jon said with a nod.

"Not at all," Eden said to Harry, "In fact, Sheriff Highfather has been most pleasant company."

"Ah, you caught him on a good day I see. So, Jon, what do you think of our new school teacher?"

Highfather smiled at Eden, "I guess you weren't kidding about all your worldly possessions in that bag. Welcome to Golgotha, Miss Crane." The look she gave him in that moment branded him, marked him forever.

"Please," she said. "Eden."

"Got anything that might help me, Mr. Turlough?" Jon asked.

Clay Turlough, Golgotha's resident liveryman, taxidermist, and amateur scientist, had a wild fringe of hair swirling about his liver-spotted pate. Clay always smelled faintly of sour chemicals and decay, but he was the smartest man Jon ever met, and if there was anyone in Golgotha who might be able to suss out who the Angel of Death was, it was Turlough.

"Please, Jonathan, just Clay's fine," Jon had ridden out to Clay's place at the end of Duffer Road. He found Clay puttering about in one of the barns he had converted into a makeshift laboratory. He was examining two of the shattered doors from the homesteads of two of the victims. Clay had scattered some odd powder over the broken doors.

"What you got, Clay?"

"I examined the doors of the victim's homes," Clay said, "I was looking for ridge impressions."

"Impressions?"

"About nine years ago, this British administrator in India named Herschel insisted on having an inked impression of the ridge patterns on a person's thumb be affixed to any official documents along with the person's signature. He claimed the patterns are unique to each individual and could be used for positive identification. I figure if our murderer is knocking these doors open, maybe they are leaving their mark on them."

"Well don't that beat the Dutch! You find anything?"

"Some smudges, probably left by fingers, most likely in gloves—looks like heavy gloves, maybe made from some kind of...chain mail?

"Chain mail? You mean like King Arthur?"

Clay shrugged, "I'll examine the impressions in greater detail and see if I can glean anything else for you Jonathan. I know how important catching this villain is to you. I'll help however I'm able. I should probably examine the interiors of the homes as well to see if I find anything useful."

"You do that, and thanks, Clay." Turlough looked at him oddly, like he didn't quite understand the words, and went back to his examination.

Highfather had built the cabin just off Absalom Road as a honeymoon present for Eden, the beginning of their new life, the life that never happened. Most nights he slept in a vacant cell at the jail. He came here when he needed to clean up, or a change of clothes.

It was getting dark, and the Angel would be out again tonight. This time he came for the book. It was on the fireplace mantle beside a bunch of long-dead flowers, the stems wrapped in a blue hair ribbon. Jon took the book down gingerly. It was old, its cover brown and faded. The spine read in flaked, gold-leaf letters, *Sartain's Magazine 1851.* Jon sat at the edge of his cold, unmade bed and opened the book carefully, reverently. The poem was bookmarked with a scrap of paper. Eden's delicate ornate handwriting had faded a little, but he knew every word written in the margin of the page:

My Jonathan,
I will wait for you in our kingdom by the sand.
My Love Always,
E.

The poem was by Poe. Jon never heard of him before Eden—another gift she gave him he could never properly thank her for. He rubbed his eyes—he hadn't slept in two days. He read the first line, heard it in her voice. It crashed into him, like a wave. He remembered—there was never a time where he could forget.

"Golgotha has a rather unsavory reputation, Jon," Eden said as Highfather handed her a slice of apple. Class was dismissed for the day and the children were gone. Jon had come by the schoolhouse, just off Rose Road, with a basket of food prepared by his landlady, Gillian Proctor. "I heard quite a bit about it on the coach ride. At least two of the people on the stage urged me to not come here." She laughed; it was a beautiful sound. Jon shrugged and dabbed his lips with a napkin. "Another prayed over me, entreating protection from the evil forces that reside here."

"I got told the same thing when I showed up here last year," Jon said. "Funny thing is the folk who are the loudest ones to tell you to leave are the ones who turn out to have stayed here the longest."

"Is it really that bad?" Eden asked.

"It can be. This place, it draws the best and the worst of everything to itself. The bad can be...really bad." A memory stabbed him, and he almost winced from it. "Really bad."

"And the good?" Eden's eyes were blue-gray. They made Jon think of the sky before a storm. Jon swallowed hard. Just looking at her made his heart jump. She was the most beautiful woman he'd ever seen. Looking at her chased the horror of the memory away.

"The good, is very, very good."

"Is that why you stayed? Became sheriff?"

"That's a long story," he said. "and not a very pretty one for a picnic."

"I love a good story," she said, a smile playing at the edges of her lips, "and I must confess a fondness for stories of the macabre." Her eyes widened and she stood. "That reminds me, I have something to share with you."

"Please don't turn into a giant gila monster," Jon muttered under his breath.

"What?"

"What?" Jon hastily responded.

Eden handed him an old book, hardbound with a frayed, brown, cloth cover. "I wanted to share this with you." She opened it to a bookmarked page. "This poem, it made me think of you."

"Really?" Jon said. "I've never really considered myself the poem-type."

"Well, you are, Sheriff. Get used to it."

"Okay. Don't tell Mutt. He'll tease me."

She began to read. Her voice, soft but strong, filled the empty school-house, "It was many and many a year ago, In a kingdom by the sea, That a maiden there lived whom you may know by the name of Annabel Lee..."

Jon listened, caught in the spell of her voice and the melancholy words. It was a beautiful, terrible view into one man's ultimate love and loss. It spoke to the broken parts inside Jon left from the madness of the war, the death of his brother, his loneliness. He looked into her perfect face, her perfect eyes. It all seemed unreal, too good. Too good for him, too good for this world. A pale bloom defiant against the harsh winter. It took him a moment to realize she had finished. Eden looked at him as she lowered the book.

"Why me?" he muttered.

"What?"

Jon shook off her spell as best he could. "Why...does that remind you of me?"

"You'd wait," she said. "Come what may, you'd wait."

Alone at the edge of the bed they had shared for such a short time, Jon thought he had long ago emptied himself of tears, that the well of his pain was dry. He was wrong.

"It may seem odd to say it, but the actual killings are a mercy," Dr. Gorgon said.

"What?" Jon said. He was several days past exhaustion. Another night had passed in Golgotha, another three people were dead, with no sign of the Angel, no trace of his passing other than the corpses. Jon and Mutt met the doctor at his office to see if his examination of the victims to date yielded any clues.

"How the hell you reckon any of this a mercy, Doc?" Mutt asked.

"The incision used to end their lives is quick, simple and relatively painless, Deputy," the town's doctor said. Gorgon was a tall, austere man, seemingly washed out of color. He was well-respected among the towns-folk of Golgotha as an excellent physician, but Jon heard more than one of the locals mention that the doc was something of a cold fish. "It is the postmortem wounds that seem the most severe. Each victim is disem-boweled, their livers or spleens excised with, I must say, expert precision. Your killer has exceptional skill with a knife, Sheriff." Gorgon noted the look both men gave him at the remark. "I assure you gentlemen, if I was your Angel of Death I would not point that out to you."

"Thanks, Doctor," Jon said.

Outside Gorgon's office the business of Golgotha continued like any other morning. Wagons clattered along the muddy thoroughfare of Main Street while riders on horseback darted between them. Cowboys, Chinese laborers, and Mormon shopkeepers flowed past the two lawmen on the wooden planks that were Golgotha's sidewalks, a river of human-ity. Any one of them could be the Angel of Death. No, not anyone, Jon corrected himself. Someone who knew how to use a knife as a profession, someone who probably used chainmail gloves to protect his hands from cuts and nicks while working. Highfather blinked in the bright sunlight and tried to make some sense of it.

Mutt's voice was low and gruff near his ear, "Jonathan, let's get some grub. You ain't ate squat in a spell. C'mon, I'll spring. How's a hot pot of coffee and a pair of steaks sound?"

Jon turned to his deputy as if coming out of a trance, "What? What did you say?" The image was sharp in his foggy brain. Steak, meat, cuts.

Eden's skin felt like a partner to his own. When he held her, when he explored her, it was like discovering a lost part of himself. One kiss led to a second, to a third, each more hungry, more insistent than the last. They were in the bed in the cabin he built for them. Nothing, no one, ever felt as right, as complete as she did. In the darkness, their faces close, he whispered, "I love you." Her blue eyes caught the moonlight like stained glass.

"I love you," she said, "I always have. I always will."

It felt as if all the spirals, all the motions of heaven and earth turned, locked, and Jon knew a peace and a happiness he had never known in all his days.

"Always," he said.

Bill Ferro's ranch was on the outskirts of Golgotha in the ribbon of living land that ringed Argent Mountain before the withering hand of the desert re-exerted its domain. Jon rode his horse, Bright, up Argent, past the squatter encampments, full of the destitute, desperate men and women who lost their livelihood and their hope when the Argent mines went bust. He took Backtrail Road down the western slope of the mountain and reached the farm well after noon. Jon had sent Mutt off to talk to Professor Mephisto, the owner of Golgotha's only playhouse, and something of a local expert on the preternatural. They wanted to see if perhaps there was something significant to the days involved in the onslaught last year and again this year. Tonight was the Angel's final night to hunt if his pattern remained the same and they were running out of daylight. The last night he would appear perhaps for another year, perhaps forever. If Jon was wrong, and they had to split up, there was too much ground to cover. Eden died a year ago this night.

Ferro was a rancher. He slaughtered and butchered his own stock, as well as doing it for others in and around Golgotha for pay. He even supplied clients as far away as the town of Hazen.

A butcher—someone who knew his way around a knife and who was an expert with precise cuts. Every butcher Highfather had ever known always made sure her wore protection as the blade slid and danced under his command. A stay slip and you could lose fingers or worse. It wasn't much to go on, but it was all he had.

Jon had only heard of Ferro, maybe saw him in a crowd a few times since he became sheriff. No one ever said a cross word about Ferro, no one ever mentioned anything odd or out of the ordinary about him, but Jon was already beginning to understand one of the unspoken rules of Golgotha—everyone here carried a secret, a hidden face.

The teeth of the desert peaks were already biting at the edges of the bloating sun as the sheriff rode past the main gate of Ferro's ranch. Jon's hand drifted to the stock of the sheathed rifle he carried on his saddle. He noticed the gate was adorned with animal skulls - cattle, coyotes, desert hares, and foxes.

There was a main house and several outbuildings and barns. It appeared the cattle had already been brought in for the evening as the fields were empty. He slowed and halted Bright near the well that resided between the cluster of buildings. He dismounted, Winchester in hand, looped Bright's reins to a post and let the horse lap at the watering trough.

The ranch was still. The wind whistled off the plain and gently jingled a bit and bridle that hung on the awning post to the closest building. Jon saw no signs of any ranch hands, of anyone.

He pushed open the door and stepped inside. The late afternoon sunlight poured down through the windows. Shadows filled the large room. Something creaked. Jon leveled the rifle and moved further inside, leaving the door open. Jon carefully navigated the blind corners, past walls of baled hay, making sure each shadow was empty.

Toward the center of the room, he discovered a massive, heavy wooden table about three and a half feet off the ground. The table had a raised five-inch lip all the way around the edge. Near the table was an easel and a small shelf crowded with books. Jon rested the Winchester on his shoulder as he puzzled over the strange drawings on the easel. They looked like anatomical drawings of two organs with notes in Latin pointing to hundreds of different spots on both. Jon wished he had learned more of the ancient language growing up, but he only comprehended a smattering. He looked down at the table and noticed the dark stains ingrained in the table's surface. The floor groaned and Jon began to turn, when a brilliant light flared behind his eyes and a terrible pressure struck his skull.

Jon, Jon. It was Eden, her voice, the smell of wildflowers and soap on her skin, the caress of her lips, like the flutter of a bird's wing—the sweetest kiss he'd ever tasted. *You have to wake up now, Jon. Please, my love. This isn't your end, the end of your poem. Please, wake up.*

"I want to be with you," he muttered, "stay with you."

We are a verse, darling, but not the final one. Such a sweet verse though.

"Is this a dream?"

It's all a dream, she said.

He was on the table, his wrists and ankles bound, his shirt removed and the numerous bullet-wound pockmarks and raised, white knife scars on his chest visible. He managed to focus his eyes with some effort and great pain. Standing over him was Ferro, an unremarkable man, easy to lose, or mistake, in a crowd. Thinning brown-gray hair and a fringe of a beard. Eyes the color of muddy water. He wore chain mail gloves that went to his elbows, fastened by leather garters. The gloves caught the light of the lanterns that were now lit as night had come. He was searching Highfather's face intently.

"Where were you?" he asked, his voice surprisingly gentle.

"A better place," Jon said. "You're under arrest, Mr. Ferro."

Ferro nodded but didn't smile. "More than you may ever comprehend, sheriff. You're the last, for now. Until it is demanded of me again, until the great wheel spins in the heavens. Golgotha will be safe. I hope that gives you some comfort."

"Why? Why all of them? Why her?"

"The universe is wrought with channels of cause and effect, they pull on us like the strings on a marionette, moving us, guiding us. Even as a boy I could see them, see their interplay. With time..." he nodded toward the easel, "and study I came to understand their intent. We all play roles, Sheriff, we all have a part, like notes in a symphony, and we play those parts again and again and again."

Jon's arms were above his head and held fast. He moved his numb fingers as best he could and felt the hob nail that the ropes at his wrist were attached to. He tried to keep Ferro's eyes on his own as he began to work the knot of the ropes against the nail, pushing it into the heart of the binding.

"You, most of all, Sheriff. Your part is extensive, and complex, no simple melody. We will have this discussion again many times before the stars burn out and fade."

"You're trying to tell me it was those people's fates to die at your hand? Who the hell made you god, Ferro? She was one of the finest people I've ever met in this slaughterhouse of a world, she had a good heart. Of all the things that are golden in this life, you have any idea how rare a good heart is, a true love? She deserved to live a damn sight more than you do, than I do."

"There is no god, Jonathan," Ferro said, tearing up. "There is our time, our motion. No morality calls the dance. It is cause and effect and we are its slave—me, most of all."

The nail began to spread the knot, loosening it.

"For whatever it may mean, you two were destined. We dance this reel in grand circles, Jonathan, and the song plays again, and again." Ferro raised a long, narrow, and very sharp blade into view, the lamp light catching it. It was made to cleanly and quickly butcher a carcass. "I will see you in the next stanza."

The blade moved toward his neck, but Highfather drove his freed fist into Ferro's jaw before the steel could kiss his vein. The butcher stumbled back, hitting the post that held one of the lamps and smashing it, fire and scattered light engulfed some of the bundles of hay. Jon sat up, his head swimming from the sucker punch Ferro had given him earlier. He fumbled for the six-gun at his belt. Ferro, partly on fire, wreathed in smoke, and seemingly oblivious to his state, advanced. Jon's nostrils flared at the stench of crisping flesh. Ferro's eyes were clear and free of pain even as his skin snapped and popped like a knotted log tossed in a stove.

"Jonathan! Jonathan, you okay?" Mutt called from near the door. Jon aimed the Colt at Ferro's chest, thumbing back the hammer. Ferro froze.

"Drop it," the sheriff said as he freed his feet from the rope with his other hand. The fire was beginning to catch, smoke drifted everywhere. Ferro nodded, as if answering some unheard question.

"Next time," he said and lunged forward. The pistol retort was like the hammer of an angry god, smashing apart worlds.

"Sumbitch was as crazy as a loon with sun poisoning," Mutt said. The whole building was a pyre, sending sparks drifting upward to the silent stars, like an offering to cold, mute gods. Many of the neighboring ranchers had seen the blaze and come running to fight it. Their shouts and cussing were audible over the roar of the blaze, as were the cries of many frightened animals. "Come on, Jonathan, they got this. Let's let Doc Gorgon take a look at you."

Highfather walked unsteadily away from his deputy, silently out into the field, the blaze at his back and the cold sea of darkness ahead of him. "Jonathan?"

He heard the poem, her voice, her laughter. He felt the joy of her skin, the taste of her lips, the sweet fullness of her love, and the treasure of being lost in something greater than one heartbeat, one breath. He understood the words of the poem better than he had ever thought he could. He'd never seen the ocean, but Highfather felt what it felt like to stand alone at the edge of such yawning emptiness, understood, here in his kingdom by the sea.

AMORE

L. MARIE WOOD

Too hard.

In the end, it was too hard and he couldn't use it.

There was no way it would ever feel right, ever move right, ever be... right.

She wouldn't have held her arms that way, on her hips in that unnatural pose.

She never would have turned her leg out, knee facing forward, sassy.

She wasn't sassy.

Well, she was, but he didn't like that she was sassy. Not at all.

Sassy wasn't who she *really* was – what she was *really* about. It was part of someone else, this made up woman, the one that she wanted the world to see. She liked for them to think she was sassy, sharp-tongued, almost mean with the way she quipped, always with a sarcastic smile on her lips. Always ready to cut. But he knew who she really was. He knew that her words weren't real, that they weren't what she meant to say even if she said them often and to anyone who would listen. He knew because she told him. She spoke to him in private even in the middle of a room full of people.

He knew Trina better than she knew herself.

And that's why he couldn't use the mannequin even if he had paid good money for it off a junkie who didn't even remember how he'd gotten it – probably hadn't gotten it himself at all, probably found it in a dumpster behind some store that went out of business. Yeah, that was probably how he had gotten it but it didn't matter- he wanted the green Max was offering up for it and he would say whatever he needed to say to get it. Rory couldn't use that mannequin because Trina wouldn't stand that way and he couldn't change that; the legs couldn't be repositioned on this old model from the 70s. Trina wouldn't cock her head that way either, her chin tilted to the side, her jawline accentuated, sticking out, jutting out, challenging. Well, maybe she would have done that. As he thought about it, he knew she would have, and he hated it. He hated the way she looked when her chin was sticking out defiantly, like she was going to do whatever the hell she wanted to do regardless of what anyone else felt, regardless of what someone else told her to do. She would not listen to anyone unless she wanted to and as much as he hated that about her, he loved it too. Maybe she would tell *him* what to do. Maybe she would whisper in his ear and tell him all the dirty little things she wanted him to do to her, with her, for her and he would do it. He would tell her he didn't want to but she wouldn't listen to that because she was that kind of girl, that kind of *woman* who did whatever the fuck, whatever the hell – wait...

Rory heard his breathing filling the cab of the truck – it was rapid and hot, almost like a dog panting. He had gotten excited again, damnit, and this time he was outside where people could see him. He couldn't help it, though. Just thinking of all the things he might have tried to tell Trina to do and her telling him to kiss her ass and then he'd do it, right then and there, even if they were in the middle of the street. Even if they were in his mother's goddamned living room, he'd kiss it if she told him to. That she might push him away and say that she didn't mean for him to really kiss her ass, that it was a figure of speech, that he must be dumb to think otherwise, and who the fuck *was* he anyway – that was just one of the games they played. He knew she didn't mean those words just like she didn't mean the words she said to those men who definitely wouldn't kiss her ass in the middle of the goddamned supermarket if she told them to. Definitely not.

But the mannequin was too hard and anyway it would take the right tool to make it look the way it should. He'd have to scrap it.

On to plan B.

Really, plan F, if he was being honest. But that didn't matter. He would do whatever he had to do to make it work because that's what she really wanted and he knew that. She told him with her eyes.

Pretty eyes.

Light brown, kinda yellowish, with this dark brown ring around them.

Rory felt like he could fall into them.

When she stared at him with those beautiful eyes under those eyebrows she worked so hard to maintain – she liked to say they were snatched. She laughed at Rory when he said snatched, said he might as well say on fleek, or cool, or fly. Said he sounded old school. Well, she didn't say those things to him, not like that, but she told him all right, told him through the mirror, told him as he looked in on her at her job and she was easy to see because her beautician's chair was near the back door, the back door where there was a window that was just big enough to see in without seeming like you were trying to take a peek. And Rory did look in on her because he knew she wanted him to and he heard her tell him that he wasn't cool but that she loved him anyway. Those beautiful brown eyes. She knew just how to make his heart sing with them.

He had to try something else.

He had to calm down.

People were watching.

People were always watching.

He saw them, all the time watching her. She couldn't go anywhere without someone scoping her every movement. It was terrible. Sometimes he wondered if she could feel their eyes on her, and if she could, he wondered if she liked them. Of course not. She wasn't the kind of girl to want people to look at her all the time, to be on stage, in front of a camera, sitting there like a fish in a fishbowl. She didn't want people always watching her, always talking about her, always following her or friending her or liking her pictures or tweeting or snapping or whatever the hell else they were doing with her. Tik-toking her – at least that's what he thought it was called.

Whatever.

Eye-fucking her. In the end, that's all it was.

She didn't like all of that and he knew it. He could tell by how dead her eyes looked in the pictures she posted… how vacant.

Trina was like that when she danced too – her eyes so far away. Except when she saw him looking at her, saw *him*, knew he was there, knew she was safe. And when she took her clothes off he didn't look, well, at least not directly, not the way they did, so obvious so she could see them doing it, because she was looking at him and she needed him to be looking back to get through it all. Even though she smiled up there on that tiny little

stage, just enough space to twirl for the slobbering mob, like wolves sali-
vating over a fresh kill, the bastards; even though she smiled when they
gave her money, pushed it into her G-string, copped a feel when they
weren't supposed to touch-

don't touch –

never touch –

he knew she wasn't looking at them, wasn't interested in their nasty,
groping, dirty hands.

She wasn't looking at them, she didn't want them, couldn't stand them,
in her red sparkly bra and panty set with the rhinestones or the black see-
through thing with the fur he liked. She wasn't looking at them, didn't
care if they liked what she was wearing – what she was taking off. But she
cared about him, cared if he liked what he saw. She wore it for him. She
licked her lips and blew all her kisses to him and not that guy in the front
row with the greasy hair and a wad of dollar bills. She rubbed her titties
for *him*, not the one-eyed piece of shit at the corner of the stage that liked
to bend down and see if he could look up at her snatch when she leaned
over, to get a closer view of what she was hiding behind that thin strip of
material.

She looked at Rory and no one else. And when the downers threatened to pull her into slumber before she finished the lap dance for the
college boy that came in and thrusted up against her, trying to get his
rocks off before the guard noticed, it was his eyes she looked into, Rory's
eyes that gave her peace.

The plaster was easy to buy, but the mold was harder. He ended up
just doing the head because it was the only thing he could find a model
for, especially after he got rid of the mannequin. Too fast, maybe he had
gotten rid of it too fast. He could have used the torso, probably, though
not the arms – the angle was too weird, too unnatural. Whatever. He'd get
another one. Get something else. He'd figure it out. But he realized all too
late that he needed a head. Easy peasy once he broke the picture window
at the hair salon. They wouldn't miss one of those heads he saw her
working on when nobody was around, trying to figure out how to put in
microlocs.

He only needed one.

Rory tried to get the one she used most of the time, tried to get all the
way to her chair and snag it, but he had broken a window at the front of
the store, not the back, and he got nervous. He just took the one closest to
the broken window and called it done.

He couldn't get caught doing something stupid.

He couldn't get caught at all

Because then who would she look at? Who would she have to help her through all the shit she dealt with, help her know she was ok, help her see the truth about everything?

Rory couldn't get caught.

He couldn't.

So he took whatever head he could reach and ran, ran like hell, ran like there was a gun trained on the back of his head, ran like he might die if he slowed down.

It didn't matter which head he took.

It didn't matter because she would love it anyway.

Burned.

That shit burned Rory's nose more than he thought it would. There in the cab of the truck, he felt like he might cough up a lung, was sure he would soon start spitting up blood if he didn't stop unscrewing the top to the formaldehyde but he couldn't help it. He needed to touch, needed to feel it under his fingers and well, shit, if a little burning and a little coughing, a little runny nose, and watery eyes – if that was what he had to bear to get close, so close, closer than anybody ever had before, then he would just have to do it. Because that's what she wanted him to do. She wanted him to touch, to feel her flesh beneath his fingertips, to know her that way, better than anyone else. He already knew she did, and had been wanting him to do that for a long, long time. He had been teasing *her* for a change, making *her* wait. Making *her* want. Nobody ever seemed to do that – they always let her take the upper hand and control the way things went, but not Rory. And that's what she liked about him: that he took control. That he wasn't afraid to do exactly that, if the situation called for it, and boy, did she know how to make the situation call for it. One time she walked right by him like she hadn't seen him there. He had even whispered her name and she didn't turn her head, acting like he was just some guy on the street, some unimportant man who was there, just there . Rory guessed she had to do that because she was meeting some guy for a date, some guy she was planning to let take her out and feed her a fancy dinner, give her money, whatever – money she would probably use to buy her Rory something nice. Maybe that turntable he was looking at and some records so he could go back to DJing again because she liked when he was a DJ when they were in school together and he used to play all the parties and make all the girls get up and dance. Yeah, she used to look at him from across the room even back then, those pretty brown eyes staring him down like she wanted to kiss him, fuck him there in front of everyone. And she would do it, too, if he let her but they were in public and he didn't want everyone to see her body like that – he didn't want her to show everything that was his, so he didn't answer her call when she looked at him like that in front of people because, you know she could be impulsive and their shit was theirs so he wanted to preserve it even if she couldn't control her own self.

But yeah, she was gonna buy him something like that – he knew she was saving up for something special, like maybe even a car or some shit and they could take it and drive across the world and have babies in France, but that was ok, he didn't need all that to be happy with her. He knew what they needed and he would just have to show her so she would understand.

She would.

If he showed her right, she would understand.

His smart girl Trina.

She would understand everything.

The plaster took a long time to set, but that was ok. Once it was done it was perfect, exactly what she would want it to be. He just had to show her.

The jar was almost too full of that stuff when he added to it, casting it off on the surface like putting one of those paper lanterns in the lake. Delicate-like. Because it was precious cargo. In contrast with the rough skin on his hands, dirt crushed under his fingernails and in the lines that swirled on his fingers, he was gentle then. Some of the dirt that was so much a part of him, he didn't notice it came off in the formaldehyde and he was sorry for that. It made him upset to see the crud dancing around her corneas, clinging to, cleaving to, embedding in the pink of her optic nerve. Like a cable, that thing was. He'd had to cut it out of her head to get the whole thing. He even took some of her brain, not much – just the part that was connected to her eyes by the fleshy cord because that's the part that would have known him best. He figured if she was going to see him, really see him and him alone, she would need everything she had used before and then some.

He set some flowers in the plaster, pretty and pink, just like she liked.

When her eyes went cloudy on him, her corneas blocking that beautiful brown that he loved so much, he tried to fix it with food coloring. He found a syringe in an alley in the city, one that she would have been damned angry about if he ever told her how he'd found it lying in a puddle filled with what could have been piss just as easily as it could have been rainwater – anyhow, he filled the syringe with yellow and a little bit of this brown food coloring he found at one of those cheap stores where nothing costs over .99 cents. Some off-brand thing that literally looked like shit when he squeezed it out. He mixed that together and shot that into her eye to bring the color back but it didn't work. He'd try it again but the first time had gotten to him a little. They were hard to poke, those beautiful eyes, and he spent more time than he wanted jabbing at them only for them to roll away in the formaldehyde. When he did get the needle in and pushed the weirdly greenish muck all the way, it seemed like all the color went behind the cloudiness, depositing it in front of the irises he loved for safekeeping and doing nothing about the white film. Her eyes were gross now, snot-like white over some weird backdrop of haze on lime greenish shit.

At least he hadn't dyed the whites by mistake. He might have vomited then and she wouldn't have liked that at all… not one bit.

He'd have to try again once he set them in the plaster.

After his eyes stopped burning.

Trina was looking at him and she liked what she saw.

He'd have to fix the hair the way she wanted it and make her a body before too long, but that would all come. And she'd wait for it because she was happy. He could tell. She told him with her eyes.

RED (QUINCY'S VERSION)

JOHN G. HARTNESS

CHAPTER ONE

W hat the literal fuck is *that?*" I asked, shivering inside my Level Three Antimicrobial Containment Airlock Suit, or whatever the fuck the real name was for the oversized yellow Hefty bag with a windshield I was wearing. It was hotter than Satan's nutsack, with Atlanta clinging to its ball-melting summer heat and humidity like a bridesmaid fighting for a tossed bouquet.

I stood in an abandoned warehouse looking down at a corpse that might have been human at some point, but now was mostly just a rat's nest of hair, disconnected bones, and flesh that didn't seem to be where it belonged. I was pretty sure I could find an eye in the muck, and there was something that might be a femur, but most of it looked a lot like human soup stock. Whoever had done this was a bad mamma jamma.

"That seems to be the remains of one Lawrence Hetrick, a securities broker with an office downtown and a condo in Buckhead," said an officious skinny man similarly attired in a bright yellow trash bag.

"What happened to him?" I asked. "Because that's pretty fucking nasty."

"Is this what constitutes an expert opinion in your division, Deputy Director Flynn?" the snotty little prick asked my boss, Rebecca Gail Flynn. Becks is the Deputy Director for the Department of Homeland Security's Paranormal Division. The prick was Carl Segan, pronounced like Sagan but without any of the cool space stuff. He also worked for

Homeland for fifteen years after transferring over from the Treasury Department. He was very much a by-the-book kind of agent, which meant he and I were not going to like one another. I had a head start on him, though - I'd met him three minutes ago and already hated his guts. I didn't think he'd had time to form a real opinion of me yet.

"Mr. Harker has a..." Becks started.

I interrupted her. "Very particular set of skills, shall we say?" I put as much menace into the words as I could, channeling my inner Liam Neeson to the best of my ability. Must have worked, because Carl took a quick step back out of arm's reach. "Now why don't you quit trying to piss on the corpse to mark your fucking territory and tell me what you know, so the grownups can fucking work?"

He was obviously affronted, and perhaps a little appalled that someone would drop f-bombs so fluently in his vicinity, but I didn't care. He was a prick, and I'd been hauled out of bed in the middle of the night, flown to Atlanta on a private government jet, shoved into a Hefty bag, had a goldfish bowl stuck on my head, a SCUBA tank strapped to my back, and shown to a crime scene that looked like leftovers at a Dahmer family buffet. I wasn't happy, so I didn't care what the career bootlick thought about me.

"We...actually have no idea, Mr. Harker," Segan said, with the good grace to look a little embarrassed. "We were only called in because one of the monitors your group provided the local police department detected something anomalous and sent a signal to the local office. We secured the scene and contacted your people in Washington, as per protocol."

While I was pretty sure that this guy followed protocol in every aspect of his life, right down to taking a dump, I was glad for his adherence to procedure in this case. Our tech geeks had cooked up magical "sniffers," handheld devices that cops could use at strange crime scenes to detect hints of magic or supernatural activity. We told them it was to check for explosive residue, radiation, and biologicals, the unholy trinity of crime scene terrors. Any cop finding something like that wanted to hand it off to somebody else as fast as possible, so we made literally thousands of "sniffers" and equipped every major metropolitan area in the U.S. with them. In theory, the "sniffers" let cops know when to loop Homeland in on a case. In reality, if one detected something kinky, it automatically sent an encrypted message to the nearest DHS office and instructed them to call 1-800-555-2386, the fictional number for Ghostbusters. That last bit was just for my amusement, but the number did come to our office in D.C.

Carl and his crew got here, secured the scene, and called in the pros from Dover, as it were. Except when the body was discovered less than fifty miles from the Centers for Disease Control main office, a few other departments showed up to the party. Me, Becks, Carl and what remained of Mr. Hetrick might have been the only people inside the building, but there were literally dozens of folks in uncomfortable yellow suits milling around outside wondering what to do and how the hell they were supposed to scratch their noses. Or anything else.

"Okay, Agent Segan, we've got it from here," Becks said. "Please have your people continue to keep everyone who isn't part of my team out."

"How will we know they're part of your team?" Segan asked, simultaneously pissy about being kicked out of the crime scene and obviously relieved to be able to get as far away from the Hetrick pieces as possible.

"They'll be the ones with DHS badges who don't work in the same building as you, dipshit," I said, kneeling by the body and slipping into my Second Sight. The room exploded in a kaleidoscope of colors as I peered at the body in the magical spectrum. There was some serious fuckitude happening here. This guy was wreathed in reds, yellows, greens, and some kind of smoky orange aura that I'd never seen before but was instantly wary of. Put that together with the damage done to the body, and we had something seriously vile afoot.

I heard Segan leave, his tasseled loafers clicking across the concrete floor in a precise march toward the door. "You didn't have to be such a dick, Harker," Becks said.

"Three hours ago, I was in Charlotte with a gorgeous woman lying mostly naked beside me. Now I'm in Atlanta wearing a Level Three Containment Suit, sweating my balls off, looking down at the punchline to a frog in a blender joke. I kinda felt like being a dick."

"Well, do you see anything useful, Mr. Grumpypants?"

"No, which doesn't help my mood. There was serious magic thrown around here, but I can't tell if it all was directed at this guy, or if some of it came from him, too. There's definitely something supernatural about him, but I can't tell what it is."

"What's the next step? Is there any magical trace evidence we can use to follow our bad guy? Or to trace this guy backward to where whatever was done to him happened?"

I stood up and turned to head outside. "Let's talk to the first cop that found the body. Is he still around? Maybe he can tell us what brought him out here, and how he happened across Mr. Hetrick's...remains."

"She, and yes, she's here. She's been quarantined ever since backup arrived." Becks led me out of the warehouse and across the parking lot to a big tent with zippered sides. We stepped into a portable airlock, got the outside of our suits sprayed down with chemical disinfectant, and passed through a clear zippered wall to where a young police officer sat on a folding cot. Becks pulled a camp stool up in front of her, while I stood by the "door."

"Officer Semper?" Becks asked, holding out her gloved hand. The woman, a pretty brunette with a glowing smile, shook it.

"Hi," she said. "You can call me Sheelagh. No need to stand on any formalities, given the circumstances." She waved a hand around the interior of the tent.

"Sheelagh, I'm Deputy Director Rebecca Gail Flynn with Homeland Security. This is my associate, Quincy Harker." Becks gestured back at me and I gave a little wave.

"Pleased to meet you," Semper replied. "Wish it were under less... stringent circumstances. What can I do for you?"

"How did you find the body?" I asked. "This isn't exactly a normal patrol route for the graveyard shift, I'd expect." We were in a heavily industrial part of town, with practically no third-shift activity, so I felt pretty safe in thinking there weren't often a lot of cops down here this time of night.

"The alarm company called it in," she said. "Something tripped the alarm on the warehouse, door breach and motion sensor, so dispatch sent me to check it out. I found the body, but it didn't look like *that*. He was just a dead guy, facedown in the middle of the floor. I rolled him over, and things got weird. This funky green cloud rose up out of his nose and mouth, and he started to...well...*dissolve.* That's when I knew something seriously bad was going down. I called in HazMat and told them not to approach without the full gear. I made sure everybody was in their little plastic suits before they got close to me, then we brought out the testing equipment. One of the thingies your people gave us went nuts when I put it close to the body, so here we are."

Here we were indeed. The system worked, in that only one person was exposed to whatever this shit was, but I felt bad for Officer Semper. She seemed nice, and I was going to feel really shitty if she turned up a pile of bones and goo in the floor like Hetrick. I slipped on my Sight again and gave her a once-over.

That sucked. She was *covered* in the same magical shit that was all over the body. The same colors and the same striped arrangement of magics, like there were layers to whatever spell was used to do this. The only difference was that on Semper, the magic was still active, and it was *hungry*.

We can't let her out of here, I "said" to Becks over the mental link we share. *Whatever killed Hetrick is all over her, and it really wants to spread.*

You mean it's sentient? Like The Thing?

Do you mean from the comics, or the John Carpenter movie? Sometimes my immersion in popular culture slows down investigations just a touch.

The movie. Where the pudding cups ate people, or whatever it was.

I didn't bother correcting her recollection of horror movie plot devices, because she was close enough for government work, and we did in fact work for the government. *Sure, that'll do*, I replied. *She's not a danger to us in our suits, but she absolutely can't be let out until we figure out what this shit is and how to stop it from spreading.*

I noticed you didn't say find a cure...

You can't cure magic. If we find the caster, we might be able to persuade them to reverse the spell, if that's even possible. But I don't know. Most of the time, magic can be cast and some types can be dissolved, like wards, but it's really hard to undo. Hard to put the pin back in a grenade after it's thrown, you know? What we do fucks with the laws of nature, and that stuff's pretty hard to un-fuck.

So she's going to die?

Almost certainly.

Badly, and in excruciating pain.

Probably. Unless you want me to...

No. Not yet, anyway. Let's try to find out what's going on, then if you have to...

I'll do what needs to be done. That's what I do. I do what needs to be done, no matter the cost to my soul. That's why I'm Quincy Fucking Harker.

Thirty minutes later, I was stripped to the waist in a newly erected portable tent, this one with opaque sides zipped down so no one was exposed to the glory of my masculinity. More like to protect the assembled mundanes from being blinded by my pale chest, but I'm sticking with masculinity. I sat cross-legged in the center of a chalk circle, with my hands on my knees and my eyes closed. Because magic and technology don't mix well, my phone lay outside the circle, softly playing the *Lord of the Rings* soundtrack as I sent tendrils of magic out from my core, reaching, exploring, seeking the threads that connected Metric's corpse to Office Semper in her plastic quarantine room and hopefully back to whoever cast the spell that disassembled Hetrick in the first place.

Salt. The taste of brine flooded my mouth, and I knew it was a sympathetic reaction to something my magic found. I drew back all the other questing fingers of my power, pulling everything back except the thread that triggered the weird taste in my mouth, and sent more power in that direction.

Silver, now. Layered in with the salt was the tang of silver, and something else. Garlic? Did I have a dead werewolf with a marinara fetish on my hands? No, there was something else, something heavy, dead-tasting, like a weight, dragging on my power. *Cold iron.* I had a source of divine disruption in salt, a substance lethal to lycanthropes in silver, a pop culture myth that garlic harms vampires, and the one thing known to be lethal to the fae. And it was all rolled up in a spell that turned Lawrence Hetrick from a shithead stockbroker into a disconnected bag of bouillon and soup stock.

What the *fuck* was going on here? It felt like someone cast a spell on Hetrick that was designed to destroy any supernatural creature it touched, no matter their origin. But instead of instantly rendering Hetrick into his component parts, it somehow passed to Officer Semper *then* killed Hetrick. This was some complicated shit, and I had to figure out who cast this shit before Officer Semper ended up melting like the Wicked Witch of the West.

Fortunately for me, all magic leaves a trace, and now that I knew what sickening blend of poisons this spell contained, the trail was easily visible. Unfortunately for whoever cast this particular piece of assholery, I was now good and pissed at being dragged out of bed for a magical assassin. I was ready to go do what I do best - fuck shit up.

I blinked a few times to drop my Sight and shift everything back to the mundane spectrum, then stood up and crossed out of the circle, dragging a foot across the boundary to depower my protections. I turned off my music and stepped through a slit in the side of the tent into the commotion of the quarantine/crime scene.

"Hey love, could you grab me a towel or something?" I asked a young crime scene tech as I emerged into the sweltering night air. I was soaked with sweat, my hair plastered down across my forehead and rivulets of water running down my chest and abs.

The young guy, a cute blond man in his late twenties, froze in his tracks, looked me up and down, then stammered a reply, not moving. "Hey, kid. My eyes are up here," I said. His gaze snapped up to my face and I repeated, "Towel?"

"Oh, yeah. Um…sorry, Mr. Harker," and he scurried off, red blossoming in his cheeks.

That was a little cruel, Harker. Jacob's been crushing on you since his first day with us, Becks said inside my skull.

Really? I asked. *I had no idea. I'm flattered. But all I really wanted was a towel before I throw my t-shirt back on. Otherwise I'm going to be sticking to my clothes all day.*

Threaten me with a good time, cutie.

Pretty sure that's sexual harassment, Deputy Director.

You want me to stop?

Literally never, I said. I took the towel from Jacob, who managed to look only in my eyes as he handed it to me. I dried the sweat off, grabbed my tattered Four Horsemen t-shirt off the ground and slipped it on. "Thanks, Jacob," I said to the kid, trying not to notice the red creeping up to the tips of his ears.

I walked back over to the exterior wall of Officer Semper's quarantine tent and knocked on the fabric wall. "Sheelagh? It's Quincy Harker. Can you come over to the side of the tent? I don't want to put that garbage bag suit back on but I have a couple questions I need to ask you."

I heard the scrape of metal on pavement as she pulled her folding chair over to the wall. "What can I tell you, Mr. Harker? I'm afraid I don't know anything else about Mr. Hetrick or this building."

I lowered my voice. "This is about you, Sheelagh, and I'm going to need you to be completely honest with me about this. There will be no judgment, and no backlash toward you for your answer. This will be completely between you, me, and Deputy Director Flynn. I need to know—"

"I don't know why it's any of your business, but I'm straight. Not every female cop is a lesbian. Not even most of us. Sure, there might be greater representation among females in law enforcement than in the general population, but—"

Well, that went somewhere unexpected. And completely unhelpful.

"Sheelagh, I don't give a fuck if you're gay, straight, bi, whatever. That's not what I need to know."

"Oh. Sorry. It's a question I've had to answer a lot. Hell, my own dad asked me if I was gay when I told him I wanted to be a cop. What do you want to know?"

I was going to try to lead into this, but I guessed that ship had sailed. "Are you human?"

There was a beat of silence, which was really all the answer I needed. "What are you talking about, Mr. Harker?"

Still not a "yes." "I need to know if you are totally, or partially, even the smallest part, cryptic, fae, divine, demonic, supernatural, or otherwise paranormal in nature. Are you a vampire, faerie, lycanthrope , demon, angel, or any part of any of those?"

Longer pause. She hadn't denied anything, she hadn't laughed, she hadn't called for a paramedic to check me for a head injury, and she hadn't yelled for a supervisor to get the crazy fed away from her tent. She was definitely not completely human, but keeping that fact hidden was such a huge part of her life that she didn't know how to come out of the closet, so to speak.

"Sheelagh, I need to tell you something about me, and maybe you'll get an idea why I'm asking." I held up a hand, right against the wall of the tent. "Can you see my hand a little? The tent is almost opaque, but not totally, right?"

"Yeah."

I channeled power through my palm. "Do you see the purple light?"

"Yeah."

I cycled colors through the glow around my hand, and heard a gasp from the other side of the tent wall. "Is that…you?"

"Yeah. I'm a magician, but not like David Copperfield. More like Gandalf, without facial hair. And I think there's something special about you, too. And that might have something to do with this murder. It's a vague theory right now, but vague theory is all I've got for the moment."

"My grandmother was a faerie. It's pretty diluted in my generation, but our ears are a little pointy, we don't like iron, and every once in a while we get flashes of intuition. So, yeah, I'm mostly human, but a little bit faerie, too."

Something in her words resonated. "Did you get one of those flashes tonight?"

A sharp intake of breath. "Yes. Right before this call came in. I felt like

I *had* to take it, even though I wasn't the closest unit. I responded, and waved off the other officer who was closer. He was happy to take a doughnut break, and I ended up in this stupid tent."

Something in this was really tickling the back of my head, but I couldn't quite pull all the threads together yet. "Okay, thanks. I won't tell anyone; it's not anyone's business. But now I have to ask Mr. Hetrick a few questions."

"Um, Mr. Harker? Hetrick's dead."

"Then he probably won't lie to me much," I replied. I patted the wall of the tent. "Hang in there, Sheelagh. I'm gonna figure this out and get you out of there. I promise."

How can you promise that, Harker? You have no idea if you can cure her or not.

I never promised to get her out of there alive, I replied, my tone as grim as the look on my face.

I walked back over to where the remains of Lawrence Hetrick lay in the warehouse, ignoring the panic-stricken looks of the CDC employees as I blew past them with zero protective gear. If my theory was right, I was completely safe. If not...well, I guess Sheelagh and I would see how roomy her tent was.

Hetrick was, unsurprisingly, right where I'd left him. Which was good, because when people start reassembling from component parts and walking around, that's when I'm getting a motorcycle and a crossbow and going all *Walking Dead* on the world. And nobody needs that. I'm not even a good show with a crossbow. I knelt by the puddle of corpse, trying to keep the knee of my jeans out of the blood and goop. It's surprising how much surface area you can cover with one human body if you spread it out thin enough, and Hetrick had definitely started to ooze a bit.

I looked at the body in the magical spectrum a bit, and just like I'd suspected, the magic that killed him was fading fast. All the bands of red, green, and yellow that had swirled around his corpse when I first examined it were gone, and even the moldy green-black splotches on his aura were shrinking and vanishing. And underneath the magic of what had been done to him, I could see hints of the magic that he *was* poking out. That's right, Lawrence Hetrick was not your run-of-the-mill human. He was a lycanthrope. Obviously I couldn't tell what kind of shifter he was, but nothing in his background screamed "predator" of any type. He was probably something kinda tame, like a goat shifter or something. Maybe a were-sheep.

Lycanthropy's weird. It's a disease, but it's a magic disease. It's not like the weirdo possession that makes people into vampires, but it's got enough of the hallmarks to be in the same neighborhood. Someday maybe I'll go hunting for the O.G. Alpha wolf, and maybe they'll be like my Uncle Luke, who lost his wife, and made a grief-stricken deal with a demon that turned him into the world's most famous cryptid — Count Dracula.

But that was a problem for another day. Now I knew a little more than I had when I started. Someone had cooked up a magical plague, it was transmitted by supernatural or paranormal beings, and it was currently contained in a quarantine tent in the parking lot of a warehouse district in Atlanta. But who made it, because this was *definitely* manufactured, and what was their plan to use it?

And did they have more stashed away? Was this just a test run?

CHAPTER TWO

Here's what we know so far," I said to the screen in the dash of our DHS Suburban. "This thing was definitely manufactured, and it is either designed to attack magical beings and cryptids, or it uses them as carriers and then kills the hosts once it's passed on."

"How do you know that, Harker?" Skeeter asked from the screen. Skeeter usually ran tech support for our...coworker Bubba, another Homeland contractor based out of Georgia. He would normally have been the one called in to check this out, but he was off in Asheville, North Carolina, looking at wedding venues with his fiancée, Agent Amy Hall, Becks' second in command in the Southeastern Region. With Bubba off evaluating China patterns or whatever people do when they're going to get married, we got to borrow his nerd.

"When I looked at the living victim's aura in my Sight, I could see tendrils of this shit stretching out to both me and Becks, but the colors were different. The stuff trying to get to me was reddish-purple, like a bruise. The vines of awfulness reaching for Becks were black, tinged with green, like mold or rot."

"Well, that's disgusting. Thanks for not telling me that when I was close to the shit," Becks said from the driver's seat.

"Good news is that none of the cops were infected. Sheelagh's quick thinking in getting her tent set up and staying far away from everyone may have saved us from an outbreak of whatever this shit is." When I mentioned that to her, she credited the same intuition that made her take the call in the first place. Seemed like her intuition had more to do with her grandmother's fae blood than our officer likely realized.

"So what's next?" Skeeter asked. "It's real early, and I'm pretty sure you didn't interrupt my Frosted Flakes just to tell me that something shitty happened in Atlanta. The day ends in a 'y,' so something awful is probably happening in every major city in the world. Because people suck."

"Wow, that's way more a Harker attitude than a Skeeter attitude, buddy," Becks said. "Everything okay?"

"Just boyfriend troubles," Skeeter said. "He's not from this world, you know? When stuff gets weird, sometimes it freaks him out."

"And you work with Bubba, who carries a cloud of chaos around him even bigger than mine," I said. "Your guy is in a perpetual freaked out mode, right?"

"Yeah," the skinny man's dark face was somber. "I don't know if it's gonna last much longer. He's getting real tired of my best friend almost dying."

"Probably not near as tired as Bubba is," Becks said, trying to lighten the mood. "Be sure to tell the big goofball hello from us."

"Just her," I said. "Can't have the big idiot thinking I like him. Might ruin the mystery in our bromance."

"Yeah, because that's what y'all have," Skeeter said with a snort. "A bromance. More like the most epic pecker-measuring contest in the history of magic."

He wasn't *wrong*. Bubba and I were too much alike to be really good friends, but he was someone I knew I could count on in a fight, and I hoped he understood the same about me. I might not be sending him Christmas cards, but I'd happily stand shoulder to shoulder with him when shit went sideways. And shit was perpetually sideways in our world. "Anything on the symptoms we described?" I asked, trying to get us back on track. Or on track in the first place, I guess.

"Not really," Skeeter said. "There are hemorrhagic fevers that can liquify internal organs. Ebola is the most famous of these, but not the only one. It might be some kind of hemorrhagic disease cocktail mixed up special just for this hit, or it could be something brand new. Without more time and testing, I can't know."

"Okay, magical ebola," I said. "That's a starting point. We can work from there. But we need to figure out if this shit is designed to take out supernaturals or humans. I can tell you that the disease, or spell, can't live long in the host's remains. It was less than an hour between Officer Semper discovering the body and when I walked over to the pile of meat that used to be Hetrick, and there wasn't enough infectious material left to hurt me."

"That was a stupid risk, by the way," Becks said, and I knew that she was speaking aloud not just to drag me on the carpet in front of Skeeter, but to put her bitching me out on the official record. She was pretty pissed about me wandering over to a potentially lethal pile of human remains without even a pair of latex gloves for protection. I was going to hear about this one for a *while*. "You had no way of really knowing that the infection was dead when you went back over there."

She was right. It was stupid. I didn't know for sure if the infection was dead. But I could either worry about the consequences of my actions, or I could blunder about like a meth-addled elephant in a china shop like I'd done all my life. One of those methods had kept me going for a century and a quarter, so I doubted I was switching to the cautious approach anytime soon. "But it was, so we're good. Now, how can we figure out if this was an accident, a dry run, or part of a massive terror attack?"

"I start with the victim," Skeeter said. "I'm running deep checks on Hetrick and his financials, his work, his family…everything about this guy. I'll have everything in a few minutes, go through it all real quick, and get back to you."

"Meanwhile I'll talk to the local LEOs and see if there's anything happening within the next few nights that would be a good target for a mass casualty event. I'm sure there will be several, given the size of the city," Becks said.

"I'll talk to Sheelagh a little more, see if she knows anything on the faerie side of things, although from what I've seen, the full-blooded fae aren't terribly welcoming to their mixed-race relatives."

"You can say that again," Skeeter chimed in. "You should have seen how psycho some of Bubba's weird-ass fairy relatives got when we went for a little visit. Made my family look normal, and I'm a gay Black man adopted by white hillbillies in rural Georgia." His screen winked out.

"I'm sorry," I said to Becks. "I really am. I didn't mean to scare you. I had a hunch it would be fine."

"Next time you have a hunch, maybe back up that hunch with a *tiny* bit of thought about how fucking pissed I'll be if anything happens to you. Please?"

"I promise," I said, leaning forward for a kiss. She pressed her lips to mine, and as I sat there in the front seat of a government SUV making out with my fiancée, my mind flickered back across all the years of rash shit in my life. Maybe if I'd had somebody like Becks through all of it…but I did have somebody. A pale face framed with brown hair swam to the front of my memories. Anna. My first real love. My greatest regret and my deepest sorrow. The woman who was ripped from me by a Nazi asshole almost eight decades past. I couldn't bring her back, couldn't make right what was done to her because of me. But I could try my damnedest to be better this time around. I gave Becks one last kiss and slid out of the Suburban, determined to do better. To be better.

And to find whoever infected this nice part-faerie cop with what seemed to be a horrible fatal disease, and murder the everloving fuck out of them.

CHAPTER THREE

Eight hours later, I cracked my neck, checked that my pistol was tucked firmly in its holster at the small of my back, and looked around, a tiny droplet of sweat rolling down the line of my back as I got out of my rented Maserati. "You know I fucking hate dressing up, right?" I asked.

A voice crackled in my left ear with a soft laugh as my fiancée replied. "But you look so good in formal wear, Harker. You cut a dashing damn figure, even if you wouldn't go for the bow tie."

"You got me in a tux, babe, and I even got the pleats on my crumb catcher right side up. I draw the line at bow ties, though. I never got the hang of them, and my father would climb out of his grave and slap me silly if I was ever caught in a clip-on. So no ties. And no patent leather rental shoes, either." I looked down at my gleaming Doc Martens. I had sprung for a shoe shine from the guy at the formal wear store. My boots looked less like the well-worn asskickers that they were and more like a fashion statement.

I don't make fashion statements. Unless flames and blood spatter can be considered fashion. But this wasn't the kind of shindig where I could just waltz in and blow everyone up, at least not before a little recon. I was walking up to the Bellington Mansion, an antebellum monument to shitty race relations on the outskirts of Atlanta, one of the few buildings of any size that General Sherman hadn't used for kindling on his famous march.

Skeeter's research had discovered that tonight the mansion was playing host to a fundraiser for one of the most famous cryptid research facilities in the Northern Hemisphere, The Oberon Institute. The Obie, as no one but me ever called it, was created to scour the globe for species previously thought extinct or mythical, like Sasquatch, Yeti, the Loch Ness Monster, and any of a hundred other critters that I'd crossed paths with at some point in my ridiculously long life. That was the Institute's stated purpose, anyway.

The real reason the Institute existed was in response to a bunch of bad apples within DEMON, the now-defunct super-secret government agency tasked with keeping the things under the bed from coming out into the light. When DEMON's director went rogue, in part thanks to encouragement from an old enemy of mine, the Institute was created by a rich faerie who wanted to have a foothold in the mundane world to protect his people from the nasty humans. A laudable goal, as long as they didn't get too faerie about their protecting.

The fae aren't nice people. They aren't people at all, and it's important for humans, and those of us who are close enough to pass as humans, to remember that. The Oberon Institute's goals usually aligned with those of my employer, the Department of Homeland Security's Paranormal Division, but I harbored not a single illusion about whose side the Institute would be on if there was ever a serious conflict between humans and cryptids. Hint—it wouldn't be the ones with rounded ears. And now that there was some kind of engineered super-plague out there that could turn lycanthropes into smelly Jell-O, that was exactly the kind of thing that the Oberon Institute would either have their fingers in or be pissed as hell about, depending on where the disease was aimed.

I was making an appearance not just as a representative of the DHS, but also as Quincy Fucking Harker, to very clearly not say that we are keeping an eye on the Institute. The only problem was I was also making an appearance at a five thousand dollar per plate fundraiser with neither five grand in my pocket nor an invitation, a fact that was about to be brought to light when I gave my name to the gorilla in a rented tux standing by the door. I could tell it was a rental because if you get your tux custom made, like I did, you get it cut a little loose under the arm to hide your shoulder holster. Both gorillas flanking the door had the telltale bulge of a piece under their left arms.

"Name," Gorilla One said, holding a clipboard.

"Quincy Harker," I replied. *Here it comes.* I thought. I hadn't even made it across the threshold and I was about to get in my first fight.

Gorilla One ran his finger down the list, shaking his head. "Not on the list. Can I see your invitation, please?"

At least he was polite. Maybe I could get him to move out of the light so I didn't have to beat his ass where everyone could see. I opened my mouth to reply, but Gorilla Two spoke up. "Check the special guest list, Mikey," he said.

Gorilla One, Mikey, flipped to the back page on his clipboard, ran his finger down that list of names, and nodded. "Got it. Welcome to the gala, Mr. Harker. You can check your coat if you like, and if you have a firearm, there's a gun safe to check that as well."

My eyes widened. I wasn't on any guest list that I knew of. I sent a mental message to Becks. *Babe, am I on the list?*

Not that I know of. Did he say you were on the list?

Yeah, he just waved me through and told me where I could check my gun.

Don't check your gun.

Don't worry. I'm even less inclined to go in here unarmed than I was thirty seconds ago. I nodded at Mikey and asked, "Will there be a problem if I don't check my gun?"

"No, sir. This is Georgia. We're not Texas, but we one hundred percent support your Third Amendment rights," Gorilla One replied.

"Well, that's a relief," I said, stepping past before we got in a debate about constitutional law. I was happy to hear that no one was going to ask me to house soldiers in my home tonight, but I was pretty sure he meant that he was supporting my Second Amendment right to bear arms. Which I'm not sure that I technically have, since not only am I not a citizen, I'm not even quite human. I'm also not interested in paranormal case law, but if I didn't have to fight to keep my piece, I'd take the win.

I stepped into the massive foyer, complete with mansion-styled double curved staircases and giant crystal chandelier, and handed my long coat to a smiling Korean woman who gave me a claim check. "Would you like to check your firearm as well?" She asked, her Georgia drawl thick.

"No," I said. "I'm working."

"Not a problem, Mr. Harker. Enjoy the party."

Does everybody here know me? I asked Becks.

I don't know, Harker. I'm out here. But you are a little famous, remember?

She wasn't wrong. In the hundred years or so that I'd been hunting demons and other nasty things that chase down humans and use them as appetizers, I'd developed a certain level of notoriety. It really should come as no surprise when the staff at a gala for monsters, magicians, and other weirdos recognize me.

I left the foyer and followed the sound of a string quintet into a massive ballroom, the kind of room more at home in a convention center than a private residence, and stopped in the doorway, stunned at the riot of imagery before me. The party was *packed* with cryptids, fae, and super-natural creatures, most of whom made zero effort to hide their appear-ance. It was a lot like walking into an elaborate costume contest, except the contestants weren't wearing costumes. The wings, the horns, the pointed ears, the jewel-toned skin…it was all real, and all on open display here at the massive fundraiser.

Oh, there were mundane humans floating around, too, but they were significantly in the minority. Hell, even folks that looked human, like me, were pretty thin on the ground. I recognized a few faces from some magical gatherings I've snooped on over the years, and there were even a couple of demons from the upper Circles making their way through the crowd. I recognized them, but when I gave what I thought of as a friendly nod to one of them, he quickly scurried away and vanished down a hallway.

That's interesting, I thought to Becks. I spotted a familiar face across the room and started in that direction.

Interesting lethal or interesting cool?

Interesting interesting, I replied as I walked up to the bearded mountain of humanity standing in a corner.

"James," I said to the large bald man with more tattoos than I have scars.

He looked down at me and nodded. "Harker. Good to see a friendly face."

"Same," I replied, giving him a brief handshake. "What are you doing here? I can't much imagine the fae hoi-polloi going in for much in the way of ink." James was my tattoo artist, but he was unlike any ink master I'd ever met. His tattoos were more than just decoration, they were spells woven into the wearer's flesh. In my case, he tattooed sleeves of magical batteries up both my arms and across my chest and shoulders. The process was lengthy, expensive, and nut-shrivelingly painful, but having more magic to draw on that I can handle naturally has saved my life on more than one occasion. Still, he looked even more uncomfortable in a tux than I was, and I still wasn't sure he'd be picking up much new business here.

"I'm a donor for the Oberon Institute. A big one. So I get to come to the gala every year and eat shitty food paid for with my very not shitty donations."

I'd never thought of James as being all that philanthropic, but it made sense. Magical tattooing was a lucrative sideline, and if there were no more magical creatures or people, that money would dry up. Of course, he might be a donor just because it was a good thing to do, but I don't believe in pure motives. Ever. "That's cool, James. Protecting the bottom line is smart," I said.

The big man gave me a steady look, and I could tell that I'd definitely put a foot wrong. "My best friend and business partner is a faerie, and I'm an ink witch, Harker. It's not just about the money. If anybody like your friend Director Shaw rises to power again, I'm gonna find myself in a Martin Niemöller situation real quick. It's self-preservation for me as much as it is for anybody here. I might be mostly human, but what happens to the fae matters to me." He gave me a little half-smile. "And it does protect my bottom line, which both Mandy and I are very interested in."

He gestured to the gorgeous Asian woman beside him. She held out her hand. "Amanda Burns, Mr. Harker. James has told me a lot about you."

I took her hand, bent at the waist, and kissed it. "Much to my chagrin, it's probably all true," I said with a smile.

Careful, Romeo, Becks said in my head.

She's the faerie James was talking about, and she's powerful as fuck, I replied. *I definitely do not want to piss her off. Magic rolls off her like a cheap cologne, only even more likely to knock you on your ass.*

Flirt all you want. Just remember who you're coming home to.

No doubt about that, love. I turned my attention back to the faerie smiling up at me. "I didn't know James had a business partner."

"I tend to be more silent than most partners," she said. "James is the expert on body modification. I provide entrée into markets where a human, no matter how magical, would never be allowed. In return, his shop provides a safe place for my family to work on their glamours and assimilation into human society. Most of his shop managers are young fae learning how to function in the human realm."

That explained why I had to teach the guy how to run a credit card last time I got my ink freshened up. The problem with having magical tattoos as batteries is that the magic is in the ink. When I drain them, the tattoos fade and I have to get the damn things completely redone. James has probably spent upwards of a hundred hours tattooing me over and over again at this point. Still better than dying.

"If you gentlemen will excuse me, I have some people I must speak with," Amanda said, then moved off through the crowd, shaking hands, kissing cheeks, and generally working the room better than I've ever managed to do.

"So you're in league with the fae, huh?" I asked James.

"And your uncle is a vampire," he replied. "We all have our weird friends and family."

"Ain't that the truth."

"What are you doing here, Harker? This gala happens every year. I've been to the last eight and never seen you. What's going on tonight that brings the scariest motherfucker in two hundred miles out to a party?"

I glanced around, but quickly realized that it didn't matter if anyone was standing nearby. With as many witches, wizards, magicians, faeries, and cryptids as were in the room, if anybody wanted to eavesdrop, they could cast a spell. Or hell, maybe just stand a hundred yards away and listen in.

"I'm not sure. I might be on a wild goose chase. A body was discovered early this morning, or maybe last night. I'm so sleep-deprived I can't really tell anymore. But it was a shifter, and he'd been turned into a messy pile of bits. From all we could figure, it was like some kind of magic Ebola. If it's a weapon, this seemed like the most likely place for it to be deployed. I'm just not sure if the attack is going to be on the Institute…"

"Or if the Institute is going to attack Atlanta," James finished for me.

"Yeah, that," I said. "Anything with the name Oberon attached to it is automatically suspect, but I don't know if this is something the Faerie King cooked up to take out his rivals , or if somebody wants to take out the biggest fish in the southeastern supernatural pond in one shot."

"Anything I can do to help?" The big man asked. I raised an eyebrow, and he shrugged. "I don't have offensive magic. Hell, I don't even have defensive magic. I pour energy into ink and the designs do what they do. It's kinda like paint-by-numbers, except the numbers are really compli-cated and I'm using nuclear paint. But I'm six-eight, I look like I eat babies for breakfast, and I didn't check my piece at the door." He pulled back his jacket to show a nickel-plated Colt 1911 on his hip.

"Is that your dress gun?" I asked with a grin. "Awfully shiny."

"Got 'em from a friend," he said, revealing an identical pistol on his other hip.

"Just stay here and menace the fuck out of the buffet," I said. "But keep an eye on me as I wander. If my hands start to glow purple, then it's probably time to let those boys out to play."

"If you pull power through your tattoos first instead of using your internal reserves, I'll feel a twinge and know you're in trouble."

I nodded. "Got it." That made sense. Magic was a sympathetic manipulation of energy, and it left a little bit of the caster in every spell. It followed logically that James could sense whenever I pulled on the stored power in my body art. The fact that we were in close proximity tonight meant he could feel it more strongly.

And just like that, I have backup, I sent through my mental link to Becks.

He doesn't look nearly as good in an evening gown as I do.

No question about that. Until we know if this biological thing is geared to infect humans or paranormals, I'm not letting you anywhere near it.

But it's okay for you to go running in without any hint of protective gear. Chauvinist much?

One person's chauvinism is another one's chivalry. And let's be real. If I catch this Uberbola virus and die, you'll be pissed and visit all kinds of pain and suffering upon whoever invented it.

True.

But if you get sick and die? I don't remember what happened the last time someone I loved this much died, but by all reports, the body count was in the triple digits. And I'm much better at mayhem now than I was in the 1940s. It's better for the entire state of Georgia if you stay at least a little bit safe.

There was a long moment of "silence" across our mental connection as I felt her mull that over. *Okay, that was flattering enough for me to let the chauvinism slide. This time.*

I took the win.

CHAPTER FOUR

I headed toward the bar, figuring that the bartenders usually knew what was going on in any crowd. This guy, though, he looked like he couldn't decide if he wanted to crap his pants or if he was going to have a nerd-gasm at all the weirdness around him. He was a skinny kid, maybe mid-twenties, with a shaved head and a trim goatee. He gave me a dazzling smile as I walked up, and I was reminded that a lot of movies were shot in Atlanta nowadays. This kid had "struggling actor" written all over him. His name tag said "Jeremy."

"What can I get for you?" he asked as I walked up.

"Johnny Walker Blue Label, neat please, Jeremy," I said, sliding a twenty across the bar to him.

"It's an open bar, sir," he said as he looked at the note. "And we aren't allowed to take tips at this event." His face revealed his disappointment, but he very carefully slid the bill back in my direction. That's when I noticed the latex gloves. Not exactly standard issue for caterers.

"Boss told you not to take anything from anyone here, under any circumstances, didn't they?" I asked, folding the twenty back into my pocket. "Good call. You don't want to be in anyone's debt here, no matter how innocent it seems. And you're not supposed to touch anyone or anything they've handled with your bare hands?"

He looked side to side, as if trying to make sure I wasn't some kind of bizarre secret shopper. "Yeah, that's right. Weirdest damn load- in I've ever seen, then the guests started arriving…man, it's like Dragon Con or something!"

"Except these dragons really will eat you, kid." I took the highball glass of whiskey and sipped it. "Thanks. I do have a question for you, though."

"I kinda figured you weren't trying to tip me twenty bucks for a free drink."

I chuckled. Kid was no dummy. He might even live through the night if he paid attention. I discreetly flashed my Department of Homeland Security credentials. "Something weird is happening in town tonight, and our intel points to it coming from here. Have you seen anything out of the ordinary?"

He laughed and waved a hand around the room. "Dude, I don't see anything that's *not* out of the ordinary, do you?"

"Jeremy, that might be the greatest understatement of your life," I replied. "But I meant before the guests arrived. Any rooms that were off limits, any weird devices getting loaded in, anything like that?"

He thought for a moment, then shook his head. "No sir, nothing like that. Should…should I be worried? I take care of my grandmother, and if anything happened to me, I don't know what Gram would do."

"Keep an eye on me as I'm walking around the room," I said. "If you see my hands glow purple, or if I start throwing fireballs, you should probably hand in your resignation. Preferably as you're running for the nearest exit."

"Dude, I'd laugh, but after the shit I've seen already tonight, I don't think you're joking," he said.

"I think for all our sakes, we really want me to be," I replied, downing my drink and putting the glass on the bar. "But you might as well top me up, because I'm not joking and I think before the night's over I'm really gonna need the drink."

He refilled my drink just as the music stopped and a clear baritone voice filled the room. I turned to see a thin man step to the center of a riser I hadn't noticed before. It was on one end of the room and gave him enough elevation to be the focus of everyone's attention.

As if being the most attractive man I'd seen in a century and change wasn't enough to stop most conversation in the room. I mean, this dude was *pretty*. Wavy dark brown hair perfectly styled to seem unruly yet never messy. Piercing blue eyes that I could spot from across a huge ball-room. A tux that fit like it was made for him, with the perfect taper between his shoulders and his waist. And atop his head, once you made it past the perfectly manicured goatee, the razor-sharp cheekbones, and the sculpted eyebrows, a plain silver band with a blue gem in the center sat atop his head, framing the pointed ears at the side of his skull. This was very obviously the Head Motherfucker In Charge, and he was as obviously a faerie as anyone I'd ever met.

He cleared his throat, and the two demons in a back corner who had still been whispering to each other fell silent. "Thank you all for coming, I am Oberon Aestas, founder of The Oberon Institute. We are here to celebrate the wild, the weird, the magical, and the mysterious. Despite everything the mortal world has done to keep us down, we are here, we are thriving, and we *will* protect our people!"

A cheer rose up from the crowd of supernaturals, and I saw Jeremy shrink back a little behind his bar. Good call. This felt a lot like being in a local's pub when the visiting team scored a last-second goal to snatch a win from the beloved homers.

There was no microphone in evidence, but when Oberon spoke again. his voice carried effortlessly to every corner of the room. "Tonight we begin to take back what is ours!" Cheering. "Tonight we lay claim to parts of this world where we once roamed freely!" More cheering. "Tonight we revel like we did in the wild times, before men ruled this plane!" The cheers were verging on deafening now.

"But first," Oberon said, holding his hands out over the crowd as if in a blessing. "First, a toast!" And just like that, there was a champagne flute of crimson liquid hovering in the air in front of every person and being in the room. "Please join me as I raise a glass to humanity!"

The King of the Faeries held out a hand, and there was suddenly a glass in it. He downed the red liquid, smashed the glass to the floor, and shouted, "For the fae!"

A thousand humans, faeries, demons, and cryptids all shouted back in unison, "For the fae!" and slammed down their drinks, throwing the glasses to the floor. They shattered, exploded into glitter, then faded away completely.

I didn't drink. I've dealt with faeries before, so I knew better. Just for good measure, I knocked the drink out of Jeremy's hand before he got it to his lips. "No drinking, remember?"

He shook himself, like he was coming out of a trance. "Oh yeah. What was I thinking?"

"You weren't thinking," I replied. "That was kinda the point. You were under his spell. It happens."

"But why? Why would he want me to drink...whatever that stuff was?"

"Kid, I have no idea, but I think finding the answer to that question is the whole reason I'm here."

I waggled my whiskey glass at Jeremy, who refilled it. I'd just knocked back my third drink, letting the heat scorch my throat and start a lovely little fire in my belly when I saw the first body drop.

And then the screaming started.

CHAPTER FIVE

I whipped my head around, trying to pinpoint the source of the screams. It took me several seconds of scanning the crowd to focus in on a young female waiter standing over a pile of shattered glass and a discarded drink tray, pointing at the young man standing next to her and screaming. When I got a good look at the guy she was pointing at, I knew exactly what she meant. This dude was *fucked up*.

What is it? Becks asked.

Not sure, but there's no way it's good. I'm not typically known as a master of understatement, but I was hitting on all cylinders this time. "Not good" was the mildest way to express what I was seeing. "Totally pants-shitting terrifying" was way more apropos. The screaming woman was pointing at a man who I assumed was another waiter, judging by the ill-fitting tux and cheap shoes. He stood stock-still in the middle of a growing circle of emptiness as people backed away from him, and his face was the stuff of nightmares.

He was melting from the inside out. I've set a lot of people on fire, and on more than one occasion I've stuck around to watch the results, either out of a desire to make sure the bad guy was really dead, or out of pure spite. But I'd never seen anything like this shit before. This dude wasn't burning. He *oozed* blood and pus and body fat from every orifice, and if the droplets of crimson popping out on his forehead were any indication, he was about to be literally sweating blood. His mouth opened in a massive scream, but no sound came out. Blood fountained from him like a sanguine firehose, covering everyone within five feet of him. He dropped to his knees, flopped over onto his side, and shrank in on himself, drawing knees up to his chest in a fetal position as he continued to bleed out from absolutely no visible wound. He let out a long, liquid, rattling breath, then his body relaxed as he died.

The whole thing took maybe thirty seconds. From scream to death rattle, less than half a minute. And all this less than a minute after Oberon's toast. I looked to the stage, where the Faerie King stood with a huge smile stretching his countenance.

"Well, that worked more quickly than anticipated. I suppose we'll have to bring in the cleanup crew early. Goblins!" He snapped his fingers. A rift opened up on the stage behind him, a tear in the fabric of our dimension, and a dozen three-foot tall green-skinned little shitheads with no hair, pointy noses, and elongated ears and teeth designed for nothing more than rending flesh appeared and made a beeline for the corpse.

Four other waiters dropped to the ground in a crash of glass and cutlery before the goblins could even reach the first body. By the time they had it rolled into a body bag and hauled away, every other member of the catering staff was on the floor bleeding from the eyes, ears, nose, mouth, and every other possible orifice. The only server, bartender, or busboy still standing was Jeremy, who stared around the room with wide, but fortunately bloodless, eyes.

"What the fuck just happened?" he asked in a whisper.

"Kid, I have a hint of an idea, but the short answer is—nothing good," I replied. "Hey Oberon!" I yelled over the low rumble of the crowd. "If you didn't like the canapés, you coulda just stiffed them on the bill!"

"Ah, Quincy Harker," he replied. You would have thought he was Moses, or at least Charlton Heston, the way the crowd parted to make a path straight from Oberon to me. He stepped off the stage and started walking my way. "I wondered how long it would be before you made your presence known."

"Pretty sure you knew about my presence the second I walked up, since I was on your super-secret guest list," I called back. The fae ruler was still the better part of a hundred feet away, and I was good to keep him at that distance. I've tangled with faeries before, and they're difficult opponents in the best scenarios. Here, surrounded by a fuckton of other faeries, demons, cryptids, and spell-slingers? Even if I could somehow best Oberon, which was by no means guaranteed, I'd be open to attack from most of the rest of the assembled crowd. I was more outnumbered than even I was comfortable with.

"I did indeed know the moment you stepped through the door, Mr. Harker," Oberon said, his pace implacable as he walked toward me. He didn't look angry or upset. In fact, his expression was downright placid, which is not the reaction I usually get out of monsters when I show up at their parties. "I knew you were here, I knew you couldn't stop my plan, and I knew you would eventually attempt to do just that, regardless of how futile the attempt would be. What I didn't know was whether or not you would survive the initial exposure to my little spell. And you have, so that's one of the tiny mysteries of the universe solved."

"What's that?" I asked, genuinely confused.

"Why, whether or not you're human, of course. If you weren't supernatural to some degree, you would be writhing on the marble floor gasping for breath around a lungful of blood and bile, like these poor waiters. But as you're still standing, I believe it is safe to say that the one thing you are not, Mr. Harker, is human."

"Took you this fucking long to figure that out, Obie?" I asked, and my inner twelve-year-old reveled in how annoyed he seemed to be that I didn't use his full name or any of his honorifics. "I'm over a hundred and twenty years old, I throw fireballs around like Babe Ruth threw fastballs, and I've gone toe-to-toe with the baddest motherfuckers across a couple of dimensions. Of course I'm not human, you stupid wanker. I'm the fucking Reaper. Tell me exactly what the fuck is going on here, or I'm going to show you exactly how I got that name."

He actually stopped approaching at that, which was better than I thought I was gonna get. I figured he'd laugh, walk over to stand right in front of me, and snap my neck or something equally gruesome and unpleasant. But he stopped his advance and looked at me for a long moment. "Okay," he said.

"Okay?"

"Okay. You would like me to explain what's going on, to give you the grandiose villain monologue so you can concoct some devilishly clever method by which to thwart my nefarious plan. Is that it?"

I was a little on the back foot by how blasé he was being about all this, but decided to go with it. "Sure, if you've got the time," I said, folding my arms over my chest.

"I most certainly do. I'm not sure you do, but just because you're never leaving this building alive is no reason for me not to indulge your infantile desire to know how and why you're dying."

He was nothing if not confident, I had to give him that much. "I'm waiting," I said, waving a hand in the air in a "get on with it" motion.

He laughed. I hate it when the bad guys laugh and I don't know what they're laughing about. It makes me feel like they know something I don't. And in this case, he definitely knew something I didn't. Like what the fuck was going on.

"The drinks were poisoned," he said simply, leading to a collective gasp from the assembled crowd. "Not to you," Oberon quickly clarified. "No, the magic I imbued the liquid with is harmless. To supernatural beings, cryptids, fae, demonic or divine creatures, and animals."

"It only kills humans?" I asked. "Seems like a little bit of overkill to take out half a dozen waiters."

"Oh, don't worry, Mr. Harker. I have no intention of stopping with just the dead humans in this room. In fact, once I explain how my spell works, everyone here will be very highly motivated to spread my disease to the farthest corners of the globe." A low murmur rippled across the crowd. "You see, Mr. Harker, humanity came after us, and they failed. They tried to eradicate all paranormal beings from the face of the planet, but they couldn't get the job done. Now I think it's time humanity felt the boot of extinction pressing down upon their collective throat. And I think everyone in this building will agree with me. We were here first, and these round-eared bastards will not replace us!"

The roar of the crowd was palpable, and the wave of rage that came from them almost bowled me over. *Becks,* I said through our link. *Lock this place down and keep* everyone *the fuck out of here. Whatever is going on in here is super-lethal to humans, and I think it's contagious. If anyone gets out that isn't me, James, or the waiter I was talking to—kill them. I don't know what Oberon has up his sleeves yet, but it's starting to sound a lot more like a biological weapon than a mass poisoning.*

That makes sense if the dead guy we saw earlier was a test run. But why didn't it kill Officer Semper as soon as she touched him?

I'm not sure, but I think Oberon—

Silence. Becks was gone. Not in my head. Not unconscious, and not dead, because that kind of severing of the connection has backlash attached to it, and this didn't feel like when Anna died, or when Becks was almost killed a couple years ago. No, this felt like...yep. When I

241

looked back at Oberon, he was smirking like a cat with a belly full of canary.

"Can't have you calling for backup, *Reaper*," he leaned into the nick-name, and the Pavlovian response from the gathered monsters and magic-users was a threatening rumble. "No, we're going to have to keep your little mystical bond on hiatus until we've put the final stage of our plan into motion. Now, where was I?"

"I think you were about to start goose-stepping and talking about a Final Solution," I said. This shit is *old*. Older than me, older than Luke, and it never fucking changes. I heard it in Germany in the thirties, I heard it in America in the sixties, I heard it in a dozen shitty countries all across the globe. Most recently, I heard it from the mouths of literal Nazis in America who wanted to eradicate every faerie, angel, demon, cryptid, witch, or person with even a drop of supernatural blood. Now it looked like Oberon found the DEMON playbook and decided to turn the tables on the humans.

Unfortunately for everyone here, and maybe everyone everywhere, the humans that ran DEMON's nasty plan were all dead, courtesy of yours truly and my friends. That meant that whoever Obie wanted to make dead, they weren't going to be the people responsible for his rage. Which was just going to piss him off more, which was going to lead to more corpses. Nothing about this looked good. And it started to look way worse when he smiled at me, raised a hand, and said, without ever raising his voice, "Nazis? You compare my grand plan to eradicate humanity to that pathetic little house painter's bigotry? No, Mr. Harker, I am not the second coming of Hitler. I'm no genocidal maniac like him. I am the asteroid that killed the dinosaurs. I am what your scientists call an extinc-tion-level event. The second one of my new carriers comes in contact with a human, they'll spread my little gift like wildfire. And on the off chance someone here comes down with a conscience and decides not to infect humanity, I've built a safeguard into the disease. If they pass the disease to another supernatural, they die a horrific, painful death. If they don't pass the disease to anyone within twenty-four hours, they die a horrific, painful death. If they try to counteract the spell or the symptoms of my disease—"

"Yeah, yeah," I interrupted. "Horrible, painful death. I get it. So the only way to stop this disease is for me to kill you and then everybody in the building?" I looked around and cracked my knuckles. "Okay, I suppose I can deal with that."

Oberon glared at me. Obviously I was not appropriately terrified. Not that he could see. My bowels felt like water and a line of sweat ran down the inside of my dress shirt, but I was happy to know that I still looked like I couldn't be intimidated. He raised his arms and gestured to the crowd, easily three hundred supernaturals of various flavors . "You heard him, my children. Quincy Harker would rather save humans than protect his own kind. He is the worst type of race traitor, one who thinks nothing of who he really is, currying favor with those in power. You know what to do. Kill the Reaper." He slashed his arm down through the air, opened up a portal back to Faerie, and stepped through, leaving me in the Ebola ward with a lot of angry paranormal folk.

All alone in a room full of people that want me dead, with no backup. Becks can't even darken the door without getting a dose of magic Ebola and dropping dead. Guess it's a good thing I got my tattoos recharged recently. I called power through my ink, sheathing my hands in glowing purple spheres of magic.

"Okay, fuckers," I said to the monsters moving slowly in my direction. "Let's dance."

CHAPTER SIX

Any time you're fighting a mob of bad guys (or good guys, if you happen to be the bad guy, and I understand better than most that sometimes even though you're the hero of your story, it's pretty easy to become the villain of someone else's), the first few seconds are the only easy ones. And I'm not talking in some kind of "the only easy day was yesterday" hoo-rah crap, I'm speaking literally. The first few seconds of a big fight are usually the easiest.

Because the stupid ones charge in first. If you're facing down a bunch of enemies, the ones who come at you without any hesitation at all are either going to be overconfident, supremely *un*confident, or just completely psychotic. Two of those three types of opponents are easy to handle. The real psychos are a challenge, because they're often too bugshit nuts or too stoned off their tits to feel pain, so they take a little more work to put down.

But the cocky ones and the terrified ones? Those are easy-peasy, chicken greasy. And that's what rushed me the second Oberon dropped the green flag to start the Reaper 500. A handful of Reaver demons literally leapt over a line of faeries and shifters to come at me, and I cut all but one of them down with a narrowly focused line of pure force blasting from my hands. The last one I grabbed by the throat, impaled it on one of its own claws, and flung it back into the crowd to keep the next round of attackers at bay for an extra half-second.

After the Reavers came a couple of half-shifted werewolves, slashing the air with their claws and snapping fangs in my general direction. They were a little more cautious, so I put them down in the "scared of what will happen to them if they don't come at me" column. Didn't matter. I summoned my soulblade and chopped off limbs and heads with abandon. They knew nothing about how to fight as a group against a single opponent, which was weird, because wolves are pack animals. I guess their Alpha sucked.

The faerie knight who came striding in next was more of a threat, but he wore his arrogance like a suit of plate armor, summoning his own magic sword out of thin air and assuming a fencer-like combat pose in front of me. "Quincy Harker, on the orders of the Highest Lord of the Fae, King Oberon, prepare to die."

I wondered if Titania knew that her boy toy was styling himself supreme ruler of Faerie to a bunch of basement-dwelling incel faerie warriors, then decided I didn't give a shit about fae politics, because this skinny fuck charged me. Unlike the rest of the first wave of attackers, he was actually decent. He came at me high, then reversed his strike after I bit on his feint and slashed across my midsection. If I hadn't wrapped myself in a shield of pure energy, he probably would have cut me in half. As it was, my trailer park mage armor kept me from getting dissected, but the power behind his strike still doubled me over.

I rocked back on my heels and threw myself back, landing flat on the floor with my arms spread, trying to disperse as much of the impact as I could while avoiding the downstroke that would have severed my head. I managed to keep my head from slamming into the marble floor, but still dazed myself a little when I landed. I raised my hands, palms out. The knight pivoted and slashed down at me. I channeled energy through my palms, draining some of the color from my tattoos as I pulled on the power stored there, and blasted a fist-sized hole through the faerie's chest. He froze, looked at his midsection in confusion, then slowly toppled to his left. He landed with a meaty *thwap* on the floor.

I hopped to my feet, hands glowing with power, and spun in a slow circle. "Who's next?" I asked. "Because you fuckers aren't leaving this building to infect humanity. You can either die right now, die a horrible death once the virus turns inward and eats you, or you can open a portal to Faerie for me to go after Oberon and get him to reverse this shit. What's it going to be?"

I scanned the crowd, looking for even a hint of a friendly face, but all I saw was James and his fae friend Amanda standing shoulder to shoulder by the main exit to the room. James had both his pistols in hand, and judging by the four corpses in a heap in front of him, there had already been a few people who tried to get out that way. Otherwise, pretty much every face I saw looked like they wanted to jump rope with my intestines.

Except one. A pale man in a custom tux stepped forward, the crowd parting before him wordlessly. "Do you know me, Quincy Harker?" His voice was cultured, with a European accent. He had dark hair, high cheekbones, and the bone-white skin of someone who hadn't seen the sun in decades. His hazel eyes were piercing, and as I stared at him, trying to place the face, he smiled, showing a hint of elongated incisors. This was a vampire, and I could feel power radiating off him in waves. This dude was *strong*, which meant he was very old.

"I don't," I said. "I have no idea who you are. I know what you are, though."

"My people and I have a great deal to lose if humanity is eradicated, as our food source would vanish," the vampire said.

"Yep," I said. "Wouldn't be a good time for the shifters, either, since they need humans to keep diversity coming into the gene pool. And demons wouldn't have anyone to tempt, so no new souls in Hell. That means a lot of bored archdemons looking for someone to torture, with no more humans on the menu. Honestly, I think the faeries are the only ones this shit benefits."

"Which is typical of Oberon," the vamp said. "He puts forth a false image of generosity, which ends up only being generous to him and his subjects. And only to his subjects if he is feeling particularly magnanimous."

"If you think so little of Oberon, why did you show up to his party?" I asked. I didn't really give a fuck why he was here, but the longer he prattled, the longer I had to recover my expended energy and think of a way to end this without killing everyone in the building.

"I was curious, especially when he informed me that you would be here. After all these years, the opportunity to meet my old rival's protege in the flesh for the first time was more than I could pass up."

I gaped at him for a moment, then said, "You mean Luke?"

He gave me the pitying look people reserve for the truly, egregiously stupid among us. "Yes, Luke. Luke, Vlad, Dracula…whatever name he is using these days. I have known your…uncle for many years. Longer than you've been alive. Longer than your parents were alive. I knew him before there was an America, when we roamed the land as kings of the night, feeding as we wished, ruling over the weaker-willed as was our right!"

There it was. I was waiting for the batshit crazy to start to leak out of this guy's pores, and right on time, there it was. Maybe he did know Luke from way back in the day, and maybe they had been friends in the fifteenth century or some bullshit. Luke didn't talk much about the time before he'd met my parents, and when he did it was almost always to remark on how different a person he was today. This guy seemed like he had painted a thin veneer of modern sensibilities on his old megalomania , but if you scratched the surface a little bit, the old lust for power would come bubbling up.

"Are you gonna try to kill me, are you gonna help me fight off the restless demons behind you, or are you going to stand here and reminisce about the good old days? Because one of those is less useful or interesting than the other two," I said. If you're going to talk shit to a megalomaniacal vampire while surrounded by hundreds of paranormal creatures who want to rip you limb from limb, it's best to pick one with a sense of humor. Or to get lucky and happen upon one with a sense of humor. Since I didn't even know this bloodsucker's name, I got lucky. He threw back his head and laughed.

"We will not interfere in your battle, Quincy Harker. Neither I nor my minions, nor any who wish to conduct business with my people, shall attempt to harm you or hinder you in your quest to reverse Oberon's curse. We also won't aid you in any way, but we will do nothing directly to harm you. On this, you have my oath." He walked over to a cluster of round tables and waved for a waiter. Eight vampires followed, and I watched as a couple dozen other cryptids, shifters, and witches took seats to watch the show. I didn't know what kind of businesses this guy ran, but it went straight to the top of my "Shit I Need to Investigate" list.

That only left about a hundred and fifty demons, monsters, and faeries looking to gut me like a fish. And I'd already slaughtered the stupid ones. Shit was about to get real.

CHAPTER SEVEN

The flat *crack* of a pistol boomed through the ballroom. All heads spun away from me to stare at the bald, tattooed mountain of a man standing over a corpse by one of the side doors. "Harker says nobody leaves," James called out, leveling the pistol in his right hand at the face of a nearby faerie. "So nobody leaves. I've got Thelma here," he wiggled his right-hand gun. "Loaded with silver. Her best friend Louise," he raised the barrel of his left-hand pistol. "Is packing cold iron rounds. If you're not vulnerable to either of those things, let's consider for a moment how much it hurts to have a forty-five caliber round punch a hole the size of a dinner plate in your back as it tears through your body. Doesn't matter if it kills you or not, that's gonna hurt like a sumbitch."

The mass of supernaturals stacked up in front of James at the door took a collective step back, and the big man nodded. "Good call. I don't have enough ammunition to kill all of you, but I'm a good enough shot to take out a couple dozen. Unless you want to be part of that number, go sit the fuck down and behave."

"What if I think you're just another punk-ass human who's about to shit his pants for seeing us in our real forms, baldy?" asked a skinny demon with blue skin, red horns, and yellow eyes all clashing wildly with his pumpkin-orange foot suit and massive wide-brimmed pimp hat. He looked like he took his formal wear cues from a rerun of *The Mask* at two in the morning.

"I think you're going right back to Hell, dipshit," James said. He swung both pistols around in front of him and dotted the demon's eyes with forty-five caliber ink. The back of the monster's skull blew out in a shower of acidic black blood and filthy green brain matter, proving that the demon couldn't even color-coordinate his viscera. The fashion nightmare fell straight backward, landing in a puddle of ick and starting to dissolve into an even larger puddle of ick.

I caught movement out of the corner of my eye and snapped attention back to my current dilemma. James might have bought himself a few seconds to spare, but that motivated the crowd of assholes near me to try harder to escape and unleash a disease that would make the Black Plague look like the sniffles.

There was a diminutive faerie creeping toward the door, sliding along the wall almost invisibly, using their glamour to blend in with the architecture like a chameleon. Except when it looks like the wallpaper is moving, you're either in a Charlotte Perkins Gilman short story or something is cloaking and coming up on you. Since I was mostly sure this was real life, I cut a line of power across the wall and sliced the faerie into a couple chunks. His glamour fell away as his head did the same, and he fell to the ground dead.

That was the trigger, right there. Every asshole in the ballroom decided to go for it at once. The melee that ensued was like a dozen Royal Rumbles, only without referees, without a pause between entrants, and without a script. So nothing like a Royal Rumble, but everything like a goddamned pitched battle. I dimly heard James's pistols fire again and again, interspersed with a few screams and shouted spells from his fae friend Amanda, I suppose . Most of my attention was focused on the matter at hand.

That being a hundred monsters trying to rip me to shreds so they could get out of the room and spread death and destruction across the globe. Silly monsters—spreading death and destruction was *my* gimmick. It was right there in the name. I was the Reaper. It was time to get reaping. I summoned my soulblade in my right hand and channeled power through my left to build a massive shield of pure magic, put my back foot up against the door and started hacking. It was like chopping firewood, if the firewood wanted to chop you back. Hack, stab, block, chop, hack, stab, block, chop—I can't tell you how long that went on before my arms started to get tired. Even swinging a blade of pure energy can be exhausting if you're cutting through flesh and bone with every stroke.

"Harker, I'm out!" James called from across the room.

"I'm running low on magic!" Amanda shouted.

Time to finish this. There were dozens of dead cryptids, fae, and demons on the ground before me, but at least fifty still coming at us across the room. "If you don't want to get roasted, you should probably hit the deck!" I yelled to the vampire and his friends sitting at tables commenting on the fracas. A couple of the snarkier of them had made scorecards and were holding up napkins with "9", "10", and "1" scrawled on them like they were Olympic murder judges. Well, motherfuckers, get my gold medal polished up.

They hit the floor, as did James and Amanda. I pulled every ounce of magical power I had in myself, in my tattoos, and anything I could pull from my surroundings into one final spell. This was a doozy, one that I'd concocted a long time ago but had never used because the timing was never right. I needed an enclosed space, a lot of enemies, and no allies in the path of my spell. I also needed to not have any other fucking option, because if this went sideways, I was going to be defenseless except maybe for my soulblade, if I even had enough gas left in the tank to conjure that.

I held my hands out in front of my chest, palms to the floor, fingers out with my thumbs touching. I channeled power through my hands, shouted *"Arcus Infernus!"* at the top of my lungs, and let the magic fly out of me. And fly out it did. Fire leapt from my fingertips in an expanding semicircle, sending a line of flame a foot high and several feet wide out from my hands. But this wasn't me flinging some weird fire boomerang, hoping that it would blast a few bad guys to pieces and scare the rest.

Nope, this was a moving, growing curtain of mystic flame stretching from my hands and growing wider by the second, still anchored to me and still feeding off my power, getting more and more vicious as it moved out from my body. And it wasn't just fire. I've learned far too often demons don't mind getting blasted with fire. It kinda makes them feel all cozy and homey. No, I wove the fire around a core of pure mystical force. Even when my magic fire-scythe slammed into a creature that was immune to fire, it still cut it across with magic, slicing the top from the bottom and leaving two pieces of demonic prick dissolving on the floor.

Demon, shifter, cryptid, faerie, and spellcaster alike fell beneath my blade. They wanted to call me the Reaper, well now they fell like so much wheat before my magical blade. Their shouts of rage turned to screams of terror and howls of agony as I cut through the assembled monsters like... well, like a scythe through a wheat field. It took maybe twenty seconds for my spell to slam into the farthest nook and cranny of the room. I released my hold on the magic and sagged against the sealed door behind me, nearly spent.

A few of the smartest or shortest monsters slowly poked their heads up from the scattered mounds of corpses, but none of them looked interested in a fight after I wiped out over a hundred of their compatriots in one fell swoop. The only creature on its feet except for me was the mystery vampire, who stood up, dusted off his tux, and turned to me, applauding lightly.

"Well done, Mr. Harker. Your uncle would be quite proud. It seems you have surpassed even your mother in magical ability. I am truly impressed," he said. "But there is still the—"

I interrupted him before he could get too deep into his monologue. "What the fuck are you talking about? My mother wasn't a magician."

His eyes widened slightly, but he was otherwise unfazed by my remark. "Oh? My mistake, then. I thought you were the child of Wilhelmina Murray Harker, one of the most powerful witches in all of Europe. I must have been mistaken. Regardless, there is still the matter of our current predicament, namely that of enforced quarantine. How do you intend to sort out that little challenge?"

Okay, this dude was definitely raising some questions that I was going to want answered, but he was right. I had a bigger issue on my hands at the moment, namely needing to figure out some way to reverse Oberon's curse before I ended up stuck in this ballroom for the rest of my life. "Yeah, I'm working on that. But as soon as I figure out how we're reversing Obie's spell, you and I are going to have a conversation."

"I look forward to that moment," he said, returning to his table as unruffled as if we'd been talking about the weather.

"Okay, are there any faeries left alive?" I called out over the room. Nobody answered, which wasn't a surprise. Mystery vamp and his coterie of neutral party supernaturals were all vampires, shifters, or something else. James and I weren't fae, and the few survivors who'd been smart enough to hit the deck and let my magical scythe pass over their heads were mostly scheming demonic types, little shifty fuckers who were pretty useless in a fight but very handy when you needed to screw someone in a contract.

That left only a couple of options. Jeremy was only part fae, so it was doubtful he'd have a master key to Faerieland, but that still left…"Amanda," I called over to where James and his silent partner stood by the room's other door. "Can you help us out here? I need to get to Faerie, so I can punch Oberon. A lot."

She stepped away from James's side and walked to the center of the room, right about where Oberon had stood and monologued before popping out of this dimension. "I believe I can do a little better than that, Mr. Harker. Oberon!" She shouted, and her voice *rippled* with power. I staggered a little, leaning more heavily against the door. I glanced down at my arms, and saw that my tattoos were nothing more than bare outlines now. If Obie came back pissed, all I was going to have was my soulblade and my charm, and Oberon had proven immune to my charisma up to now.

"Oberon!" Amanda repeated, her eyes taking on a green glow. "Get your ass back here, *now!*" She seemed to grow taller before my eyes, and her hair shifted from dark brown to a lighter, honey color. Her skin tone and features changed as her glamour fell away, until I wasn't staring at a beautiful Asian woman in a red dress, but a stunning being with honey-blond hair cascading in loose curls down her shoulders, a dress of mottled emeralds and yellows, and a face that managed to be at once stunningly beautiful and terrifyingly inhuman. She was the definition of the uncanny valley—close to looking human, but just off enough to be truly disturbing. The thing that caught my eye was the golden diadem on her brow, a massive carved emerald sitting in the center of her forehead.

Legend held that no faerie save the highest royalty were allowed to wear crowns, and only the true rulers of the fae wore jewels. Mab was reported to have a white gold crown with a ring of faceted sapphire spikes around her skull, while the Queen of Summer was said to wear a simple crown, resembling nothing more than a golden circlet of flowers, with a lone emerald in the exact center. Exactly like the one now resting atop the head of my friend's "business partner."

This wasn't any mid-level faerie investing in a tattoo shop. This was the motherfucking Queen of the Summer Court. I was standing in front of Titania, one of the most powerful rulers of all the fae. Oh, and she was married to Oberon, the dickhead who started this whole shitshow, and she'd just called him back to the scene of the crime. Was she bringing him back to kick his ass and make him undo his spell, or to finish the job and do it right this time?

No matter what her intention, I was about three seconds away from having a pissed-off faerie king standing in the room with me, and I had about as much real magic as David Blaine. Fuck.

CHAPTER EIGHT

A shimmering line appeared in midair, and seconds later, a chastened Faerie King stood amidst the carnage he had wrought. Okay, I'd really wrought most of it, but it was his fault, not mine. And this time I mean that.

"What the *fuck* were you thinking?" Titania asked, and if the glowing tendrils of yellow and green magic floating off her head and shoulders were any indication, the Queen of Summer was *pissed*. "You unleashed a goddamned extinction-level plague upon the human world without consulting me? Without consulting Mab? Without consulting *anyone?* You ignorant fuckwit. I should have married the donkey."

Oberon opened his mouth, then closed it again with an audible *snap* as Titania raised a finger. "You speak when I fucking tell you to speak, you ambulatory dildo. Jesus of Fucking Nazareth, sometimes I wish I was a human so I could die and *haunt* your stupid ass. Explain yourself, and this better be good, or I'm going to let Peaseblossom and Mustardseed use you as as a sex doll for the rest of the century."

For some people, spending the next seven and a half decades getting banged by a pair of faeries would sound great, but if the expression of unbridled terror on Obie's face was any indication, he wasn't one of them. Maybe he knew what they were into, and it wasn't anything pleasant. "I… my Lady, I just…"

"You just what? Wanted revenge on Director Shaw because some of your trollops got killed in her plans? To punish all of humanity because you didn't protect your little faerie side pieces? For fuck's sake, Oberon, what is *wrong* with you? You were married to Mab, couldn't deal with her brand of crazy, defected to Summer, managed to worm your way into my bed, and now *that* isn't enough for you, either? I should turn your pitiful little spell back on you and watch your insides turn to liquid, you ignorant, philandering, cockweasel!"

Oberon opened his mouth again, then dropped to one knee and bowed his head. "I am sorry, my Queen. I thought this would please you. How can I make it right?"

"You thought this would please me? *Please* me?" The Summer Queen's voice hit a whole new register when she got this level of pissed, and I started to worry about all the glassware in the building. If the chandeliers started coming down, I wasn't sure I could shield myself and James, much less anyone else. "You might be the stupidest walking cock I've ever deigned to attempt to pleasure myself with. I swear, at least the plastic things the humans developed don't talk or come up with idiotic genocidal plans. Why would this please me, you stupid prick?"

"I know you were fond of Ivy, and Shaw's scientists tortured her, drove her mad, and then Quincy Harker slaughtered her. I thought if I killed him, and wiped the world free of the taint of humanity, that you would feel justice had been done." Oberon looked up at the gloriously furious Titania, hope blossoming in his eyes as she didn't immediately lop off his head.

She took a deep breath. Her hair, which had been floating out to the sides à la Drew Barrymore in *Firestarter*, settled around her shoulders. She seemed taller in her Titania form than in her Amanda Burns form, too. She looked down at the kneeling Oberon and patted him on the head. "You poor idiot. I did love Ivy. She was loyal, loving, and incredibly good in bed." She slid her hand around to grab Oberon's pointed ear and twist, yanking him to his feet so their foreheads were touching.

"I can say none of those things about you, my idiotic, useless meat cock of a consort. You are neither loyal nor loving, and when it comes to fulfilling the *one job* I keep you around for, you're only mediocre at that. You are going to reverse this spell, cure everyone in this building of this plague you have created, and go back to Faerie, where you shall immediately report to the dungeon beneath my castle and await my punishment."

"My Lady, there is no dungeon—"

Titania snapped her fingers, and I felt a wave of power like I'd never witnessed in my life flow out of the pissed-off queen. "There is now. Do it, Oberon. Do as you're told, and you might be allowed to feel the sun on your skin again in this millennium. But don't count on it."

Oberon, his face an abject portrait of terror, waved his hands through the air, then clapped them together once. A wave of red sparkles flew from his fingers, dancing through the room, circling everyone, dead or alive. As it wove through the ballroom, the stream of magic grew larger, swelling to an enormous snake of crimson glitter floating through the air, winding around and around until it had touched every single person, no matter their level of humanity, or in the case of some of the first demons I killed, their level of dissolution. After several long minutes of this, a four-foot sphere of glowing red energy floated in front of Oberon. He plunged his hands into the giant orb of magic and breathed in, drawing all that power back into himself.

I could almost taste the power as he absorbed it, and watched in awe as he took it all in. That much magic would have split me at every seam and scattered my atoms to the far corners of the galaxy, but Obie sucked it in like a Hoover. This dude could handle that kind of power and he was still scared shitless of Titania? Holy fuckbiscuits, Batman. She was *strong*.

For a long second, I thought Obie might take the opportunity, full of reclaimed magical energy, to step to Titania. I mean, it was the perfect opportunity. They were away from Faerie, so her power was somewhat lessened. Every faerie in the place was likely more loyal to him than to his queen, so she had little backup. And her strongest allies in the room were a tapped-out wizard and a human tattoo artist with two empty pistols. I felt the tension in the room grow until the sound of a clearing throat drew my attention.

"My dear Oberon, that would be a spectacularly bad idea." The words came from the mystery vampire, the dapper motherfucker who talked like he knew my family and exuded age and power just like he dripped class. "I allowed your little game to progress as long as Quincy and his friend were able to mitigate the danger to the world, but if you attempt to attack Titania, I am afraid certain arrangements I have made with your...wife will require me to put an end to your hostilities. Permanently."

I was definitely going to have to talk to Luke about this motherfucker. He acted like he had Dracula-level juice, but I'd never met him or heard of another vampire with this kind of authority, much less the actual power to stand up to a faerie noble. Oberon obviously thought he could back up his threats, because after a long moment, the Faerie King's shoulders relaxed and he dropped back down to one knee.

"A wise decision," the vamp said. He walked back over to his table and sat down, no more excited than if he'd asked the waiter for another bottle of wine.

Titania walked over to me and looked me in the eye, something not many people can manage. I'm pretty tall, but the Summer Queen had no problem meeting my gaze. "Quincy Harker, you have done the Summer Court a service tonight. It would have been…inconvenient for me to lose James to this disease. He is an important ally, and his shop provides a safe haven for my people to learn how to interact with the human realm. For this, we thank you, and we are in your debt. Should you need my aid, you need simply grasp this crystal and speak my name three times." She handed me a necklace with an emerald pendant. I dropped it over my head, and it felt warm against my chest.

"Thank you, Your Majesty," I said, bowing a little. I didn't kneel. I'm not a faerie, and not one of her subjects. We aren't equals by any stretch, but I didn't kneel to the Archangels, and they're about the most powerful beings I've ever met, so I wasn't going to kneel to Titania, either. Even though she certainly seemed to have enough juice to give Michael a run for his money in the power department. "There is one thing I would request before you go, though."

Titania looked amused rather than affronted that I had a favor to ask so soon. "And what would that be?"

"There's a cop, part fae, that got exposed to Oberon's virus during what we think was a test run. Going by what he told us when he cut his little disease loose on everyone, if she doesn't infect a human within the next twelve hours or so, she's going to die. Horribly."

"We are aware of Officer Semper's infection, Quincy. She has been cured, and will be none the worse for wear once the sun rises. In time, she will forget all about my consort's little…indiscretion." The black look she gave Obie told me that Sheelagh might forget about it, but Titania was going to remember this shit for a long, *long* time.

"Okay, then," I said. "Thanks. But…why didn't you step in before I slaughtered a roomful of supernaturals? You could have stopped Oberon before he ever got started with his plan, but you let him make the first couple moves without any interference."

She laughed, then reached out and stroked my cheek. Her touch felt like a warm sunbeam, and the smell of honeysuckle trailed after her

256

fingertips. "I wanted to see what you could do, of course. You are something new and interesting, Quincy Harker. There's never been anything like you in any dimension. James and I were here to make sure nothing went too far, but I wanted the chance to evaluate you firsthand, to see if all the stories were true."

So the dozen dead waiters and hundreds of dead cryptids, demons, shifters, and other supernaturals were just collateral damage so the Summer Queen could check me out? Mab might be the Winter Queen, but Titania was pretty goddamned ice cold herself. "I'm not sure whether to be flattered, appalled, or terrified," I said honestly.

"All of the above, Mr. Harker. All of the above." She turned to Oberon and snapped her fingers. "Open the path home, worm. You have a lot of apologizing to get to."

Oberon did as he was told, waving his hands in the air and opening a portal to Faerie. He tried to stand up to cross over, but Titania slapped him on the back of the head any time he got off all fours. Eventually he just crawled home on his hands and knees.

Becks? I reached out through the link between us, and felt her relief flood back.

Harker, thank God! I could hear you, but I couldn't communicate at all.

Yeah, I think Obie wanted you to know what was going on, but not be able to do anything about it. More torture, I suppose.

What an asshole.

Yeah, but I almost feel sorry for him now.

Seriously? That piece of shit could have wiped out the entire species, and you feel sorry for him?

You didn't see the look in Titania's eyes. I think after a few hundred years of whatever she's got planned for him, he'll wish he never learned how to spell "apocalypse."

Good. Becks can get a little testy when the existence of all of humanity is threatened. Me, I've been around for enough really awful shit that it only kind fazes me anymore.

But one thing still tickled the back of my head. When the portal winked out of existence I walked over to where James stood by the door. "Dude, your silent partner is the fucking Queen of Summer?"

The big man had the good grace to look a little embarrassed at keeping it a secret from me. "I usually don't refer to her by her title. Or her name, for that matter."

"What do you call her?"

"I...usually just call her Grammy. It kinda drives her crazy, but I get away with it because I'm her favorite." He slapped me on the shoulder, almost driving me to the floor. "Come by the shop tomorrow before you leave town. We'll touch up those tattoos for you. No charge."

I shook my head and walked out into the pinkish light of the oncoming dawn.

ACKNOWLEDGMENTS

Thanks to Lynne Hansen for the amazing cover, and to all our awesome Kickstarter backers. This book would never have emerged from the shadows without their kind support. You're the best!

Adam "Chili" Stevens
Aleah Hanafin
Alex Rath
Allison Charlesworth
Amy Claflin
Andrew Oprysko
Andy Bartalone
Anthony A. Hauck
Anthony Bannon
April Baker
Ashleigh Floyd
Ashley P. Long
Ashley M.
Bee Crampton
Becky Young
Berta Platas
Beth Wojiski
Bill Feero
Billy Coley
Bobby Zamarron
Boris Veytsman
Brendan Lonehawk
Brita H.
Cameron Dockery
Candi O'Rourke

Carol Gyzander
Carol Mammano
Carole Stokes
Carolyn Rowlan
Catharine Clark-Sayles
Cathy Green
Cerise Cauthron
C. Ess
Chad Bowden
Chant Layfayette
Chip
Chris Fletemier
Chris Kovski
Christina M Fernandez
Christopher M. Palmer
Christopher Wolfe
C.K. Eichel
Corey Zanotelli
Cursed Dragon Ship Publishing
Daniel C. Webb
Danielle Ackley-McPhail
Darin Kennedy
Darrell Z. Grizzle
David Bedwell
David Myers
Dean Hsu
Debora Herlihy
Deborah Torrance
Deborah Wade
Deena Cates
D. Hildreth
Diego Riley
Dino Hicks
Edward Abbott
Elizabeth Chaldekas
Elizabeth Donald
E. L. Winberry
Emily Leverett
Emily Turner

Emmy
Eric P. Kurniawan
Eric Shivak
Ernie W. Cooper
eSpec Books
Finley Fisher
Finley Ymir
Frank Lewis
"FU" Mark Wilcox
Gabriele Caredda
Gary Mitchel
Gary Phillips
G. Hebson
GhostCat
Giusy Rippa
Glen Beattie
GMark C
Gravey
Hannah Fulbright
HashtagFarmlife
Henry de Villiers
Hildy Silverman
Holly Thomas
Hordlings of the House of Croft
Howard Blakeslee
Ida Umphers
Irina Kebreau
James Burns
James Palmer
Jenna E. Miller
Jen "Loopy" Smith-Pulsipher
Jennifer Halbman
Jennifer Roshek
Jenn Whitworth
Jessica A. Enfante
Jessica Bay
Jessica Nettles
Jim Reader
Jim Ryan

JJ Broenner
Joe Compton
Joelle M. Reizes
Joey & Matt Starnes
John R. Muth
Jonathan Gensler
Jonathan Mendonca
Joseph Procopio
Josh Durairaj
Joshua Palmatier
Julie Pitzel
Justin J. "Wookiee" Smith
J. Yamil Camacho
Kacy Woody
Kaden Koba
Kandice Williams
Karen Lloyd
Karen Carothers
Kari Blocker
Kathryn McLeer
Kathy Anderson
Kayla G.
Kelly Snyder
Kevin A. Davis
Kevin Sargent
Kiersten Keipper
Krista Fox
Kristiana Marcopoulos
Kristina Meschi
Kymberlie R. McGuire
Lara Young
Larina Warnock
Laura Ducolon
LauraBeth Brogdon
Lex Morgan
Linden Vimislik
Lisa M. Gargano
Lisa McEwen
Little Shop of Horror NC

Lori Padgett
lukeender1978
Lynn Kramer
Lynn Gietz
Madison Metricula
Maria V. Arnold
Mark Corum
Marlaina Cockcroft
Mary Kearney
Matt Lauterbach
Matt Thomas
Matthew Cortland
Megan Harris
Megan McKinley
Melanie B.
Melanie Duncan
Meredith Carstens
Michael Axe
Michael Bodrie
Michael DeCuypere
Michael G. Williams
Michael J. Grey
Michael Mendoza
Michelle Lee
Michelle Palmer
Mollie Christian
Molly Otto
Murky Master
Mx. Allie Ogle
Nancy Knight
Nasreen Alkhateeb Nhonami
Nicholas Stephenson
Nick Crook
Nijeara "Ny" Buie
Pal Patti
Patricia Casey
Patrick Dugan
Paul Staples
Peter Jockel

Philip Lebow
Philip Reed
pjk
Ptahmet Pyndan & Roxy Wülffe
Rachel A. Brune
Rachel Near
Raven Oak
Ravyn Crescent
R. C. Briggs
Renee Portnell
Rev. D. Sellers
Rhel ná DecVandé
Richard Leis
Richard Novak
Rick & Suzann Schrader
Robert Claney
Robert S. Evans
Ronald H. Miller
Roth Schilling
Rune
Ruth Ann Orlansky
Ryan C.
Samantha Bryant
Sandy LeMay
Sara T. Bond
Sarah Hudgins
Sarah Thorstad
Scarlett Letter
Scott Hendershot
Seamus Sands
Shanda Douglas
Shane W. Graham
Shannan Ross
Sharon Shawn Reardon
Sheelagh Semper
Sheryl R. Hayes
Shyam and Tommy
Sirrah Medeiros
S.M. Hillman

Solange Hommel
Stephanie Creed
Stephanie Taylor
Stephen Saffel
Steve Pattee
Steven J. Horstman
Susan C.
Susan K Jolly
Susan Rawlings
Susanne Stohr
Tanya S.
The Fall of the House of Croft
The Nightmairs
Theresa Glover
Thomas Gerlick
Tiffany Gray
Timothy J. Stanley
Tina M. Van Dusen
Todd & Lisa Rich
Tom Eaton
Tony Sarrecchia
Tracy Syrstad
Tyler Hulsey
T. Zablan
Valentine Wolfe (Sarah and Braxton)
Vee Luvian
Venessa Giunta
V. Hartman DiSanto
Vincent E. M. Thorn
Walter Pavlik II
William C. Tracy
Zack Fissel
Zel Zia King

ABOUT THE EDITOR

✦

MISTY MASSEY is the author of the Mad Kestrel series of rollicking magic adventures on the high seas. Her second novel, Kestrel's Dance, was the 2023 Palmetto Scribe Award winner for Best Novel. She was a co-editor of The Weird Wild West and Lawless Lands: Tales of the Weird Frontier and she edits for Falstaff Books and Mocha Memoirs Press. When she's not writing or editing, Misty is a cast member on the Authors & Dragons podcast. She's a sucker for ginger snaps, African coffee, and anything sparkly.

ABOUT THE AUTHORS

R.S. Belcher is the award-winning journalist and author of the Golgotha series (*The Six-Gun Tarot, The Shotgun Arcana, The Queen of Swords, The Ghost Dance Judgement,* and *The Hanged Man* (TBA), the Nightwise series (*Nightwise, The Night Dahlia*), and The Brotherhood of the Wheel series (*Brotherhood of the Wheel, King of the Road*),currently in development for television at Fox Entertainment. He is author of the adaptation of the Men in Black International movie, and of the *The Queen's Road*—an original audiobook for Audible. He can be reached at rs-belcher.com, as well as on Facebook, Instagram, Patreon, and on X @AuthorRSBelcher.

Michele Tracy Berger is a professor, an award-winning writer, a creativity coach and a pug-lover. Her main love is writing speculative fiction, though she also is known to write poetry and creative nonfiction, too. A few places her work has appeared include: 100 Word Story, Glint Literary Journal, The Wild Word, Apex Magazine, Blood and Bourbon, FIYAH: Magazine of Black Speculative Fiction, Ms. Magazine, various anthologies. Much of her work explores psychological horror, especially through issues of race and gender. Her short story collection will be published by Aunt Lute Books in fall 2024.

Rachel A. Brune is the founder and chief editor at Crone Girls Press, an indie horror micropress specializing in anthologies. She also edits the Falstaff Dread line of horror fiction at Falstaff Books, a Charlotte, NC-based regional indie press. She lives with her spouse, two daughters, one reticent cat, and two flatulent rescue dogs. Her werewolf secret agent novel, Cold Run, was published in 2022 by Falstaff Books. She holds two additional graduate degrees, a Masters of Criminal Justice and an MFA in Creative Writing.

R.E. Carr is the award-winning author of over twenty fantasy, science fiction, and horror comedy books. When not changed to her writing desk she can be found running after her horde of furry overlords.

Alexander Gideon's writing style can best be summed up by the phrase "and many people died". He writes in a myriad of genres, from dark fantasy to sci-horror, and everything in between. He enjoys exercising, taking long walks on extraterrestrial beaches, relaxing demon hunting trips, and fishing for Old Ones.

Jason Gilbert is an author and film critic best known for his action-packed and often irreverent *Coldstone Case Files* series and his dark urban fantasy/alternate history Clockworks of War series.

Jason streams on Twitch as Failflix with OhHaiMark and TheGreyCat on *Terrible Movies with Wonderful People.* His influences include horror cinema and video games, dark beer, and heavy metal music.

L.R. Gould was born in Upstate New York and raised on a family dairy farm. She studied mechanical engineering at the Virginia Military Institute and is a professional engineer. L.R. Gould writes science fiction and urban fantasy and is the author of the Peterson Apostle Monster Hunter series and The Adam Initiative: A Gen-Ship Endurance Story.

Bram Stoker Award® finalist **Carol Gyzander** writes and edits horror, weird fiction, and science fiction with strong women in twisted tales that touch your heart. She co-edited Even in the Grave, a ghost anthology, and A Woman Unbecoming, the horror anthology inspired by the reversal of Roe v. Wade, which benefits reproductive healthcare services. Her short stories appear in various magazines and anthologies, including Under Twin Suns, Weird Tales 367, Weird House Magazine, and Tangle & Fen. Carol is HWA NY Chapter Co-Chair and co-hosts their monthly Galactic Terrors online reading series. CarolGyzander.com or on social media @CarolGyzander

John G. Hartness is an author, publisher, and editor from Charlotte, NC. He is the author of multiple series, including the award-winning *Quincy Harker, Demon Hunter* series. He is also the publisher of Falstaff Books, and founder of the SAGA Genre Fiction Writers' Conference.

EM Kaplan writes quirky, dark-humored mysteries, including the Josie Tucker series and the new Virtual Vigilante series from Falstaff Books. She lives in coastal North Carolina with her family, where she likes to collect craft supplies but never use them, think about donuts, hide from pollen, watch murder shows, and intend to wake up early on the weekends. You can find her on the Authors & Dragons podcast or at JusttheEmWords.com.

Nicole Givens Kurtz has been called "a genre polymath who does crime, horror, and Science Fiction and Fantasy (Book Riot)." She's the recipient of the Ladies of Horror Grant, the HWA's Diversity Grant, and a two-time Palmetto Scribe Award winner. She's the editor of the groundbreaking anthology, SLAY: Stories of the Vampire Noire and Blackened Roots: An Anthology of the Undead with co-editor, Tonia Ransom. She's written for White Wolf, The Realm and Baen. She enjoys reading scary stories and mysteries.

Gail Z. Martin writes urban fantasy, epic fantasy, steampunk and more. Together with Larry N. Martin, she is the co-author of Iron & Blood, Storm & Fury (both Steampunk/alternate history), the Spells Salt and Steel comedic horror series, the Roaring Twenties monster hunter Joe Mack Shadow Council series, and the Wasteland Marshals near-future post-apocalyptic series. As Morgan Brice, she writes urban fantasy MM paranormal romance, with the Witchbane, Badlands, Treasure Trail, Kings of the Mountain and Fox Hollow series. Gail is also a con-runner for ConTinual, the online, ongoing multi-genre convention that never ends.

Day Al-Mohamed's first novel, "Baba Ali and the Clockwork Djinn: A Steampunk Faerie Tale," co-written with Danielle Ackley-McPhail was released September 2014. In addition to speculative fiction, she writes comics and film scripts. She is an active member of the Cat Vacuuming Society of Northern Virginia Writing Group, Women in Film and Video, and a graduate of the VONA/Voices Writing Workshop.

Day is Senior Policy Advisor with the federal government. She loves action movies and drinks far too much tea. She lives in Washington, DC with her wife, N.R. Brown, in a house with too many swords, comic books, and political treatises.

When she's not writing or being a freelance fiction editor and writing coach, **Kat Richardson** wanders through the mountains of Western Washington in a trailer with one hound dog and a husband—it's even her own husband. She has been a builder of paper automata, journalist, editor, actor, singer, diamond expert, and Renaissance faire performer. She's the author of the bestselling Greywalker paranormal detective novels, one award-winning SF novel, a historical noir novel due out in November 2024, a slew of short stories, and a few unspeakable things that live in an electronic trunk. Trust me: it's better that way….

James R. Tuck writes books and tattoos professionally. He used to throw people out of bars for money.

Michael G. Williams writes queer horror, sci-fi, and urban fantasy about outsiders finding their people, including A Fall in Autumn (Manly

Wade Wellman Award), Perishables (Laine Cunningham Award), Through the Doors of Oblivion, and many short stories. He lives in Durham, NC, with his husband and a variety of animals.

L. Marie Wood creates immersive worlds that defy genre as they intersect horror, romance, mystery, thriller, sci-fi, and fantasy elements to weave harrowing tapestries of speculative fiction. She is the recipient of the Golden Stake Award, a MICO Award-winning screenwriter, a two-time Bram Stoker Award® Finalist, a Rhysling nominated poet, and an accomplished essayist. Wood is the Vice President of the Horror Writers Association, the founder of the Speculative Fiction Academy, an English and Creative Writing professor, as well as a horror scholar. Learn more at www.lmariewood.com.

FRIENDS OF FALSTAFF

Thank You to All our Falstaff Books Patrons, who get extra digital content each month! To be featured here and see what other great rewards we offer, go to www.patreon.com/falstaffbooks.

PATRONS

Dino Hicks
John Hooks
John Kilgallon
Larissa Lichty
Travis & Casey Schilling
Staci-Leigh Santore
Sheryl R. Hayes
Scott Norris
Samuel Montgomery-Blinn
Junkle

Printed in the USA
CPSIA information can be obtained
at www.ICGtesting.com
CBHW020847030424
6258CB00004B/15